Tikiri

Copyright

• • • •

THE GIRL WHO FOUGHT To Kill
The Red Heeled Rebels Series
Book Three
All rights reserved.
Copyright ©20209 Tikiri Herath
Edition: 2020
www.RedHeeledRebels.com

• • • •

LIBRARY & ARCHIVES Canada Cataloging in Publication
ISBN: 978 0 9938152 7 0

• • • •

AUTHOR: TIKIRI HERATH
Publisher: Nefertiti Press
Copy Editing & Proofread: Stephanie Parent
Cover Design: Angela Oltmann
Back Cover Headshot: Aura McKay

• • • •

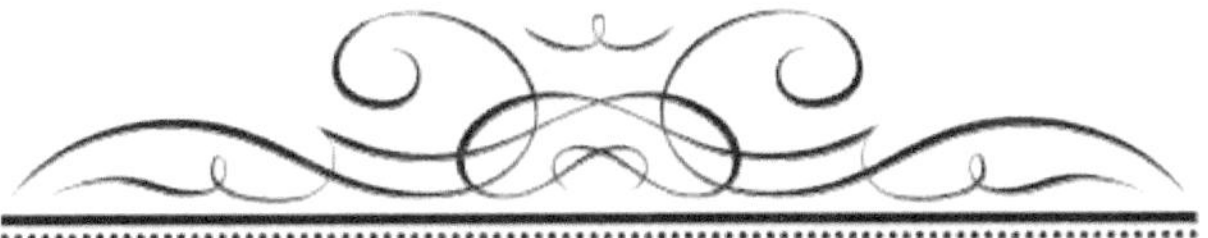

The Girl Who Fought to Kill

Book Three
Red Heeled Rebels Series

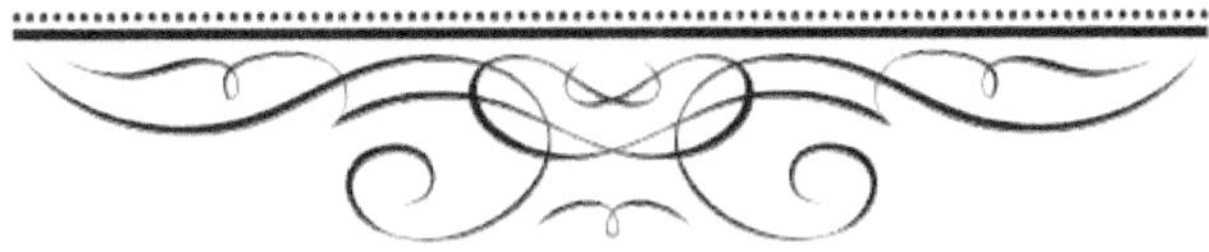

Formerly titled EXILED.
This is the third book in the Red Heeled Rebels series. You'll enjoy
it more if you've read the previous books.
You can learn about the full series here.
www.RedHeeledRebels.com[1]

---

1. http://www.RedHeeledRebels.com

Your Gift

Have you got your hands on the CIA dossier on the Red Heeled Rebels yet? Access the Top Secret document at the back of this book and learn why the most powerful intelligence agencies in the world are after them.

Other Titles by Author

• • • •

The Red Heeled Rebels Novels[2]
The Girl Who Crossed the Line
The Girl Who Ran Away
The Girl Who Made Them Pay
The Girl Who Fought to Kill
The Girl Who Broke Free
The Girl Who Knew Their Names
The Girl Who Never Forgot

• • • •

The Accidental Traveler
An anthology of personal short stories based on the author's sojourns around the world.

• • • •

The Rebel Diva Nonfiction Series[3]
Your Rebel Dreams: 60 Days to discover your purpose and passions and power up your life.
Your Rebel Plans: 30 Days to create a masterplan for your career and life change.
Your Rebel Life: 100 habit hacks to transform the ten most important pillars of your life.
Bust Your Fears: 3 easy tools to conquer your fears and upgrade your career and life.

• • • •

---

2. http://www.RedHeeledRebels.com

3. http://www.RebelDivas.com

Collaborations

The Boss Chick's Bodacious Destiny Nonfiction Bundle
Dark Shadows 2: Voodoo and Black Magic of New Orleans

Part ONE

No river can return to its source, yet all rivers must have a beginning.
Native American Proverb

Chapter One

"**H**alt!"

I swung around.

It's a cop!

My heart beat a tick faster.

No, it's an immigration agent.

I was sure of it, given his peaked pilot cap and that gun hanging from his belt. If we hadn't been in an airport, I'd have thought he was a paunchy, middle-aged police officer, rather than someone who checked passports for a living.

He marched toward us with a deep frown on his face. I watched him stride up with a sinking feeling in my stomach.

Does he know who we are?

I glanced over at Luc. His face had gone pale.

My gut screamed to turn and run. *But where would we run to?* We were in the international terminal of Mumbai's airport—a wide, open hall as big as a ballroom. There was no way we'd escape him. Plus, the man had a weapon.

At least my friends were with me.

Katy, Luc, Win and I had just disembarked after an exhausting thirteen-hour flight from Marseilles. Other than a stopover in Amsterdam where we'd had a panic attack when we thought Win had been kidnapped again after she'd gone to the washroom without telling us, the journey had been uneventful.

We were bone tired. None of us had slept or ate or even talked on the plane. After what happened in France, all we could do was shift in our seats, struggling to come to terms with what we'd just done.

I'd only seen Tetyana's back for a moment before the French police whisked her into the police car. I'd wanted to run after her and scream at them to let her go, but Luc and Katy had grabbed me and pulled me away before I did something stupid.

We can't help her if we're all rotting in jail, they told me.

They were right. But all I could think of was how I'd abandoned a friend who'd been ready to kill for us.

How could we leave her like that?

When the plane finally landed in Mumbai, we stumbled down the staircase in a daze. India enveloped us in a steamy tropical fog that smelled vaguely of jet fuel and cow dung. I struggled to breathe.

Funny, I thought as I staggered across the hot tarmac that was threatening to burn my soles, *everything's so foreign*. India was my second home. Well, sort of. For three years of my childhood, anyway. *Have I been away that long?* It was a relief to get inside the air-conditioned terminal.

A few people stared as we shuffled in. We were a conspicuous crowd. Katy the redheaded Canadian, Luc the lanky French guy, Win the petite girl from Laos and me, the half-Indian woman.

Our plan had been to pretend to be clueless tourists and ask for visas on arrival. Luc had suggested Win hack into the Indian immigration system beforehand to get us all proper visas, but our departure had been so rushed, it hadn't been possible.

We'd been lucky so far.

Katy and Win had cleared customs with no questions asked.

The officer who took my Indian passport handed it back with a cursory glance. I'd forgotten to remove Preeti's letter tucked between the pages before passing it to him, but he hadn't even noticed. Luc was last in line. He was standing right behind me.

I surveyed the area.

Katy and Win were waiting for Luc and me under a sign that said *Baggage Retrieval*.

We had nothing to retrieve. We were each carrying our worldly possessions on our backs, in the small hiking backpacks bought in Luxembourg only a few days ago. We had our passports, a change of clothes, toiletries and a few bars of dark chocolate Luc had sweet-talked the first-class flight attendant into giving us.

We were on the run. This meant essentials only. And chocolates counted.

So far so good. No one had followed us. Nothing had seemed out of the blue.

Until now.

"I am talking to you!" The man in the white uniform stepped up to Luc and glared at him.

A second man in a white uniform was walking toward him with a long-snouted beagle on a leash.

This is not good.

"Me, sir?" Luc said, giving the officer an innocent look.

"Yes, I talk to you!"

What do they want from him? I was the one with a false visa and a passport made by someone who faked these things for a living. Everyone else had proper documents. If anyone was liable to get arrested by a customs officer anywhere in the world, it had to be me.

"*Merde!*" I heard Luc say under his breath. *Shit.*

"What's going on?" Katy mouthed silently at me. I shrugged.

"Did we tell you pass the gate?"

I turned around to see the officer standing five inches from Luc now, breathing heavily as if the exertion had been more than he could muster.

"I'm so sorry, Officer, but I thought we were done." Luc spread his hands. "Was there anything else?"

Respectful words. I noticed he emphasized his French accent, which usually charmed everyone he met. But this officer didn't seem impressed.

"Yes, there is very good reason," said the man, his face stern. "You know very well why we want to talk to you."

Luc's eyes flickered. He gave me a nervous sideways glance. My stomach sank. I hoped Luc hadn't brought any of his white stuff with him. *He couldn't have made that mistake, could he?*

The second officer with the dog was standing a few feet away, one hand on his hips, where he kept his gun.

"I will ask you again now," the first officer was saying, enunciating each word slowly. "Do you have anything to declare?"

Two local men stopped to look at the commotion. They smirked to see a foreigner in trouble. One whipped out his phone to take a video but bolted as soon as the second officer waved him away.

Thank god. The last thing we needed was our faces splashed on the Internet.

My heart raced. *I've got to do something. But what?*

"I'm, I'm clean," Luc stammered. "I'm really clean, sir. I have nothing to declare."

With a snort, the first officer reached over and yanked Luc by the shoulder.

"Hey!" Luc cried, pulling away. "What are you doing?"

I found my voice.

"Let him go!"

Ignoring me, the officer pulled a struggling Luc toward the back area, followed by his partner and the dog.

Motioning Katy and Win to stay right where they were, I rushed after them.

"What do you want with him?" I called out from behind.

The first officer gave a grunt.

"Where are you taking him?"

"Not your concern," he barked without even a glance at me.

"Yes, it is! You can't just arrest someone like that!"

He stopped and turned around, wringing Luc's shoulder as he did so. Luc grimaced in pain.

"Let my friend go!"

"Your friend is going to jail for very long time."

I stared at him in shock.

"And he knows exactly why."

Luc went limp and a look of resignation crossed his face.

I gave him a desperate look. "Luc—"

"Sorry, Asha."

Before I could say another word, the men hauled him through a doorway into a darkened corridor behind the customs desk.

The door slammed in front of my face.

The sign over the doorway said, "Immigration Police. No Entry."

Chapter Two

Katy and Win were staring at me from across the hall, their faces a picture of fear. I didn't know what to say.

"Miss, you come with me."

I looked up to see the younger officer with the dog, now holding the door open. One hand was hovering over his holster, as if daring me to disobey.

I gaped at him.

He turned and looked over to where Katy and Win were standing.

"Miss," he called out, motioning to them, "you both also. Please to come right now." His words were polite but his tone said he meant business.

We looked at each other in alarm.

Around us, people were shuffling, rustling passports, too jet-lagged or anxious to catch their next flights to care. But a few had perked up when Luc got pulled away. They were gawking at me now. I turned away, feeling like a criminal. I guess I was. Only, no one was supposed to know.

"Come, please."

With cautious sideways glances at each other, Katy, Win and I silently followed the officer through the Immigration Police doors.

We stepped into a busy working area. It was a messy place with half-opened suitcases and boxes carelessly lying on the ground. Paperwork was spread all over desks and old-fashioned phones and walkie-talkies sat on the tables. Uniformed men and women bustled around, all talking at once—a cacophony of official talk in a language I didn't understand.

"In here." The officer was pointing to a small side room with its door ajar.

"Where's our friend?" I asked.

"You're with that white boy, no?" the man replied, ignoring my question.

"You mean Luc?" I asked.

"We must better understand the purpose of your visit."

I looked at him, trying not to blink, my nervous tick. *Did we escape traffickers in Europe to only get arrested in India?*

The guard opened the door wide for us. "You will wait here."

I followed Katy and Win inside.

It seemed all interrogation rooms looked the same. Bare. Stark. Intimidating. They made you feel like a felon for just being here. Though it was warm, I felt a shiver run down my back.

"Passports, please."

We reached into our bags and pulled out our documents.

Every time I looked at my passport, my stomach churned. I was sure I was only minutes away from getting hauled into a detention camp—one with barbed-wire fences, spotlights, and armed guards. People with no countries, I used to think whenever I saw them on the news. I was one of them now.

"Please to take a seat."

We scraped back the metal chairs and sat down quietly while the officer flipped through our passports. He didn't seem too rushed.

I turned to Katy, my fiery, redheaded friend. Her face was flushed and the worry lines on her brow had deepened. She looked exhausted and a lot older than her nineteen years. But she was sitting ramrod straight, alert, observing the officer carefully from the corner of her eyes, ready for anything like she always was.

Katy was the only person I trusted with my life. We went back all the way to Toronto, where we'd worked for Dick and Jose at the drug-dealing enclave fronting as a bakery. We'd gone to high school together, taken the same classes. We'd even lived in the same apartment. I knew her better than she knew herself, sometimes.

Luc was different. I'd wondered how he'd ended up in a seedy brothel in London with Tetyana and Win, but he never told us his story. Come to think of it, I hardly knew Luc.

I looked over at Win, who was sitting across the table from Katy and me. She gave me a wide-eyed look, like a baby deer caught in a snare.

She was the youngest among us, but she'd gone through more than any normal adult would in a lifetime. Born in Laos, sold by her father to Chinese traffickers, and brought over to Europe to work at a brothel, she still held on to life like she believed in its promise. But she lived in fear. Ever since our escape, she'd clung to us like glue. *Can I trust her to do the right thing?*

"I will have to ask you to please give your bags for secondary inspection."

I looked up. The officer was holding out his hands. "I will take them now, please."

One by one, we passed our backpacks to him.

Thank goodness I put Preeti's letter in my pocket.

They could take my bag and even my passport, but I couldn't lose the two most precious links I had to my cousin, the only living family I had left now.

Preeti's letter and the ankle bracelet she gave me the night before my fateful wedding day were my lifelines to her. She gifted me two anklets that night, but I'd clasped the second one around her right foot. "Like a friendship bracelet," I'd told her. "We'll stay connected then, no matter what."

She hadn't known I'd get on a plane and be out of the country the next morning. I hadn't known that was the last time I'd see her either.

"Is this some uniform?"

I looked up to see the officer staring at our feet. We were all wearing the same red shoes we'd bought in Luxembourg. I instinctively pulled my feet back. Win had already tucked hers under her chair, looking even more frightened than before.

"It's our college color," said Katy, casually. She sounded friendly but her eyes were sharp.

"Your college color is red?" the officer asked, slightly amused.

"It's our volleyball team's official color."

"Ah," he said, giving an appreciative nod. "Volleyball is very good game for girls."

I tried not to make eye contact with Katy or Win.

"Stay here, please."

Without another word, the man turned around and left the room, taking our passports and bags with him. The door closed with a click.

Did he just lock us in?

Win looked like she was about to burst into tears.

"Is Luc gonna be okay?"

"It's just routine checks," I said, unconvincingly even to myself. "We'll figure it out soon."

"I don't want him to get hurt," said Win, her voice rising.

I squeezed her arm.

A tear rolled down her cheek. "I'm so scared for him," she said. "I'm scared for Tetyana too. Do you think she's okay?"

Tetyana had been our leader. Of sorts. At twenty-one, she was a couple of years older than Katy and me and the most experienced of our group. Being trained as a soldier, she could handle a gun. She could also tackle the men following us. If there was anyone who knew how to get out of a bad situation, it had to be her.

"It's the police, sweetie," Katy was saying. "Not some crazy gang. They won't do anything illegal." She squeezed Win's hand and gave her a weak smile. "This is the Indian immigration office."

I looked away.

Sometimes, I thought, it was the authorities who were the worst, who turned a blind eye and even took part in the evil for their own benefit. But I didn't say anything. This was not the time to get paranoid or make things worse for us.

"I'm so glad you let me come with you," Win replied, wiping her tears. She reached out and clutched Katy's hand and mine. "I don't wanna lose you guys too."

I felt a pang of shame for doubting her. *She's just a kid.*

"It's gonna be okay," I said. "I promise we'll stick together. We'll find a way to get Luc and Tetyana out."

"Promise?"

"Pinky finger promise," said Katy with a small smile, grabbing on to Win's smallest finger. I did the same.

Holding tightly to our fingers, Win put her head down on the table and closed her eyes. We sat silently holding each other across the table for a long time.

The only other person I'd been close to like this was my cousin Preeti.

There was only one reason I was in this country—a reason that had pulled me from continent to continent ever since I'd discovered her letter hidden in Mrs. Rao's home two years ago.

Since then, I'd made new friends, escaped some tough places, raced across Europe, and fought the men who'd captured us. A heck of a lot of crazy things had happened between then and now.

The door banged open. We all looked up.

It was a female customs officer wearing the same peaked cap and a pistol on her belt like the officer who'd taken Luc. Her face looked tight and cold.

I swallowed.

"So, you are all accompanying Mr. Segal?"

Katy and I glanced at each other.

"Yes?" She seemed impatient. "Answer my question, please."

"Yes," I spoke up. "We're traveling together."

She looked me up and down. Her eyes moved over to Katy and then to Win. She squinted.

"How old are you?"

"Fif...fifteen," Win stammered.

The woman shuffled the papers on her clipboard, pulled out Win's passport and flipped through it. She looked up with a frown.

"Who is accompanying you? Where are your parents? What about adult guardians?"

She spoke fast and in a thick accent I had to strain to understand.

"Er..." Win gave Katy and me a desperate look.

"She's with us," I said quickly. That much was true. We were Win's family now.

"We are her guardians," added Katy.

The woman raised her eyebrows.

"Where are you all traveling to?"

"Goa," I replied.

The woman turned to me, her face stony. She didn't look convinced.

I cleared my throat. "It's my hometown. I'm visiting my family and they're all my guests, including Luc."

Her brows knotted.

I guessed I didn't look like a typical girl from Goa, or from India for that matter. I'd cut my hair and died it reddish brown to make it harder for anyone to spot me. Instead of a beautiful, colorful sari or traditional dress, I wore US Army cargo pants and a plain white T-shirt.

I wasn't the only one who'd gone through a transformation.

Win had cropped her hair short and dyed it purple. Katy had her long red hair jammed under an oversized baseball cap. We were all wearing the same army cargo pants and T-shirts we'd picked up at the Luxembourg sports store, but given the grime we'd accumulated sleeping in airports and planes, we probably looked like we'd come from a weeklong boot camp.

"Can you tell us where our friend is, please?" Katy asked in a polite voice.

"What did you do to Luc?" Win asked plaintively.

"Your *friend,*" the officer said and paused, "has an arrest warrant from the Netherlands. We're putting him on the next plane in handcuffs."

Chapter Three

W e stared at her in shock.

"Are you sure you don't have the wrong person?" I asked.

"Luc's never done anything wrong," Katy added, half-truthfully. "He's a nice guy."

"He may be a *nice guy*." The officer smirked. "But he's a known criminal."

She looked us over, one by one, a stern expression on her face. "And I want to know what you were doing with him."

Win looked like she was about to hyperventilate. "He's our friend," she wailed. "He's my best friend!"

With a sigh, the officer pulled a chair and sat down at the table, her holster making a clanging sound against the metal.

"What do you know about your friend?"

No one said a word. Whatever Luc had done in the past, it had been to save his own skin. Just like all of us.

The woman sighed again. "Did you know he had an international arrest warrant?"

We shook our heads.

Luc was a small-time drug crook who only used his bad habit to get out of sticky situations. He was nothing like Zero, Vlad, Franky, Mrs. Rao or any of the black-hearted men and women who dealt in human trafficking and brothel running. Rape and murder were their business. Now that was real crime this officer should be going after.

Win looked at her with pleading eyes. "Can you please let him go? Please? He's always been there for me. He's..."

I nudged her under the table with my foot, hoping she'd get the point and not say too much. We couldn't afford to get locked up. Not in a foreign jail. Not now.

"The evidence is clear," said the officer. "He was arrested because we found a packet of cocaine in his bag."

Win gasped loudly.

Katy took a sharp breath in.

I stared at the officer wordlessly, an angry knot forming in my stomach. *How could you do this, Luc?* If he'd been nearby, I'd have slapped him.

"It's less than a gram, but it's enough for us to keep him and do a search." The woman looked at her clipboard. "Your bags came clean though."

No one spoke.

"How are you all related?"

Win opened her mouth to say something.

"We go to college in Toronto," I replied quickly. "That's where we all met. I promised to show them India for spring break."

"Really? Where's your home?"

"Vasco da Gama."

"You speak Hindi?"

I shook my head. "Some Konkani and a bit of Tamil."

"Address?"

I shared the apartment number and street name of my grand-mother's old home. The woman grunted but took it all down.

"How long do you plan to stay?"

"Just one week and then we have to go back to Canada. School starts soon."

I was really stretching things and it took some effort to maintain eye contact. Her phone rang and she looked away before I was forced to.

We waited silently as she spoke rapidly into her mobile. Then, she pulled back her chair and got up. Cradling the phone between her head and shoulder, she walked out of the room. Before we knew it, the door closed with a click behind her.

The three of sat still, staring at each other, not daring to breathe.

"I guess we'll be here for a while," Katy said.

She was right. It was a full two hours later when the officer returned. We had our heads down on the table when she came in, opening the door with a bang like before. I lifted my head and looked at her with bleary eyes.

"Here." She plopped our passports on the table. "We can't keep you." Her voice was as cold as before but was laced with irritation now, like we'd wasted her time.

I blinked and looked at Katy, who gave me a confused look back.

"You may go."

"But what about...what about Luc?" Win asked.

"Can we see him?" I asked.

Someone knocked on the door.

The officer turned around impatiently. "Yes?"

It was the younger officer who'd escorted us here earlier. "Madame." He hesitated. "The boss...er...wants to talk immediately, madame."

She gave him a nod and turned back to us.

She leaned across the table, her eyes steely, her mouth in a thin line. "Your *friend* is going straight back to Amsterdam. Unless you want to join him in jail and get deported too, you should leave now."

We stared at her.

"You two." She pointed at Katy and Win. "You are only permitted to stay in this country for seventy-two hours. Do you understand?"

Katy and Win nodded.

"Do you understand?"

"Yes, ma'am," said Katy quickly. Win nodded her head mournfully. The officer gave them a satisfied look.

"You." She turned and pointed at me. "Remember, you're back in India. This is not America where you can play around." She gave me a flinty look that reminded me vaguely of Mrs. Rao. My throat felt dry.

"Obey the rules or I'll have the entire Indian police after you."

She scraped her chair back and stood up, still glaring at me. "Our jails are overflowing, but I am sure they will be very happy to take you lot in."

Chapter Four

W e stumbled out of the airport in a daze.

The heat hit us as we stepped out of the sliding doors and onto the tarmac. I felt like I'd walked into the world's largest outdoor sauna.

Outside, taxis, shuttles and private cars were pulling in and out, honking loudly as they did. People were rushing around us, hurrying to find their ride home. The noise of so many people talking all at once made my head hurt.

My mind was still racing. *What's going to happen to Luc? Are they really going to send him to Amsterdam? And what in god's name made him think it was okay to bring contraband when we were running away from thugs and the police?*

The three of us stood for a minute, trying to take in the pandemonium around us.

I felt Katy and Win step closer toward me. It was comforting to have them near me. They were all I had now. And Preeti. I knew she was still alive. Somewhere in Goa.

"We have to find Preeti," I called out over the din.

Win gave me a wild-eyed look and shook her head. "But we can't leave Luc behind."

"Let's go find my cousin first," I said. "Maybe she'll know someone who can help us get Luc out."

Win's eyes screwed up. "Let's go talk to that policewoman again. Maybe if we—"

"I don't think it's smart to argue with her," Katy said, shaking her head. "I'm sure Indian jails are worse than hell."

I nodded. I hadn't seen inside a jail yet, and I didn't want to start here.

"How do we even find your cousin?" Katy asked, looking around with apprehension in her eyes. "And how the heck do we get anywhere in this mess?"

By now, Win had traveled through two continents and I'd been on three. We would have called ourselves part of the jet-set crowd, except our trips had typically been in shipping containers, stolen vans, or in coach class with fake passports. But at least we were used to seeing different places.

Katy was different. Born and raised in Toronto, she'd never left her hometown until recently. Neglected by her mother, abused by her uncle, she'd run away at nine only to land in the hands of small-time drug dealer, Dick, and his Colombian partner, Jose. Katy had hopelessly fallen for the suave Jose. It had been a rude awakening for her to learn he'd been negotiating to sell her to the highest bidder all along. Now here she was bruised inside and out, standing in the most foreign land she could imagine.

"Hey," I said. "Don't worry. I know my way around."

For the hundredth time that day, I wished Tetyana was with us. I had the piece of paper she gave me at the Marseilles airport just before they hauled her away. It was safely tucked into my pocket. I took a deep breath in. *She's not here, so I've got to take the lead.* This was my father's country after all. It was mine too in a sense, though it had rejected me in so many ways.

I stepped off the curb and walked toward the taxi line, gently pulling Win and Katy with me.

"You want car?" said a slimy voice.

I jerked my head around, on full alert.

"Hullo, preetty girls."

"Where you going?"

In a matter of seconds, five scruffy men surrounded us.

"I can give you good ride, haa?"

"You come with me, nice girls."

"No, thanks," I said. "We don't need a ride."

One of the men leaned dangerously toward Win. She huddled closer against me.

"Thai?" He leered at her.

"Leave her alone," I snapped, glaring at him.

He didn't seem to hear. He got closer, so close I could smell his curry-laden breath. He smiled a wicked smile.

I scanned the area, looking for a police officer, someone to call for help.

"You beautiful."

I jerked my head around. A second man was standing a few inches from Katy, his black eyes focused on her like laser beams. His hand moved up as if to touch her lips. Katy withered next to me.

"Don't you dare touch her!" I shouted.

He stepped back, rattled that I'd call him out.

"Leave us alone, you creeps!"

The man who'd been near Win gave me an evil look and spat on the ground. The others stepped back, their ogling eyes replaced by angry, sullen expressions.

"Go away or I'll call the police!" I shouted. "Git out!" My heart was beating fast. I was ready to fight if I had to.

A few passersby glanced our way but scuttled along as if this was not their problem. Still, that seemed to unnerve the men.

"We only want to help," growled one man, giving me a disgusted look.

"We don't need your help," I snapped back.

"Stupid American girls," he muttered as he stepped away.

We've got to get away from here.

The sound of a bus revving its engine nearby made me turn around. From where I was, I couldn't see any signs to say where it was heading. Like most public buses in India with no air-conditioning, the doors were open. The driver signaled to pull out and turned the wheels.

"This way!" I yelled, running toward the bus.

"Wait!" I shouted.

I jumped in and grabbed on to the steel bar, just as the bus rolled out.

Chapter Five

The airport bus driver didn't blink an eye to see a trio of foreign girls jump into his vehicle while it was moving.

He was too busy maneuvering around people and cars that weren't obeying any rules. He wouldn't answer any of our questions or take the dollar bills we offered for our fare.

We sat close to the front door waiting for a good time to get out. As soon as we spotted signs for a train station, we jumped off.

"Found it!"

I looked to see what Katy was pointing at. The sign said *Currency Exchange* in English. It was above a hole-in-the-wall shop in an alleyway next to Mumbai's main train station.

"Let's go," I said, running toward it.

Before we got to the booth, I pulled my friends into a nook nearby. While Win and I shielded Katy, she pulled out one thousand dollars from her bra. Most of the money we carried was split into hundred and five hundred euro and dollar bills. Each of our chests had expanded a few inches since we'd left Brussels, but Katy's had grown the most.

I walked up to the grimy glass counter and paid a hefty fee to buy rupees. I breathed a sigh of relief to have local currency in my hands. It made life so much easier.

The first items we bought with our new money were three burner phones from a nearby street stall—*in case we get separated*, insisted Katy. Then, we walked over to the train station to get two-way tickets to Goa.

We found a quiet corner on the platform to wait for the train to arrive. The three of us huddled on a bench, tired but alert, still coming to terms with Luc's sudden arrest.

Win sat staring at her hands, her face a picture of sadness. Katy looked out into the distance with an expression of confusion, overwhelmed by the strangeness of this new place. The smells and sounds were overpowering even for me, who'd lived in this country for a few years.

But things had changed during my absence. The roads looked cleaner. Swanky new high-rises were going up everywhere and luxury cars weaved in between the three-wheelers and errant motorcycles. Yet, the din of traffic, people and hawkers was still as loud as I remembered. And there were still cows wandering along the streets, although not as many as I saw as a child.

I felt a peculiar mix of emotions as I watched people hurry by. It was as comforting as unsettling to be back in India.

The trip from Mumbai to Goa would take eight hours. We could have taken a flight. We had the cash, but we didn't dare return to the airport in case the border guards changed their minds and wanted to arrest us too. We had less than seventy-two hours before Katy and Win were due back, and I desperately wanted to find Preeti before then.

"What about Luc?" asked Win. "We can't just leave him like that."

"We can't go storming into the airport either," said Katy thoughtfully. "I mean, can we?" She gave me an inquiring look.

It wasn't a silly question. After everything we'd gone through in London and Brussels, it seemed like anything was possible now.

"We'll need weapons and ammo," she added. "And we'll have to think of a fast escape."

"We'll need a really good plan," I said. "And a way to—"

"But maybe they've already sent him back to Europe!" Win cried out. "Maybe we'll never see him again."

"They can't make him disappear like that," replied Katy. "It's the Netherlands, not Russia or India."

"Holland's good news," I said, nodding.

"How's that?" asked Win.

"A jail in Holland is so much better than a jail in India. Plus, we'll have more options to appeal and all that. Things will be aboveboard over there. Luc will be safe at least."

"But he's not going to get away easily if he brought crack with him," said Katy, frowning. "Do you think he really did that?"

My headache returned in full force.

"I think it was a mistake," said Win. "Don't we all make mistakes?"

I nodded. "Shall we try this one step at a time?" I said, massaging my temples. "That'll give us time to figure out how to get him out."

If it had been Zero, Vlad, Jose or even Franky, we could have fought back. We could have done *something* to stop them. But when it was the authorities who—

"You know what Luc did for me one day?"

I looked over at Win. Her eyes were filled with tears.

"He stopped Zero beating me."

I stared at her. Every time I heard about her past, I felt like throwing up. It made me believe the entire world was evil. *How can humans be so cruel? How can this kind of thing happen?*

Win wiped her nose. "This client wanted me to go into a room with four men and I said no. Zero said he was going to thrash me to pieces but Luc saved me."

I shivered. All I could do was nod numbly.

"I'm scared they're hurting Luc right now," said Win. "I'm so scared for him."

"Tetyana would know how to deal with these border police," Katy said quietly. "She work—"

"Oh my god!" I sat up. I reached into my pocket.

It's still there!

I pulled out the piece of paper and unrolled it on my palm. Katy and Win leaned over. I held the paper gingerly in my hand like it was a precious artifact. I had to smooth out the wrinkles carefully before we could make out the numbers. They were already fading. I'd been so busy brooding over Luc's arrest, I'd forgotten all about this.

Katy pulled out her phone and turned it on. "What's the number?"

"Seven-oh-five-eight-eight-one-eight," I read the numbers aloud while she dialed with trembling fingers.

We waited.

Nothing.

"Not working," Katy said.

I repeated the numbers.

Again, nothing.

"Did you use the international code?" Win asked, taking the phone from Katy. She punched in a series of codes and asked for the number again.

"Seven-oh-five-eight-eight-one-eight."

She dialed and handed the phone back to Katy.

When we heard the first ring, it was like a jolt of electricity passed through us all. I sat up, praying to hear Tetyana's voice. Anytime now.

The phone rang and rang. No one breathed. We let it ring for thirty seconds. Then tried again.

Nothing.

"Text her," Win said.

Katy brought up the messaging app. Within seconds she'd sent off a note saying, "Hey, are you okay? We are in Mumbai now."

"Should we tell her about Luc?" she asked after hitting send.

I shook my head. "Not now. She's got enough problems to worry about."

Katy turned all notifications on and was just about to pocket the phone when it buzzed, making us jump again.

With shaking hands, Katy turned on the screen and read the text that had just come.

"Are you all OK? Urgent. Need \$60K. Email to 75694@gmail.com. Can you do it? Repeat urgent."

Chapter Six

"Attention passengers!"

Our train was rumbling into the station with a thunderous sound.

"Attention passengers. The train to Karmali is approaching on platform three. Please step back."

People flocked to the train before it even came to a stop, fighting with the surge of travelers trying to get out. A man waving a green flag marched down the platform calling out something or other.

It was a colorful crowd surrounding the train: women in saris and shawls jostled with men balancing suitcases on their heads. Scattered here and there were tourists in beach shorts and T-shirts, some in dreadlocks, carrying backpacks twice their size.

The man with the green flag walked by us and gave an inquiring look. "Goa Express?"

"Yes," I said, getting up.

He pointed at the train before walking over to a lone tourist standing in front of the schedule with a confused look on his face.

Win and Katy were still gawking at the phone screen.

"Sixty thousand dollars?" gasped Win.

Katy shook her head in disbelief.

"Let's get on the train first," I said, shouldering my bag.

"Why does she need all that money?" Win whispered as we followed the other stragglers toward the train.

"Where would we even find it?" Katy mumbled. "We're not carrying that much."

"What if..." I said, more to myself, getting a sinking feeling in my stomach. "What if that's not *her*?"

"Oh, my god," I heard Win say from behind me.

We stepped onto the train.

Everyone had been fighting to get on, but there was still space here and there. We walked the length of the car looking for three seats together and found them at the back. Win took the window seat, Katy slipped into the middle and I sat near the aisle.

A few people stared as we settled in. Three oddball girls, unwashed and unkempt, probably looking like runaways, which wasn't far from the truth.

It was a good thing we were heading to Goa. Goa has always been a destination for nomadic hippies everywhere. With our grungy looks, we could have easily been tourists heading for a full moon rave at the beach.

The car was full so we couldn't talk openly without calling attention to ourselves. Seated across from us was a family of four, but the parents seemed more preoccupied with getting their kids to eat than paying attention to the strangers in front of them.

The smell of something hot and spicy wafted to our noses. My stomach growled and as if on cue, Win's tummy followed.

The woman in front of us smiled shyly and held out an open tiffin box toward us. I peeked in. *Samosas!* My stomach rumbled louder. She gave a little laugh and covered her mouth. I smiled sheepishly and reached in to take one.

"*Dhanyivaad*," I said with a slight bow of my head.

The woman thrust the container toward Win and Katy next, who took one each with beaming smiles. We hadn't eaten since the dry sandwiches we got on the plane, and that was a long time ago.

The kids finished their snack and lay across their parents' laps. Very soon, the adults' heads nodded as they dozed. The movement of the train lulled Win to sleep almost instantly. Eventually, even Katy fell asleep, leaning to the side, her head touching Win's, one hand clutching her phone in case Tetyana called back.

I tried to relax.

Nobody had bothered us so far. The men who'd initially stared when we walked in were now engrossed in a card game. But my eyes refused to stay shut.

Curled up in my seat, I stared out the window. I didn't see the green landscape flashing by. Instead, it was Tetyana's arrest at the Marseilles airport that kept playing over and over again in my mind.

I'd never truly known her other than she'd been a junior school teacher in the Ukraine turned rebel soldier to fight the Russian army, or the *red thugs*, as she called them. I'd seen her wield a pistol like I'd pick up a pen, and it was hard to picture her teaching English to a roomful of kids.

After the red thugs captured and tortured her and her younger brother, they released her, telling her to bring ransom money in exchange for her brother's life. That was the only reason someone like her would end up in a brothel in London.

I gently pried Katy's phone from her hands and looked at the screen again. What did she mean by "Urgent. Email to 75694@gmail.com. Need $60K?" After we'd gotten settled in the train, Katy had texted her several times, but the message box had remained infuriatingly silent.

Is it really Tetyana? Or someone pretending to be her? If it's her, what does she need the money for? Is it ransom for her brother's life? Or is it bail money to get out of the French jail?

I had no answers. I buried my head in my hands and let out a big sigh.

Maybe we should have stayed in Europe and found a way to help her out. My mind shifted to Luc and a guilty pang shot through me. He wouldn't have gotten arrested then. I could have spoken up more, resisted more, demanded they both get released. Instead, I'd slinked off like a coward.

The authorities scared me more than the trafficking gangs. I knew it wasn't smart to fight the police. That only got you into more trouble, the kind you'd never get out of.

But the real reason I'd walked away from my friends, if I had to be brutally honest with myself, was because I'd waited my entire adult life to find Preeti. I was so close and nothing was going to stop me now.

I shuddered to think of what her life was like. Preeti's teachers used to boast how she'd become a star medical student. It had been her dream.

I remembered the day she showed me her secret pink diary. She'd come across a magazine article about a female doctor, a rarity in the country those days, and had ripped out the photo and stuck it to a page. She didn't let anyone touch that dream book of hers, except that day when she showed the photo to me.

I reached down to touch my anklet. A hot tear rolled down my cheek.

"Sorry, Preeti. I'm so sorry," I whispered to myself. "I'm sorry too, Tetyana." I swallowed a sob. "Luc, hope you're okay." It seemed like everyone I'd come into contact with got into trouble. *Am I cursed?*

"Hey, did you sleep at all?"

I jerked up. It was Win. Katy was still asleep, her head nestled on a sea of her red curls against the seat.

"Kinda," I lied, quickly wiping my face.

"I had a dream," Win said, sitting up, rubbing her eyes. She noticed the phone in my hands. "Is that's Katy's?"

I nodded.

"Did she call?"

I shook my head.

She reached over and plucked the phone from me.

"What are you doing?" I asked.

Win turned the phone on, and said in a low voice, "Tetyana will know how to get Luc out. So I'm gonna help get her out first."

I did a quick check to see if anyone was listening. The family in front of us were asleep. The rest of the passengers were either buried in their own phones or in deep slumber.

Win started to click away on the phone, her face taking on a strange expression.

It was a look I recognized.

"Hey, Win?" I whispered. "What's your idea?"

The quick shake of her head was almost imperceptible. Other than her eyes moving across the screen at supersonic speed, her face was still, like she was in a trance.

Chapter Seven

"**M**ay I have your attention, please. We are approaching Karmali station. Please be prepared to disembark at platform number three."

The announcement came first in Hindi and English and then in Konkani, the language of my grandmother.

I shook Katy awake gently.

Win was still absorbed in the phone and hadn't taken her eyes off it for the past hour.

"Hey, Win." I leaned over. "We're getting off now."

She gave a quick nod. With a swipe of the screen, she turned the phone off and handed it to a surprised Katy. Then, she stood up and put on her backpack.

"Good thing we've got data," she said, as she squeezed past us to follow our seatmates who were now pulling their sleepy kids toward the doors.

Katy looked at the phone on her lap and gave me a puzzled look. "What was that all about?"

I shrugged.

I knew to leave Win alone when she was in this state. She'd given up explaining the intricacies of her online activities to us a long time ago, exasperated by our blank looks and stupid questions. I also knew every time she got immersed in a phone or on a computer, she had a breakthrough.

"Best to leave her be," I said as I picked up my own bag.

Besides, I had other things to figure out. We had to find transportation that would take us to Vasco da Gama, the seaport town where my grandmother, aunt Shilpa, and cousin Preeti used to live. It was a half hour drive away and time was ticking. I followed Win out of the train with Katy right behind me.

As soon as I stepped onto the platform, my childhood memories came rushing in. The scent of lush tropical Goa filled my lungs.

This was where the sun drenched the land and the sound of the ocean called out to you. This was where I lived and played with Shilpa and Preeti. I remembered our walks along the beach and our visits to the vegetable markets. I remembered how once we three got on a motorcycle taxi and went for a crazy ride—something you'd never see in Toronto, London or Brussels. I could almost hear our nervous giggles as we held on while the driver zipped in between cars and cows.

Tears welled up in my eyes. Even with all the things I'd gone through during my last year here, I felt an affinity to this place I couldn't describe.

It had not been easy for me as a girl. It had not been easy walking down the streets fearful of being catcalled, whistled, or groped. It had not been easy living with a grandmother who called me a half-breed. And it had been terrifying to get pulled out of school to be sold off in marriage at fifteen. But those warm and cozy feelings of my times with Preeti and Shilpa overrode all those difficult memories.

"Shuttle, miss?"

It was a ticket hawker, one of the young men who hung around train stations pretending to help tourists but demanded a sizable tip in return.

Katy and Win looked at me.

The signs on the shuttles were in the local language, a language I'd learned a long time ago but had lost touch with. Next to us, a group of German students were haggling with a bus driver. All of a sudden, I felt the events of the past few days, weeks, months heavy on my shoulders. I was too exhausted to hustle my way through this.

I nodded to the man. "Sure."

"Panaji?"

"No, Vasco da Gama, please."

"Vasco?" He gave me a curious look. Most tourists didn't travel to areas beyond the resorts and the beaches. "Okay, no problem, miss." He gave that sideways Indian head nod and smiled. "I find you right bus, haa?"

We followed him, winding our way through vans, taxis and the ubiquitous motorcycles to a small shuttle bus parked under a tree.

"This is our bus?" I asked our guide.

"Yes, miss. Take you direct to Vasco. No problem."

We walked up to the bus with our mouths open. It was adorned to the hilt with psychedelic flags, gaudy plastic flowers, and pictures of Hindu gods in all their celestial poses. I wondered how the driver saw through the heavily decorated windshield. Maybe he thought all those gods would guide him.

"A hippie ride," Katy said, a small smile breaking out for the first time since we arrived in India. "So fun."

"Oh, my god. I love it!" said Win clapping her hands.

Seeing them forget their troubles, even if only for a moment, was worth the exorbitant tip. I handed our guide the cash he'd been waiting for and followed my friends into the bus. Inside were mostly locals. We settled in at the back.

The ride to Vasco was as wild as the bus itself. Squeezed in between Katy and Win, I clutched onto the seat in front, hanging on with every twist of the road.

"He's toking up in front, I'm sure," Katy whispered after one furious turn when we tilted on just two wheels.

The driver calmed down as we got out of the city and onto the main road. I leaned back and prayed for things to go right from now on. First, find Preeti. Then, contact Tetyana. Finally, get Luc out.

Sunny Goa unfolded around us. We settled in our seats quietly, looking out at the swaying coconut groves, long silvery beaches and colonial white churches, relics from the Portuguese era of centuries ago. The smell of the sea instantly reminded me of my grandmother's cooking—her delicious curries, vegetable patties, and her spicy cut-lets.

A pang of sadness crossed my heart. Aunty Shilpa and Grandma were gone now. Even though she mistreated me, my grandmother was still my grandmother and her death bothered me.

From my pocket, I dug out Preeti's letter written on her signature pink paper. I read it for the thousandth time, soaking in her swirly handwriting. Something told me things had changed between the time she wrote that letter and now.

I hadn't realized by how much.

Chapter Eight

"Chef Pierre's looking for you."

Katy and I glanced at each other in surprise.

"What?" I put down my cup. "*Chef Pierre?*"

"Uh-huh." Win nodded.

"What does he want?"

"Come. I'll show you." Win pointed at the row of ancient computers lining the back of the dingy café, where she'd been busy for the past half an hour.

After getting off the psychedelic bus at the Vasco da Gama station, we'd walked over to a small restaurant called "Good Eats, Lodging, and Internet." It had a mix of locals and tourist clients which meant we wouldn't stick out.

I was itching to run over to my grandmother's old home. I wanted nothing more than to find Preeti, grab her and take her far away from this place. But I had no idea if the tyrant Kristadasa or any of his goons would be around. I had to hatch a plan. Besides, the samosa on the train had been our only meal for almost twenty-four hours. We had to get food and water and take stock.

While Katy and I were trying to figure out our next steps, Win had disappeared to one of five Internet stations.

We pushed our plates away and got up to follow her. Win ran back to her computer, plopped down on her chair and tapped away at the keyboard. It was an old beige computer that belonged in another century, but it obeyed Win's commands quickly. Katy and I snooped over her shoulder.

"What's going on?" Katy asked.

"I was trying to find Tetyana. That's how I saw Chef Pierre's note."

"What did he say?" I asked, leaning in.

"He wants to talk to you," she said, pointing at the screen. I followed her finger to read a tweet from Chef Pierre, himself. "Seeking extraordinaire Canadian baker in Europe. You know who you are. BTW, you're not even on Twitter! WTH. Asha, will you please contact me ASAP?"

"Wow," Katy said.

"That could be for anyone," I said.

"Called Asha?" said Katy with a raised eyebrow.

"So, do I reply?" Win asked, her fingers hovering over the keyboard.

"No," I said.

"Why not?" Katy asked.

"We don't have time for this."

"No point in burning bridges."

I shook my head. "I'll never see him again after what happened in Luxembourg. I'm finished with that business."

"Why's he trying to find you then?" Win asked. "He liked what you did."

That was true. Until two years ago, all I'd wanted was to bake cakes for a living. It was a talent I'd inherited from my mother and perfected from trying out all of Chef Pierre's recipes to satisfy Mrs. Rao's sweet tooth back in Toronto.

I'd dreamed of owning a bakery one day, maybe even a series of bakeries just like my idol, Chef Pierre. Because then, I could help my aunt Shilpa recover from her illness, get Preeti through med school and buy them a grand house in the upscale part of Goa.

That dream had come crashing down the day I learned what happened to them. And now, all I wanted was to take revenge on the people who'd hurt my family.

"Hey," Katy said, giving me a pointed look. "Maybe he can help us."

"Right," I said, with a sarcastic smirk. "Remember the last time I tried to get the Diplomatic Dragon Lady to help us? That didn't go so well, did it?"

"She was using you," Katy said, her green eyes boring into mine. "Chef Pierre *wants* to talk to you. Would it kill you to say hi? Who knows, maybe he's got connections in Holland to help us with Luc."

"Connections?" I stared at my friend. *She's right. She's absolutely right. I need to listen to Katy more often.*

I turned to Win. "Can you tell him I said hello and will be in touch? But please don't promise him anything, okay?"

Win nodded.

"Do you guys want to see what else I found?" she asked, lowering her voice. She opened another browser page. Katy and I leaned in closer. Strings of numbers and letters filled the screen.

"What's all this?" I asked.

Win lowered her voice some more. "The entrance to the accounts."

"Which accounts?" Katy whispered.

"What entrance?" I whispered.

"The ones in Costa Rica," Win said in a voice that clearly meant, *Don't you know?*

I glanced at Katy.

She shrugged.

"Is that Tetyana's account?" Katy tried again.

Win let out an impatient sigh. "Yes, it's her money, but Zero locked it in his account."

When we rescued Win from Zero and Vlad, I'd thought she was just another young girl caught up in the gruesome sex industry. But I hadn't accounted for her intelligence or skills. Even in those horrifying circumstances, Win had discovered a way to keep her mind off what she was being subjected to.

Zero was a technophobe, so he used the girls he'd exploited to do all his paperwork. Win had become so good at the job he'd made her his personal assistant. She set up his secret forums, created covert chat lines, answered his emails and even transferred money to tax havens. Getting immersed in the tech stuff was her escape from the evil surrounding her.

While he'd kept the more important passwords to himself, he hadn't known Win had taught herself how to hack her way into anything in the six years she'd been with him. Inside that damaged girl's body was a brilliant brain. She'd sponged up everything and even learned English from her clients.

"Hey Win," I said. "Katy and I are a little slow today. Can you explain how you got here for us?"

"I found their accounts," Win replied, her voice slightly smug, "in Costa Rica."

"I thought they put their money in an offshore Swiss account," I said.

I remembered how Tetyana had lost access to her hard-earned money because it required passwords from all three—Zero, Vlad and herself. But when we left Brussels, both Vlad and Zero had been incapacitated and not able to share passwords, or anything else for that matter.

"Yes, but every month Zero made me move money from the Swiss account to this one."

"Are you kidding me?" Katy exclaimed. "The double-crosser."

"There's more than sixty K here," Win said, pointing at the screen. "See?"

Katy and I squinted at the rows and rows of numbers and letters. All I could make out was a gobbledygook of alphanumerical characters. *How can she even read this?*

Win saw my face. "This is the back end," she explained. "They'll see me if I go through the front, so I found a way through a side door."

Katy and I looked at each other with raised eyebrows.

Someone coughed next to us, making me jump.

Sitting at the computer to the right of Win was a local boy, around ten years old. He had his headphones on and was playing a game that had both racing cars and dinosaurs.

To Win's left was a paunchy middle-aged tourist, watching a grainy YouTube video with earphones. The screen was flashing an orgy of flesh, more than the typical Bollywood movie. He saw me look, grinned and cocked his eyebrows. I gave him a nasty glare. Within seconds, he shut his computer and shuffled off.

Good.

I wanted to take his seat so no one else would come over, but I didn't dare touch it.

"How did you do that? I thought these places were like vaults," Katy was asking Win. "Real vaults."

Win nodded. "The Swiss one is. I tried but couldn't get in. This one was easier," Win said, tapping away. More gobbledygook scrolled across the screen. "Can't stay here too long. They'll find me."

"How much is in there?" I asked.

"Eight hundred thousand."

Katy let out a low whistle. "US?"

"Uh-huh," Win said. "There's more in their Jamaican account," she added, turning to us in earnest. "You want me to get in there too?"

I looked at her in surprise. Zero and his gang certainly had tricks up their sleeves. Win had been so used to doing their dirty work, this all seemed normal to her.

"No."

I touched Win on her arm and lowered my voice.

"That can be our backup plan. Plus, we don't want to send too many red flags. Take out eighty grand from Costa Rica."

"Do we need that much?" Katy whispered.

"I've got a funny feeling," I said. "There's Luc we've got to get out somehow." I turned back to Win. "Can you do all this without getting traced?"

"Yup!" she said and happily pounded on the keyboard while Katy and I watched in awe. "I know how to steal stuff."

"This is not stealing," I said. "This is taking back what's owed to Tetyana and you."

"This is *blood* money," Katy whispered hoarsely.

Her face was drawn. I'd heard her say this before when we ran off with Dick and Jose's drug money in Toronto.

"This is for all the work Tetyana, you, Luc and others did for those thugs," Katy said to Win. "For all the work you were *forced* to do for them."

I wasn't sure if Win heard Katy, but her fingers were flying over the keyboard a hundred miles per second.

My brain whirred. We still had to find a way to access the money easily in local currency.

I leaned in and whispered, "Hey, can we transfer this cash to an Indian account afterward?"

Win nodded and went back to tapping, switching through several pages. It was hard to keep up.

I turned around and stood with my back against Win's chair, watching people come and go. They were mostly backpackers seeking a place to stay or something to eat and kept the two workers behind the counter busy. No one noticed us. If anyone did, they probably thought we were looking up tourist information.

Whatever happened, I didn't want Win's fingerprints on this. She'd already paid a price of a lifetime.

She was nine when the traffickers kidnapped her from her village. Just like a baby elephant tied to a pole is conditioned over time to never pull away, Win had stayed loyal to her captors. She could have called for help or ran away, but she hadn't known any other way of life.

While Win was busy, I turned to Katy and whispered, "Hey, can you message Tetyana back?"

She pulled her phone out.

"We need to check if it's her first," I said. "Need to ask her something only she'll know."

Katy nodded. "I know what to ask."

She clicked on the messaging app and typed her question. "Pls confirm: who are we?"

To our surprise, a reply came back immediately.

"The Red-Heeled Rebels."

Katy and I sighed in relief.

"It's her," I said. "It's Tetyana."

Katy messaged back. "Thank god, it's you! Are you okay? Where are you now? Call us!"

No answer.

"Maybe that didn't go through," Katy said, trying again.

Within half an hour Win had moved the money to a shadow account. From there, she transferred sixty thousand to Tetyana's email, broken into ten transfers spread across seven days. It took her another fifteen minutes to transfer the remaining money into a local bank account, and memorize the new numbers and pin codes she'd set up herself.

Meanwhile, Katy sent a series of messages to Tetyana telling her what had happened to us since we left France.

With a sigh, she put the phone away. "No replies."

"Maybe she got on a plane," I said. "Or is somewhere she can't talk."

My mind raced. *Is she still in jail? How come she has her phone if she's still locked up? Maybe the red thugs got her again?*

As if on cue, a troupe of Russian tourists strolled in, looking like they'd come from a night out at a casino. They took over the café tables, talking loudly. One of them looked our way curiously.

I picked up my bag and lowered my voice. "Time to get out of here."

Chapter Nine

"**A**re you seriously doing this?" asked Win, giving me a shocked look.

"After all we've gone through, you wanna walk in there?" asked Katy, her face scrunching up in disapproval.

We were a few feet away from a government building. With its bright yellow facade and Christmas-like lights strewn across the exterior walls, it didn't look imposing, but the sign in front was clear. It said, "Vasco Police Station."

Lounging on the rough gravel patch outside the main entrance were a handful of officers in wrinkled khaki uniforms. None of them noticed us lurking behind the juice stall at the street corner, sipping on coconuts through straws.

We might have looked like casual tourists to anyone passing by, but I could feel Katy and Win's nervous energy. We'd cut across continents, escaping untold danger by ourselves, never once getting help from the authorities. In fact, the police seemed to want to chase us as much as the bad guys. I understood why Katy and Win felt the way they did. But I had no choice.

Franky was too organized. Kristadasa was too dangerous. And both of them had too many friends here. I was on their home turf now. I'd be stupid to think I could walk in and rescue Preeti by myself without harming her further or putting bystanders in danger.

Hurting others through my actions seemed to be my thing. I was determined once and for all to put a stop to that curse.

It was time to do the right thing.

I handed my half-finished coconut to Win and stepped forward.

I'd asked them to stay right where they were, hidden behind the stall. We couldn't have the officers get distracted or confused by the presence of foreigners. I, at least, could get away with looking like a local.

One of the policemen turned around as soon as I walked up. He squinted his eyes when he spotted me. All of a sudden, I felt self-conscious, wishing I'd changed into a salwar kameez or even a sari, but it was too late now.

All eyes were on me.

"Yes?" one of them snapped.

"Good afternoon," I said in the local language. My accent was off, but I couldn't help that.

They stared, eyes running up and down my clothes, trying to place me.

"I need your help, please," I said, speaking slowly and deliberately. "My cousin is in grave danger."

"Who are you?" one of them asked.

"My name is Asha, and my cousin's name is Preeti. We live in the government complex on the east side of town."

They gave me a blank look.

"What's wrong with your cousin?" asked one.

"She was..." I swallowed. "She was kidnapped."

"Kidnapped?"

I had their full attention now.

"Yes," I said. "They forced her to marry an older man in my village."

The men's faces cleared as if that explained everything.

"This is happening right now?" asked one of the older men in the group.

"Yes!" I paused. "Well, three years ago. The marriage, I mean."

"Oh? And she is still married?"

"As far as I know, yes."

One man who'd been smoking threw his cigarette butt on the ground and snorted. "Domestic issue, haa?"

"No." I shook my head. "She was forced to marry him."

I half wondered if I should switch to English. From the reactions of bus drivers and restaurant workers, I'd learned that English immediately raised my credibility in their eyes. Besides, I could explain myself better, but I didn't want to come across as alien to these officers. I needed them to trust me.

"Tell her to ask for a new sari or gold bangles and stop complaining."

"But you don't understand," I said, feeling slightly sick. "She was only sixteen."

"It's the way they do things in the villages. What to do?" said one man with a shrug.

"All my aunts got married at sixteen," said another. "Fifteen is practically a woman."

"At least she's not ten," said a third.

"Maybe it's a marriage counselor she needs, no?" asked another.

I felt my face go warm. I switched to English without even thinking. "They pulled her out of school and forced her to marry this vile old man. She was a child bride!"

The men raised their eyebrows and looked at me with renewed interest.

"American?"

"Yes!" I said, stepping forward. *Might as well invoke the strongest country on earth. Maybe that'll get them to pay attention.* "This is a serious crime!"

One of the officers sighed and shook his head. "You Westerners always come here to intrude and give us trouble."

I stared at him.

"That's village tradition," he said. "You come here to fight tradition?"

"But—"

"Look, you look like a good Indian girl," said the older officer, giving me a fatherly look that probably meant well. "Why you behaving like a Westerner and making trouble for yourself?"

"Since when is reporting a crime making trouble?" I snapped.

"Coconut!" cried out a younger man to the guffaws of his pals. "We have a coconut!"

I glowered at him.

"Hey, don't get so insulted," he said, seeing my face. "So many coconuts in India now. Brown on outside, white on inside. Ha ha!"

"Do you have any evidence for this accusation?" asked the older officer, ignoring his colleagues.

I shook my head, racking my brain for anything that would persuade them to take this seriously.

"I know where they live," I said. "I can show you their house and you can speak to her directly. And you can speak to the man too. You'll see when you meet him what kind of a criminal he is."

That brought another round of chuckles from the younger officers.

"You think we can go into another man's house like American Rambo and ask him about his own wife?"

"But she's not his wife," I said. "She never wanted to get married in the first place. She was just a kid. Look, I have a letter from—"

Before I could finish, someone hollered through the main doors. The men turned and shuffled back in, grumbling, throwing their half-smoked cigarette butts on the ground.

The older man turned around. "You might as well go and file a report with the office, then." With that, he marched inside and shut the door behind him.

I looked back toward the juice stall. Win and Katy were still there, pretending to be tourists. They didn't dare wave. I didn't either.

With a heavy sigh, I walked up to the door of the police station.

No one said this would be easy.

I stepped into what felt like an oven.

I was in a narrow corridor with a row of plastic chairs set against the wall. The room was airless. Two thin men in dirty sarongs and ripped shirts sat in one corner looking forlorn. At the other end, a gray-haired woman in a sari sat bent over with her head in her hands. Next to her was a flustered young woman. She gave me a nervous glance as I walked in.

The public area was separated from the office by a concrete barrier that came up to my shoulders. A glass panel made up the top half of this wall. Through this, I could see the officers assembled in a corner in what looked like an urgent meeting. While it was sweltering in the public area, half a dozen ceiling fans were buzzing inside the office.

"Yes?"

I turned my head. It was a policewoman. She'd appeared behind the glass barrier with a notepad in one hand and a walkie-talkie in the other. She looked too harried to be interrupted.

I leaned in and pressed my nose against the glass. *Finally, a female officer.* She'd understand, I was sure.

"I'm here to make a report. I need to rescue my cousin. She's in trouble. A forced marriage."

She raised her eyebrows.

She looked like she'd actually listen to me. I opened my mouth and before I knew it, my mouth was blabbing faster than my brain could keep up.

"My grandmother signed a contract to marry me off to a man called Kristadasa. But I ran away before that happened and Preeti, my cousin, was forced to marry him instead. He's an evil man. He was already married too. And Preeti was only sixteen. She was a child bride. I have a letter from her saying what happened."

I paused to take a breath. For the second time that day, I wished I'd stopped by a store to get local garb so I wouldn't look so foreign. I felt like I had to explain further.

"Franky, who owns the Good and Fast Immigration Broker near the Vasco bus stop, promised to help me. He said he'd send me overseas so I could escape but in the end, he stole all of my parents' money. I didn't know it then. I was only fifteen. He told me he'd use the money to send Preeti to school and help my Aunty Shilpa get her medication. She was really sick, almost dying. But he lied to us. He stole my money and never helped my family."

I faltered, running out of breath. The woman was staring at me silently as if I was an alien. She hadn't understood a word I'd said. I might as well have been speaking Chinese.

I tried again. "Please, may I speak with a police investigator or the inspector? I really, really need your help."

With an incredulous look, she turned and called out something to the men in their huddle. I heard a snort from somewhere in the back of the room. A couple of men looked up, peered my way and shrugged their shoulders and went back to their meeting.

The female officer put her walkie-talkie down with a sigh. She rifled through a stack of papers on the bench in front of her, pulled out a sheet and pushed it through the small opening in the glass window.

"You must fill out this form and we will look at it," she said.

"But this is urgent," I said, "Look, I'd like to speak to the inspector—"

"You cannot just walk in to see the inspector on these matters," she said, turning to walk away. "Fill the form to show how this warrants police attention. That is the process for family matters."

"This is not a family matter!"

The woman gave a resigned shrug, turned around and disappeared into a back office.

I stared in her direction, feeling numb.

Chapter Ten

"**I**s that your home?"

Win was pointing at a low terracotta brick building.

"Ours was smaller. And older. And uglier."

After leaving the police station, we'd wandered for an hour, trying to find my old apartment complex. My search hadn't been as easy as I'd expected.

The landscape had changed. In place of shanty compounds, new office buildings with parking lots had sprung up. The narrow gravel paths of my childhood had disappeared under two-lane asphalt roads now buzzing with motorcycles, auto rickshaws, cars and buses.

We'd returned to the bus stop to buy bottles of water and ask the local vendors for directions to the apartment complex.

I turned to Win. "Hey, can we take some of that cash out now? Kristadasa will probably ask for money to release Preeti."

"Like ransom money?" Katy asked.

"My grandmother got paid for giving Preeti to him. He'll want that back."

"Your grandma *sold* your cousin?" asked Win, her eyes widening.

Interesting. She'd been sold off by her own father, yet she was confounded that the same thing had happened to someone else. *Win's holding onto her humanity,* I thought, feeling both relieved and sad.

I shrugged. There was nothing to say.

Everyone stared silently at the ground for a moment, letting it all sink in, I supposed.

"Hey, are you sure Preeti will want to leave?" Katy asked.

The possibility that she wouldn't hadn't even crossed my mind. "She's Kristadasa's *slave,*" I said, after a pause. "Why would she want to stay?"

"Just wondering. Stockholm syndrome and all that. You never know," said Katy in a quiet voice. "Don't want you to get disappointed."

I slipped my hand into my pocket and felt Preeti's letter. I knew every word on it now. She hadn't been unhappy when she wrote that letter. She'd been *tormented*.

"She'll want to get out. I'm sure. One thousand percent."

On our way to my grandmother's old apartment, we found a bank machine. Win's hard work was paying off and the cash had come to our brand-new account. The money had been transferred to Tetyana as well, but we still hadn't heard from her.

"There!"

I stopped and stared at the cheaply constructed, seven-story concrete block.

I'd seen that graffiti-covered facade a thousand times before. This complex had been built just before an important election decades ago. One political party had promised to get slum dwellers into better housing and had won by a landslide. Just as quickly, they'd forgotten the very people who put them in power. Every time the plumbing broke, or a crack appeared in the wall, Grandma would huff, "Our government's corrupt. Useless buggers. I was better off in the slum!"

A crooked coconut tree stood in the front yard, looking as lonely as I remembered it. Its leaves rustled in the wind as I watched. I wondered if it had witnessed the short wedding ceremony supposed to have taken place in this yard the day I'd run away. I wondered if it had watched as they took Aunty Shilpa away in a stretcher to die at the hospital. I wondered if it had seen my grandmother's funeral.

"Asha?"

I turned around to see Katy and Win staring at me.

"Are you okay?" Katy reached over and touched my shoulder.

"Fine," I mumbled, swallowing something that had stuck in my throat.

At least I had one family member left. My heart quickened. I could already see Preeti's face with those expressive dark eyes and her beautiful smile. *Will she be excited to see me? Like I am to see her?* I couldn't wait to hug her and tell her how much I missed her.

But will Kristadasa be with her?

My hands involuntarily clenched. I'd been much smaller and much younger when he'd tried to attack me. If I'd pushed him back then, I could do it now. I shook my head to remove the old cobwebs of memories trying to strangle my mind. *I'll deal with him when I see him.*

"Let's go," I said in a firm voice.

I didn't walk to the building. I marched forward.

Around me, I could hear children playing in the backyard. I could even hear the sound of the ocean from far away.

My heart was beating faster now, but I kept striding. I felt the comforting presence of my friends right behind me. *We're going to be fine*, I told myself as we arrived at the main door.

The entrance was unlocked. My heart thumped faster. I pulled on the knob and opened the creaky door. Inside, the bulbs had gone out and it was dark.

I stepped in. The fixtures had been removed or stolen and the only light coming in was through the open doorway.

A door banged somewhere in the building, making us jump. I felt Katy take a sharp breath in.

My grandmother's apartment was at the end of the corridor on the ground floor. Every time I'd come home from school, I'd smelled her mouthwatering cooking from the hallway. There were no such smells now, just mold and a faint trace of a dead animal. I sniffed. *A rat?*

I walked toward my former home.

Our apartment had been a simple affair.

It had an open fire stove in one corner and a sofa bed in the other where Preeti and I practically lived. It was where we'd done our homework, giggled over schoolgirl gossip, read our books, and slept curled up against each other for warmth. Aunty Shilpa and Grandma had slept on a straw mat in the only room of the apartment. *Room* was a generous word. It was the size of a closet, large enough to fit a mat and a tiny shrine for the Hindu goddess, Kali.

Kali, the Mother of the Universe, my grandmother liked to call her. She believed she warded off all evil. Preeti and I were glad the statue stayed inside their room because the goddess wasn't a pleasant sight. She had four arms, one of which carried a bloodied sword and another which held the bleeding, severed head of a human. With her bulging eyes, lolling tongue, and necklace of human skulls, she used to give me nightmares.

I didn't realize how long I'd been standing at my old door, frozen, until I felt Katy's hand on my arm.

"Do you want me to knock?" she asked softly from behind me.

I shook my head. No, this was my mission. I lifted my hand and rapped on the door.

We waited.

Nothing.

The silence was eerie.

The walls of this building were so thin we used to hear Fartybag's loud music pumping from the floor above us. Many nights, we'd also hear the man in the third apartment down the corridor beat his wife. Her cries kept Preeti and me up. On those nights, my grandmother used to sleep with the corners of her sari pushed into her ears.

But it was midday now, a time when anyone with a job was out and everyone else was in the backyard seeking the cool breeze in the shadows of the building.

I knocked again, louder this time.

After Grandma and Aunty Shilpa's death, this apartment should have gone to Preeti. I banged louder. This was my home. *My family home.*

I banged again.

"Open up!" I shouted.

The door creaked open.

Chapter Eleven

K ristadasa's first wife stared at me.

She was stooped over, like a hunchback wrapped in a dirty orange sari. She had aged since I'd last seen her, the lines on her withered face making her look older than even my grandmother used to.

She gave me a shocked look.

"What are you doing here?" I asked her in Konkani.

She put a hand over her mouth and let out a surprised cry.

Blood rushed to my head. "Where's Preeti?"

She threw her hand up to shut the door. I thrust my foot in to stop it from closing.

She looked behind her in panic, like someone was watching her from back there.

I felt a jolt of anger go through me.

I stepped inside, pushing her roughly aside.

I swirled around the apartment. There was no one here.

The place looked smaller and more squalid than I remembered. There was a mat on the ground where the sofa bed used to be with a dirty shawl draped across it. My grandmother's cooking pots were all gone. The kitchen looked like it had barely been used in years.

I felt disoriented. There were all these strangers' things here now. Someone had moved in. Outsiders. People who'd swindled my family. People who'd stolen my cousin. People who'd *killed* Grandma and Aunty Shilpa.

A fire roared in my gut, a fire that had ignited the day I received Preeti's letter. It was flaming inside me now.

"Preeti!" I shouted. "Preeti! Where are you!"

A peculiar noise came from the small room where Grandma and Aunty Shilpa used to sleep. Someone had installed a door now. I marched toward it.

"Preeti!" I screamed.

I yanked the door open and stormed in.

Where Grandma used to sleep, I found Kristadasa. Lying on the same mat she used to.

The stench of alcohol fumes and cigarette smoke made me gag. Kristadasa turned with a grunt and gave me a bleary look. His eyes were bloodshot from too much Fenni, the strongest drink you'd find on this side of the planet.

But it was the girl next to him that stopped me on my tracks. She must have been twelve, thirteen at most. She was curled in a fetal position in the corner of the room, half-naked, like a piece of bad meat thrown away to rot in a dumpster.

She gave me a frightened look and quickly covered herself with her shawl.

I felt like retching.

Years of built-up rage pulsed through my veins mixed with vomit-inducing nausea.

"You pedophile!" I roared. "Where's Preeti? Tell me! You disgusting creep!"

Kristadasa gave me a glazed look and stood up, holding on to the wall. He swayed and belched.

I never believed in any of the one hundred and one gods my grandmother used to pray to. I especially detested Kali, whom I felt looked like the devil himself. But the fury of Kali was rising in me now. My eyes felt like they were streaming molten lava. I was ready to rip this man to pieces.

"What did you do to her?" I screamed at him. "Where is she! Where is Preeti! Tell me!"

The man growled—a low guttural sound you'd hear from a caged carnivore.

My hands clenched, ready to hit him till he fell to his knees, till he bled to death right in front of me.

"Tell me, you bastard!"

Kristadasa was quicker than I expected. I felt the knife before I saw it. It slashed my stomach, but I felt no pain. The adrenaline rushing through me numbed any feelings.

I jumped back and just as quickly lunged forward to kick him.

"Asha!" I head someone shout. It might have been Katy. Might have been Win. I didn't have time to find out.

Kristadasa slammed me against the door and wrapped a dirty paw around my throat. "Get off me!" I gargled, kicking furiously, hitting him wherever I could.

His hand pressed down on my nose. My head felt like it was about to explode.

Someone was beating against the door. It pulsated behind me like an army was banging on it.

"Asha!" Someone screamed my name again.

But I focused on the monster in front of me. I fought back, trying to pry his hands off my throat, kicking nonstop. But he was strong.

Froth streamed from the sides of his mouth like in a rabid animal. He was trying to say something but was either too drunk or too surprised to.

I saw the fist come over my head. He was going to pummel me to death. I didn't have time to think. I blocked it with my left arm and screamed as the searing pain went through me.

My arm may have been crushed, but I didn't care. I punched his nose with my other hand, targeting the soft part. Once. Twice. Three times. Hard. *Harder.*

He rocked back on his heels, trying to steady himself. He swayed but maintained his grip on my neck. Then, he belched, the vile smell filling the room.

I was hyperventilating. *I want to breathe. Breathe. Let me breathe.*

Then, something in my brain kicked in.

I stopped fighting. I stopped kicking, punching and screaming and forced myself to breathe normally. In and out.

As I slackened, the hand on my throat relaxed. Kristadasa glared at me with those ugly beady eyes. A shudder went through me as I remembered those same eyes on me when I was fourteen years old. But I stared right back, unwavering, getting stronger with every breath.

To my child's mind, he'd looked like an enormous ogre who ate girls for supper. I now realized I hadn't been too far off. He was a heavy-set man and if he'd been sober, this fight would have been over in seconds.

It was now or never.

I dug my nails into his palms and twisted his hand away.

"Aaarrrg!" he yelled.

Summoning every ounce of Kali energy in me, I gave a left hook on his ear. Right hook on his nose. Left jab on his Adam's apple.

Those martial arts lessons I'd got back in the international schools in Africa were going to be helpful after all.

Jab. Jab. Jab. Hook. Nonstop. A kick on his kneecap.

He faltered. I kicked his knees again, this time making him buckle.

He backed off, looking at me with hate-filled eyes, and let out a snarl like a vicious animal.

He swiped at my face.

I ducked.

I grabbed at the knife but he pulled away.

Another swipe.

I ducked the other way.

I felt my cheek burn but only for a second. If he was going to kill me, I was going to take him down with me.

"Asha, open the door!" Someone was screaming from somewhere. I focused on Kristadasa.

From the corner of my eyes, I saw the knife coming toward my face again.

I ducked and stomped on his toes.

He let out a yell. I thrust two fingers right in his jugular, screaming as I did. He rocked back. I kicked him in between his legs. Right in the balls. Then another kick. And another. And another.

With a screeching howl, he dropped his knife and slithered to the ground, clutching his groin.

I didn't wait. I grabbed the knife from the floor and plunged it right into his stomach.

The roar was deafening. He doubled over.

I stood over him, the knife in my hands. "Tell me!" I screamed. "Where is Preeti? What did you do to her?"

Kristadasa gurgled, holding on to his sides.

He shot me a dark look. "Smashed her face. Thrashed the little—"

I was no longer thinking. I was no longer human. Kali was strong in me. I pulled the knife out and plunged it right in between his legs and sliced sideways.

With a piercing howl Kristadasa came crashing down like a massive tree, his head hitting the floor two inches from the young girl's feet.

She shrieked. The man bellowed. The girl huddled against the wall and stared at him in horror.

Kali got the better of me. She was in control of me now.

With a roar to gather all my remaining strength and my eyes flashing fire, I lifted the knife high, aiming for his throat.

In the split second I lunged at Kristadasa, the door banged open.

Chapter Twelve

Win and Katy flew into the room yelling at the top of their lungs, like a tornado had hurled them inside.

"Asha!" Katy yanked the bloodied knife from my hands and pulled me away from Kristadasa.

"Oh, my god!" Win cried, staring at the young girl.

The older wife came in screeching after them.

She pushed us away roughly and let out a wail at the sight of her husband incapacitated on the ground.

She fell to her knees, calling out his name, beating her chest. She didn't even glance at the terror-stricken girl huddled in the corner, sobbing.

"My god, are you okay?" Katy asked, grabbing me by the shoulder and looking me over.

"You're bleeding!" Win cried out.

"I'm fine," I replied, panting, trying to orient myself. "I'm... Don't worry about me."

I glanced at the man on the floor clutching his genitals, yelping like a dog in pain.

He was alive all right, but his breathing was raspy. He was not in a state to talk. Even if he had been, I doubted he'd have shared Preeti's whereabouts with me.

I crouched down next to the old woman.

"Hey," I said. "Can you please tell—"

She turned around and slapped me across the face. I reeled back, stunned.

She shot me a venomous look. "You filthy whore!"

I stood up, rubbing my cheek. "I had no choice. He—"

"You good for nothing slut! I wish he killed you!"

"Listen," I said, taking a deep breath. "Do you know what he was doing to that little girl—"

I didn't get to finish my sentence. She jumped up and slapped my face again so hard I fell back.

"Asha!" cried Win.

"Stop that!" yelled Katy, darting in between the woman and me.

I stared at the wife. She glared back.

I wanted to be angry, but all I felt was sorry for her. *What a life she must have had to think this kind of existence is normal. What would make her defend such an evil monster like Kristadasa?*

I shook my head. "Look, I didn't come here to hurt anyone. I only want to find my cousin. I want to find Preeti. That's all."

"That bitch is gone!" the woman cried in a shrill voice. "Ran away like a coward little slut."

"Where did she go?"

"May Vishnu strike you dead, you mongrel."

The hate in her voice was startling.

"Just tell me where she went!"

"To the streets, you black bitch!"

A chill went down my spine.

"Please tell me," I said, pleading, "Do you know where she is? Is she in Goa? Mumbai?"

With a nasty glare, she stepped up to me, pulled me by my hair and spat in my face.

"Hey!" Win cried.

"Stop this!" Katy yelled, pulling me away from the woman.

I stepped back and wiped my face with the back of my hand.

With an angry scowl, the woman squatted back down next to her husband and started to wipe the blood from the knife wounds. He was sniveling like a child.

I was not going to get anything from her.

I looked over at the girl cowering in the corner.

"Hey," I said softly. "You don't have to stay here."

She gave me a terrified look and retreated even further into her corner.

"Don't be scared. I can help you."

I took a step forward, but before I could get any closer she scampered to the other end of the room on all fours like a wild animal.

I stopped moving and knelt down. I held out a hand to her. The girl whimpered and pulled down her scarf to cover her face.

"*Tugele naav kasale?*" I asked. *What's your name?*

Ignoring me, she crawled over to Kristadasa and his wife. She turned her back to me and huddled against the old woman's body.

I watched her in shock. *What made her do that?*

"Let's go," Katy said softly from behind me, but I didn't move. I couldn't. My mind whirled. *How can I convince her to get away from this hellhole?*

I felt Katy gently pull me by the arm. "There's nothing you can do here."

The girl buried her head in the older woman's lap. I guessed the devil she knew was more comforting than the devil she didn't.

I looked down at my torn and bloodied clothes. My foreign accent, unusual looks, and the way I'd subdued that man, probably meant I wasn't safe to her.

I still had to find Preeti. She must have run away and was replaced by this little girl. *But when? And where is she now?* There was nowhere they could have hidden Preeti here. She was gone. She'd been gone a long time. I felt in my bones.

Katy and Win were at the door, urgently motioning to get out. After one last glance at the little girl, I followed them out.

Behind us came a loud wail from the first wife.

"He's not dead. Why's she acting like he is?" Win whispered.

I shrugged. For what he did to my family, my cousin, and that girl, I wished he was dead.

"Let's get out of here."

Katy took me by one arm and Win by the other.

Blood was still pounding in my ear from my fight with the brute. Something hurt near my stomach and my left arm felt numb.

"It just grazed you," Katy said, examining me briefly.

"But that's a lot of blood," I heard Win say.

"We need help," said Katy.

My knees felt like they'd give way at any moment. I closed my eyes and let them escort me out.

Part TWO

I knew I was going to take the wrong train, so I left early.
Yogi Berra

Katy and Win hailed a tuk-tuk taxi and took me to a private clinic in town. It was a good thing we had extra cash. Travel insurance had not been at the top of our minds when we dashed across Europe looking for the best escape route.

A friendly nurse cleaned and dressed my wounds and pressed a vial of painkillers into my hand.

"Just flesh wounds and a few bruises," she said. "They'll heal in a week or two."

Katy had told her I'd walked onto a busy intersection and got hit by a motorcycle. The nurse's face said she didn't believe us, but she didn't say a word.

She probably got her fair share of tourists who'd come after a beach brawl or a drug-fueled moonlight party. Silence, I was sure, was part of the service for the high price they charged. They'd even let us wash up, change and rest for a few hours in cots in the back until I felt well enough to walk by myself.

But time was precious.

We didn't have many hours left before Katy and Win had to be at the airport and on a plane out. And I didn't want to look for Preeti alone. Without them, I'd have murdered a man in cold blood, while he was lying on the ground gasping for breath.

I needed Katy and Win with me. I badly needed Tetyana and Luc too, but they were fighting their own battles. I could only help them once I'd finished my personal quest.

Though my head hurt and my mind felt woozy, I was ready to do whatever I needed. My only remaining hope was The Good and Fast Immigration Broker. Everyone else I'd known in this town had either died or disappeared.

After a meal of bland rice and vegetable stew served at the clinic, we hopped into a taxi and drove to where Franky's fake immigration office had been. This was where I'd met his son, Fartybag, the name Preeti and I had given to him a long time ago. I still didn't know what Fartybag's real name was and didn't care to find out. I'd hoped to never have to deal with him again, but I couldn't have been more wrong.

We got out of the taxi and walked into Vasco's main bus station. I'd come to this place every morning to go to school with Preeti. The bus shelters and platforms looked cleaner and the buildings around the area more modern. There were also more people than before, busy chatting on their phones or rushing somewhere important.

But one thing was glaringly missing: the homeless beggars who used to squat near the entrance. They were all gone now. On the wall, above where they used to sit, was a picture of a man in a loincloth begging for alms with a thick red line drawn across it.

I wondered about Meena, the flute-playing *hijra* who used to sit cross-legged on the ground, playing beautiful music no one seemed to hear but me. I'd been transfixed by her songs ever since I'd first heard her play.

Over time, I'd learned how similar we were. We were both outcasts. I was a foreign orphan trying to fit into a strange land, and she was a transgendered woman in a culture that vilified them. Other than Aunty Shilpa and Preeti, few had shown me kindness in this country. She was one of them.

What happened to Meena? Where is she now? I wondered as I scoped the area.

I searched for Franky's office sign, but it no longer said *Good and Fast Immigration Broker.* In place of the faded, garish sign stood a swanky, multi-neon lit one that said, *Gadget Mart, Best modern dealer in Goa. Get your cool mobiles here!*

Did Franky move?

There was only one way to find out.

I motioned to Katy and Win to follow me.

We climbed up the dank stairwell to the shops on the second level, above the station. We walked up holding our breath. The lighting was better than I remembered, but the smell of urine and diesel pervaded the stairway just like before.

To my surprise, the second-floor landing opened up to an ultra-modern electronics store.

Gone were the faded travel posters, the statues of Hindu gods and colonial furniture. Instead, there were LCD screens on the walls flashing the latest gadgets. Rows and rows of mobile phones of every conceivable brand sat on pristine white shelves. Two lanky teens bustled around the shop, rearranging merchandise, helping a lone customer. It could have been any electronics store, anywhere in the world.

I looked over to where Franky's bureau had been. In its place was a sleek chrome desk. And behind this sat Franky's son, immersed in his phone.

He was wearing a gaudy gold chain and sporting a tight-fitting T-shirt with a picture of Arnold Schwarzenegger in full military gear. He'd grown wider than he had tall. The T-shirt only covered half his belly, exposing rolls of excessive good living.

He looked nineteen, twenty at most. But to me, Fartybag would always be the obnoxious boy with the pockmarked face who used to urinate at the corner of the bus stall, catcalling any girl who'd walk near him. I wondered what had happened to his two companions who'd loved to harass the schoolgirls at the bus stop. That is, until the day I punched Fartybag on the nose and made them stop.

Taking a deep breath in, I walked up to him. I hoped he'd forgotten that incident.

Chapter Fourteen

Fartybag was sitting back, feet on his desk. He held a greasy donut in one hand and was about to take a bite when I strolled up. On his table sat a large teacup nestled among a pile of papers.

I cleared my throat.

He looked up and dropped the pastry. He pulled his feet off the desk and stared at me like he'd seen a ghost.

I crossed my arms and stood in front of him, feet apart, shoulders straight and chin up, just like Arnie would have before an enemy. I now knew the dirty games he and his father played, and I had no reason to believe they'd changed for the better.

"Where's Franky?"

I chose to speak in English deliberately.

Fartybag wiped the donut crumbs on his cheek, only to smear them on his face even more. His eyes were wide in shock. He looked like a kid who'd been caught doing something wrong.

"Oi," I raised my voice. "I asked a question. Where's your father?"

His eyes flickered from me to Katy and Win, who were standing behind me, and then back to me again.

I stepped closer.

"Have you forgotten how to speak?" I snarled. What I really wanted to do was punch him in the face, but I needed information first.

I took a deep breath and leaned across Fartybag's desk. He drew back, his eyes now larger than his teacup.

"I'm here to find Preeti, and I think you and your father know where she is."

"Oh?" He looked relieved. "Is that why...?" He cleared his throat and put his hands up. "No idea."

"Don't lie to me. You live over Grandma's apartment. You know everything that goes on in that building."

He cracked a nervous laugh. "We don't live in dump no more. We live in real place now." A visible change went through Fartybag. He sat up, shifting from shocked to his more cocky self.

"We moved to big house."

He looked smug.

"Just tell me where Preeti is."

"I told you. Don't know this." His eyes slithered toward Win. "Chinese?" He leered. "Thai girl?"

"Oi!" I snapped my fingers in Fartybag's face. "Pay attention, boy."

"And why you all got red shoes?" he said, with a snicker. "A stupid girly uniform?"

"That's none of your goddamned business." I scowled. "You and your father orchestrate everything in this town. You turned my family's life upside down. You killed Grandma and Aunty Shilpa!"

"Your aunty died because she got AIDS. She was—"

"Shut up!" I banged my hand on his desk. He jumped. "One more word and I'll do you in myself!"

I glared at him. He gave me a confused look. I guessed he'd never had a woman talk to him like this.

I felt everyone's eyes on my back now. The store had gone silent, but I was long past worrying about witnesses.

"Cut the bull crap. I know exactly what you did to my cousin. I know your father brokered the deal so she'd be married off to that creep after I ran away."

Silence.

"Answer me, boy!" I cried. "You ruined my family and stole my parents' money. That's what paid for all this!"

He shifted uncomfortably in his seat and shot a nervous glance at his team.

I looked over my shoulder. Bunched in a far corner and safely out of range were the two young workers, staring at me with wild eyes.

They huddled even closer to each other when they saw me turn their way.

I noticed Katy and Win were standing their ground, legs apart, arms crossed, with don't-mess-with-me, unsmiling expressions on their faces. I knew they were dog-tired from searching for someone they hadn't even met, but they'd stuck with me. I couldn't have asked for better friends.

I turned back to Fartybag. "Your father's nothing but a criminal."

He shook his head, a serious look on his face now. "No, no, no. Appa is good man. He was only helping you. For that we need to take a cut. It's for all the service, you see."

I realized then all he worried about was not getting caught for the money he stole from my parents. Preeti's disappearance, the child bride brokering and the human trafficking his father was involved in were all minor issues in his world.

"I know a hell of a lot more than you think!"

"Appa did so much for you. He give you good life. Without him, you'll be on street." He gave me a sad look—an emotion I didn't think he was capable of. "You were like family to him. In Indian culture family is utmost important, you know."

"And that's why he finished mine?"

He looked down at his desk.

I gritted my teeth.

"Tell me now. Where's Preeti?"

"Only Appa knows."

I took a breath to calm myself. "Okay, where is Franky then?"

"Mumbai," he mumbled. "At Aunty Rao's funeral."

It was my turn to be shocked. "Mrs. Rao from Toronto?" *The woman who kept me captive for almost two years as her servant?*

Fartybag nodded forlornly.

"Aunty killed herself two days ago. Appa brought her body to Mumbai. That's where he is." He wasn't making eye contact any more. "Please, our family is in mourning."

Aunty? Family? Were all these people related?

"I don't believe you," I said. "You're lying to me again."

My eyes swept the desk where the teacup, half-eaten donut and his mobile phone lay. Before he could make a move, I leaned in and grabbed the phone. I held it out to the side.

"Oi!" he called out in surprise.

Without taking my eyes off the man, I said, "Win, can you get Franky's address, please?"

I felt her step up and pluck the phone from my hand.

Fartybag stared at me, open-mouthed.

I wondered if this was the first time he'd experienced a woman get the better of him. I glared back.

I lowered my voice. "I will tell the whole world that you built your fortune from the money you stole from my parents. You and your father are nothing more than common thieves. Do you understand what I'm saying?"

Sweat streamed down his oily face.

He was at least twice my size and could have easily tackled me, but he was a coward. And cowards never fight when cornered.

"I don't know what you talking about..." he faltered. "This is intimidation, you know."

I let out a coarse laugh. "Intimidation? We can talk about intimidation, if you want. You double-crossing basta—"

"Done."

Win stepped up and deposited the phone back on the desk. She gave me a quick nod. "I've got it."

I gave one last nasty glare at Fartybag. "You're going to regret you ever met me."

An angry flicker passed over his face, but he said nothing.

I turned around.

"Let's go."

Chapter Fifteen

I heard the music when we got halfway down the stairwell.

I was still reeling from my encounter with my childhood nemesis. My mind was trying to decipher lies from truths, imagining conspiracies and games. That was when I heard the song. It was like a siren call.

"Meena?"

I stopped to listen.

It was faint, coming from someplace far away, but I recognized the haunting melody.

"Meena!" I yelled.

I stumbled down the stairs with Katy and Win running behind me, asking *what the heck's going on now?*

The music stopped for a few seconds. In my mind's eye, Meena had paused to take a sip of water from the broken tin cup she always kept nearby.

Then, the flute song started again. It was a beautiful, ethereal sound coming from that tiny instrument of hers. It was like her soul was weeping.

"Meena!" I cried, looking around me. "Where are you?"

I was about to vault across the road when a bus rumbled in front of me. I felt two hands pull me back just in time.

"Watch out!" Katy and Win called out at the same time.

"I'm sure it's her!" I said, jogging on the spot, waiting for the bus to clear our path.

"Who's Meena?" Win asked.

"Another one of Franky's friends?" Katy asked, with a hint of exasperation in her voice.

The bus drove off, leaving us in a plume of diesel smoke. I jumped across the road and ran to where the beggars usually sat. But the spot was empty.

Black dust and exhaust fumes hung in the air, creating a haze around us. I spotted a security guard strolling nearby with a wooden baton in his hands. He looked bored and was swinging the stick gently, in time to the music.

Where is she?

"Come," I said to Win and Katy. "She's got to be here, somewhere."

The guard gave us a curious look as we rushed past him. For a moment, I worried he'd stop us. But he didn't. We scampered out of the station and onto the street, following the music. It was coming from around the corner near the bazaar.

There!

I stopped in my tracks.

Leaning against a lone frangipani tree, I saw the outline of a woman sitting cross-legged on the ground. Next to her sat a gray-haired beggar man in a loincloth, quietly nodding to himself, lost in the song.

With my heart in my mouth, I walked over slowly, each step dragging more than the one before. I'd had so many disappointments, I didn't want this to be another one.

I got closer.

It was her. It was Meena.

Her eyes were closed, focused on the song.

I remembered how eerie this music had sounded when it had echoed through the station during those rare times when things got quiet. That exquisitely surreal sound was now being drowned out by car honks, street hawkers and the irreverent revving of motorcycle engines. Despite all this, her head was moving back and forth gently to the tune, like the music had her completely.

It seemed obscene to interrupt.

Meena was wearing a saffron-colored sari. She had the same bright red dot on her forehead she'd worn before and didn't look a year older than when I saw her last.

I felt a surge of emotion go through me. A sob escaped from my mouth. How I'd missed all these good people I'd left behind.

Katy and Win stood next to me as I listened with tears streaming down my face. Neither the beggar man nor Meena noticed us.

Then halfway through a note, something made Meena stop and look up. Maybe she'd felt our presence.

She shielded her eyes to peer at the three bedraggled girls standing in front of her. She squinted at me.

"Asha?"

I dropped to my knees and put my hands together. Meena let her flute fall to the ground, reached toward me and pulled me close.

I fell into her arms sobbing.

Chapter Sixteen

"**W**hat in Shiva's good name happened to you, my girl?" Meena reached out and touched my cheek. The fresh knife cut was small but visible.

We were sitting on a concrete block next to a chai wallah stall, sipping hot tea.

I looked away. "It was an accident. I saw a doctor and she patched me up."

She scrunched her face. "Really?"

"It's nothing. I'm okay." I didn't want to burden her with my story. My fight with Kristadasa was too raw. Too scary. Even Katy, Win and I avoided talking about it. "Just a small traffic accident."

Meena's critical eyes passed over my pants and shirt. I'd changed at the clinic but I still looked like someone who'd run a marathon in a dust bowl. "What happened to your overseas job? They didn't take care of you, my girl? Haa? They didn't know what a godsend you are?"

I half smiled to myself. If she only knew what the past few years had been like for me.

Seeing Meena was like reuniting with an older sister, a sister who lived a very different life, but one who deeply cared for me. I'd spent a few good minutes letting myself go and crying into her sari folds under the frangipani tree. It was a cry I had badly needed.

Meena hadn't changed a bit. Her lips were brightly painted in pink and her eyes were heavily lined with black kohl I'd never dare use myself. She'd covered the knife scar she'd gotten as a child with a heavy dose of baby powder. Behind all that cheap makeup lay a warm face and an even warmer heart.

She clapped her hands and giggled in glee when I introduced Katy and Win to her. She'd seen tourists pass by to get onto buses and taxis, but she'd never met anyone from outside of India. We huddled over chai and sweets, Meena asking us a million questions and me translating as much as I could so Katy and Win could follow along.

Meena was mesmerized by Win.

"Your face!" she said with a tsk. "Vishnu has blessed you with an angel face, but you have scratched it so badly! What ungodly things have you girls been doing?"

Win gave me a curious look. I translated.

Katy and Win had had their own fight with Kristadasa's first wife while I was battling him inside the room. She'd slapped and scratched them, but we hadn't stopped to notice the marks she'd left on them until the nurse examined us at the clinic.

"She was in the accident with me," I blurted.

Meena turned to Katy next, fussing over her "exotic" amber hair, touching it and exclaiming in wonder. Win and Katy seemed happy to be the center of all this sudden attention. They giggled and laughed along with her.

Just as we finished the tea, Meena's face took on a serious tone. She pulled out a small paper bag from the folds of her sari. "I have something for you," she said to me. "Something special."

She deposited it carefully in front of me.

"What's this?" I asked.

Win picked up the bag before I could.

"It's a book," she said, slipping it out of the bag. "A pink book."

I frowned. *What does that remind me of?* I leaned over her shoulder to see.

"It's a journal of some sort." Win flipped through the pages quickly. "Or a scrapbook," she added. A photo of an Indian doctor in a sari flickered by.

"Go back," I said. "Slowly."

Win turned the pages back one by one.

"Preeti's diary!" I exclaimed, grabbing the book from Win's hands. "Where did you get this?" I cried, turning to Meena.

"She wanted me to give it to you if...when you returned."

I grabbed Meena's hand. "Where is she?"

She shook her head sadly. "She was in a hurry that day."

"When? Where? Why?" I wanted to shake her. "Please tell me."

Win was staring at us quizzically.

"What's going on?" Katy asked, seeing my agitation.

"Tell me from the beginning," I begged Meena. "Tell me everything. When did you see her? What did she say?"

"I was playing the flute at the station that day," Meena replied, her eyes lowered as if the story was too hard to tell.

"I saw her come very early in the morning. For one moment, I thought it was you." She raised her eyes to give me a wistful look. "I thought you returned from your big overseas job."

I reached out and squeezed her hand.

"But it was your cousin. It was an hour before the school bus came, so I knew something was different that day. She looked scared." She paused. "Very scared."

I turned to Katy and Win and translated quickly.

"She'd been crying," continued Meena. "She had a big bruise on her face. Her lips were swollen. She didn't look well. She came and sat next to me quietly like you used to long ago, remember?"

I nodded, still holding her hand. "Yes, I remember," I whispered.

"She told me she had to go."

"Where?"

Meena shook her head. "She handed this book to me and told me to give it to you if I ever saw you again. Then, she left."

"Left to go back home? To school?"

"No, she jumped on a different bus that day. Not the school bus."

"Which one?"

Meena's frown deepened.

"She didn't tell me. And I'm not a woman who can read bus signs. I'm not smart like you, Asha."

Then, I remembered. Like Aunty Shilpa and my grandmother, Meena never learned to read.

"I'm trying to help you." She gave me an earnest look. "All I know is she was running away. She got on the bus that all the foreigners get into."

I sat up. "The one to Mumbai?"

Meena gave me a blank look.

"The one going to the airport?"

She shook her head. "I don't think we'll ever know where she ran off to."

"No! Don't say that. I'm going to find her!"

Meena gave me a sad look. "You just have to accept it as god's will. For your own sake, forget she ever existed."

Chapter Seventeen

I t was a long train ride back to Mumbai from Vasco da Gama.

My heart felt heavy with sadness for leaving Meena behind. But she'd refused to come with us.

"I've got my routine," she said, one she'd been living for more than two decades, ever since she was chased out of her home as a troubled child. She told us the gods had found her a place on earth.

Playing songs to harried workers and making strangers smile to hear her music was her drug of choice. It was also probably the only way a low-caste transgendered person could make a living in that city, or in this country, I thought.

I hated the idea of leaving Meena on the streets. She knew I was on a mission and wasn't fazed when I told her I wasn't going to stop looking for Preeti. She merely pressed her hand on my forehead to give me her blessing.

While she was preoccupied saying goodbye to me, Katy quietly slipped all of our remaining rupee notes—equivalent to ten thousand dollars—in the brown paper bag that had held Preeti's diary. We knew Meena would never accept the money directly. It was a good thing she didn't speak English, or she'd have heard us hatching our little plot in between our conversation.

"Don't forget this," I said, slipping the bag into her hands just before we got on the bus to Mumbai. "It's a small gift from all of us."

The last I saw her, she was standing at the edge of the bus station, her flute tucked into her sari waist, one hand holding the brown bag and the other waving at us. I waved back, wondering if I'd ever see her again.

"This is it."

I double-checked the address on my phone. Win had not just memorized Franky's coordinates but programmed it into the GPS.

"Wow!" Win said, gaping at the glass tower rising above us. It could have been a building right out of Manhattan, like the ones I'd seen in Mrs. Rao's fancy travel magazines.

The glistening facade and the art deco style screamed multi-million-dollar luxury. For a second, I got a flashback to Toronto. It was only the incessant sounds of traffic honking and food hawkers calling that reminded me I was in the middle of a busy Indian metropolis.

"Do we buzz in?" Katy asked, running her fingers down the names of the residents displayed in a glass box outside.

"There's no Franky here," Win said, peeking over her shoulder.

"Check Fanibhusan Sardindhi," I said, dredging up his real name from my memories of long ago. He used "Franky" because it had been easier to pronounce. The man's hyena-like smile and crooked yellow teeth flashed into my mind. He'd played me well. For the hundredth time, I thought, *I should have never trusted him.*

"Found it." Katy reached over to push the button on the intercom to his apartment.

"Wait!"

She turned around in surprise.

"This is my fight," I said. "I'll go in alone."

"But that's scary," Win said, her eyes wide.

"And dangerous," added Katy.

"I can't have you guys involved in this," I said, shaking my head. "I've already taken you on a long ride. It's not like you need more crazy stuff in your lives."

"But Asha—" Katy started.

"No, stay here." I looked around me. "Maybe behind that side wall so no one can see you. If I don't come down in half an hour, go back. Find Tetyana and get Luc out."

"Maybe we need to call for help," said Katy, giving me a desperate look.

"Who do we call? The police? I tried that, remember?"

"But...but what if you need *our* help?" Win said.

I hesitated. "To tell the truth, you guys will distract him. Besides, I think he'll be more honest if I'm alone."

Katy and Win stared at me.

"You can be my backup. How does that sound?"

They nodded silently, but neither looked happy.

"Hey, I trained in martial arts as a kid, remember?"

That didn't seem to cheer them up.

"Okay, you'll have to get out of sight now."

I waited until they stepped over to the side of the building and were well concealed from anyone opening the front doors.

I silently counted to ten and reached up to push the buzzer. And then waited.

Silence.

Maybe he's not in. Maybe we got the wrong address.

I buzzed again, holding the button down longer.

This time, the intercom crackled.

"Haaa?" a woman's voice answered. She sounded irritated.

I stepped up.

"Hello," I said, unsure how I was going to even start this conversation.

"Ha?"

"I'm here to see Franky," I said in English.

"Franky?"

"Fanibhusan Sardindhi."

"Oh?"

"This is Asha."

The intercom made a crackling noise like someone turned it off. Silence.

It was three long minutes before I heard a loud click and the front door opened in slow motion, like someone had pushed an automatic button from inside.

A slightly built, nervous-looking woman peeked out, holding on to the doorframe as if she was afraid to get locked out. She looked me up and down, her mouth curling in distaste.

Is this Fartybag's mother?

I never saw her at the old compound. Dressed in a bright maroon sari and adorned with a heavy gold necklace and gold-colored sandals, she looked too posh to have lived anywhere near Grandma's old apartment. She also looked too young to be Fartybag's mother.

"Yes?" she snapped.

"I'm here to see Franky."

"Asha, haa?" She gave me a disapproving once-over, making me feel self-conscious.

"Okay, you come," she said, finally.

I stepped toward the door.

I walked into the ritziest lobby I'd seen in my life. A glass chandelier hung from the high ceiling and everything sparkled of marble and granite. The interior looked so swanky, I felt bad stepping inside with my dusty shoes.

After an awkwardly quiet elevator ride to the fifteenth floor, I found myself in front of an ornate wooden door.

The woman pushed open the door and stepped inside.

I followed her in through a corridor toward the main living room, walking on the most cushiony carpeting I'd ever felt. On the walls were old Indian paintings. Antique bronze statues of Hindu gods and goddesses stood silently along the walls, some in erotic poses, playing out the Kama Sutra in its glory. Franky was living the life of hedonistic luxury.

"Welcome! Come, come!"

I looked at the man sitting in an armchair in traditional garb—baggy pants and a long shirt. Franky flashed his crooked yellow teeth at me.

He's gloating.

I looked like something the cat had dragged in while he was sitting in his princely throne, probably bought with my own parents' money.

I felt the bitter taste of bile in my throat. I swallowed and took a deep breath. *I didn't come to fight. I came to get information.*

A telephone rang, distracting all of us. It was coming from the coffee table near Franky's chair. Scattered on the table were an open laptop, pads of paper with scribbles all over them, sticky notes, pens, two sets of eyeglasses and three cellphones.

The woman bent over to pick up the phone. Franky stopped her with a dismissive wave.

"We have an important guest. That can wait."

He turned to me.

"My son told me you were coming."

His hyena smile widened.

Chapter Eighteen

"Tea?" Franky said, his head nodding sideways in that amenable Indian manner.

"I'm here for only one thing," I said, giving him a pointed look.

"But we must not forgo good tradition," Franky replied, giving a nod to the woman. She disappeared into the corridor with a sullen look on her face. "It's such a long time, no? Come, Miss Asha, sit down and we can talk. Please."

He beamed at me.

"I'm not here to chat," I said.

It took all the energy in me to not shout at him. Self-control was not my strongest suit, least of all at this point. But I had to remain calm.

"Aah?" Franky nodded sideways again and flashed a fake smile. He was on his best behavior. Of course, he was. He stole what was mine. "But you are back in India now. We do hospitality very properly here."

"Where's Preeti?" I snapped.

He looked surprised. Something clanged loudly in the kitchen. The woman was not happy to make me tea, whether I wanted it or not.

"Preeti?" asked Franky. "Who is that, please?"

"You know exactly who she is." I gave him a stern look. What I really wanted to do was lunge at him and punch those teeth out. But that wouldn't get me far.

I took a step closer.

Franky's eyes flickered.

"You said Preeti would go to medical school. You said Aunty Shilpa would get her medicine. You said you'd take care of my family."

Franky spread his arms wide. "I only did my very best for your family, Miss Asha. My absolute, extreme best. But circumstances change, you know—"

"You lied to us then. You're lying to me now."

Someone cleared her throat.

I turned my head.

The woman had come in with a tea tray. Something about her, the speed with which she'd returned with that tea and the way she was looking at me, sent a shiver up my spine. It was a fleeting feeling but I had more urgent matters at hand.

"Ah, there we are," Franky said, as if in relief. "Let's sit down now, shall we? Make yourself comfortable."

I turned back to him and glared.

"You killed my aunt and grandma! You condemned my cousin to a horrible life!"

So much for self-control.

"But now, how could you say such hurtful things?" He gave me his most innocent look. "I helped you when you were just a little girl in so much trouble—"

"You sold Preeti to Kristadasa!"

"What a terrible accusation, Miss Asha. I never did any of that." He put his arms up in defense. "What happened to her was not in my control. Not at all. I never do evil things. I am a god-fearing Hindu." He gave me a pleading look. "Please. I think my son already told you. My family is in mourning right now. We have a funeral to prepare."

"I didn't get to even bury my aunt or my grandmother! You sent me away so you could steal my parents' money. You're nothing but a criminal!"

I was frothing at the mouth. But Franky was unusually calm given the accusations I was lobbing at him. Something was not right. The woman was still standing, tea tray in hand, a grimace on her face.

"I understand you're very, very upset by the death of your aunt. That's a terrible thing. But as you know...." He paused and licked his lips. "She was dying with that terrible sickness, anyway."

My eyes flashed in anger.

"You're evil. I also know exactly what you were plotting with Dick and Jose. I know about your human smuggling ring. I heard every word when you were trying to come up with the right price for us. You can't get away with this!"

"You got it all upside down, my dear miss." He shook his head sadly. "I never worked with Mister Dick. Him and Mister Jose are the common gangsters. I am an honest man. Only a middle broker. That Mister Dick is a full and complete criminal and that's why he is in Toronto jail already."

"Good," I said, giving him an icy stare. "That's where he belongs."

Franky gave a slight nod, as if he agreed. *What a charlatan.*

"And where's Jose right now?"

"Oh, that man is very smart. Very smart. Outwitted everybody, even police. He went somewhere in Africa. Found very good job for non-profit."

"A non-profit?" *That fast-talking, drug-dealing crook working for a charity?*

Franky let out a deep sigh like this was all too much to take in and motioned to the woman to bring the tea tray over. She stepped closer, watching me from the corner of her eyes like I was a rabid animal.

She carefully set one cup on Franky's coffee table and turned to me. Her eyes shifted between her tea tray and me.

"Why don't you try the chai? This is excellent quality tea you will never taste anywhere else in the world." Franky smiled, motioning to the tray.

I didn't move.

"You came from a very long journey and you must be very tired. I can understand why you are feeling this way. I implore you to sit down and have some tea first. Then we can find good solutions. Come. Sit. Sit."

"I didn't come for a tea party," I said through clenched teeth. "I came for information."

Franky let out a sigh of exasperation. "Okay, I will tell you the truth."

I looked at him in surprise.

Franky was giving me a regretful look, an almost fatherly one. "She told me not to say, but I can see you are so disturbed. So, I will tell you what happened." He paused. "Your dear cousin came to me to ask for help. And I helped her. Gave her genuine help."

My stomach did a nauseating flip. *Preeti approached Franky for help?*

"She wanted to leave the country. Just like you."

Is he lying again? His face was inscrutable.

"So, at her behest, I found a nice family in England who wanted a maid. I was absolutely upfront. Never would I lie to your cousin. I was trying to help her."

"You mean you sold her off as a maid."

"Maid is better than her life here, no? Staying married to that man? That was a big mistake."

"You pushed her into it!"

"Look, this is Indian custom only. When one sister or girl cousin runs away from an important wedding, the next girl is given." Franky spread his arms expansively. "Who am I to go against tradition? This was not my doing."

"Where is she now?"

Franky hesitated only half a second. "Hollingdon. Near Heathrow Airport."

I stared at him, unsure of what to think. "You sold her like you sold me to Mrs. Rao."

"Aah." Franky gave me a sad look. "Please, let us not talk about the dead inappropriately. My sister was always a little ill in the head and now she's—"

"Your *sister*?"

So Fartybag had told the truth? Or was this all an elaborate game?

"Mrs. Rao was my sister. But, alas, she is gone now." He lifted his arms and turned his face to the ceiling. "To the heavens."

"I doubt that," I said, more to myself.

But he didn't hear me or pretended not to. He had a faraway look on his face. "She had a hard life. You see, her mother...our mother worked in the...how do you say it...red district light."

Why is he sharing this?

"When I was boy, the Madame asked me to help her. I taught myself to read so she got me to do some small jobs. Her paperwork. That was me. When she died, I took the management. I didn't want my sister to become prostitute so I married her off to a businessman who worked for me."

I don't have time for this.

I looked around me. Other than Franky and the woman, the apartment seemed empty. *Maybe there's information on Preeti somewhere here. If only I can look around....*

"She never even knew she was my sister," Franky was saying. "She never knew her mother. Only I knew. And now she's gone. But my mother's ghost is still with us." He put a hand over his face as if he was trying to stop himself from crying.

"You're lying," I said. "As usual."

"On my dead mother's grave, I will never lie to you. I know you're angry with me and I know things didn't go as you wanted—"

"That's the understatement of the century."

"But, Miss Asha, I can promise you this. I can at least offer you some very good compensation."

He was studying my face as if to find a weakness, a clue.

So that's why he let me in. To bribe me into silence.

The front door clicked open.

Franky broke into a wide grin, his eyes still on me.

I whirled around.

Two police officers walked in and silently took their place behind me. They looked like thugs on standby, waiting for a command.

Chapter Nineteen

The woman looked at me with a superior smile on her face.

She turned to the men and put her hands together. "Namaste."

They greeted her in return.

A frisson of fear went through me. *Franky had been buying time. All those stories were just that. Stories till his paid goons came.*

Franky was watching me, fingertips together. His face said *checkmate.*

He smiled. "You think I have big operation like this without protection? I'm not an uneducated man like you think I am."

From the corner of my eyes, I saw the men step closer.

From their uniforms, I could see they were low-level officers. They weren't carrying any weapons, not openly anyway, but their fists would be enough. I clenched my hands and straightened my back. *If I'm going to go down, I'm going to go down fighting.*

"You only had to drink this very good tea and we would not have to make things so...." Franky hesitated, seemingly trying to find the right word. "Difficult."

So, the tea's poisoned. I've walked right into his den.

But I didn't show my fear. At least I hoped I didn't. "So you've got the local police in your pockets now, do you?"

Franky let out a crude laugh. "You're still just a silly child." He leaned back in his chair with a satisfied smile. "You think you can scare a big man like me?"

My mind whirred. I had to stay strong. I had to think fast.

Something buzzed in my pocket, making me jump. I pulled out my phone and stared at the screen.

"Unknown number."

Who's calling? No one has this number except for Katy and—

I turned it on and held it to my ear.

"Get on speaker now."

Bizarre. That was Katy's voice, urgent, commanding.

I pressed the speaker button.

"Agent two-nine-one-three." Katy sounded crisp. I noticed she was stressing her American accent even more than usual. "Do you copy? Agent two-nine-one-three. Please confirm. Do you copy?"

"Copy that," I said, trying to not sound flustered.

"Do you require backup? We are on standby and ready to move in." There was some noise in the background. Katy's voice came again, this time to the side but loud enough for us to hear. "Radio for second air cover immediately."

"Yes, ma'am!" Win's voice came clearly from the background.

What are these two up to? I focused my eyes on the phone, trying to keep as straight-faced as possible.

Katy was barking into the phone again. "Agent two-nine-one-three, we're prepared and waiting for your signal. We'll be there in three-point-five seconds."

Without looking up, I spoke in a steady voice to the phone. "Thank you, Agent five-six-eight-one. Stand down for now."

"Copy that."

I squared my shoulders and looked up at Franky. He was staring at me. The woman next to him was scowling darkly again. I didn't dare to turn back, but I felt the hostile presence of the two men behind me. It was like the air in the room had amped up, frizzing with electricity. One false move and things could get bad fast.

"I didn't come here unprepared either," I said to Franky, looking him in the eyes. "Did you really think I only baked cakes in Toronto?"

His eyes narrowed. I could see he was vacillating between anger and confusion. He cleared his throat. "Do you know how powerful I am in this city?"

"Not powerful enough."

I'd stashed Preeti's diary in the right thigh pocket of my cargo pants. I knew it formed a nice bulge right now, but no one here knew what it was. I slowly and deliberately moved my right hand toward the pocket and kept it hovering, ready.

Franky glowered. I could feel his hate in my bones.

"I have connections everywhere," he growled. "If you do anything to me, my people will hunt you. They will torture you so you wish you were never born."

"There are things that would scare the life out of you if you only knew, Franky," I said in a low voice, keeping my eyes steady on him.

I pulled the phone back up to my mouth. "Coming down. Stand by till I give the signal."

Without another glance, I turned around and marched out of the room. The men in the back didn't make a sound as I passed them. I felt their eyes burn into my back as I walked out.

I closed the main door of the apartment with a click and scanned the corridor quickly. I had seconds, if at all. I strode up to the fire exit and yanked the door open.

Then, I ran down.

"Coming down fire exit!" I screamed into the phone as I scrambled down.

The elevator would have been nice, but Franky could have his men waiting for me at the bottom. The stairwell was brightly lit with handlebars on both sides and, most importantly, more escape routes to choose from.

Halfway, on the seventh floor, I felt a cramp on my left side. I clutched my waist, desperately wanting to collapse, but my mind screamed *go, go, go!*

At the bottom of the stairs was the main fire exit door. I pushed on the steel bar and ran out.

I'd opened a side door of the building. In front of me was a freshly mowed lawn. To my relief, no one was around. I scanned the facade quickly, wondering if Franky or his goons could see me from above, but it was hard to see the fifteenth floor from where I was.

"Where are you?" I screamed into the phone.

I heard a rustle behind me and looked back to see my friends running toward the side exit.

"This way!" Katy yelled, motioning me to follow her.

She dashed around the building, with Win and me trying to keep up with her long strides. We slipped in between the cars in the back parking lot and ran toward the busy street.

I didn't dare look back. And I prayed Franky hadn't alerted his men.

K aty stopped a taxi.

"Go!" I said to the driver, once we'd all jumped in. "Go!"

"Where?" The man gave me a confused look. "Where you want—"

"Tourist district!" I yelled.

We tried to catch our breath while the driver honked and fought his way through traffic. I kept a sharp eye on the cars around us. After a few minutes of careening in and out of traffic, I realized it would take a miracle for anyone to tail us.

"Thanks, guys," I said, turning to my friends. "You're super geniuses, you know that?"

"It was Katy's idea," said Win with a grin.

"You both played really well," said Katy.

"You saved my life," I said.

"When we saw those two men come in, I knew something was up," said Katy. "They came in an unmarked car and changed their shirts into police ones. That smelled fishy."

"Are you serious?" I said. "So they weren't real police?"

Katy shrugged. "We'll never know."

"Did they see you?"

"Nope," said Win. "But we could see them."

In fifteen minutes, the driver screeched to a stop in front of the palatial entrance of the local Hilton.

"Here," he said with a satisfied grunt. "Tourist district."

Win and Katy looked at me.

Now what?

I looked at the luxury facade and realized this was exactly where people like Franky and his corrupt friends would hang out.

"No," I said, shaking my head. "I'm so sorry. This is the wrong hotel. Please take us to the backpackers' district."

With a resigned sigh, the driver obliged.

He looked relieved to get rid of us when we disembarked from his car in the shabbier part of town. It was more crowded here and we could easily pass for student backpackers.

We stopped at a cash machine to get money out and walked into a dingy motel off a side street that looked like the perfect budget tourist hangout. Win wanted to find an Internet café so she could create another account and transfer more money, but that would have to wait.

I was partly relieved and partly amazed Franky hadn't tracked us down.

If his goons had followed us, we didn't know. So far, I'd banked on him believing our bluff, or at least being thrown off enough to not want to take the risk. But something didn't feel right. My intuition said Franky still held all the cards.

My mind felt woozy. I hadn't slept in over twenty-four hours. While Win and Katy had napped on the train, they looked ready to drop any moment too. We were beyond exhausted, and that was when we were liable to make dangerous mistakes. We couldn't afford that, not after coming this far.

We bought a stack of chapatis and a large bowl of chickpea curry from a street vendor and holed ourselves in the motel room. We ate silently in front of the television tuned to the local news channel with the sound off.

Katy was now sound asleep on the couch and I was mindlessly flipping through Preeti's diary. We'd offered Win the only bed in the room, but she refused to sleep and instead squeezed in between us on the couch, her nose firmly stuck to her phone screen.

I couldn't sleep either.

Every time I closed my eyes, the image of Kristadasa lying at the feet of the horrified little girl sprang to mind. And every time, that knife in my hand looked bigger and bloodier than before. I wished I had finished him off. For what he'd done to Preeti, that little girl and who knows how many others, he didn't deserve to live.

I looked down at the diary on my lap and tried to imagine what Preeti's life would be like now. I hoped she'd found a better family than what I'd encountered in Toronto.

At least she's not with that pedophile, I thought with a shudder.

I wondered about the little girl we'd left behind. *Where's her family? Was she an orphan they picked from the streets? What will happen to her?*

The way she crawled toward the older wife told me she didn't have anyone of her own. Otherwise, she'd have jumped at the chance of getting free and finding her family again. I shook my head. *I can't save everyone.*

I turned the pages of the diary without really looking, my mind whirling with one phrase over and over again.

"Hollingdon. Near Heathrow Airport."

Win had checked the map on the phone but it was hard to pinpoint anything. Most of the area was farmland with nothing nearby for miles, except for a few lonely sheep farms. *Maybe she's at a farm. Don't they use migrant labor at farms?*

That was the best explanation I could think of.

So the UK is our next stop, I thought, frowning. *But can I believe Franky?*

There was one other worry. I'd entered the UK illegally only a few weeks ago. *Do they have an alert on me?* I wondered. *How am I going to get to Preeti if they arrest me at the airport? Can Katy and Win find her for me?*

I shook my head. I knew they'd say yes in a heartbeat if I asked, but it would be unfair to even think of it.

I massaged my tired brow. Tetyana and Luc had far more street smarts than the three of us combined. One good thing about returning to Europe was we'd get closer to both.

That was, if Luc was already in Amsterdam. But I doubted it. The police paperwork alone would take weeks, even months. *He must still be in a detention center at the Mumbai airport.* My head hurt just thinking about it.

"Hey."

I looked over at Win.

"Chef Pierre really wants to talk to you. He's been tweeting like crazy. Something about a new café launch in New York."

I arched my eyebrows. "Are you kidding me? We're in the middle of this hell ride and he wants to chat about cakes?"

"I can tell him to stop bugging you."

"Yes, please."

"Okay."

"No, wait!" I said, and paused. "Tell him to give me one more week. Tell him I've got a big cake catering gig in Mumbai right now. But I'll contact him in a week."

"Sure," Win said with a nonchalant shrug and went back to her screen.

"No, wait!" I said again, as a new idea crossed my mind.

"What?"

"Tell him I'm being offered a really awesome deal to open a cake shop here in Mumbai. But I haven't signed anything yet. Ask him if he can share more info about his offer."

Win turned back to her phone and tapped away.

Though I'd met Chef Pierre just once in Luxembourg, after a lifetime of following his work, I felt I could trust him. But I couldn't be sure if the authorities were using him, twisting his arm, to get at me. If this was a ruse for me to walk into a trap set by EUROPOL, they'd have to work hard for it.

I massaged my temple again. I was getting paranoid. I'd turned into a deranged neurotic.

The buzz of Katy's phone made us both jump.

"Oh!" Win exclaimed, grabbing Katy's phone.

"Oh my god!" She waved it in front of my face. "It's Tetyana!"

"What?" Katy asked, stirring awake. "What's going on?"

"Got a message!" Win said.

We peeked at the small screen over her shoulder.

Win read the message aloud. "Leaving France."

"And?" I asked.

"That's it. *Leaving France.*"

"Is she coming here?" Katy asked, with hope in her voice.

Win tapped into the message box. "Are U gonna join us, Tetyana? We miss U."

And we waited.

Nothing.

"What does this mean?" Katy asked, rubbing her eyes. "She's got out of French jail somehow?"

"I think that sixty thousand was bail money," I said. "But sixty K is a fair amount. Maybe part of it is the ransom for her brother."

"Got another!" Win cried.

Katy and I leaned in.

Win read out loud. "Not yet. Heading east. Love you all too."

Katy and I looked at each other.

"East?" said Katy. "East of France? East of Europe?"

"Could also mean Asia, no?" I said, raising my brows.

"Ask her how she's doing? And if she's okay," said Katy.

Win nodded and started tapping again.

"Sent."

"Maybe she's going to Russia, where they're holding her brother," I said, thinking out loud. "That's the only reason she's not joining us."

My head was throbbing even harder now. I moved Preeti's diary from my lap onto the couch and got up to go to the bathroom to take my nightly painkillers. The bruises on my arms and legs from my fight with Kristadasa were turning purple now. They still ached but it was the headaches that hurt the most.

When I walked back to the room with a glass of water in hand, Win was showing something shiny to Katy.

"What's this?" I asked.

"Information," Win said, looking triumphant.

"Where did you get that?" I said, squinting at the silver phone Win was holding. That didn't look like any of our cheap throwaway models.

"Fartybag's phone," Win said matter-of-factly. "You gave it to me."

I stared at her. "But didn't you put it back on his desk?"

"No, I picked that one from a shelf in the store," she said as if she'd done the most natural thing in the world. "I kept his phone in my pocket."

"But won't they track it back to us?" I asked, frowning at the phone.

"Disabled the tracking," she replied with a shrug.

Katy and I burst out laughing.

"You're one crazy, super-smart girl," Katy said.

Win flashed a grin. She loved it when we complimented her brains.

"I didn't even see you do that," I said.

"'Cuz you weren't watching," she quipped.

"Can I see it?" I asked.

I bent down to take the phone, forgetting the glass in my hand. It tipped over, splashing water across the couch. Katy and Win sprang up.

"Oh, no!" I cried, looking at the damage.

Katy pulled Preeti's diary away from the couch and shook the water from the book.

A silvery paper escaped from in between the pages. It floated gently to the floor and came to rest next to my feet.

Chapter Twenty-one

"What's that?" Win asked, bending down to pick up the paper.

I took it from her and rubbed the soft foil paper in between my fingers.

A rush of memories came to me. "Hershey's Kisses tinfoil wrap," I whispered.

Katy shook the book again and a half a dozen more pieces of silvery chocolate wrapping paper floated to the ground.

The three of us stared at the debris of wrappers on the ground.

Preeti had told me the story of these wrappers a long time ago. She was in grade five when a team of teachers from an American organization had visited her school. They'd come with books, pencils, school bags, and most importantly, bags and bags of chocolate kisses.

She'd shared the chocolates with Aunty Shilpa but had kept the wrappers, flattened them out and pasted them in her diary. She told me they were her favorite sweets, even tastier than gulab jamuns, those heavenly Indian sugary balls doused in honey that melted in your mouth.

Win picked up the wrappers from the ground and wiped them with a bathroom towelette.

"Hey," she said, putting one up to the light. "Look on the other side. There's something here."

I scrutinized the back of mine. There were words etched in pencil, so faint I could hardly make them out under the dim motel lamp.

"Wish we had better lighting," I mumbled.

Win shined her phone's light on my paper. "Here," she said. "That should help."

The writing was in English. I read the words out loud.

"He beat me again today. I'm a slave. That's what I am."

Katy and Win drew a breath in.

I knelt in front of the couch, collected all the loose wrappers and placed them facedown on the floor. The three of us huddled over the silvery collage in front of us.

I placed a second wrapper under the phone's light and read it out loud. "Hate my life. God, I want to die like Grandma and Aunty Shilpa."

"Oh, my god," I heard Katy say next to me.

I picked the next one.

"Wait!"

I looked at Win.

"See?" she said, focusing her light closer to the bottom of one paper. "There are numbers here. We need to read these in the proper order."

I hadn't even noticed the date squiggled in the corner of each paper.

Win held the phone steady while I rearranged the papers chronologically. When I was done, she trained the phone's light on the first wrapper.

I picked it up and read it out loud.

"Wish I was dead. Why is this happening to me?"

I took a deep breath in.

"Today I threw up four times. He'll kill me, I know it."

My heart dropped.

"I'm going to run away. Just like Asha."

I felt goose bumps on my arms as if the temperature in the room had suddenly dropped ten degrees. But I kept reading.

"I can't take it anymore. I'm going to leave this hellhole."

If I hadn't run away, Preeti would have stayed in school, graduated and become a doctor like she'd always wanted to. And I would have been the one writing these heartbreaking notes instead.

A river of guilt washed through me. I struggled to breathe but I picked up the next wrapper.

"Isn't it weird she wrote in English?" said Katy.

"Maybe she didn't want anyone else to read them," said Win. "Like a secret code."

"She was amazing at school," I said. "She could read and write in three languages."

I placed the next wrapper under Win's light.

"Franky said he can help."

I felt I'd just got stabbed in the chest.

"He promised to get me a visa and passport for free."

A tremor went through me as I remembered being promised exactly the same only a few years ago.

"Fartybag's pushing me to sign all these papers. I'm scared. I wish Aunty Shilpa was alive so I could ask her for help. What do I do?"

I moved on to the next one.

"Franky's sending me to the UK. Wow. If Kristadasa finds out he'll really kill me for sure."

"Franky's acting strange. I don't think he's telling the truth. I don't trust anyone right now."

"He beat me again today. He forbade me to leave home so neighbors won't see my bruises. Will this nightmare never end?"

"I stole all the money from Kristadasa's drawer."

"She's plucky," I heard Katy say, "Thank goodness for that."

I picked up the next wrapper.

"So sad to leave home. I'll miss Grandma and Aunty Shilpa but they are gone for good anyway. They won't miss me."

Win handed me the next one.

"Franky's in Mumbai. I stole my passport from his office. Fartybag's too stupid to suspect anything."

"Wow!" said Win.

"Wait. Why did she steal her passport?" asked Katy. "Wasn't Franky going to give it to her anyway?"

"Dunno." I shook my head, but I had a funny feeling I knew where this was going. Preeti was doing what I wished I'd done years ago.

"I got my ticket! Tomorrow's my last day in India."

I picked up the last wrapper.

"Franky thinks he's sending me to London, but I'm going to follow Asha. Can't wait to see her again."

I gulped. *Did she go to Toronto looking for me?*

I stared at the wrapper, feeling numb.

"Did she know you were in Canada?" Katy asked.

A sudden realization came to me. I shook my head, a sinking feeling in the pit of my stomach.

It took me a few seconds to speak.

"Franky told everyone I was going to Tanzania," I whispered, almost to myself. "He switched my plane ticket at the last minute just before I got on the plane. I was so scared and desperate to get away I never told Aunty Shilpa where I was going."

I remembered finding all the letters I'd written to my family stuck in Mrs. Rao's desk—unstamped and unsent. She'd been wily. She'd kept my hopes up, saying my letters had gone out. She'd told me the only reason I wasn't getting letters back was because the Indian postal service was so slow and inept.

I pulled out Preeti's letter from my pocket. It was still in its original envelope. I traced the faded words with my finger.

"Dar Es Salaam, Tanzania," I said, reading the last line in the *To* address. "I don't think Franky told anyone where I was."

"How did you get Preeti's letter then?" asked Win.

"Mrs. Rao got tons of packages from India, many from Franky," I said, scrunching my face as I thought. "Maybe someone, whoever worked for him threw it in by mistake? I can't think of any other reason."

"And Mrs. Rao kept it?"

"She hid it with all my other letters. She was a pack rat and couldn't throw anything away. You should have seen her home."

"So, where's Preeti now?" Win asked, frowning. "I'm confused."

"I don't think she's in the UK," I said, speaking slowly. "Or in Toronto."

"Hey, are there any more of these messages?" Katy asked.

Win grabbed Preeti's book and flipped through the pages, pulling out every image stuck inside. Katy examined each paper, double-checking both sides, while I watched them in silence, too stupefied to speak.

There were cutouts from newspapers and magazines, mostly pictures of beautiful homes and exotic destinations Preeti had dreamed of. But there was nothing in the back.

Win pulled out every picture until they lay at our feet like a broken jigsaw puzzle. We sat and stared at them for a while.

It was Katy who broke the silence.

"Franky lied to you," she said, with a sober look. "He wanted to send you on a goose chase."

Chapter Twenty-two

Katy gave me a concerned look. "They could arrest us for this, you know."

"Do you have a better idea?" I asked.

Though our problems were as daunting as the night before, my mind was clear that morning. Franky had to have figured out our bluff and would be after us soon. We couldn't sit around, ruminating, worrying or planning for all eventualities. We had to get to work.

That morning, while Katy and I went to find breakfast, Win worked on her phone using the motel's patchy Internet service. She masked her entry through virtual pathways into foreign banks on the other side of the world.

She was good. Really good. If Zero and Vlad had truly understood her talents, they'd have used her for work that didn't force her into getting abused by their sick clients. I shuddered to think of what she must have endured at the hands of those men, those *animals*.

Typically shy and timid, Win transformed into a completely different person when she got in front of a screen or found a keyboard in her hands. Her face became taut, her demeanor confident and her eyes turned into laser-like pinpricks, fully focused on what she was doing. Maybe this was how she blocked the past horrors from her mind.

Breakfast that day was masala dosa with chai tea. Katy and I also found Win's favorite Indian sweet from a nearby food stall. She'd developed a taste for the Indian funnel cake, a honey-colored pretzel, crispy on the outside and syrupy on the inside. I was sure it was terrible for you, but who were we to begrudge her this simple treat?

Win now sat in bed with her nose stuck to the phone, her hand stealing into the paper bag occasionally to pull out a sticky funnel cake. I made a mental note to wipe down her phone once she was done.

Within sixty minutes, Win had transferred money to three new accounts. This would sidestep withdrawal limits and wouldn't raise red flags. At least, that was what we hoped. Afterward, we walked over to three different cash machines near the motel to take the money out.

"Do you think this is enough?" asked Win, pointing at the stack of rupee notes on the motel couch, now dry after last night's mishap. She'd been counting and recounting the money for the past ten minutes just to make sure.

I nodded. "That should be enough for our flights out, including Luc's."

"What if he's already gone?" asked Katy.

"I doubt it. Government paperwork takes forever, especially in India. Even longer if they have to make arrangements with another country. I'd be shocked if they'd figured everything out in just two days."

"You do realize he's, er, a liability?" Katy asked, giving me a worried look.

"What do you mean a *liability*?" Win whipped her head around and frowned at Katy.

Katy sighed. "What I mean, sweetie, is...." She spoke slowly, choosing her words carefully. "He didn't tell us everything, did he? Plus, he's got himself and us into trouble more than once now."

Win's face flushed. "He didn't mean it. It was a mistake. He'd never betray us. I know him!" She looked like she was about to cry. She got up, picked up her backpack and gave us a stubborn look. "I'm not going anywhere without Luc."

Katy and I glanced at each other. Though it felt like we'd known Luc, Win, and Tetyana for a lifetime, we'd all only met a few weeks ago. I wondered how many secrets everyone was hiding that we still hadn't figured out.

I gave my head a small shake. I couldn't go around distrusting everyone, especially not those who'd been with me through all the craziness of the past few weeks.

"Let's put half of that cash in an envelope, shall we?" I said. "We'll need to pass it in a hurry at the airport."

Katy and Win stared at me.

I spread my arms. "Well? Are you both in with me?"

"Yup," Win said with a quick nod. "I am."

"Sure," Katy said with a shrug, not sounding at all sure. "Like you said, we don't have many choices."

"And if we get arrested, we'll get to see Luc!" Win said, with a bit more enthusiasm than I'd have liked.

It took us half an hour to find a taxi and get to the airport.

"We need a meeting place," I said, looking around the arrival lounge.

"There," Katy said, pointing to the huge Starbucks logo on a far wall. "Easy to spot."

"Excellent," I said. "Are we all ready?"

Win and Katy nodded. After quick hugs, Katy took off to the ticketing counters while Win and I headed in the opposite direction.

We walked silently. With every step, I wondered if I was putting my friends in more danger than they already were.

Chapter Twenty-three

There were two ways to contact a customs officer. From what I'd dug around the Internet the night before, I knew the first way was to walk up to an official desk and ask to speak to one. But that idea was out. So, we had to try the second way.

After a short walk through the terminal, Win and I got to the international baggage retrieval area.

Passengers who'd just disembarked were straggling out of the sliding doors after clearing customs. Two airport staff members were near the baggage carousels, moving luggage and fielding questions. Neither looked like they enjoyed their jobs, stopping every few minutes to check their phones and show each other whatever they were scrolling through.

We stood near the sliding doors, watching, waiting for the right moment. There was no other staff around.

Then, the right time came.

A frustrated American couple strode up to the two workers, complaining loudly about lost luggage, their indignant voices rising above the din. The men reluctantly turned toward the tourists, looking like they'd rather be anywhere else but here.

"Now!" I said, moving swiftly. Win and I slipped in at the same time a troop of schoolkids came out.

Inside the customs clearance area, it was busy.

The place was teeming with people. It seemed that several planes had landed all at once. A handful of uniformed airport staff was trying to herd everyone into proper lines, but no one was paying any attention to them or their lines.

Perfect.

We slipped through the crowd and got close to the sign that said "Baggage retrieval"—the same sign Katy and Win had waited under for Luc and me to join them. Except Luc never made it.

We leaned casually against the column. With our cargo pants and backpacks we looked like we'd just stepped off a long plane trip too. We stood there for fifteen minutes, keeping an eye out for the customs officers.

"Hey." Win nudged me.

I looked in the direction she was discreetly pointing.

It was the young officer with the dog, the man I was looking for. I'd worried it had been his day off or he'd been sent to work elsewhere. He was perfect for the job I'd planned. He was a junior officer, most probably underpaid but believes he deserved more.

He was walking around with a junior member who was holding the dog's leash. Both were wearing the same uniforms, peaked caps and sidearms on their belts.

We watched him instruct his colleague, who then turned and commanded the dog to sniff a traveler's backpack. After ten minutes of this, he stopped following his trainee around and stood back, arms crossed, watching her and the dog in action, occasionally stopping to give more instructions.

Signaling to Win to stay where she was, I stepped away from the column and strolled toward the officer. Just as he turned around, I walked deliberately into him.

"Oh, sorry!"

It worked like a charm. He gave me a cross look but stopped.

I leaned over and touched him on the forearm. "Hey, do you remember me?"

He pulled his arm away like I'd stung him. "I, er, how can I help you, miss?"

"Could we go to a quiet spot to talk?" I said, giving him my most charming smile. Smile, Katy had said, but not too much and not too little. For a minute, I wondered if I looked more like a crazed foreigner than the charming young woman I was trying to portray.

"Er...did you want customs papers?" he said, stepping back.

My palms were sweating and my heart was beating a tick faster. Katy was so much better at this than me.

"No," I said, "but I have something special for you."

"Huh?"

"I brought a gift. I think you'll like it."

He scrutinized me. And I put on my most innocent look. It was a good thing I was no taller than five feet. As a petite Asian woman, I was used to being underestimated. And sometimes, that was a good thing. A very good thing.

"What do you want, miss?" He paused, his curiosity getting the better of him. "What do you have for me?"

"Can we go to a quiet corner?" I asked, pointing to a spot away from the crowd. "Please?"

He hesitated only for a second. He surveyed the room quickly and nodded.

"Got to check something out. Be back in a minute," he called out to his trainee before following me.

I walked over to where Win was waiting. She looked nervous but was standing her ground.

"You have our friend," I said, when he joined us.

"What?"

"Two days ago, you took our friend into custody. Do you remember?"

"I don't know your friends. I thought you had something for me."

"The French citizen you were going to deport to Amsterdam. You said he was charged for carrying cocaine."

His eyes cleared as he remembered, but he didn't say a word. He stood with his hands on his hips and a frown on his face.

"What do you want from me?"

"Is he still here?" I asked, pointing to the offices behind the customs desks.

"Is he doing okay?" asked Win.

He stared at us as if trying to figure out how to respond.

"We'd like to bail him out," I said.

He raised his eyebrows.

"Can you make it happen?"

He looked at me, then Win, and then back at me, and let out a loud sigh. "It's not easy," he replied, speaking slowly. "Or cheap."

"We're ready to pay," I said, turning to Win. "Do you have the envelope?"

Win pulled out a thick brown envelope and opened it to show him what was inside.

The officer's eyes grew wide.

"How much?" he asked.

"How much will it take to get our friend out?"

He arched his eyebrows again.

"Officially..." He paused, rocking back and forth on his heels. "Officially, you'll need a lot of money."

"Unofficially?" I asked, my heart racing. *This was where he was going to arrest me.*

His eyes traveled to the envelope in Win's hands.

I wished she'd not stand so close to him.

"How much is in there?" he asked, lowering his voice and stepping closer.

"Three hundred thousand rupees," I said, giving Win a side glance, hoping she'd get the message to step back.

His eyes grew wider. From my research the night before, that was half his annual salary.

"That's all we have," I said. "There's no more where that came from. And you have to promise first."

"Let me check this," he said, grabbing the envelope.

"Hey!" Win cried out, her face flushing pink. "Give that back!"

Oh no.

Standing in front of us, he opened the envelope and started counting the money, his mouth moving silently.

People walked by, not giving us a second glance. Two harried-looking airport workers were cordoning off an area for a new batch of passengers to disembark from their planes. The junior officer with the dog was busy with some tourists in one corner. Another officer was checking passengers' passports before directing them to the customs counters.

No, we couldn't create a commotion here. They'd surround us in a heartbeat and throw us in jail.

"So?" I said, when the officer was done counting. "Are you going to get our friend out?"

He stared for a moment like he was trying to make up his mind. Then he nodded. "I can help you."

"We'll wait here with this then," I said, giving him a steely look and reaching over to take the envelope.

He pulled his hand back. "I need this to convince my superiors to let him go."

"Oh, really?" piped Win.

"How do we know you're going to help us?" I asked. "We don't have any guarantee."

"You have to trust me," he said, shoving the envelope quickly into his pant pocket. "You wait right here, please. I'll bring your friend."

With that, he turned around and marched smartly toward the back office.

"Hey, wait!" I called out, but he didn't look back.

"He's running away with our money!" Win cried. She was ready to lunge after him.

A few people turned and looked at us.

"Shh..." I said, holding her back.

I watched the officer disappear into the immigration offices in dismay, feeling like I'd been duped.

"We'll never see Luc now!" Win slipped to the floor with a cry.

I joined her. There was nothing else we could do now except wait, if we could believe him.

Fifteen minutes passed.

We kept our eyes peeled on the doors to the offices, waiting to see either Luc come out and join us or a handful of armed agents run out and arrest us for attempted bribery.

I was beginning to think we'd been had. *Win's right. The man's run away with our money.* I felt a sinking in my stomach. Double-crossed again.

A buzz from Win's pocket made us both jump.

She pulled her phone out and put it to her ear.

"Hello?"

Someone mumbled on the other end.

"Katy!" Win cried.

I leaned in to listen.

"Get out of there now," I heard Katy say.

I turned my mouth to the phone. "Where are you calling from?"

"Near Starbucks. You guys gotta leave. *Now.*"

"What's going on?" Win asked.

Katy's voice came over the line crisp and clear. "Luc's here."

Chapter Twenty-four

Win and I scrambled to our feet and walked out of the sliding doors behind an extended Indian family.

No one stopped us or questioned us. The officer who'd taken our money was still nowhere to be seen.

Once outside, we ran to our meeting place, my mind in a whirlwind.

How did Luc get out? Did our bribe work?

The café was busy. All the tables were taken and there was a long line up to the counter. It took a few seconds to find them.

There.

Luc and Katy were sitting at an isolated table in a nook in the back. I noticed Katy had an annoyed look on her face.

"Luc!" Win cried as soon as she spotted him.

She ran up to him and threw herself around his neck. He grabbed her and lifted her while she giggled in glee.

"Oh, my god. Are you okay?" Win asked. "I thought something terrible happened to you!"

"Nah." Luc gave her a floppy grin. "Wasn't all that bad. They even served me tons of chai."

I looked him over.

His clothes were crumpled. His hair, normally preened more carefully than that of a top model in Milan, was now standing on end, unbrushed, unkempt.

"I found him in the departure area," Katy explained with a pained expression on her face.

Luc looked sheepish. "I, er, thought you guys abandoned me, so I was gonna find a ticket to France."

"How did you get out?" I asked. "That officer helped you just now?"

"You won't believe this," Katy said, shaking her head.

"They let me go," Luc replied, with a wonky smile. "After one night."

"What?" Win and I exclaimed at the same time.

The officer stole our bribe after all.

"And here I thought they were beating you up in jail."

He gave me an accusing look. "I looked everywhere for you. Thought I'd never see you all again."

"Sorry," I said. "I had something important to take care of."

"More important than me?"

"We got back as quickly as we could." There was too much to say and now was not the time. "But how'd you manage to get out?"

"They said I could make one call. And after that, they were super nice to me. They even let me out!" He grinned.

"Who did you call?" I asked, narrowing my eyes. That sinking feeling came to my stomach again.

Katy sighed. "This is where the news goes bad."

A slight pink color came to Luc's face.

"Luc," I said, looking him in the eye. "I need you to tell me everything, okay?"

"I just asked for help." He shifted his feet, not looking at me anymore.

"We just risked our lives and handed over a nice packet of cash to a border guard to get your ass out of jail. He could be looking for us right now."

"I don't think so."

"Why do you say that?"

He was silent for a moment.

"Stop playing hide and seek. We're all on the same side."

"Okay, okay." He shot me a nervous look. "But you're not gonna like it."

"Try me."

"They kept telling me they were going put me in this horrible detention camp with murderers and stuff, so I told them I had connections..."

"And who'd that be?"

He averted his eyes, like he was too ashamed to admit what he was about to reveal. "I called Fred's lawyer."

I looked at him in shock. "You could have called us!"

"You don't have a phone!"

I stared at him. *He's right.* We got our burner phones only after we left the airport.

"I called him 'cuz they're the only people I know who can help. These people have got me out of pickles before." Luc smoothed his hair, looking uncomfortable. "Besides, he knows the COP here."

"COP?" I asked.

"Chief of police," Luc said, giving a quick glance around him.

I remembered Luc's connections with the drug gangs of Europe. I also remembered how scared he'd been when he learned the drug dealers were after him for not delivering the goods he'd promised. It had been a small transaction, but these gangs were vicious and took things very personally.

"And now," Katy said in a low voice, her lips in a thin line, "Fred knows where we are."

"I didn't have a choice and I didn't wanna rot in an Indian jail!"

I reached out and put my hands on Luc's shoulders, suppressing the desire to shake him. "Hey, I want you to promise me something."

His eyes widened.

"I want you to tell us everything about your past, the people you know, and the kind of stuff these people are up to. Everything. Otherwise, we've no idea what we're up against."

Before Luc could answer, Win glanced in alarm behind me.

"Oh no!" she said, her hand flying to her mouth.

I turned around to see two officers in white customs uniforms rush by the café, panning the area as if they were looking for something or someone.

"Time to get outta here," Katy said, getting up. "Let's go everyone. We can chat later."

I turned to Luc. "Are you clean? We can't go through this again."

He spread his arms. "They took everything from me. I'm super clean."

"This way," Katy said in an urgent voice. "I had a backup plan and now we'll have to use it."

She led us out of the café, in the opposite direction of where the officers were heading.

We quickly got lost among the crowd.

Katy seemed to know what to do and I had to trust her. Her job had been to find out how to get us out of India quickly.

I turned around to see the officers disappear through the departure gates that led to the taxi stand outside. *Maybe they think we were returning to the city? Maybe they're after someone else?*

I caught up to my friends, who were now heading toward the ticket booths. Instead of going to the main counters, Katy walked up to an automatic kiosk in a corner. It was so small, I hardly noticed it at first.

A small sign above the station said, *"Sri Lankan Airlines."*

Chapter Twenty-five

"**I** swear to god I saw him."

I looked at Katy's troubled face.

She'd been saying this for a while now but like the others, I wasn't sure if she'd become a little paranoid. Like we all were.

I leaned back and closed my eyes with a sigh. I'd been running on adrenaline for the past few days, but it was all catching up to me.

I'd found a first-aid kit from a convenience store at the airport and cleaned myself in the washrooms. The painkillers were helping, but once in a while the stings from my cuts and bruises made me want to crawl somewhere dark and quiet and sleep. Just sleep.

"He saw me. I'm telling you he looked right at me," I heard Katy say. "He was watching me when I was buying tickets to Dar Es Salaam. Why do you think I made a plan B?"

She was sitting next to me on one of those uncomfortable airport benches, leaning against the wall. "He was wearing that same stupid Arnie T-shirt. I know I only saw him once, but I'll never forget that shirt or that pudgy face."

I kept my eyes closed and tried to think this through.

Doesn't Franky have thugs to do his dirty work for him? Besides, shouldn't he be happy we were leaving the country and getting out of his hair? It didn't make sense. *Unless,* I wondered, *he wanted revenge for what I did to Kristadasa and for having hoodwinked him.*

I opened my eyes and turned to my friend.

"Hey, what happened to those tickets to Dar Es Salaam?"

"Ditched them in the Starbucks bin," she replied.

We were far away from Tanzania now. Instead of traveling west, we'd headed south, closer to the Equator.

There were only two flights from Mumbai to Dar Es Salaam, Tanzania every week. The next departure was not for another forty-eight hours. Katy had thought we could sleep in the airport till then, like we'd done before. But as soon as she suspected we were being followed by Franky's men, she hatched an alternative plan.

There were three daily flights from Mumbai to Colombo, a hop and a skip from Mumbai but altogether in another country, a place no one would suspect we'd go. All we had to do was jump on the next flight that day.

It was the shortest flight I'd ever taken. Soon after we'd taken off and settled in, the pilot announced our arrival at Colombo's International Airport. It had been a relief to get off the plane and wash India off me.

We made a beeline to the ticket counters and found a flight to Tanzania via Dubai that day. After getting our boarding passes, we took over a small corner of the departure lounge, sticking close together.

Katy and I huddled on a bench while Luc and Win sat on the ground in front of us, leaning against the window.

Luc had taken a strategic position, so he could see the entire lobby from where he was. His eyes constantly swept the room. Cuddled next to him, with her head on his shoulder, was Win. Her face looked drawn. Her hand was holding tightly to Luc's, as if afraid she'd lose him again.

My heart did a little flip to see them like this. They'd been abandoned, sold by their families, and had grown up in a brothel with no one to trust but each other. That was until Tetyana had come along.

But even she hadn't been able to save them, too focused on rescuing her own brother first. I could only imagine how Luc and Win had coped all these years.

"Oh!"

We looked at Win in alarm.

She slapped her forehead.

"What?" Luc asked, swiveling his head. "Who? Who's here?"

I peeked nervously at the lobby. *Did Fred or Franky's men follow us here?*

"We forgot to message Tetyana," Win said. "She's got no idea we're in Sri Lanka now."

I pulled out my phone. "What's the number, Katy?"

They all stared at me.

"Where's your phone?" I tried again.

"I ditched it in the bathroom bin near the gate before we boarded," she replied.

"Me too," said Win.

I stared at them, realizing what I'd done. "If anyone's tracking—"

"Pass it here," said Luc, taking it from me. "I'll go trash it."

He got up and walked over to the men's washroom.

"But we still have her number, right?" Win said.

Katy nodded. "There's a phone booth near the ticket counters. We can call her from there."

I thought about it for a moment and shook my head. "We're boarding soon. We'll try her from Dar Es Salaam. Best to lie low till we get out of here."

"Hey." Katy gave me a worried look. "Do you think they know where we are?"

"Who?" I asked, trying to think of all the people on the hunt for us. "The customs officers? Franky? Fred?"

"All of them, I guess."

"Won't customs just check plane logs to find out where we went?" Win asked, wrinkling her brow. "That's what I'd do."

"That's if they are chasing us," I said. "We don't know for sure. And that guy who took our money probably isn't saying anything to anyone right now."

"And Franky?" asked Katy.

Luc chuckled as he sat back on the floor and took Win's hand in his. "That Franky guy's probably pissed because they never thought you'd take on that Krista-whatever-his-name like that." He raised his eyebrows at me. "Didn't know you were such a kick ass."

I felt a shiver go through me. I didn't need to be reminded of that fight.

"What about Fred?" Katy asked. "He worries me the most."

I turned to Luc.

"How close are the Indian customs officers to your, er, friends in Europe?"

"It depends." He was silent for a minute. "It depends on how easily they can be bought and how much the goons are willing to pay. In this biz, information is expensive."

I leaned back with a resigned sigh.

"Why would Fred and his men spend time and money chasing us down?" Katy asked out loud. "We're not worth that much trouble, are we?"

Luc gave her a strange look. "I don't wanna scare anyone, but..."

"But what?" I said.

He turned to Win. "They're probably really after you, Win."

"Me?" she said, looking perplexed. "Why me? What did I do?"

Luc pulled her hand close to his chest, clasping it in his own. "If they know you've been hacking their accounts and taking their money, they'll want to stop that. And they won't be nice about it."

Win's face went pale.

"I'm here now," he said, putting his arm around her. "I won't let those bastards touch you."

"Wait," I said, sitting up. "First, how do they know it's Win? They'll have to be really good to trace that back to specifically her, us. Second, those bank accounts belong to Zero and Vlad. This has nothing to do with Fred."

Luc raised an eyebrow. "They're all connected. How do you think the COP in Mumbai knew Fred's lawyer?" He looked at me pointedly. "You told me to tell you what I know. Okay, here's what I know. Europe has the EU, Asia has the Pan Pacific and America has a boy's club with Canada and Mexico, right?"

I nodded.

"Don't you think the goons have their own international boy's clubs?"

My headache returned in full force. I massaged my forehead with my thumbs, trying to make it go away.

"It's like a mafia, black market boys' club. And they're bigger and stronger than some countries. It's how they don't get caught. Their power is in their connections. You've no idea how scary this is."

Katy and Win closed their eyes. Either they were digesting this information or had tuned it out, too much to take in right now.

Luc kept watch, holding Win close.

I'd been hoping to get some shut-eye before our next flight, but this conversation was not helping. My body wanted nothing more than rest but my mind was refusing to cooperate.

Everyone had fallen silent now, lost in their own nightmares.

I surveyed the departure lounge. Colombo was not as busy as Mumbai. Most people around us were families and couples or businessmen and women, chatting, snacking or sleeping. No one seemed remotely interested in us.

The airport tarmac lay behind the panel of floor-to-ceiling glass windows in front of me. A handful of planes were waiting in line on a runway to take off. Singapore Airlines. Air France. Air India. Behind the planes and the airport, far away on the horizon, I spotted tall coconut palm trees and the lush tropical greenery surrounding this area.

I gazed into the distance. I could almost hear the rustle of the palm tree fronds, feel the sun on my skin and smell the island sea breeze. This was my mother's country. *My Ceylon,* she used to call it fondly.

For a minute, I wished I could drop everything and just walk out. *One day*, I told myself, *one day, I'll come back to see what my mother's childhood home is really like.*

My headache slowly receded and my mind floated to more pleasant memories. I recalled those sunny Sundays when I helped my mother bake little cupcakes. I remembered how we'd gather around our kitchen table in Dar Es Salaam to drink cups of Ceylon tea and eat freshly baked cakes with my father.

Whenever I thought of my parents, it was that vision of Sunday treats I remembered the most. I'd buried the darker emotions somewhere deep inside.

But suddenly, the image of my family car on fire with my parents still inside flared across my mind. A deep sense of dread washed over me. That had not been an accidental car crash.

For months, my parents had been worried about being followed, just like I was now. Instead of human traffickers and drug overlords, they had been chased by the goons who worked for the large mining monopolies. When my parents reported the child laborers in the local camps, they had rattled a cage. A very large one.

They hadn't been the only people in town who'd been targeted. Every expatriate worker with Environ Africa had left the country, paying heed to mysterious threats. But as my mother had said many times, we had nowhere to run. Our home was in Africa. Tanzania.

Though my mother was from Sri Lanka and my father was from India, Africa was where I'd been born. Until my parents' death, I'd never imagined leaving that continent. And here I was now, returning to it.

I slipped my hand into my pocket and felt Preeti's letter between my fingers. I was sure she was in Dar Es Salaam. She was resourceful, smarter than all the girls in our school combined. She'd got herself out of a horrible situation by her own wits. She was far away from

Kristadasa and Franky. I got goose bumps thinking of how close I was to her now.

My hopes rose.

I'd get to see Chanda, my childhood best friend, again. I'd get to visit Mrs. Ngozi, her mom, who used to cut my hair at the market and babysit me whenever my mother got busy. I'd get to reconnect with Mr. Mudenda, my caretaker, the one who stayed by my side, night and day, after my parents' deaths.

They were all pulling me over the Atlantic, to the land where my parents lay buried.

"This is a boarding announcement for Flight 9822 to Dubai. We are inviting passengers to come to the gate now. Please have your boarding pass and identification ready."

Win stirred awake and sat up. I nudged Katy and got up to grab my bag.

"That's our flight," I said.

I took one last look at the waving palm trees in the distance and promised them I'd be back. *Soon.*

Part THREE

If you can remain calm, you don't have all the facts.
Unknown

"Chanda is our first stop," I said. I felt uplifted for the first time in days. "She'll help us out."

I hadn't seen my childhood friend for years. I was sure she'd gone on to a brand-new life, but I knew in my bones she'd never forget me. Like I'd never forgotten her.

"Who's this Chanda?" Win asked.

"My best girlfriend when I grew up here," I said. "Her mom, Mrs. Ngozi, took care of me when my mother got busy. She has a hair salon at the market. I loved hanging out there with Chanda."

I paused as I remembered my last days in Tanzania.

"When I was planning to get away after Grandma planned my wedding to Kristadasa, I wanted to come back here. I wanted to live with Chanda and her mom. They're like my second family."

We were rattling toward the main market in a van filled with people, suitcases, and baskets full of live chicken and vegetables.

Katy had wanted to take a taxi but Luc's warnings about Fred and his well-connected, cross-border matrix haunted me. I wondered if Franky was part of this loose international brotherhood too. Either way, we had to make it difficult for anyone to track us down, and being in a crowded bus with locals was a far safer bet than sitting in a car where we could be easily ambushed.

We'd hung around the Julius Nyerere airport for hours to get our visas on arrival. The line had been long and the customs agents had taken their time to ask a million and one questions.

We were college students on our mid-semester break, excited to visit East Africa for the first time—that was our story and we stuck to it. Since I was traveling with my Indian passport, they had no records of my previous stay here. Franky had done a good job with the fake documentation. That was his specialty after all.

Once we got through the first hurdle, we took a bus into Dar Es Salaam's city center to find an Internet café.

Win created another bank account and transferred money over while Katy and I went to find food, safari hats, and sunglasses. It wasn't as crazy hot and dusty here as in Mumbai, but the hats and glasses would give us the tourist camouflage we needed. Luc stayed at the café, never moving more than five inches away from Win, constantly on alert.

Once Win had the accounts figured out, Katy and I walked over to a few cash machines and withdrew Tanzanian shillings. We didn't care about the exorbitant fees or exchange rates. Neither did we feel guilty about digging into Vlad and Zero's cash hoard. As Katy said, this was *blood money.*

In sixty minutes, we were ready to head out.

I looked out the van's window as the East African landscape unraveled in front of us. And my heart filled with mixed emotions. Delight at returning to a familiar place of my childhood. Sadness at remembering why I left. And hope. Lots of hope at the thought of seeing Preeti, Chanda, and everyone I loved again.

I sat back in my seat, breathing in the smells and sounds of my old home. I smiled to hear Kiswahili spoken around me. I didn't speak it as well as before, but I understood a fair amount.

"Did you keep in touch with her all this time?" Katy asked.

"Who?" I said.

"Your friend, Chanda."

I shook my head. I hadn't kept in contact with my family, let alone my friends.

"Just before they buried my parents," I said, dredging up memories from long ago, "I asked Mr. Mudenda, my psychologist at the hospital, to arrange for Chanda and her mom to adopt me. I begged him not to send me to Goa. But he said I didn't have a choice because

I had a living family. And that was it. I never saw Chanda or her mom again."

"Hey." Katy leaned in toward me. "If you hadn't gone to Goa, you'd have never ended up in Toronto. And if you'd never come to Toronto, you'd never have met me."

Win nudged me from the other side. "And if you hadn't come to London, you'd have never found me."

"Or *me*," said Luc with a wry smile. "But you're probably super sorry about that."

I smiled back. "Hey, no regrets. We're family, remember."

I stared out the window. Outside, along the dusty road, a half a dozen boys played a pickup soccer game using a deflated football. Further down the road, we crossed a troop of girls carrying oversized aluminum pots on their heads.

I felt like I'd come full circle.

I remembered how I used to wave at these girls as I rode in the back of my parents' little Fiat to school. I'd always wished I could jump out and join them.

Carrying heavy pots long distance was an immeasurably more appealing thought than going to a class filled with snotty jet-setting girls who loved to bully me. This was one reason my best friend hailed from the local farmers' market and not from my school.

"Can't wait to see Mrs. Ngozi again," I said, trying to think what she must look like now. Gray hair? Wrinkles? Either way, I hoped she was happier. It was Mrs. Ngozi who gave me the multicolored braids I'd pined after for months—the same braids Chanda had. I wondered if Chanda still wore her hair the same way.

"Market!" the driver shouted out from the front.

Though the van was still moving, the passengers got up and scooped up their belongings. At the back, we shouldered our backpacks and waited patiently for everyone to get off.

"Thank you," I said to the bus driver as I climbed down. *Asante sanna.*

"Asante!" echoed Win and Luc after me.

"Asante," said Katy in a more reserved voice.

The driver's face broke into a wide grin to hear foreigners speak his language.

He pulled away with a friendly wave, leaving us standing uncertainly in front of the entrance to the dusty open market of Dar Es Salaam.

The smell of open barbecues and the calls from the fruit vendors came our way. For a minute, I teetered on my heels, feeling a little dizzy. It was like I'd been transported back to my childhood. I remembered how impatiently I'd waited for my father to park the little green Fiat at this spot, under the tall mahogany tree, so I could jump out and run off to find Chanda.

This is home. I felt a tear roll down my cheek.

"You okay?" Katy asked, reaching out and touching me on the shoulder.

"All good," I said, swallowing a small lump in my throat.

I looked at my three friends who were quietly waiting for me to take the next step. *What would I have done without them?*

"Thanks for sticking with me," I mumbled.

"Hey," Luc said, punching me gently in the arm. "We're family, remember?"

I took a deep breath and stepped inside the market with the others following me.

It was still a noisy, bustling place, but some things had changed. Most of the stalls had white canopy coverings now. There were more men than women behind the stalls than before, and everyone was wearing Western clothes and fancy shoes and carrying swanky mobile phones. Shifty-looking young men were hawking electronic goods from the back of expensive European cars parked next to the stalls.

The market, it seemed, had lost its soul.

I missed the multicolored Chitenge gown-wearing women with their impressive headdresses and even more impressive voices selling vegetables and homemade wares. They were larger-than-life goddesses to me. The bosses of the market, I used to call them, much to my parents' amusement.

"This way," I said, pointing at the path that led to the spice stalls. "Mrs. Ngozi's salon is a few stalls down."

I led the way while the others fell in step behind me.

An hour later, we had circled the entire market, poked our noses into all the stalls and talked to as many people as were willing to speak with us. We'd even walked into the "forbidden area" where the old Saudi man in the long white robe used to sit among his luxury items—the one place in the market that had been off-limits to us children. Mrs. Ngozi's and my mother's warnings had been burned so strongly into my mind that I hesitated passing by that stall even now, as an adult.

But the old Saudi man was no longer at his store. In his place were two Arab men who could have been his sons or younger brothers, wearing the same long white robes and desert head scarfs. They were too busy hustling their wares to even notice us.

There was no sign of Mrs. Ngozi.

Her presence at the market had been completely erased. The stall where she used to sit with her cutting and crimping tools was a mobile phone mart now. The man at the stall had no idea who or where Mrs. Ngozi was but was happy to sell us prepaid burner phones.

We walked over to sit at the base of an acacia tree to take stock.

Now what?

"First thing," Katy said, "is to let Tetyana know where we are."

"I'll do it," said Win.

She began to tap on her phone, speaking out loud as she typed.

"Hey, you're not gonna believe it. We're in Dar Es Salaam. That's in Tanzania. Long story. Had to run away from those crazy men again. So much to tell you. Where are U? Are U OK? Are U coming to join us? Miss U. Bisous."

I surveyed the area and tried to think of our options. *Maybe Mrs. Ngozi got a job and moved? Maybe Chanda got a job somewhere and took her mother with her? If not them, who can help me find Preeti? Where would I have gone, if I were Preeti searching for me, looking for safety?*

A shriek from Win startled me.

"She wrote back!"

Chapter Twenty-seven

"That's unusual," I said. Tetyana was always slow to respond.

"Shit!" said Luc. *Merde!*

"Oh, my god!" Katy's hand flew to her mouth.

I squinted at the screen to see what the others were reading, but the sunlight blinded the words. "What's she say, Win?"

Win read the text out loud. "How does Fred know where you are?"

A cold shiver went through me.

"They've followed us here?" Katy whispered in a horrified voice.

I looked at Luc in dismay.

"Wait," Luc said, knotting his brows. "Fred knew I was in Mumbai. But he doesn't know we're here. Plus, we cut through Sri Lanka and Dubai. That's not possible."

The phone pinged. We peered at the screen.

Katy read out loud, "What the hell are you doing in Dar Es Salaam, anyway?"

Win started typing furiously. "Hey, where are U?? How do U know about Fred? Are U with him? Can U talk to us? Are U OK????" She clicked on the send button. We waited huddled around her, without breathing.

Nothing.

"God, he'd better not have found her," said Luc, shaking his head.

"She's a fighter," said Katy. "Do you remember what she did to Vlad and Zero?"

"Not good enough," said Luc gloomily. "She's by herself. Fred's got teams of men. Crazy, freaky men."

I reached over and took the phone to re-read Tetyana's messages. Maybe there was a clue in them somewhere. *Why does she have to be so maddeningly cryptic?*

"Someone's followed us from Mumbai to Colombo to here," Katy said, looking around nervously.

But other than a few friendly smiles from locals passing by, no one was paying close attention to us. A dozen tourists with backpacks strolled through the market, haggling over wood carvings, Masai beads, and Chitenge cloth. We didn't look too out of place.

"Still no reply?" Luc asked.

I shook my head and handed the phone back to Win.

Tetyana was a like a ghost. I didn't blame her. I could only imagine the hell she must be going through to rescue her brother from a Russian jail. I imagined her running through the streets of Europe, jumping on trains, escaping on boats, getting on planes. It was a miracle she even wrote back to us.

"So, what do we do now?" asked Win.

"Become more careful," I said. "And find Chanda's home."

"Where does she live?" Katy asked.

"Bit of a walk from here," I said, squinting through the dust. "It's been a long time but I have a general idea."

Chanda and her mom walked to the market every day along a tiny gravel path that led to their village, an hour from here. I'd only been there a few times and once, I'd walked with Chanda from the market to her home. That was all I had to go by.

"Can we take a cab?" Katy asked. "We have the cash."

I shook my head. "Don't have the address. Sorry, I don't even remember the name of the village. But I think I can trace the path from memory."

That's where we found ourselves half an hour later, walking in single file along a chalky road, with me carrying the biggest flower bouquet I could find in the market for Mrs. Ngozi.

For the second time that day, I felt thankful for the presence of my friends. None of them had to follow me on this wild and convoluted goose chase, yet they never wavered.

I walked in front and Luc took the rear, scoping out our surroundings like a bodyguard on duty. The only people we met along the path were locals carrying sacks of produce or goods to the market. They all looked surprised to see us but other than a polite hello, they didn't stop to talk.

We took an hour and a half to get to Chanda's village. We'd paused to rest under a shady tree and gulp down water more than a few times along the way. *How did Chanda and her mother do this every day?*

I was relieved to spot the thatched huts huddled in the distance. They looked familiar. I quickened my pace, almost giddy at the thought of seeing Chanda and her mother again.

I kept walking, searching for the landmark etched in my head. A tall tree under which my parents, Mrs. Ngozi, Chanda and I had shared a spicy pumpkin stew made in an open fire pit right outside Mrs. Ngozi's hut. It had been the most memorable meal I'd had in Tanzania. I wondered if she'd invite my friends and me for supper that day.

"That's it!"

I stood and stared at the little house.

It was like time had stood still. The hut looked the same as before. Maybe a little smaller than I remembered. The tall tree was still beside it, holding its massive branches over it, protecting it. My legs felt shaky as I walked up to the wooden door.

I knocked softly.

Not a sound.

I knocked again.

Nothing.

"Chanda?" I called out with a slight tremble in my voice. "It's me."

I knocked again, louder this time.

"Mrs. Ngozi?"

A bird chirped on a tree branch. Other than that, no one was around. Everyone was at the market, working, making a living.

I turned the doorknob gently. There were no locks in these huts. Everyone expected everyone else to respect their privacy, and here I was doing the wrong thing.

The door creaked as it opened. I called out softly, "Hey, Mrs. Ngozi?"

Silence.

"Hello?" I said a bit louder. "It's me, Asha."

I opened the door wider and peered inside, letting my eyes adjust to the darkness. I could see the outline of a small figure sleeping on a cot at the other end of the room. My heart leaped.

"Chanda?"

Oh my god, Chanda!

I opened the door wider and stepped inside. She was fast asleep. I tiptoed toward the bed not wanting to scare her. My heart beat faster as I approached her.

When I got to the cot, the person turned and looked at me.

I stared back in shock.

Oh, god. I've made a mistake.

I took a step back.

"I...er...I'm so sorry..." I spluttered. "I thought this was—"

"Asha?"

I stopped.

It was a murmur of a sound, but I'd heard it. I stared at the woman in the cot who was struggling to sit up. She looked sickly. Sunken eyes and botched skin, more a skeleton than human. A whisper of a shadow rather than a person.

"Asha?" The voice was cracked, feeble.

The woman raised her head.

My throat went dry.

"Mrs. Ngozi?" I leaned in closer. "Is it....is it really you?"

Her eyes lit up ever so slightly.
I ran to the bed and fell to my knees.

Chapter Twenty-eight

S he used to be so beautiful.

I remembered her flawless ebony skin, full lips, and hair done up like a queen's crown on her head. Compared to my prim and petite Asian mother, Mrs. Ngozi had looked bigger than life.

I'd secretly wanted to be buxom and beautiful like her when I grew up. But when I told Chanda that, she'd pointed out how impossible that would be given my boy-like hips and nonexistent boobs.

Mrs. Ngozi was staring at me like she was seeing a ghost.

"Are you okay?" I asked in a soft voice. "You look...so..." I swallowed.

She tipped her head as if trying to recollect something.

"It's me, Asha," I said, pointing at my chest. "Chanda's best friend."

"Chanda?" she whispered more to herself.

"Do you remember me?"

"Of course, my child," she said in a hoarse whisper.

I looked at her sadly. I remembered her rich and confident singsong voice that called out to her friends to join her for a cup of rooibos tea every Saturday afternoon. Or that shouted out to Chanda and me to behave.

I scrutinized her carefully. Her skin was sallow, her eyes jaundiced and her body half the size it once was.

She reached out to me with a skeletal hand. I took it in both of mine, holding her gently, worried I might hurt her.

"So good to see you."

"You too, Mrs. Ngozi." I badly wanted to ask what happened to her, but it seemed too impolite. Too soon. "Where's Chanda? Is she here?"

She gave me a weary look like it was too hard for her to speak. After an excruciating silence, she said one word.

"Gone."

"Gone?" I raised my eyebrows. "Where?"

She shook her head and let out a melancholy sigh.

Still holding on to my hand, she lay down and closed her eyes. I watched her silently, listening to her raspy breathing for a full minute. The house was eerily quiet. My friends hadn't come in but I could feel their presence crowding the doorway.

Just when I thought she'd gone to sleep, she coughed, a rough cough that made her whole body shake. Her grasp on my hand tightened. Holding on to me for stability, she lifted her head, turned to the other side of the cot and spat. Then, she turned around and collapsed like that simple act had exhausted her.

I stood up and peeked over. On the other side of the cot was a broken clay pot on the floor. Even in the dark, I saw the red liquid inside it. *She's spitting blood.* Next to this bowl was a bunch of long, dried twigs and a feather-bound whisk I'd seen before as a child. Village shaman tools, I remembered.

Mrs. Ngozi coughed again and covered her mouth, her face wincing in pain.

"She needs a doctor," I said out loud.

Katy stepped inside and walked over to the bed. She knelt down and gently touched Mrs. Ngozi's forehead.

"Fever," she said in a low voice.

Mrs. Ngozi kept her eyes closed. Her body twitched every few seconds like she was in pain.

How long has she been lying here? What sickness does she have? Why isn't Chanda with her mother?

"Should I get an ambulance?" I heard Luc say softly from behind me. "I can call a car or a taxi."

Before I could answer, the door creaked open.

We whirled around.

A small dark face peeked in through the door. My heart leaped.

"Chanda?" I called out.

The door opened wider and a wizened old woman stepped in. She stared at us in shock.

I let go of Mrs. Ngozi's hand and stood up.

The woman took a step back and stood at the threshold, her eyes cagily drifting to each of us, taking us in, assessing us.

I walked slowly toward the doorway.

"*Shikamoo*," I said, dipping one knee in a mini curtsy and clapping my hands twice. That was how I remembered adults greeted each other here. I hoped I got it right. The woman's face relaxed slightly but her eyes still looked wary.

"*Shikamoo*," she greeted me back.

"Mrs. Ngozi…" I racked my brain, trying to remember my childhood Swahili. "What's wrong with her? She looks very sick."

The woman nodded hesitantly.

"I come from far away. I came to see Chanda and her mother again."

She looked startled. "Chanda?"

I pointed at my chest. "Chanda's *rafiki*." *Friend.*

Her face cleared. "Aaah." That seemed to have broken the spell.

The woman spoke rapidly, gesturing madly. As her hands moved up, so did her voice. I strained to listen, trying to make out the words, but she was speaking too fast. …*Bedridden…spirits….bad….daughter…*

Mrs. Ngozi coughed. I turned around to see her spit to the side of the bed again.

I walked back to the cot, followed by the old woman.

I knelt in front of the bed and touched Mrs. Ngozi's hand. "Hey, are you okay?"

She barely nodded.

The woman knelt next to me, put her hand on Mrs. Ngozi's forehead, closed her eyes and began to mutter to herself, in a low guttural prayer.

Mrs. Ngozi reached out to me, her hand weak, trembling. "She's my neighbor. Village shaman," she whispered, "she helps me."

I nodded.

She took a deep breath. "I'm so happy to see you."

"Me too," I replied, "you have no idea."

I didn't expect her next few words.

"I'm dying, my child."

"No!" I cried out.

The old woman prayed louder.

I felt like someone had just reached in and scooped everything out of me. "Don't say that!"

Mrs. Ngozi looked at me sadly. "It is what it is."

"You just need help. That's all. And you'll be okay."

The woman's chants got even louder.

"Why didn't you call a doctor?" I looked at the old woman accusingly, but she was too busy with her incantations to even notice me now.

"Oh, my child," Mrs. Ngozi said in her tired voice and gave me a weak smile. "I prayed to see you before I go. And with god's blessing, I can go now."

My body went cold. Tears rolled down my cheeks. "You can't just die here!"

"Hey, the ambulance is coming."

I swiveled around and blinked. Luc was standing at the doorway with a phone in his hands. "I got the village name from someone outside. They said they can be here in twenty minutes," he said in a quiet voice.

I turned around to see Mrs. Ngozi struggle to sit up. "Stop this, my child," she said. "This is not necessary."

"I'm not leaving here until we get you to a hospital," I said.

The old woman turned to me and said something.

"Sorry, I don't understa—"

Mrs. Ngozi nodded. "It's too expensive. We can't afford it. Stop this silliness."

I shook my head, holding tightly to her hand. The shaman may have her mantra. I had mine.

"You're coming with me," I said. "We're going to get you help. No matter what."

It took fifteen minutes to convince Mrs. Ngozi to get in the ambulance when it finally arrived. It took another half an hour to take her to the Dar Es Salaam General Hospital.

Luc and Win rode shotgun in front with the driver while Katy and I squeezed in the back with Chanda's mother and the first responder. We were paying cash for this trip. The promise of a substantial tip gave us more latitude than normal.

While the paramedic hooked Mrs. Ngozi up to the machines and monitored her vital signs, I held on to her hand, squeezing it once in a while to remind her I was still here.

The old woman in the village had refused to come with us, balking at the very idea of an ambulance in her neighborhood.

In broken Swahili, I tried to explain. "She's going to see a doctor at the hospital." She shook her head unhappily as if nothing would help Mrs. Ngozi, and disappeared as soon as the first responders disembarked from their vehicle.

But the nurses at the hospital emergency didn't waste any time.

As soon as the ambulance stopped, they pushed us all aside, hauled Mrs. Ngozi out on a stretcher and rushed her inside.

I ran after them. Before I could catch up, they took her through a door with the words "Emergency Personnel Only" written in large red lettering. The last nurse to go in put her palm out, stopping me.

"What's your relation?"

"I, er..."

"Family?"

"Not really, but..."

She turned around and disappeared inside, the doors swinging back and forth in front of my face. I could no longer see Mrs. Ngozi.

After hanging around the corridor for half an hour and failing to get anyone to talk to me, I turned away. I felt weighed down, like I was carrying a giant boulder on my shoulders.

I stumbled back to the emergency entrance to reunite with my friends. They'd paid off the ambulance workers and had settled in a corner of the waiting room.

"Is she going to be okay?" Win asked.

I shrugged and plopped down next to her.

I was too shaken to speak. It was the first time I'd seen Mrs. Ngozi in years, and I'd lost her with no clue if I'd ever see her again.

"What about Chanda?" Katy asked. "Where's she?"

I shook my head. "It's strange she's not around," I said, rubbing my face. "She'd never abandon her mom like this."

"She never wrote to you?" Katy asked.

"She has no idea where I went...."

I sat up. *That's not true.* Seven years ago, I gave a letter to Mr. Mudenda at the Dar Es Salaam airport with strict instructions. *Did he keep his promise?*

"I think I know how to track Chanda and Preeti," I said, standing up and picking my bag.

Chapter Twenty-nine

If Mrs. Ngozi was a whisper of her former self, Mr. Mudenda was brimming with health, even with his graying hair. He reminded me of a younger Morgan Freeman.

I remembered how kind and caring he'd been to me, a strange girl thrust into his temporary care after my parents' death. His words had always been gentle and his voice soothing.

"Asha!" he cried, his voice echoing through the room. He pushed his chair back and stood up, spreading his arms wide. "What in god's good name are you doing here?"

I'd been hovering at the doorway of his massive office, wondering if I should knock. We'd managed to slip past the front desk and get into the elevator while his staff were preoccupied with a mail delivery.

I ran to him and threw my arms around his waist. He scooped me up and hugged me back, a hug I'd been wanting for a very long time. I swallowed a sob and squeezed him tight. Mr. Mudenda was the closest I'd get to seeing my parents again.

He pushed me back and held me by the shoulders to inspect me. "Look at you! Taller than I remembered and bigger now. All grown up. But still the same little girl, no?"

His smile turned into a frown as he noticed the state of my face and my clothes. The bruises on my arms and face were a bright purple now. They hurt less but showed more. His frown deepened.

"What happened to you, my girl?" He shook me by my shoulders gently and gave me a stern look. "What's going on? When did you get here?"

I wiped my eyes. "This morning."

"What happened to you? Why are you here?"

"I came because...." I stopped. I'd come back to Africa for so many reasons, but this was not the time to share all of that. "I'm just so glad to see you again, Mr. Mudenda."

He stared at me for a second before pulling me in for another hug. "I don't know what's going on, but you're here now. That's all that matters." I burst into tears, crying a hot mess into Mr. Mudenda's chest.

No one in the world would replace my parents. But after the car crash, it was Mr. Mudenda, the children's hospital's only psychologist, who'd visited me every day to make sure I was getting the proper care, bringing me books to read, telling me stories to put me to sleep and doing his best to comfort a lone twelve-year-old.

I'd only known him for a few weeks, but I'd clung to him like a newly orphaned baby animal would cling to anything that moved.

"There, there, child. You're a grown woman now. What are you doing crying like this? We should be celebrating a reunion, should we not?"

I pulled away, choking back my tears.

"S...sorry," I stammered. "It's been a long trip."

"I can see that." He gave me that stern look again. "And I want to know all about it."

Someone cleared their throat behind us.

We turned. Mr. Mudenda stared at the raggedy group of people who'd gathered at the doorway and were waiting politely.

"They are with you?"

"Yes."

"These are your, er, friends?"

I nodded.

He let out a deep sigh. "Well, come in, everyone. Please come in so I can say hello to you all."

Katy and Luc walked in shyly, followed by Win.

Mr. Mudenda stepped up to shake their hands.

"My goodness," he said, surveying everyone. "If you don't mind me saying so, you look like you've been through a war zone."

Win gave him a wary look, still suspicious of adults. Katy offered an awkward smile. Luc merely looked away.

"Well," Mr. Mudenda said, shaking his head. "I guess international travel can do that to you, right?"

We all smiled weakly.

Oh yes, and much, much more.

"Take a seat. I'll get someone to make us some rooibos tea."

We were a block away from the General Hospital where Mrs. Ngozi had been admitted. It had taken us a while to locate the right office on the right floor of the right building on the hospital campus, but an hour later we'd found Mr. Mudenda. Over the years, he'd been promoted from social worker to Head of Administration at the new Children's Hospital. And that's where we were now.

"Ah, come in, son. I'm not ready to go home yet."

We all turned around.

A buff man in his twenties was standing outside the door, looking like he'd just come from the gym. His face was familiar and remarkably like Mr. Mudenda's.

"He's just finished his Kung Fu class and came to drive me home, but that can wait." Mr. Mudenda turned to me with a twinkle in his eyes. "Do you remember this boy?"

I wrinkled my brows.

"You two met each other a long time ago."

"Peace!" I said. "You look so...," I stammered, blushing, "...different."

He gave me an astonished look, surprised I knew his name.

"Don't you remember Asha, son?" said Mr. Mudenda.

Peace stared at me for a second and a wide grin broke across his face. Despite all the craziness I was dealing with at the moment, my heart did a flip—the same kind of flip I'd felt whenever Tim had looked at me with those melting brown eyes in high school.

"Asha?"

He walked over and thrust out his hand. I felt his hands grasp mine, sending a soft warm feeling all over me.

"I remember you," he said. "I remember you at the hospital. You were a lot skinnier and shorter back then." He laughed pleasantly.

He was taller, broader, and more handsome now, even with those geeky glasses.

"And you were just a puny kid back then," I said, grinning back.

Peace's eyes swept the room as he looked at my friends one by one. His eyes settled on Katy's feet. "Hey, why are you all wearing red shoes? Is this some uniform or something?"

"It's a new fashion back in Europe," said Katy with a charming smile. "Red is in."

"I love the color," said Peace.

Hi, I'm Katy," she said, giving him her hand. Peace's grin widened. Instead of shaking her hand, he took it gently in both of his and kissed it.

A pang of jealousy went through me. *What's wrong with me? I've got work to do here.*

While Peace said hello to my friends, I turned to his father.

"Hey, Mr. Mudenda. Do you remember that letter I gave you at the airport?"

He cocked his head.

"The one I asked you to give to Chanda at the market? You promised me you'd—"

"Aaah, yes. I remember very well." He paused. "I sent a member of my team to the market to find her, but your friend was nowhere to be found, I'm afraid. They told me she must have moved."

"Do you know where she went?"

"No one was willing to talk to us." He gave me a sad, almost guilty look. "Then again, villagers don't like talking to city authorities. I went to the market myself that weekend to check. It was like she didn't exist."

"Oh, no."

"I tried my best, Asha."

I frowned. "It's strange she'd disappear like that. She was just a kid."

"Maybe she went to a new school somewhere?" Peace said, settling himself on the couch, next to Katy. "Or got sent to live with relatives in another village?"

I shook my head. Mrs. Ngozi had said she was "gone." *What does that mean?* It sounded more ominous than a casual stay with family.

"I'm sure there's a perfect explanation," said Peace. "There always is, no?"

I felt Luc and Katy's eyes turn to me. There had never been a "perfect explanation" for anything that had happened in our lives, that was for sure.

"The strange thing is her mom didn't know where Chanda was either. And Mrs. Ngozi, her mother, is really sick. We just brought her to the emergency ward. They didn't let us in but she told us she was dying."

Mr. Mudenda's eyes narrowed.

"When did this happen?"

"Just now. We went to the market looking for Chanda but when we didn't find her, we walked to her village and found Mrs. Ngozi in her home. She was so ill, we called for help." I looked at Mr. Mudenda. "Is there anything we can do for her? They won't let me in the ward because I'm not family."

He leaned forward, looking thoughtful, and was silent for a minute.

"We can fix that," he said finally. "I'll have a chat with my counterpart at the General Hospital tomorrow morning."

"Thank you," I whispered.

"If she was as sick as you say she was, the emergency ward is the best place for her right now. You did the smart thing. Let them do their job. And I'll check in on her."

I breathed out a sigh of relief.

Mr. Mudenda's eyes swept the crowd in front of him. "Now that we've all met and said hello, why don't we get something to eat? I feel like you may have a lot to talk about."

I nodded. He had no idea.

Peace snapped his fingers. "Hey, I know a cool café that serves good Tanzanian beer. Just around the corner."

"Is it safe?" Luc asked.

All eyes turned to him.

"What I mean is," Luc said, "what kind of neighborhood is it in? There are no dealers or gangsters around, are..."

"Do you think all of Africa is filled with criminals?" Peace asked, looking offended.

"That's not what I meant."

"Do you think we're all terrorists too?"

Luc's face flushed. "What I mean is, what kind of people hang around there...." His voice trailed off.

"It's a normal café," Peace replied with a frown. "Caters to doctors and nurses, not drug dealers."

Mr. Mudenda got up, giving his son a look that said, *Drop it*.

"It seems to me that this is the end of a very rough voyage for you all," he said. "Let's find a nicer place than my office to sit down and chat, shall we?"

No one moved.

"It's safe here. You're with me."

Chapter Thirty

One by one, we got up and followed Mr. Mudenda and Peace out of the building.

We walked casually and silently along the pavement toward the restaurant area, taking in the local sights. It was a normal working day in Dar Es Salaam. Our past few weeks seemed like a surreal nightmare in comparison to this.

Most of the restaurants looked as clinical and impersonal as the inside of the hospital, except for one. At the end of the strip was a café with a bright orange awning. Safari photos decorated the walls and a full-sized Tanzanian flag was draped behind the bar. The tangerine color of the walls reminded me of the sun that warmed these savannah lands.

"See?" said Peace, stepping in and giving Luc a sideways glance. "Not that bad, is it? We have nice places in Africa too."

Luc looked annoyed but had the courtesy to not make a retort.

I pulled a chair at a table and sat down. Mr. Mudenda took the seat next to me. I noticed Peace pull a chair out for Katy, giving her a wink as he did so. Katy blushed. I looked away.

"So, what brings you here?" Mr. Mudenda asked once the waiter had taken our order and left.

I hesitated. *Where do I even begin?*

Katy, Luc and Win had their eyes on me now, waiting, wondering how much I'd confess to. Peace was watching me curiously, like he still couldn't make out how I'd popped up like I had.

His father waited patiently. I looked at Mr. Mudenda's kind eyes and knew I owed him an explanation. The only people I'd shared my entire life story with were Katy, Luc, Win, and Tetyana. Now, in the presence of what I felt was family, everything came tumbling out.

Over a meal of ugali, spicy fried plantains, red beans in coconut milk, a tomato salad, and Tanzanian beer, we talked and talked.

From the outside, we looked like any group of friends having a re-union over a hearty supper, except that Luc constantly swiveled his head to check our surroundings, going on alert when anyone walked in the door. I was glad he was on watch.

But sitting next to Mr. Mudenda, I felt protected.

I confessed to my original sin, how I stole a pair of ruby red slippers to make Chanda happy. I explained what happened to Preeti, Aunty Shilpa, and my grandmother. I opened up about my stay in Toronto as a bonded slave with a fake passport and visa. I told him what happened in India and why we came here, on my quest to find my cousin.

Mr. Mudenda listened intently, his face somber, nodding occasionally to show he was paying attention. Holding tightly to his beer bottle, Peace listened too, shaking his head and occasionally crying out, "That's crazy stuff!" "You can't be serious," or "I don't believe this!"

"We should have kept you here in Tanzania," Mr. Mudenda said, staring down at his plate, his face a mixture of guilt and regret.

I shrugged. What was done was done. "Can you help me find Preeti?" I asked.

"I can see what I can do," he replied with a grave nod. "I have contacts in the police headquarters. They might be able to assist us."

It was dark outside when we finished our meal. I looked down at my empty plate with a sigh, preparing to say goodbye to Peace and his father for the night.

"Do you all have a place to stay?"

Mr. Mudenda was looking at me, a concerned expression on his face.

I shook my head. "I'm sure there's a student hostel or something nearby."

"That's it," he said, getting up, "you are all coming home with me. I won't sleep a wink knowing you're wandering around town.

Besides, you've all had enough adventure for a lifetime, don't you think?"

We contemplated his invitation silently.

"Thanks." Katy spoke up first. "That's really good of you."

Win, who had been silent throughout the meal, nodded shyly. "That's nice," she said.

Luc didn't say anything, his face remaining vigilant.

"Thanks, Mr. Mudenda," I said. "Do you think we can see Mrs. Ngozi tomorrow too?"

He nodded. "But first, I must take you to your parents' graves." That look of guilt passed over his face again. "Asha, there's something you need to know

Chapter Thirty-one

I didn't sleep much that night.

I tossed and turned on the king-sized bed I was sharing with Katy in one of Mr. Mudenda's guest rooms. Win and Luc had taken the second guest room. They were becoming inseparable now. Guess I should have seen it coming.

Mr. Mudenda's house was looked after by Mama Gladness and her small team of a cook and a gardener. In her head wrap and multicolored Chitenge gown that went down to her ankles, she reminded me of the loud and bold women of the market, long ago. Katy thought she looked like a chief or queen of sorts, and Mama Gladness didn't disappoint.

That first night, she bustled into our room a few minutes before we went to bed and took all of our clothes away. She tsked with disapproval at the state of our garments. "What have you girls been up to? My goodness me!" When we got up the next morning, our cleaned clothes lay on a rack at the foot of our bed.

We showered, changed and walked into the dining room for breakfast. Mr. Mudenda was not at the table but Peace was at the head chair, slouching over his phone, sipping a glass of orange juice.

Just as we were about to sit, Mama Gladness burst in from the kitchen, humming a gospel song to herself and carrying a plate loaded with thick golden pancakes. I noticed Peace sit up straight at her entrance and quickly slip the phone into his pocket.

Mama Gladness put the plate on the table and looked us up and down with her hands on her hips.

"I've never seen girls this skinny in my life," she said, shaking her head. "How will you ever find good husbands looking like this, I tell you? I want you to eat everything I put on the table."

Katy and I nodded wordlessly.

"Eat up, now!" With a huff, she marched back to the kitchen.

I knew Mr. Mudenda had lost his wife at childbirth. Mama Gladness was almost a surrogate mother for Peace—a distant family member from their village who was helping out in exchange for room, board and a better life in the city.

Peace was Mr. Mudenda's one and only child. When he used to visit me at the hospital, he proudly told me stories about his son's achievements in school, sports, and even spelling bee contests, making me feel slightly envious. Every other day, he'd borrow storybooks from the school library and on those days he'd bring Peace with him and read to both of us, me lying in bed and Peace sitting in an uncomfortable hospital chair, swinging his legs.

"Father's already eaten," Peace said, helping himself to a pancake. "He's in his study making arrangements for you to visit Mrs. Ngozi. He said he has to make a quick trip to the hospital and will meet us at the cemetery after breakfast."

Cemetery.

I sat down in a daze. That word seemed so hollow, so far away.

The images I held of my parents in my head were solid. They were of two good people in flesh and blood, who talked and laughed and worked and played. The thought of them lying lifeless deep in the ground was unthinkable. Though the morning sun was streaming in through the windows, I shivered.

"You'd better eat or you'll get in trouble," Peace said, pushing the plate of pancakes my way.

I tried a smile but it didn't come. I picked up a pancake and doused it with syrup, my mind elsewhere. With my first bite, I flew back to a time when my mother and I baked at home. Before I knew it, I was serving myself another pancake and another, absorbed in my childhood memories, while Peace and Katy chattered next to me.

Win and Luc joined us shortly after, Win carrying a tablet she'd borrowed from Peace the night before. She plopped down on an empty chair and immediately started scrolling through it.

"Put that thing away!"

We looked up, startled.

Mama Gladness had walked in with a jug of fresh orange juice and was glowering at Win.

Win gave her a bewildered look.

"This is a dinner table, my dear."

It seemed that Mr. Mudenda hadn't shared our backgrounds with his housekeeper. I wanted to tell her this was probably the first family dining table Win had ever sat at.

"Give me that," Mama Gladness said, taking the tablet away. "When you're at my table, you're going to eat. And talk with each other. I tell you, children these days..." Muttering to herself, she plonked the device on a side table.

"Sorry," Peace mouthed to Win.

"Does anyone want more of my fluffy *vitumbua*, hmm?" said Mama Gladness, squinting into the coffee pot to see if it was empty.

"*Vitumbua*?" asked Katy.

Peace pointed at the pancake dish at the center of the table.

"You'll never eat *vitumbua* like mine in all of Tanzania. All of Africa, even. The secret is in the spices. Cardamom will refine any dish. And it's good for you too." Mama Gladness gave Win a pointed look.

"My girl!" she called out.

"Yes..?" stammered Win, her eyes widening.

"I want you to take more. You still have so much growing to do, my child."

Win quickly reached for the pancake plate. Luc passed her the coconut caramel syrup.

"Good girl," muttered Mama Gladness as she walked off to the kitchen.

"She's from Arusha. They're the nicest people," Peace whispered as soon as she disappeared. "She's like a nosy, bossy aunt but she means well."

I let the conversation drift around me and looked out the large bay windows.

Outside, a gardener was snipping the hedges. The lawn looked immaculate, like every blade of grass had been individually manicured. An overgrowth of jacaranda fell across the wall like a bright crimson waterfall. At one end of the yard was a vegetable garden and behind it, a row of smiling sunflowers stood proudly.

I suddenly felt ashamed to sit in these surroundings—ashamed at sharing my story with these people the night before. Mr. Mudenda was an executive at a hospital. Peace had just finished his political science degree and got accepted to a well-known law school in Nairobi.

Why would they have us over in their home? I'd been a slave housemaid. Katy had been an abused kid, a runaway. Win and Luc had grown up in a brothel.

I fell into a funk, eating only because I didn't want to get into trouble with Mama Gladness.

After breakfast, Peace asked us to follow him outside to his Jeep.

I trailed the group, dragging my feet. I wanted to go to the cemetery. But at the same time, I didn't want to go.

All these years, I'd conjured up a vision of my parents alive and happy, waiting for me back in Tanzania. Seeing their graves would kill that fantasy. I was the last one in the Jeep. As soon as I buckled up, Peace pulled out of the driveway.

I tried to stay focused on the scenery around me. Mrs. Ngozi's village was a far cry from Peace's gated community. In contrast to the dusty fields where boys in ratty shorts played pickup football, in this neighborhood, little boys and girls dressed in private school uniforms walked along a paved boulevard lined with palm trees.

Mr. Mudenda was already at the cemetery when we got there. He was waiting for us with a solemn look on his face.

As soon as Peace parked, we clambered out and walked over to him.

Mr. Mudenda didn't smile or say good morning. He turned to me.

"Come," he said.

Chapter Thirty-two

The sea of gravestones was a grim reminder of why I had come here.

It was a beautiful place with stately trees framing the perimeter and bushes of wild roses flourishing in between the tombstones. A bird sang high above us. I turned my face up, trying to spot it, wondering if my parents had found peace here, even if their end had been a fiery one.

"I have taken care of your parents," I heard Mr. Mudenda say.

I realized we were alone now, strolling in the middle of the park. Everyone else was standing at the parking lot by the Jeep, watching us.

We were heading toward two graves lying side by side. I stared at the two stones, wishing I could un-see them. My legs felt like lead. I stopped walking.

"Come, my child."

Mr. Mudenda put an arm around my shoulder and pushed me gently forward. Something stirred inside of me, something that wanted to rip me open. I wanted to run away, screaming, crying. I'd have done so if Mr. Mudenda had not been there to hold me.

My parents' gravestones were simple. Etched in beautiful lettering were their names, the year of their births and deaths. Someone had left a bouquet of fresh sunflowers on my mother's grave.

"I know your parents weren't particularly religious. There were scientists after all. I didn't want to insult their memories by putting anything on the gravestone," Mr. Mudenda said. "I hope that is suitable for you?"

That was when I noticed all the other graves had crosses on them, except for these two.

"Thank you," I mumbled, standing with my hands clasped behind my back, choking back something. "This is fine."

Things so significant to us when we're alive crumble like dust after death. My parents were gone for good. Nothing else mattered. Crosses or otherwise.

I got on my knees and touched my mother's tombstone, feeling each letter of her name with the tip of my fingers. My chest felt tight. I wanted to cry but no tears came out. It had been years since I'd left the bodies of my parents in this country. I'd had years to come to terms with this, but I still couldn't accept what had happened to them.

Mr. Mudenda knelt next to me. His hands hung by his side. His face looked dark.

"Asha," he said in almost a whisper. "I have a confession to make."

I looked at him in surprise.

A confession?

"The day your parents passed away...." He swallowed.

I remembered that day well—the day my world turned upside down. I reached out and touched the sunflowers, waiting for him to resume.

"The authorities visited me."

The police?

"Environ Africa, the firm where your parents worked was in trouble, lots of trouble."

I remembered my parents talking about this in hushed tones in the kitchen, thinking I wouldn't hear.

"In fact, they had disputes with the biggest mining company in this region. They went bankrupt a month after this...er...accident."

He paused.

Sophie's pretty face from long ago sprang to mind. I knew which company he was talking about. Sophie's father owned the largest mining corporation in the region. I used to have nightmares of her dragging me down dark mining shafts, forced to work with the other children they'd bought from remote villages. She was part of the school's elite clique and loved to bully everyone else, especially me.

"You see, the mining company didn't like anyone gathering information on their environmental practices and child labor camps." Mr. Mudenda let out a deep sigh. "This is not a secret. The whole country knows these things are going on. We know the government is in this racket with them. But to have evidence, now that was powerful."

He stared off into the distance. It was almost like he was talking to himself more than to me now.

"They exploit our children and take off with the riches, leaving us with broken people and an empty land." His words stumbled out faster and louder. "We call ourselves a post-colonial democracy. We're so proud about it, but we are nothing of the sort. Because if that were true, how could we let all this go on right under our noses?"

He turned to me like he'd just realized I was there. His eyes softened. He dropped his voice.

"What I have to tell you is something that will put me in danger. The reason I didn't tell you this before was because I was frightened for myself and my son."

I felt a sinking in the pit of my stomach.

"Yes, Asha, I was a coward. I'm afraid that is what I was."

He wiped the sweat beads that had collected on his forehead.

"On the day of the accident, two senior government officials came to see me. They knew I was assigned to you as your social worker. They started to monitor me. I was under their command from then on."

"What do you mean?"

"Your parents didn't die in an accident." The beads of sweat on his forehead had turned into a stream. "They threatened me with jail and torture if I told you otherwise."

A shiver ran down my back.

"The truth is the mining company killed your parents. They sent their goons to make it look like an accident."

I stared at him mutely. I didn't tell him that I'd had a strange feeling all along, a knot in my stomach, that told me something was wrong, that my parents' deaths weren't as they seemed. I'd had this uneasy feeling for years without being able to articulate it.

"The company thought all they had to do was to send a few men with guns and strong words, and the Environ Africa scientists would pack their bags and leave the country. But your parents lived here. This was their home. This was *your* home. They had nowhere to go. So the company did the next worst thing."

He turned to me with a sober expression.

"It's the reason I didn't look too deeply into Chanda's disappearance. I couldn't. They were following me everywhere. I could have told you the truth then, but you were just a child. I think you're old enough to hear this now."

I nodded. I wondered how I'd have reacted if I'd heard this news at twelve. I was struggling with it even now.

"The mining company was bringing in a lot of money to people high up, very high up. I'm ashamed to say this, but my government protected the gangsters. And they couldn't get you out of this country fast enough."

He sighed again, like he was unburdening his heart for his own sanity.

"I thought sending you to India to stay with your grandmother would be a good thing. I really did. But after what you told me last night...." I heard a choking sound and looked up to see him shaking. A grown man trying to cry, but he didn't know how. "What happened to you was a result of my negligence. I will carry this burden till my last day."

I tried to think of something to say. I wanted to tell him what happened in India or Toronto had nothing to do with him, but the words didn't come out. My head was in a whirl, trying to digest all this.

"I'm not asking you to forgive me," he was saying, "I just want you to know the truth."

I nodded wordlessly, staring at my parents' graves, wondering about the men who did this.

An image from years ago sprang to my mind. It was the sight of our little green Fiat burning among the elephant grass in the savannah. I remembered seeing my parents' silent dark shadows inside, while I screamed for help.

I felt sick at the thought of these goons running around freely after committing murder. Heinous, unspeakable murder. Without my even realizing it, Kali had crept into my head again, stronger than before, her bloodied hands and lolling tongue flashing across my mind.

A new fire ignited in my belly, a fire stronger than the one that burned my parents to death.

I'm going to find these men and make them pay. What do I have to lose now?

Chapter Thirty-three

Mr. Mudenda took his car and the rest of us piled back into Peace's Jeep.

No one asked me what we'd talked about at my parents' grave site. We sat in silence, deep in our own thoughts. Except for Luc. He kept an eagle eye out, constantly checking the cars around us.

The hospital had called that morning to say we could visit Mrs. Ngozi. She'd been given saline and painkillers and with some rest under the watchful eyes of the emergency nurses, she was faring better.

Everyone knew Mr. Mudenda at the General Hospital, and he in turn seemed to know everyone here. The first thing he did was to find a doctor to check all of us, ignoring our protests that we felt fine. After a thorough physical examination and taking our blood samples to get tested, a nurse ushered us to Mrs. Ngozi's ward.

"Tuberculosis," the emergency ward doctor told us. "TB is treatable. All she needs is proper medication, lots of sleep and good care." He shook his head. "These village shamans only make things worse. She should have come to us earlier."

Walking into Mrs. Ngozi's room gave me flashbacks to a similar room I'd woken up in, years ago. The same antiseptic smell and the cool sterile air threw me back to the fateful day that changed everything. I shivered as I walked up to her bedside.

A row of beeping machines stood on one side of the bed, their screens glowing impersonally, giving the room an even starker look. Taking notes from one of the screens was a young nurse. With a quick nod, he walked out of the room to give us privacy.

Katy and I stepped up to the bed. Win, Luc, and Peace had taken a seat on the visitor bench outside the room so we wouldn't crowd her. Mr. Mudenda was in the corridor deep in discussion with the doctor.

Though it had been less than a day since we'd seen her, Mrs. Ngozi looked different, less death stricken, more alive.

Her eyes open. She squinted at me.

"Mrs. Ngozi?" I whispered softly.

She closed her eyes with a sigh as if she'd not believed what she'd seen. I reached across and touched her hand, the one resting on the blanket nearest to my side. I gave her a small squeeze. She squeezed me back.

Her eyes opened again and a smile crossed her lips.

"How are you feeling?" I whispered.

"It's good to see you again." Her voice was hoarse.

She turned to look at Katy and reached out as if to call her closer. Katy stepped up and took her other hand.

"Nice to meet you, Mrs. Ngozi," she whispered.

"What are you two beautiful girls doing here?"

Katy and I glanced at each other.

"We're here to see you," I said. "To make sure they're treating you right."

She smiled weakly. "This will cost heaven and earth, you know that?"

"Don't you worry about that," I said. "That's being taken care of."

"By whom?" She tried to raise her head. "You're just a child. Like my Chanda."

"I'm not a child anymore." I paused. "Besides, we have help now." I peeked outside. Mr. Mudenda was still chatting with the doctor. "You'll get well soon, I promise you."

"I wish Chanda was here to see you."

"I wish that too," I said.

Mrs. Ngozi suddenly pulled my hand toward her chest. I leaned over.

"My child," she whispered in an urgent voice, tugging at my hand, "you must know I have met your cousin."

I froze.

"You... you...you've seen Preeti? Can you tell me where she is?"

"She was in bad condition."

My heart dropped.

"Is she here in Tanzania?"

"I hope so. Oh, my lord, I hope so."

"Please Mrs. Ngozi, please tell me. When did she come to see you? Was she alone? Was she okay?"

"She stayed with me for a few days." Her voice was getting hoarser. I could see she was struggling to lift her head.

"She left...she left me just like my own daughter," she said. "She followed Chanda against all my advice."

"Where did they go? Where is Chanda right now?"

Mrs. Ngozi 's sick-looking eyes welled up in tears. "The Saudi man took her."

"What?" I looked at her, shocked. "The man at the forbidden stall?"

She nodded. "I told you girls so many times not to go there. Didn't I?"

"Why? Why did he take them? Where did he take them?"

"He wanted to punish her." She swallowed as if the words drained her.

"Preeti?"

"No, Chanda. He told me she was a thief."

My blood ran cold.

"He accused her of stealing shoes. Shoes, I tell you. My girl would never do that."

No. No. I felt sick to my stomach.

I looked at her, my eyes fuzzy, my heart tearing apart inside me.

"When did this happen?" I barely managed to whisper.

"The day after you left for safari, my dear." She swallowed and didn't speak again for a few seconds. "One day you were gone, and then the next day my little girl was gone too." She squeezed my hand, but I didn't feel like squeezing hers back.

Who am I to reassure her?

I hung on to the bed rail, feeling faint. "I am so sorry..."

She shook her head. "No need to say—"

"You don't understand." I took a deep breath to steady myself. "Mrs. Ngozi, it was me who stole those sandals. It was me, not her."

She looked at me with wide eyes. "Why would do something like that? Your parents gave you everything you wanted."

"I..." The words dried in my throat. I stole the red sandals so Chanda wouldn't feel left out when my parents bought me brand-new shoes for my birthday. I stole those shoes because I knew Mrs. Ngozi would never be able to afford new shoes for her own daughter.

"I made a stupid mistake," I whispered. "This is all my fault."

Her hand slipped away from me.

I felt tears roll down my cheeks. "Will you ever forgive me?"

"Everything all right here?"

Katy and I looked up. It was the nurse who'd popped his head in momentarily.

"All is fine," I heard Katy say as I choked back my sobs. "We'll call if we need you."

The nurse disappeared back into the corridor.

Mrs. Ngozi had her eyes closed now, as if she couldn't stand to look at me any longer.

I wanted to run out and vomit. *I'm cursed.* Every person I touched was worse off after they met me.

When Mrs. Ngozi opened her eyes again, she didn't reply or look at me. She stared up at the ceiling.

"The village exiled her. My own daughter exiled because they thought she was a thief and a prostitute. Cut her off just like they cut off all those girls forced to work for the Saudi."

Chapter Thirty-four

"**I**'ve made up my mind," I said.

Everyone stopped eating and turned to look at me.

"Are you serious?" asked Peace.

"Didn't the doctor say you need to rest?" asked Mama Gladness.

"This is too dangerous," Mr. Mudenda said, shaking his head. "I cannot allow you to do that."

"I'm not the little girl you used to know." I felt my face flush. Even as I spoke, I realized the harshness of the words I was using. "I've gone through hell and back. I'm not going to give up on them now. You can't stop me."

He looked like he'd been stung.

Mama Gladness gave me a shocked look.

She had placed a row of yellow candles in the middle of the table. They quivered now as if they didn't approve of my words either.

I softened my voice. "Everything that's happened so far has been my doing. Chanda and Preeti are my friends, my family. They're the two people I cared for the most. I came halfway across the world to find them and I'm not going to give up on them now. Besides, I owe it to Mrs. Ngozi."

I looked around me. This was the closest thing to a family I'd had in a very long time. This dinner would have been a pleasant affair if I hadn't announced mid-meal that I was going to hunt the Saudi man down.

Luc broke the silence. "The only guys who'll know where the Saudi is are those two men working at his stall now. If you can get them to talk, you might just find him."

"They're probably in the same racket too," Katy said.

"There's a reason that part of the market is called the forbidden zone," Mr. Mudenda said in a tired voice. He looked like he'd gained a few more gray hairs overnight. "That's where people and weapons are smuggled. You're not dealing with petty criminals here. Even the police are wary of them. These thugs are backed by powerful gangs and corrupt industries in this region. "

I put my fork down and looked him in the eye. "The same people who killed my parents, right?"

He looked away.

No one said a word.

He put his napkin on the table, next to his half-finished plate, and let out a big sigh.

"I meant it when I said you are all welcome to stay here until you recover." He looked at each of us. "I don't care if that takes years, even decades. It's the least I can do for being complicit in your departure, Asha. If I'd only known then what I know now, I'd have fought back."

"Tsk, tsk. No one has a crystal ball," said Mama Gladness before pushing a plate of mashed potatoes toward Win. "Eat, girl," she said and turned to Mr. Mudenda. "We make decisions with the information we have at that time. What use is it to beat yourself up now? Could anyone predict what would have happened?"

I shrugged. "The past is done. I want to fix the future."

Mr. Mudenda let out another sigh. "I understand your sentiments. Believe you me, I do. But the best thing to do now is to go to the police."

"How useful will that be?" I asked. I remembered my encounter with Goa's police only too well. I also hadn't forgotten how the French police allowed Zero and Vlad to vault through the border with us imprisoned in the back of a van, in exchange for a nice bribe.

"Mr. Mudenda," piped up Luc, "didn't you say yourself the police are paid by the mining companies? You said they called it supplemental income."

The table turned quiet.

Mr. Mudenda gave me a sad look. "I finally get to see you after all these years and now you want to head straight into danger again."

"I can't live knowing I didn't do everything I could to save them."

"Would you at least permit me to speak with the police chief and look for someone who can help us? We must find the most appropriate solution. This means we will need to be patient."

"How long will that take?" Katy asked.

"Well..." Mr. Mudenda wiped his brow with his napkin. "It may take weeks."

"Weeks?" I said. "Really?"

"If I have to be frank with you," he paused, wrinkling his brows, "it may take months. We are talking about a bureaucracy, one that's very good at being a bureaucracy, I'm afraid. I will have to first find out who is connected to whom and ask the right person the right questions."

"I can't wait months," I said, shaking my head. "Every day we don't do something to get closer to Chanda and Preeti, we're letting them..." I broke off. I couldn't even imagine what they were going through. *That's not true.* Win was sitting next to me. I knew exactly what kind of torture they were being subjected to.

"I understand how you feel, my child," said Mr. Mudenda. "I know what it's like to lose someone close to you." He looked at Peace for a second. "But this is beyond a normal loss. This is an international crime we're talking about. These men commit terrible acts that only an army could fight."

I stared at him, wordless.

Everyone was looking down at their plates, not touching the food. Even Mama Gladness was no longer pushing dishes. It was like a dark, gloomy cloud had descended and was hanging over the house.

I made a decision. I threw my napkin on the table and pushed my chair back.

Everyone looked up.

"I'm going to the market tomorrow."

Mama Gladness gasped.

"And I'm going by myself." It was time to end my curse. I turned to Mr. Mudenda. "This has nothing to do with you or anyone else. This is *my* fight."

"Hey," Katy said. "You're not going anywhere alone. I'm coming with you."

Win reached over and tapped my arm. "Me too. They were stolen like I was. I wanna help."

Luc cleared his throat. "I know I haven't been the most helpful guy, but I'm coming with you all the way. I won't let you down this time. Promise."

I looked at my friends. The determination in their eyes was unmistakable.

I leaned across to Mr. Mudenda. "See, there's a gang of us now."

His eyebrows shot up.

"A *gang*?" I heard Mama Gladness say.

"A team," I said quickly. "I mean a team."

"We're the Red Heeled Rebels team," said Win.

"Rebels?" Mama Gladness gasped again.

I shot Win a warning look.

"The next step," said Peace from across the table, "is to make friends with the men at the Saudi stall and get them talking. That's going to be our first job."

"Our job?" Mr. Mudenda looked at his son in surprise.

"I can't let them go by themselves to talk to these people," said Peace. "None of them even speak Swahili."

"You start university on Monday. You have a plane to catch to Nairobi. You can't go gallivanting around—"

"It's orientation week, Father," Peace said, picking up his glass of wine. "I'm already a year ahead of everyone in class. A week won't hurt. I'll catch up like I always do."

Mr. Mudenda stared at him in shock. "Do you realize what you're getting into?"

"It's investigative work. I've read all the books—"

Luc choked on his water. He wiped his mouth with the back of his hand. "Books? Do you even know what it's like to be chased by a man with a gun?"

"A *gun*?" I heard Mama Gladness gasp.

I now wished I hadn't been so direct about my intentions. I could have quietly slipped out the next morning.

"I'm not completely defenseless," Peace snapped back. "I've got a black belt in Krav Maga and won every regional championship. I'm first in Tanzania."

"Jeez," Luc snorted. "You think getting trophies teaches you to deal with criminals?"

Peace was unfazed. "I don't need to jump into every hot mess to know what's the right thing to do."

Luc scowled.

"Enough!"

Everyone turned to Mama Gladness. She was holding her arms up, palms out, an indignant expression on her face.

"Stop this right now!"

She looked at us with bulging eyes. "Is this conversation even really happening?"

No one said a word.

"I've been listening patiently and I am not a patient woman, I will tell you that. I thought this talk was all just juvenile bravado. I was hoping that by God's good grace you will all come to your senses." She shook a finger at us. "Do you even realize what you're all getting into?"

"Yes!" I said at the same time as Katy.

"And we're not kids," mumbled Luc.

Mama Gladness turned her attention to Mr. Mudenda. "Are you going to allow these immature *children*..." She glared at Luc. "To get away with this? Your own son too. This is utter madness, I tell you!"

Peace turned to his father. "You know why I'm going to law school, don't you?"

Silence.

"You taught me about justice, Father. You told me how important it is to do the right thing. Well, I want to change how we treat our own people, how we let others treat our people. I want to see reform in our justice system. I want to see change in our policing system."

Mr. Mudenda was unfolding and folding his napkin as if it was too painful to look his son in the eye.

"So you're ready to put your life at risk?" he replied in a quiet voice.

"I made a promise a long time ago that I'm going to stand up for those who cannot stand up for themselves. *You* taught me that. If I don't help them now, how can I convince the world of what I stand for?"

"But son—"

"I want to fight for what's right," Peace said, his voice strong. He looked his father in the eye. "Or would you rather I be a coward?"

A collective gasp went around the table.

Chapter Thirty-five

Tt was not yet noon but the sun was beating down on us.

We were traveling in Peace's open Jeep in the direction of the market. Luc, Win and I were in the backseat while Katy was riding shotgun up front. Though we wore our safari hats and were carrying water bottles given to us by a grouchy Mama Gladness, we were sweating profusely and trying not to touch each other.

Peace had been keen to show us how his convertible top worked and didn't mind the sun. At least, he pretended he didn't. I had a funny feeling he was showing off to Katy more than anything else.

It had been an easy breeze through Peace's upscale neighborhood in an open car, but we were now stuck in noisy, dusty, heavy traffic, ten city blocks from the market.

Luc groaned. "Can we put up the damn top already?"

"It's not like Europe here," Peace replied with a grin. "This is Dar Es Salaam. You'll have to toughen up a bit, brother."

Luc bristled. "I can handle the heat," he grumbled from the back. "It's just everyone and their dog can see us. If anyone's following us—"

"Almost there! Be patient. *Usijali*, my brother. Relax. You're in Africa now. No one's here to follow you."

"What do you know, frat boy?" I heard Luc mutter under his breath.

I gave him a gentle nudge. We couldn't afford to bicker now.

And that included me. I was struggling with my own little demons. The way Katy chatted and giggled with Peace meant they were connecting. My jealousy embarrassed me.

Even with her auburn curls tucked into that cheap hat, Katy was her usual drop-dead, leggy, gorgeous self. She made heads turn everywhere she went. I was silly to even think of competing with her. *Besides, she's my best friend,* I thought. *And Peace is like a brother.*

If Mr. Mudenda was a surrogate father to me, that made him kind of a sibling. Didn't it? I squirmed in the backseat. Still, there was no denying he was very, very attractive, especially from the back—

"Hey, Asha, thanks for talking with my father last night," Peace called out, jerking me from my reverie.

I felt my face go warm. "I, er, yeah, no problem."

After hearing Peace's stinging comment at the dinner table the night before, Mr. Mudenda got up and stumbled out of the dining room, his head down, shoulders drooped. His son had hit him where it hurt the most.

Mama Gladness gave Peace a furious look. "What in good god's name were you thinking, boy? You dare to talk to your father like that?"

"I didn't mean it that way," Peace stammered. "It just came out…"

"I'll go talk to him," I said, getting up.

I found Mr. Mudenda in his study, sitting in his armchair, his head in his hands. I walked up and knelt next to him.

I could have ignored him, forgotten about our past, and just walked out of that house. I owed no one anything.

But the last thing I wanted was to sever ties with this gentle man who'd taken care of me when I was at my most vulnerable. The man who'd tended to my parents' graves until my return. I didn't blame him for not telling me the truth so long ago. All I wanted was his blessing to do the right thing now. Or at least to be upfront with my next steps.

I spent an exhausting hour trying to persuade Mr. Mudenda about my quest and to allow Peace to join us.

Peace was right. I needed him.

I needed them all. Peace knew the people, the culture, the language, and the roads here. He was as invaluable as Luc, who knew the ways of organized criminal gangs better than any of us. And Katy was my loyal sidekick. She'd been with me from the beginning and I could always count on her. Always.

The only person I felt guilty about bringing along was Win. *She should be in school,* I kept thinking. Mr. Mudenda disapproved of her coming the most, even more than Peace, but Win wouldn't hear of separating from us. Not now. And there was nothing much he or Mama Gladness could do to stop her.

"How'd you convince him in the end?" Katy asked, pulling me out of my thoughts.

"I didn't," I said with a sigh. "But I did promise him two things."

"What's that?" Peace asked, cautiously.

"Number one, we call the police if we suspect anything. And two, we're not supposed to approach the Saudi men at any time, no matter what."

"Doable," Peace said from up front. "Except maybe for that last one."

"We can't just walk up and ask if they run a trafficking ring," said Katy. "That's just crazy."

"How are we supposed to find out about the girls if we don't talk to them?" Peace asked.

"I have an idea," Luc said, brightening up.

I gave him a worried look. "This has nothing to do with Fred, does it?"

He shook his head. "No, but I can pretend it does."

Katy and I exchanged a concerned look.

"Here's the thing. I look like a foreigner and talk like a foreigner, right?" said Luc, sitting up.

"That much is true, brother." Peace nodded.

"I can get those guys to open up if I present them an amazing offer. A global partnership. I can tell them about a secret international channel. They won't be able to refuse, then."

"An interesting idea," said Peace.

"You're not thinking of orchestrating another drug deal, are you?" Katy asked, her brow furrowed.

"Why not?" said Luc. "It'll be a fake deal but that'll get them talking. The trick is to build trust in us."

"I don't know about this," I said, turning to Luc. "They'll go berserk if they find out you're lying. Like *killing* berserk."

"Don't you trust me to do my job?" Luc said. "I've dealt with these kinds of people all my life. I know how to play a damn good game. Let me go talk to them."

I sat back silently, trying to soak this in. *This is a dangerous game we're playing.*

No one spoke for a while. Everyone was pondering Luc's idea and no one seemed fully convinced.

"Okay fine," said Luc after a while. "Do you guys have a better plan?"

One by one, we shook our heads.

"Here we are," Peace said, maneuvering the Jeep in between pedestrians and driving into the market's parking lot. He stopped under the shade of the mahogany tree and we got off.

While Katy helped Peace put the top back on, I took a good look around the area.

A handful of boys who'd been playing football on a corner stopped to stare at us. No matter what we did, what language we spoke or how we dressed, we were going to stand out in this place. I was glad Peace was with us.

We strolled into the market casually, pretending to take in the local smells and sounds. We walked through the handicraft stalls teeming with tourists and got to the area where the city residents came to shop.

We walked past table after table laden with sacks filled with coffee beans, rice, cassava, maize, fried fish and local vegetables of all kinds. Then, we passed by the spice stalls.

I slowed down here, wishing I could stop and browse. It had been ages since I'd baked. The last time I'd made something was for the Diplomatic Dragon Lady and Chef Pierre at the Luxembourg castle. I wondered if Chef Pierre's open invitation over Twitter was serious. *What does he want with someone like me? Did he really like my cakes that much?* My paranoia returned. *Or is this a ruse to get us over there only to get arrested by the French or Luxembourg or whatever police?*

"Guys, here it is."

Peace was pointing discreetly at a large stall about thirty feet away.

I followed his finger. We'd walked to the edge of the forbidden zone. We were standing near the same tree trunk Chanda had hidden behind while I stole those ruby red sandals for her.

Two young Arab men in their white robes were squatting at the stall, engrossed in their phones. There was no sign of the old Saudi man.

Chapter Thirty-six

Luc and Peace put their differences aside to do a "team reconnaissance" at the Arab stall.

"We're going to pretend shop for new phones," said Peace, seeing my face.

"And ask a few preliminary questions," added Luc.

They seemed to be enjoying themselves, like they were taking part in a fun covert game. This made me worry even more.

While we waited for them to return, Katy, Win, and I bought mangoes from a fruit vendor and lounged next to the tree trunk as we furtively watched the Saudi store.

The stall nearest the tree trunk was selling live chickens. The smell of the frightened birds crammed into the tiny baskets was nauseating, but it was the perfect spot. We could see the Saudis and the boys, but they couldn't see us. Or, at least I'd thought.

Then, halfway through their conversation with the boys, one of the Saudi men turned around to look at us and leered.

I turned away, feeling repulsed. *What are they talking about?* I wished the boys would hurry up.

"Let's move," said Katy.

We stepped behind the chicken stall, where we couldn't see them anymore.

"Wish we had a super spy kit," Win said, licking the mango juice off her fingers.

"A super spy what?" Katy asked.

"Those things you put in your ear so you can hear what everyone's saying," said Win.

"Where'd you even find something like that?" Katy asked, incredulous. "Amazon?"

"Nope, it's a special place Zero knew," Win replied, taking her phone out. "He told me to buy one for him one day when he was meeting a policeman. I recorded everything from the car. Lemme see if I can find it again."

Katy and I exchanged a quick look. We never knew what Win would come up with next.

She really should be in school, I thought, a pang of guilt going through me. *She should be doing math, physics, and computer science, not trying to figure out how to listen in on real-world gangsters.*

"Guys?"

I turned to look. Win was staring at her phone, her face pale.

"What is it?" asked Katy.

"It's Tetyana," said Win, holding out her phone.

"Is she okay? What's she say?" I asked.

Win read the message out loud. "Yevhen is dead."

We were silent for a while.

"Her brother," I whispered. *Oh, my god, Tetyana. Where are you? What's going on?*

Another ping came from Win's phone.

She read the text. "But I made them pay. They died screaming."

We stared at the phone silently.

The third ping made us all jump.

This time, Katy read out the message out loud. "Ditch the phones. Use email. Just don't send them. Win, you know what to do."

Another ping.

"I'm coming over."

We gaped at the screen, stunned.

"Coming over?" Katy whispered.

"Here to Dar Es Sal—?" I started.

"Hey!"

We looked up.

"It's the boys," Katy said, peeping over the chicken stall.

"We're in here," she called, stepping out briefly to wave at Luc and Peace.

They came over, faces flushed and almost out of breath.

"What happened?" asked Win.

"Guess where our next stop is?" Luc asked, catching his breath.

We gave him a blank look.

"Nairobi."

"Kenya?"

"The only Nairobi I know of," said Peace. "That's where they took your cousin and your friend."

I looked at him, astounded.

"How did you find out?" asked Katy.

Peace and Luc exchanged a guilty look.

Peace spoke first. "Well, it was his brilliant idea."

Luc shuffled his feet. "It was the fastest way to get intel."

What did he do now?

"We told them we have merchandise."

"Crack?" Katy asked.

Luc shook his head.

"Cocaine?" I asked.

"No…" He paused, his eyes flitting nervously.

My chest was constricting with every second of this conversation. I'd been keeping a sharp lookout ever since we got to the market. Unless there were snipers waiting to ambush us somewhere, no one had been following us, but Luc was making me jittery now.

"Look," Peace said, taking the lead. "The only way they'd tell us where they took the girls was if we pretended we had girls too."

"You're going to sell us?" Win shrieked.

"No!" Luc cried, holding his hands up. "I'd never do that!"

"Of course not," said Peace quickly. "We just made a proposal they couldn't resist so they'd tell us how their operations worked. It was just a ruse."

I frowned. *This is what happens when you send men to do a difficult job.*

"And how do their operations work?" Katy asked, gritting her teeth.

"The old Saudi moved to Nairobi three years ago, taking everyone with him," said Peace. "He has a team that hunts girls and kidnaps kids from the villages and sends them every month to his headquarters. Nairobi is the hub. From there, he sells the kids to sex shops and mining companies."

"Except, they didn't use those exact words," said Luc. "They said they pick fresh fruit from the villages and deliver it to Nairobi."

"Fresh fruit?" I felt a chill in my bones. That was the same phrase Franky used for his business dealings. He even dubbed his trafficking company the "Super India Fresh Fruit and Vegetable Exporters of Goa."

Luc pulled a piece of paper from his pocket. "We got a name and an address in Nairobi. They said to talk to Ali Mahmood and he can connect us to the Saudi man. It's a start."

"How do you know they're telling the truth?" Katy asked.

The boys shrugged.

"We don't," said Luc.

"Except they were really impressed with Luc," said Peace. "Especially after he told them he works for Fred."

Oh no.

"What if they call Fred and ask him?" I said, my stomach twisting. "They'll find out we're running away from him."

"They've only heard about Fred through the underground grapevine," replied Luc.

"These men are small potatoes in the business and we're quite far from Europe," said Peace. "We should be okay."

Everyone stood silently as we contemplated this news.

"So, what's next, boss?" Luc asked, looking at me.

It took me half a second to make up my mind.

I nodded. "We're going to Nairobi."

Part FOUR

Our battered suitcases were piled on the sidewalk again; we had longer ways to go. But no matter, the road is life.
Jack Kerouac

Chapter Thirty-seven

The Kenyan border was a ten-hour drive from where we were.

We'd just begun our journey, and we'd already broken both of my promises to Mr. Mudenda.

Our first priority had been to get rid of our phones safely.

"They'll sniff us down like dogs," said Luc. "Trust me. Gotta dump these suckers somewhere."

"Whoever's following you guys doesn't know me," Peace said. "Can l I keep mine? Might need it as an emergency tool."

"It's also an awesome locator tool," Luc replied dryly.

"How's my father going to reach us? He's already a nervous wreck as it is."

We fell silent at the mention of Mr. Mudenda.

Everyone, I knew, was feeling guilty about running off like this. Peace had called his father at his office at the hospital on our way out of Dar Es Salaam.

At first, Mr. Mudenda had threatened to send the police after us. It was only after talking to each of us individually that he'd relented, reluctantly. Peace had promised to call him every night. He told us if we failed to call even one night, he'd unleash an official search party.

"We could get new burner phones," I said.

"We're like the Famous Five here," replied Luc, glancing around. The road was busy, but everybody was minding their own business. "People are probably talking about us at the market. Everyone will know where, when and who we got phones from."

"Aren't we acting a bit paranoid?" Peace asked Luc via the rearview mirror.

"Paranoid?" Luc looked like he could punch Peace. "You've no idea what kind of life brings the paranoia I feel right now, college boy. You've got no damn idea."

"Guys, what about Tetyana?" Katy asked loudly, deflecting an argument. "We need to tell her where we're headed."

"I've got her password for her email," said Win.

"How does that work?" I asked.

"We leave messages for each other in it," she said. "We don't send emails out, just save them in the inbox. That way, we can read them and there's no trail."

"Ingenious," I said.

"That's how Zero used to talk to his friends in other cities," she said. "He asked me to set it up for him."

We hadn't heard another word from Tetyana after her last series of messages. The only person trying to get ahold of me now was Chef Pierre.

He was tweeting daily about a brand new café franchise he was opening up in New York and LA. He was promising innovative fusion desserts and kept inviting "Asha, the Canadian-Indian-Sri Lankan baker" to join him. Any other time, I'd have jumped in with both feet. But now, I had more important work to do. Plus, I wasn't sure if there'd be a welcoming party courtesy of EUROPOL if I ever stepped foot in Europe again.

We'd been on the road for a while now. I looked at my friends in various stages of slumber in the Jeep. Peace was driving with one arm out the window, one hand on the steering wheel, focused on the road but oddly relaxed. Despite all the risks and hurdles we might face, they'd all offered their talents, their time, and most of all, their loyalty. Even Peace, the new guy on the team, was committed to my mission to find Preeti and Chanda.

Peace was not just our self-proclaimed driver but chief negotiator as well.

Before leaving Dar Es Salaam, he'd bought seven bottles of duty-free whiskey—"gifts" for police officers who manned the roadblocks.

But we only needed them twice. He'd also arranged for a place to stay in Nairobi our first night. I was glad he was with us.

"Quite the hunk, isn't he?" Katy said, coming from behind me and nudging me in the elbow.

We were at a gas station. Peace had just called his friend in Nairobi to confirm our arrival that evening and was filling up the Jeep. Luc was lurking in the shadows of the large dumpster, breaking our phones apart and dumping them in. The rest of us were looking for washrooms and water fountains to refill our bottles.

"Brains and brawns," I said, "can't beat that." I rustled up a smile. "I think he likes you. Really likes you."

Katy's face turned slightly pink. "I like him too." She gave me a funny look. "Hey, are you okay with that?"

I looked at her, surprised. "Of course. Why'd you even ask that?"

"'Cuz I see you looking at him. In a funny kind of way."

I opened my mouth but nothing came out.

"Hey, you've known him longer, so if you want me to stay away—"

"No!" I shook my head. "He's like a brother. I mean, Mr. Mudenda's like a father to me so I could never think of him like that." I swallowed, feeling my neck go warm with embarrassment.

"I've known you for a long time now. Don't lie to me."

"Katy, I want you to put these crazy thoughts out of your head, starting now, okay?" I said, giving her a playful slap in the arm. "I think you guys look really sweet together."

She blushed.

"Ladies!"

Speaking of the....

"We're ready to grab lunch." Peace was walking over to us, smiling. He stopped close to Katy, almost hugging distance.

"Hey," I said with a fake smile.

"You guys coming or are you going to sit here and gossip?" he said, pulling Katy gently by the elbow. "Aren't you starved? I know I am."

She smiled shyly.

Something in me stirred. It was good to see her smile like that, a genuinely happy, rare smile. She'd gone through enough hell, I thought. She'd been there with me at every turn of my journey and was always ready to join in on whatever stunt I was planning next. *If loyalty had another name, it would have to be Katy.*

The three of us walked to the cafeteria chatting, side by side. I couldn't ignore that empty feeling in me, but I knew I had to forget Peace. *I'm here on a serious mission,* I told myself. *Not on a dating game. Focus, girl. Focus.*

The rest of our drive was on bumpy, mostly unpaved roads filled with potholes. With no air-conditioning in the car, we all, even Luc, opted for an open ride to let the breeze through.

But this meant the sun drummed down on us, fatiguing us even more. Still, we hadn't stopped, except for the washroom break and a quick bite to eat at a roadside pit stop.

Peace drove all the way, refusing to let anyone else touch the steering wheel, asking us to rest.

But sleeping in an open Jeep on rough terrain was hard to do. Win and Luc caught a few naps snuggling against each other, and Katy snoozed for a few hours at one point. But sleep, as usual, evaded me.

The lonely landscape reminded me too much of my last days with my parents. The same glowing African sun hung in the air like an immense ball of fire, warming every twig of grass, every scrawny tree and all of us in the Jeep. And like that fatal day, Mount Kilimanjaro rose in front of us, trails of wispy clouds floating across its peak like silky scarves waving in the wind. Far off in the horizon, I spotted troops of impala and even a lone giraffe reaching out to nibble on the leaves of an acacia tree.

Every time we'd take a corner, I'd expect to come across a little green Fiat engulfed in flames. That frightening image had been burned into my brain forever.

I struggled with mixed emotions. I was happy to be back on the continent of my birth where my parents lay buried. But I couldn't ignore the flaming anger stoking my heart, knowing my parents' lives had been mercilessly cut short for the sake of corporate greed.

I didn't know anything about this mining company other than it was owned by Sophie's family who lived in Africa. In my mind, I saw a team of sharp-suited, cutthroat European and African businessmen sitting around a large oval table plotting my parents' death.

How I despised them.

"We're here!" Peace called out, rousing me from my thoughts.

Everyone slowly stirred awake.

We had pulled in front of a nondescript building with white-washed walls and a low roof. *This doesn't look like a motel or a hostel.*

The neighborhood was desolate. I hadn't noticed any houses for miles as we drove up here. We were still in the outskirts of Nairobi, so we hadn't even seen the city yet.

"Place to sleep for the night," Peace said, unbuckling and stretching his arms up.

From the outside, it looked like a small warehouse. There were no signs on the building other than a large security alarm sticker and a stern placard that said "KEEP OUT." The only door was an over-sized garage door that could have fit a truck.

The place was empty except for our Jeep. The building looked dark, deserted, and foreboding. None of us got out. We sat staring at the massive garage door, too weary to think or move.

"Hey guys?" Peace asked, looking around at us. "Are you all planning to sleep in the car?"

"Are you sure about this place?" I asked.

"Yup. Called in to check. They have free bunk beds upstairs for all of us. Coming?"

With tired groans, we got out of the Jeep, one by one. We dusted ourselves off, picked up our bags, and stumbled after Peace. Before he even got to the entrance, the garage door rolled up slowly and silently.

We stood back.

A hulk of a man in army fatigue pants, a tank top and crew cut appeared at the entrance.

His left arm was tattooed in an ancient tribal motif, and around his neck was a dog tag and a small cross. He must have been around twenty but something in his hard eyes made him look older. In the dim light, he looked like the kind of person I'd cross the road to avoid encountering.

"*Habari gani,* my brother!" Peace said, brightly—too brightly for someone who'd been driving nonstop for fifteen hours.

The stranger gave him a nod and regarded us, arms crossed, blocking our way.

"So these are your pals?" he asked, without smiling.

Chapter Thirty-eight

Is this Ali Mahmood?

The man didn't say hello or introduce himself, and seemed in a hurry.

Why didn't Peace tell us we were going to him right away?

At the man's request, Peace parked the Jeep inside the garage while the rest of us waited for him at the entrance of the building, gawking.

The inside looked like a semi-military installation. The garage housed a Hummer, two off-road vehicles, a rescue boat on a trailer and a run-down minivan, all painted in camouflage colors.

Once the Jeep was inside, our host pushed a lever on the wall to shut the garage door. As the large door slowly rolled down, red laser beams shot across the entrance.

I raised my eyebrows.

A tripwire.

Where did you bring us, Peace?

Until that moment, I'd trusted him one thousand percent. I'd entrusted him with the lives of my friends and the future of my mission. He was Mr. Mudenda's son, after all. He was an eager, idealistic college boy who only wanted to help us out, or so I'd thought. But right now, I wasn't so sure about him anymore.

We trooped in after the tattooed man to the back of the warehouse. Peace walked in front of the group with the man, neither of them talking. The two looked comfortable, like they'd known each other for a long time.

Katy followed right behind them, looking nervously around her. Win walked holding Luc's hands but Luc's face was so taut, I worried he'd snap at any moment.

I followed the crowd right at the back on full alert.

Through a door in the back, we entered a large open hall. I looked around. We'd walked into a well-equipped gymnasium.

Once we were all inside, the man barricaded the door behind us, fastening four locks, two deadbolts and adding a reinforcing bar across the door.

This was no ordinary building. And this was no ordinary room.

The floor was lined with thick rubber mats, and around the perimeter stood all kinds of training equipment.

And we were not alone.

Two men, wearing black martial arts uniforms, were inside the ring, sparring with each other. Two more men in the same uniforms stood outside, shouting instructions. They were speaking a language I'd not heard before. On the back of their shirts was indecipherable lettering, a foreign language I didn't recognize.

The men themselves looked like they could have been from any-where. The Middle East, North Africa, Southern Europe, even South or North America. All four were brawny, with muscles the size of horses'. Their faces were harsh and their eyes hard.

They stopped their practice briefly to look us over.

"What's this?" one of them called out with a smirk. "A mini United Nations tour?"

"They're my guests," said the tattooed man. His voice was low and gruff, the perfect voiceover for a military action movie. "They're here to check out the university."

I froze.

University? Is that what Peace told him?

"Where are they from?" another asked.

The man who'd opened the door thumbed at us. "Americans."

Katy and I exchanged quick looks.

The men gave curt nods as if to say they approved and turned back to their sparring.

My eyes swept the room. Three rowing machines sat gleaming in one corner. Heavy punching and kicking bags hung from the ceiling. In one corner stood a lone figure I recognized. It was Bob the rubber man I used to punch and kick during my self-defense classes at the international school in Dar Es Salaam, so long ago.

"Hey, Asha," Peace called out to me. "Are you coming?"

I turned around to see everyone walking through a narrow passageway toward the back of the warehouse. I caught up to them, my back tingling, feeling like a black-clad ninja would strike out at any moment.

On one wall of the passageway was a glass case lined with vicious daggers and swords. Each came with murderous-looking hooks and serrated blades. *These aren't kitchen knives,* I thought, staring at the collection as I stumbled by them. On the other side was another glass case that displayed handguns. Both cases were locked with electronic keypads.

What do they do here?

I followed the others through the back door and to my surprise stepped into a normal everyday setting—a galley kitchen and living room.

The kitchen was as clean as Mama Gladness's upscale one back in Dar Es Salaam, except this was much, much smaller. A round red rug covered the floor of the living area. A set of beige couches faced a gigantic flat-screen television on the wall, and the plain coffee table held neat stacks of glossy martial arts magazines. There was even a vase of flowers on the kitchen counter. It was a perfect photograph-ready IKEA set-up.

"Hey, Father must not know we're here," said Peace as soon as I walked in.

I grabbed him by the shirt collar and pulled him aside.

"Who are these people?" I hissed, shaking him. "Is this the Ali guy? Why didn't you tell me about this place?"

Luc joined us, his face in a scowl. "What the hell, man?" he whispered angrily. "We've walked into a den of—"

"Tea?"

I whirled around to see the man who'd met us at the door putting the kettle on.

Luc shot him a suspicious look. Katy opened her mouth and closed it. Win walked up to the counter, pulled out a barstool and plopped down on it.

"Yes, please," she said, in a tired voice. "I'm so dead. We had such a looong trip."

The man pushed a box of tea bags toward her. "I have all kinds. Take your pick."

"I'm starved too," she said, going through the tea collection. "Super hungry."

"There's some chocolate if you want," said Peace, extricating himself from my grasp and walking up to a kitchen cupboard. He opened it and rummaged through it to find a box of chocolates.

"You've been here before," I said.

He nodded absentmindedly, taking out the flavor guide from a box. "Hey, Win," he called out, "what's your fav flavor?"

"The ones with the cherry filling inside."

A shadow loomed next to me. I looked up.

"David."

I looked at the bear-sized paw in front of me and then up at the man's face.

I glowered at him.

"Sure you're not Ali Mahmood?"

He gave a start. "My god, no!" Then, seeing my face, he softened. "My name is David. I'm a friend of Peace."

"Asha," I said, slowly reaching out to shake his hand, half expecting him to tackle me to the ground and put me in a choke hold or something.

"Pleased to meet you," he said amiably.

I watched him introduce himself to each of my friends, even to Luc, who was decidedly very unhappy to meet him.

I shot Peace an angry look. He shrugged and held out his hands.

"What? I'm trying to help you here. I brought you here because of what you told my father and me at the café. I mean, that is some serious stuff you went through. You need real help. Professional help."

Professional help?

"What is this place?" I asked.

"The best Krav Maga dojo in the region," David said, looking quite smug, I thought.

"*Kra* what?" asked Katy.

"Israeli military self-defense," replied Peace. "Father calls it Kung Fu because he's watched too many Bruce Lee movies. But this is Krav Maga. It's what I trained in all my life."

"It's protection for the everyday situation," David said, taking out dainty teacups from the cupboard and setting them on the counter in a row. "You know, for when someone pulls a knife at you at the park or threatens to explode a bomb on the bus on your way to school."

I stared at him.

"Krav is the best personal defense system in the world." David paused his tea-making to give me a look. "If you want to find your Saudi man, you came to the right place."

I felt a chill go through me.

"How do you know what I'm looking for?"

David pointed his chin at Peace. "He said you wanted to find your sister—"

"Cousin."

"Your cousin and your friend."

I looked at Peace. "When did you share all this info?"

Peace shrugged. "I called him from the gas station."

"From a public phone?" Luc glared at him.

"Yeah—"

"Here I was getting rid of our *private* mobiles so we won't be tracked, and you go and announce it through a loudspeaker!"

"I didn't shout," said Peace, looking defensive. "I used the phone at the far end of the booth. No one was around and I spoke in code—"

"Jeez! Don't you know anything? Anyone can intercept a public call." Luc was frothing at the mouth.

"Sorry, man," said Peace, embarrassed. "I didn't think...."

Luc's eyes flared. "What do you know about anything other than the stupid Boy Scout stuff you—"

"I wouldn't worry about the call."

I whirled around.

"If it makes you feel better," said David, "every call that comes here is encrypted."

"Encrypted calls?" Win sat up with interest.

"Look, guys," said Peace. "I brought you here because David can help you. He's better than the police. He's better than anyone else you can find."

"How?" I asked. "How can you help us?"

David leaned over his teacups. "I can give you martial arts training."

"I don't have years," I snapped.

"Well, I recommend everyone learn the basics of self-defense," he said as he poured the tea into the cups. "It's like swimming or riding a bike. Basic essential life stuff."

I gave him a dubious look. I trained in self-defense as a schoolgirl. It was how I'd escaped the stickiest situations I'd got myself into the past few years. We didn't have time to go back to school. We needed help now.

"Plus," David added as if it was an afterthought, "I can give you surveillance equipment."

Win whipped her head around. "Seriously?"

"What did you say?" said Katy, squinting at him.

"Anything your heart desires," said David, opening his arms expansively.

"Like what?" said Luc.

"Secure laptops, cameras, wiretaps, drones, GPS, night vision goggles." David paused. "How about a fully equipped surveillance van with tinted windows?"

Win drew her breath in sharply.

I stared at him, stunned.

"A surveillance van?" Katy asked. "What on earth do you need that for?"

I glanced over at Peace, who was now sitting on the couch casually as if this was the most normal conversation in the world.

"See? I told you he's good," he said with a self-satisfied smile.

I scowled. *What game is he playing?*

"What I want to know is," I said to David, "what's your connection to Peace?"

"I've known him since we were nine years old," he replied, placing a teacup in front of Win.

"Where and how?"

"In grade school. A long time ago. He and his friends took me under their wing. They were there for me when I was alone in a country where I knew no one. I promised to help whenever they needed. This is the first time Peace has asked me for anything."

I looked at Peace, then back at David. There was more to this story, I was sure.

"Who do you work for?" Luc asked.

"Myself. I teach Krav Maga for a living."

"Really?" I asked. "And you own the Hummer up front?"

"That's not mine."

"So, you work for some local mafia?" asked Luc.

David pulled out a tin of cookies and opened it, studiously ignoring Luc.

"Or do you work for Fred from Brussels?" Luc said suddenly.

I wasn't sure if it was my imagination, but David's face changed for a micro second at the mention of Fred's name. He blinked ever so quickly but recovered. Instead of answering, he started arranging the cookies on a plate.

I stepped up to him. "Why do you want to help us?"

He looked at me, his eyes piercing into mine.

"Because I want to get the Saudi as badly as you do."

Chapter Thirty-nine

"Wow, wow, wow," said Win, her eyes bulging. "This is so awesome."

We were in a geek's nirvana and Win was in heaven.

David had taken us to a secure room upstairs in the dojo, which had to be unlocked with a key and a password.

Inside were electronics equipment of all kinds neatly arranged on rows and rows of shelving. There were television screens, computers, tablets, phones, headsets, earpieces, walkie-talkies, security cameras, lenses, lights, binoculars, eye goggles, helmets, and watches that I was sure didn't just tell the time.

"You work for the CIA, don't you?" Katy said, staring at the high-tech stash around us. "That's why you're so cagey."

"Where did you get all this?" I asked, looking at the boxes piled against one wall, like they'd just been delivered from a spy store, if there were such things.

"Or did you *steal* all this?" said Luc, picking up a small camera and examining the peculiar label on it.

"I don't steal," said David, "I borrow."

"From whom?" Katy asked.

"Do you want the stuff or not?" he replied gruffly.

"Aren't you going to answer any of our questions?" I said.

David shrugged. "Hey, you're free to leave anytime. The door's back there. I can show you out right now."

We stared at him silently.

He lowered his voice. "All I ask in return for this is not to tell anyone about me or what I share with you."

Before I could respond, Win squealed from her corner. "Oh, my god! This is amazing!" she said, excitedly putting on a device that looked like an odd pair of Google glasses. "Can't believe you have this! Super, super cool."

"Be careful," said David. "Read the manual before you turn any-thing on."

"So, what's your proposal?" I asked him.

"I have the Saudi man's address," he replied, giving a nod to Peace. "No need to go through an intermediary. I also know they have a delivery coming next week."

"Well, aren't *you* well prepared?" Katy said, giving him a suspi-cious look.

David ignored her. "I also know a place where we can set surveil-lance equipment to watch him and get more intel before deciding on our next steps."

Peace gave me a look that said, *See?*

"Best time to set up is at night when there's fewer people around," David continued. "Then, we can go in any time to watch them."

It smelled fishy, but his suggestion would take us leaps and bounds closer to Preeti and Chanda.

"You've got twenty-four hours to prove you're not some bad guy," I said, realizing as soon as the words came out how lame they sound-ed.

David let out a rough laugh.

"If I were a bad guy, you'd already be in trouble." His face turned serious and he gave me a hard look. "I need a team and you need the resources. We're going after the same goal. We can work together. Or not. It's your call."

I stared at him for a minute. No one breathed. Not even Win, who'd stopped playing with the gadgets and was paying attention now.

Without David, we'd have to track down this Ali Mahmood whom I didn't even know existed or could help us. I scanned the room. This place was impressive. David was a risk I'd have to take.

"Okay, I'm in," I said, with a curt nod.

Soon after, Peace was calling his father from a phone in the dojo to tell him we'd got to town safely and were getting ready to sleep. I noticed he tactfully avoided sharing exactly where we were sleeping except that we'd found "comfortable dorm rooms."

That much was true.

The school had a room upstairs with six bunk beds and a common washroom, which David said was for visiting martial arts students.

On one wall were posters of a faraway desert scape with lettering that looked the same as those on the men's black gear. Hung over the bunk beds was an Israeli flag.

Hebrew, I suddenly realized.

I turned to glance at the chain around David's neck. *Funny. It's a cross. What's his connection to this place? And those sparring men in the dojo? Who are they?*

I was burning with curiosity, but Luc, on the other hand, had made up his mind. He wanted nothing to do with David any more. His plan was to get out, with or without Peace, and find a local motel to stay the night.

Win had refused to come out of the equipment room until she inspected every gadget. So, we let her be and walked over to the dorm room. While Luc, Katy and I argued in hushed voices about David's trustworthiness upstairs, Peace and David started cooking. Soon, the smell of spaghetti marinara wafted up the stairs, making my stomach rumble.

"How can anyone who makes dinner for us be bad?" whispered Katy.

"He'll feed us now and slit our throats later," hissed Luc.

"That's some pretty heavy equipment he's got," I said. "Plus he knows the area well."

"These are exactly the kind of people you wanna stay away from," said Luc.

"David gives us firepower, that's for sure," said Katy.

"I'm not leaving without Win or you guys," said Luc. "But I really don't trust the guy. "

"Win's never going to leave this place now," Katy pointed out.

"The problem is the Saudi man's organized," I said. "He's part of a ring. He's got people and resources. We need to meet him at his level."

Luc gave a defeatist shrug.

"So, we risk it?" Katy asked.

"But stay alert," I said. "Always stay alert."

We slept at the dojo after a quiet but filling meal. But we didn't let our guard down.

Luc, Katy and I took turns to be night watch in case David or his friends snuck into the room to murder us in cold blood, as Luc had predicted.

Peace thought we were nuts. He promptly went to bed and snored throughout the night.

The next day dawned with light rain.

We had ten hours to kill before darkness fell, before we could visit the Saudi man's neighborhood. The four men who'd practiced in the ring the night before supposedly only came in the afternoon, so we had the dojo to ourselves.

David showed us around the gym, explaining how the equipment worked. Friendly but still aloof, he offered to show us Krav Maga self-defense techniques. I enjoyed kicking Bob the rubber man again. We spent all day on the mat practicing, except for Win and Luc.

Win sat on the couch, engrossed in a network she'd created with a laptop, a tablet, a phone and a walkie-talkie set she'd dug out of the high-tech storage room. She was wearing that Google glass-like device too. She was so intent on her work that no one could get anything out of her any more.

Luc slumped unhappily on the couch next to her, flipping through the sports magazines. I knew he wasn't joining us in the gym out of sheer stubbornness. It irked him that David had given Win carte blanche of the equipment plus the key and password to the special room upstairs. Because now, Win refused to believe anything negative about the man.

It was after sunset when we left the dojo on our first surveillance trip. David drove us in the camouflaged van, which reminded me too much of the one we'd been trafficked in by Zero and Vlad from London to Brussels.

I wondered if I'd been wise to trust David.

Chapter Forty

The bus was a surprise.

It was sitting next to a dilapidated building that looked like it had been abandoned during the Second World War.

David parked the van behind the building, carefully tucking it under a low tree so it would be hard to spot. Then, we picked up our gear and walked up to the bus.

The faded decal on the side read, "Mombasa Safari Tours." David reached up to the driver's side mirror and let his fingers run across it like you'd punch a password on a phone.

With a click, the door opened and he bounded up the stairs, while the rest of us gawked.

From the outside, it was a derelict coach, left to die in a heap of steel, plastic and rubber. The inside was a whole different story.

The interior had been stripped bare except for five rows of seats at the back, next to the toilet which even came with a mini shower. In the middle of the bus, someone had installed a shiny steel bench, and on this sat a bank of ultra-modern computer screens. The walls and floor were padded to keep noise levels at a minimum. But it was the driver's area that impressed me the most. It was as complex as an airplane's cockpit.

We deposited the equipment boxes and started to unpack.

Outside, next to the bus, was a row of dead cars with wheels and windshields missing. Scattered around the unkempt yard were pieces of furniture that had outlived their usefulness and then some.

We were in a private scrapyard, one that was cordoned off by a seven-foot brick wall.

Between David, Peace, and Win, and with some reluctant help from Luc, who couldn't stay away from the action too long, they'd set up the equipment and were doing a trial run.

David had also handed each of us mics the size of a penny. This way, he said, if we ever got separated, we could still keep in touch. We tucked them into our pockets.

"Test, test, test."

"All mics working."

"Camera A?"

"Check."

"Camera B?"

"Check."

"Camera C?"

I sat in the back of the bus half listening to the preparations, trying to not get under their feet. There was little room to maneuver inside anyway and they seemed to have everything under control. Next to me, Katy was pouring over a Swahili translation book David had lent us the night before. Her brows were knitted in concentration. We had to be able to communicate with anyone we met, at least at the rudimentary level.

"Someone needs to check the pivoting arms for the camera on the tree," said Win in an eager voice.

"Peace, can you take care of it?" David said, busy fiddling with a small electronic device.

"Is that a tracking device?" Peace asked, scrutinizing the pen, or what looked like a pen.

David nodded. "Got a camera inside too."

"Guys, a leaf is covering part of the camera on the Mother Ship," called out Win.

"The *what*?"

"The bus."

"On it." David pulled a collapsible ladder from an overhead compartment.

This place has everything.

"Hey, it's blazing hot in here," Luc said. "Don't you have any air-conditioning?"

"Here," David said, turning a tabletop fan his way and blasting it. "You've got to settle for a fan, my man."

"All this high-tech gear and no air-conditioning?" Luc smirked.

"You want someone walking down the road to wonder why there's a hum coming from the scrapyard?"

They sounded excited, fired up, like they were staging an epic adventure game.

It was hard for me to relate.

None of them had met my cousin or my childhood best friend.

They didn't know Preeti liked to stay up late at night, sharing schoolgirl gossip, suppressing giggles with her hand so Grandma wouldn't wake up. They didn't know how Chanda loved to practice kickboxing with the acacia tree near her home, her pigtails flying every time she jumped up and cried, *Kia!*

And none of them grappled with the guilt of knowing it was my fault they were trapped in a nightmare they couldn't get out of. I blinked away a tear.

It was dark outside now.

The Saudi man's house was just a hop and a skip from the wall that separated us. We were facing the back of his housing complex. An unused private lane carved its way toward a small gate to this compound, but the area was deserted.

Five cameras were now trained over the scrapyard wall onto the quiet lane that led to his house. Or his compound of houses.

There was a camera mounted on the rusty antenna of the bus, two on the roof of the building behind us and two more on the branches of the tree that shaded the bus. They captured all the roads leading to the compound, the gates and a good part of the inside of the compound itself.

I walked over to the computer bench.

The screens were all lit up and showing live feed now. I had an excellent view of the Saudi man's home. I took a seat at the bank of screens hoping against hope to catch sight of Preeti or Chanda.

It was a long shot, but I could still hope.

The men at the market had told Peace and Luc that the slave girls brought here were held for a few weeks before being sold off. Some were kept as slaves in the compound, but the chance I'd see Chanda or Preeti here was negligible. But at least now we could track the movement of new girls and follow the clues to see if we could find my cousin and friend.

My eyes flitted from screen to screen.

The compound was well-lit and our cameras were top of the line. From its higher vantage point, the camera on the roof of the building showed the entire layout of this place.

There were four houses inside the compound, which was surrounded by a short white concrete wall. Two houses were smaller than the others and one came with a chimney on top.

"Women's quarters and the kitchen," explained David. "They probably sleep five to a house with their kids while the men get their own houses, the bigger ones over here."

Outside the biggest house stood a man in a long white robe, smoking. Two security guards were posted at the main gate where all the traffic was coming through. A lone man squatted near the back gate, the one closest to us, eating a cob of corn. When he was done with it, he threw the cob on the ground and ambled up and down, looking bored. At one point he even dozed against the wall.

"They look more like kitchen help than guards," Katy remarked.

"They don't really need security," said David. "That's just for show. Everyone knows who lives here. His reputation is security enough. Even the police are scared to come."

"Plus, the fact he's an official supplier for the mining monopoly helps," said Peace. "You can bet no one wants to bother him."

"Money talks," I said softly to myself. "Money kills too."

I hadn't forgotten the second promise I'd made to myself. I had no idea how or what I'd do when I found the people who'd assassinated my parents. But I wanted to look them in the eye and have them acknowledge what they did, know the pain they caused, really know.

Around seven at night the lights went on inside a small house in the back of the compound. Two women covered in black robes from the top of their heads to the tip of their toes came out and walked over to the main house.

Just then, a procession of three black Porsche SUVs with black tinted windows drove toward the front gates. A guard jumped up and opened the gates. He saluted each and every car awkwardly as they rolled in.

The drivers got out first and opened the back doors to let the passengers out.

I watched the first man disembark from the SUV in front. I felt the hair on my arms rise.

"Oh, my god."

Everyone crowded around me.

"That's the man I stole the red slippers from."

Part FIVE

If you're going through hell, keep going.
Winston Churchill

Chapter Forty-one

It was Saturday morning, our fifth day staking out the Saudi man's compound.

There were still no signs of Preeti or Chanda. I was getting impatient.

We spent our days inside the bus, taking turns watching the Saudi compound and keeping logs to see patterns in their activity, in between catching up on sleep at the back of the bus.

Win sat glued to her chair in the front of screens all day, every day, rotating the cameras remotely, zooming images in and out, saving video footage and maintaining the network at its optimum capacity.

Then, in the evenings, while Win played with the gadgets in the equipment room, the rest of us worked out at the dojo after supper. David was a good teacher and Peace made a capable assistant instructor.

I noticed, though, Peace called Katy aside several times to give her individual attention. Their happy giggling told us there was more flirting than learning going on, so David, Luc and I made sure to leave them alone in their corner. *They are so cute together*, I thought, *thankful my green envy was fading.*

We only went to the gym after the sparring men in the martial arts uniforms had finished their practice and left the building. We still didn't know who they were. David described them as local workers who wanted a place to practice their skills, but something told me he wasn't telling us the whole truth.

To my surprise, he was also adamant that we learn the basics of street fighting. We spent hours learning how to grapple on the ground, escape choke holds and bear hugs and take down an opponent and incapacitate them, with Peace and David guiding us every step of the way.

The Intense daily physical activity was good for us. Even Luc joined in. I noticed it helped us let out steam and reduce any bickering that would have flared up otherwise.

I welcomed the training but still, I made sure Katy, Luc and I kept rotating night watch shifts, much to Peace's chagrin. What upset him the most was that Katy still didn't trust his good friend, but he always fell asleep quickly, snoring.

"We're wasting time," I said, at the end of the fourth day of our surveillance. "There's no one here but the Saudi family."

"They have servants in here, I'm sure," said David. "Probably chained up in the basements or kept in the kitchen. They won't let them out just like that."

I felt a chill go through me.

Katy reached over and touched me gently on the shoulder.

The women in the black robes had been our biggest challenge. Whenever they came out, Win adjusted the cameras, zoomed in on their faces, and enlarged the frames for me to check if they looked familiar.

It was hard to say from just looking at their eyes, as everything else was covered up. But I knew my friend and cousin well. It wasn't them.

A sense of despair settled on me.

All these high-tech gadgets and a team behind me, and I still didn't know where my cousin and best friend were. "They were brought here three years ago. How can we ever find out where they are now?"

"Best to wait till they bring the next shipment in," said Peace. "Then we'll know where they take the girls or how they trade them, so we can trace where Preeti and Chanda went."

I looked at everyone gloomily. "We could be sitting here for weeks for nothing."

"They come in two weeks," said David. "The next delivery, that is."

"Why make things so complicated?"

We all turned to look at Luc, who was lounging at the back of the bus.

"What are you proposing?" Katy asked, her eyes narrowing.

"We walk in and ask," Luc said with a shrug. "It's that easy."

We stared at him.

"Plus, we have a magic card to get in."

"What do you mean?" I asked, sitting up.

Luc looked at Peace. "Remember, we told those two dudes at the Tanzanian market we had high-priced merchandise?"

Peace nodded.

"It's a guess, but somebody could have mentioned that we were coming to Nairobi. We have a calling card to say hello. I say we use it."

"That sounds dangerous," said Katy.

"Do you have any other ideas?"

No one had a reply to that.

"Or we can stay here watching Saudi TV for the rest of our time," Luc said, pointing at the screens.

"You have a point," I said, slowly warming up to the idea.

We now knew the Saudi man's schedule.

He woke up late, went for a drive in the morning and entertained guests in the afternoon. They came in luxury vehicles, all dressed to the nines, looking liked mini Saudi Arabian kings. Women, of course, were never seen. When the old man himself left the compound, he did it in style, in a convoy of black tinted SUVs.

The man's wives mostly stayed inside their small house in the back. The only time they came out was in the early afternoon when they gathered in low chairs in the backyard to chat while their numerous children ran around, playing.

Then, every night, one of the guards would come to summon one of them to the main house and escort them back, later on. They were always covered head to toe in traditional garb, much like Bibi in London. They never took off their veils, even when among themselves.

"This could be a suicide mission," said Katy, looking worried.

David cleared his throat. "If you guys want to go in, we do it under one condition."

"What's that?" I asked.

"A crash course in weapons training. We'll need five days."

"Five days!" I spluttered. "We don't have that much time."

"It's been three years, give or take," he replied in a somber voice. "Five days won't make much of a difference. Plus, we'll be better prepared."

"I know how to handle a gun," Luc said, with an obstinate shrug. "Don't need no training here."

"We'll see," said David.

He looked over at Win, then tapped the wall. "Bulletproof. You'll be safe as long as you don't leave the bus."

She nodded.

"We all know you're doing your part and more already, so you don't have to come to the gun range. Only if you want to."

Win's face said she'd rather be anywhere else than a gun range.

The next day, we all, except Win, walked into the dojo to learn about firearms safety. David grilled us to make sure we'd paid attention.

Then, on the second day, he took us to the shooting range behind the dojo and had us try out an AK-47 semi-automatic rifle on top of the handguns we'd been practicing with.

"This is part of your dojo as well?" I asked, as I looked out to the walled-off range.

"It's for training," he replied, handing me my ear protectors. Training who and for what, he wouldn't say.

So far, the weapons we'd been training with had been unloaded. But now, we were using them on targets. I'd held a gun before and had even used it to threaten Zero and Vlad. But I'd never fired one until now.

I couldn't ignore the rush I got from the kick of the gun and seeing the bullet smash into the target. Every pull of the trigger sent ecstatic vibrations down my body. The reverberations of each gunshot echoed in every cell inside of me.

It wasn't just me. I noticed the wicked grin on Katy's face as she fired shot after shot after shot at the target shaped like a man. I wondered if she imagined that to be Jose.

The image in my head changed every time I fired a shot. Most times it was Franky's hyena face. Other times it was Kristadasa's ugly jowls. Sometimes Mrs. Rao, Dick and even Fartybag's pudgy face blazed across my mind as I pulled the trigger. And every time a bullet sped toward the target and hit it, I felt stronger, more powerful, like I was ready for anything to come my way.

Shooting is like therapy, I was sure.

How David got access to these weapons was a mystery, but he wasn't talking about his sources and shut down quickly when we inquired. So, I'd stopped asking questions. So far, he'd been helpful, and that was all that mattered.

But every day we spent outside with our guns seemed like an eternity, one in which we were playing with the lives of Chanda and Preeti. Still, I knew we couldn't go barging in like we'd done with Franky. I'd been lucky to get out of his place unscathed and even then, I'd got false information.

This stage of the game required smart thinking and a smart strategy.

Five days later, we were back in the bus.

Win, Katy, David and I sat side by side at the computer bench, our eyes transfixed on the video screens. Our earpieces had been set up and the cameras had been positioned. David had even rustled up a used yellow Mercedes for the foray.

That morning, after breakfast, David took out two jagged knives from the glass case on the wall, slipped them into what looked like leather sheaths and handed them to Luc and Peace.

"CIA grade," he said. "Thirty percent glass composite. With those sheaths, no metal detector's going to find them."

Peace took one of the knives and stuck it in his boots like he'd done this sort of thing before. Must be his lifetime of Krav Maga training, I thought. Luc examined the knife carefully before resheathing it and slipping it in his pocket.

Then, turning to Katy and me, David handed us a subcompact handgun each. He also made sure everyone wore Kevlar vests, even Win, "Just in case." They were heavy but thin enough to tuck under our shirts and had holsters so we could safely keep our guns on us.

Now as we sat inside the bus, we were getting two extra video feeds from the tiny cameras disguised as pens sitting in Luc's and Peace's front pockets.

Their earpieces were on. As long as everyone was within five hundred meters of each other, we could hear them and they could hear us.

"Almost there," Win said, adjusting the screen to get clearer footage.

Luc and Peace were driving up to the main gate in the yellow Benz.

Luc had a Panama hat on that made him look more like the French gangster he was supposed to be representing. Peace looked his usual self, a smart college kid who could charm anyone. At least, I hoped.

"Crossing my fingers," I said out loud. "Good luck, boys."

"We're in position," said Luc's voice in my ear.

"All good to go," added Win.

"The real game begins now," said David.

I noticed his fingers were crossed too.

Chapter Forty-two

"*Salaam Allekum*," Peace said, bowing his head.

We lost the man's face momentarily as the camera panned down, giving us a glimpse of the opulent Eastern rug.

"*Alekum Salaam*," replied the fat man on the rug.

His face was familiar. I'd seen him every Saturday afternoon while Chanda and I skipped across the market when the adults weren't watching, to peek at the forbidden zone. There he was now, more wrinkled than before, his buddha belly larger than ever, settled comfortably among plush oriental cushions, a purple hookah pipe next to him.

The room was fit for a Bedouin king.

Elephant tusks adorned each corner. Tapestries with intricate Moorish designs covered the walls. Behind the old man stood two guards, wearing the same long white robes and headdresses held by a black band. I wondered how they'd run in these outfits. *Wouldn't they get in the way?* But on their waist belts hung the longest curved swords I'd ever seen. Perfect for chopping off heads, I thought with a shudder.

As David had predicted, Luc and Peace had to pass a metal detector before entering the big house in the Saudi compound. We held our breath as they walked through the barrier, their pocket cameras giving us a good view of the entrance. They walked in without a beep.

"*Bonjour, monsieur*," said Luc in his most polite voice.

The man took a puff of his pipe and looked at Luc unblinkingly.

"So, I hear you are Fred's right-hand man?" he asked in perfect English.

Next to me, Katy gave a start. I gritted my teeth.

This was the part I didn't like.

Bringing up Fred was a mistake. I knew that in my bones. But everyone had said that was the only way we'd get in, that it gave credibility and perhaps even *more* security.

It was going to be a Plan B in case the guards didn't let them in, but since Fred was one of the biggest names in organized crime in Europe, it would also be the biggest risk we'd take.

"Monsieur Fred sends his esteemed greetings to you," said Luc with a slight bow.

"And I pass mine back to him with pleasure," said the Saudi man with a slight bow of his head.

He spread his arm grandly. "Please sit down and make yourself comfortable."

Peace was the first to sit down on the cushions, followed by Luc.

I noticed I was still clenching my fists from watching them approach the compound gates and talk their way in. Getting inside had taken longer than we'd expected.

The guard at the front gate had stood next to the Benz with a self-important look, asking a litany of questions more intrusive than any posed by a border agent. Luc had remained silent, keeping up with his mysterious European visitor persona, while Peace politely replied to the guard in Swahili.

Every few minutes, the guard would leave them at the gate to confer with someone inside the big house. David was sure they had cameras trained on the gate and anyone inside the house had a clear picture of Luc and Peace.

Fifteen minutes into this slow and intermittent interrogation, Peace nonchalantly dropped Fred's name. That stopped the guard in his tracks.

He scampered back inside the compound to talk with his boss. We saw him run into the big house and within seconds run back out and toward the gate.

The gate was opened and Luc and Peace were invited in. After passing through the metal detectors, two guards ushered them through the lavishly decorated corridors of the main house to the living room where the old man sat waiting for them.

Not taking his beady eyes off the boys, the Saudi man yelled out something in Arabic.

A small figure appeared hesitantly in the background. She'd just walked through a set of heavy curtains in the back of the room.

My heart gave a jolt.

"Oh, my god," I whispered, leaning in toward the screen. "Preeti?"

I clutched at Katy's arm, my heart pounding.

She's been there all this time and I hadn't even noticed.

"Peace, you're the closest," I heard David say quietly. "Can you get a close-up?"

Peace turned slowly and casually to look at the girl. She was wearing baggy pants and a multicolored blouse. On her head was a green scarf that covered her long black hair. She looked like she'd just stepped out of an Ali Baba movie set. She treaded softly toward the old man, her eyes cast down and shoulders drooped, like she'd been summoned into a tiger's den.

I watched her without breathing.

Something's off.

Win enlarged the video.

I shook my head. *It's not her.*

"Yes, master," she said in such a soft voice, we could barely hear.

Win turned the volume up.

"No," I said, shaking my head, feeling deflated. "That's not her. That's not Preeti."

The old man spoke rapidly in Arabic, not even looking at her. When he was done, she turned around and shuffled through the back door.

"I thought she looked Filipino," said Katy.

"They bring in slaves from all over the place," said David. "If they're very poor, they even come willingly."

Peace cleared his throat. "As you may have already heard from your Tanzanian team," he said, "we have merchandise you might be interested in."

"Ah, of course." The old Saudi nodded. "They did mention you. I expected you to come sooner. No matter. I am glad you have come now. I'm very interested to hear about these high-quality goods you bring."

Peace nodded.

"Now, tell me." The man leaned forward with a leer. "Are they young and nubile?"

"My god," said Katy. "What a sicko."

Peace and Luc were silent for a second.

The man's eyes scrunched.

"We only deal with the very best quality, *monsieur*," Luc spoke up. "We guarantee everything."

"Even virgins? Twelve and younger?"

My stomach turned.

Luc hesitated only half a second this time. "Absolutely," he said unwaveringly.

The Saudi studied his nails. "These days," he said, almost to himself, "everyone promises heaven and delivers junk. It's hard to find quality goods of any kind." He gave Luc a pointed look. "But Fred, well, he has a reputation, doesn't he?"

I held my breath and prayed that whatever reputation he was thinking of was a good one. Or our boys were in trouble.

"And we will uphold that reputation, *monsieur*," replied Luc. "You can rest assured of that."

The slave girl returned carrying a tea tray and stood silently next to the man until he noticed her. Even with the grainy picture from the pen cameras, we could see her hands tremble as she stood.

She must have been thirteen, fourteen at most. Just a child. My heart broke seeing her like this. I wondered if she'd been stolen from a village like Chanda. Or sold off by her own family like Win.

The Saudi snapped his fingers and spoke something harsh. She got on her knees and put the tray down while the old man ogled her, licking his lips.

"I can't watch this," I said, turning away, feeling like retching. "I just can't."

I felt Katy's hand over my shoulder as she pulled me in for a hug.

"We're going to find the girls," I heard David say. "We'll find them, I promise."

Peace spoke up. "We know you're also looking for new resources for Boko Mines."

"You're well informed, my young friend," said the Saudi man, raising an eyebrow.

I turned back to the video screens to see the girl was no longer in the room.

"The main reason I'm here is..." Luc paused and leaned in. "You see, Monsieur Fred, my boss, would like to suggest a long-term contract if you'd be interested."

"Oh?" The man looked at him curiously.

"We have identified a steady and strong supply from up north," said Peace. "The war has displaced many and the refugee camps are overflowing. It's an advantageous thing."

The Saudi nodded. "War always is."

"It will be a lucrative opportunity for you," said Luc, "and us."

"Ahh." The old man smiled. "I see now." He nodded appreciatively at Luc. "We're not dealing with petty goods anymore. Well, well, well. We're here to talk serious business. That is why you have come."

"Absolutment, monsieur," said Luc, his voice confident and strong.

He's really good at this.

"But first we must drink." He motioned for them to pick up the cups. He picked one for himself and raised it high. "How do you say in France?" he asked, looking at Luc. "Er...*chin chin?*"

"Sante, monsieur," said Luc, lifting his cup. "To your health. *Sante.*"

"And to yours."

They were quiet for the next minute as they sipped their drinks.

The Saudi man smiled. He stared at the boys for a few seconds and said, "In four days we celebrate an important festival for our people. I would be delighted if you would attend my festivities here."

"Careful," David said, his voice low, cautious. "Don't say no to a religious ceremony or they'll take offense. Especially them. Say yes, but get the hell out."

"We are honored by your generous invitation," Peace replied, bowing his head.

That seemed to please the Saudi. He became animated.

"We will share a wonderful feast. We also have a shipment coming that day, and I will give you any of the girls you wish for the night. We get some juicy little ones, unsoiled and fresh. You will be very happy. And we can get to know each other better and discuss business specifics, no?"

How Luc and Peace could get through this conversation without throwing up was amazing. I made a mental note to give them more credit for their acting skills.

"How generous," replied Peace. "It would truly be an honor indeed."

"Tell them you'll bring something from France," David spoke again. "It's tradition to exchange gifts."

                    TIKIRI HERATH

"And I will be sure to bring some sweet delicacies from France," said Luc. "I'm sure you and your family would enjoy some rare French cakes."

"Delighted. That would be really nice." The old man's smile widened. "You are also welcome to stay the night in my humble home for tonight if you wish."

Luc and Peace looked at other.

"Not a good idea," David said in a low voice.

"Alas," said Peace as if genuinely disappointed, "I have promised to visit my family tonight and introduce them to Monsieur Luc. As you know, you can never say no to family."

"Of course, of course, but we must eat together soon. This is not America where you shake hands coldly and walk away. We don't do business like those barbarians."

"Neither do we, in France." Luc nodded. "We would be delighted to attend your celebrations next week."

"That's settled then," said the old man, lifting his cup again.

We watched the boys bow goodbyes to the Saudi and follow one of the guards outside.

"Hey, look over there!" Win said.

I swiveled around to see her pointing at the fourth screen that was feeding video from the back of the compound. We'd been so riveted by the computer showing us live footage from the boys' pocket cameras, we'd forgotten all about the other screens.

Three women dressed in head-to-toe black robes were walking toward the parked SUVs. Behind them came stumbling three young girls carrying large baskets. They looked much smaller and skinnier than the women in black. This was the first time we'd seen these girls outside.

"Servant girls," David said.

It was hard to make out their faces because their heads were covered by scarves. Win tried to enlarge the images, but the women in black got in the way.

The two guards opened the passenger doors for the women. Once the women got in, a man pulled up the hatch in the back of the second vehicle and motioned for the girls to enter.

Maybe it was my imagination, maybe it was just pure futile hope, but I thought I saw Preeti. Or, at least someone who walked vaguely like my cousin.

"They get put in the hatch like dogs?" Katy said. "There's plenty of space inside."

"They treat them like animals," David said with disgust.

"The gates are opening," said Win.

I jumped up and grabbed my jacket.

Everyone turned to look at me.

"I'm going to find out where they're going."

David gave me a warning look.

I put on my jacket. It was hot outside, but I needed it to conceal the bulge my weapon was making at my waist.

"Pass me the van keys," I said, holding my hands out to David.

He hesitated.

"Come on. Give them to me."

"Slow down," he said. "I'm coming with you."

I glanced over at Katy and Win and shook my head. "No, you're not. I don't want them to be alone."

"We'll be fine," Katy said. "Someone needs to keep an eye on the compound." She gave a nod. "You go."

"This bus is the safest spot outside of the dojo," said David, standing up. His jacket flap opened, showing two handguns in a holster on either side of his waist. He took one out. "No one knows we're here. Besides, the walls are bulletproof," he said, checking the gun. "So is the roof."

"Why on earth would you need a bulletproof roo—" Katy didn't get to finish.

He placed the gun on the table in front of her. "There. You just got double safer."

He took a step toward the door and paused. "Just so you know, that has a silencer."

"Guys, they're leaving!" called out Win.

I banged open the door and vaulted down the stairs.

Chapter Forty-three

David and I clambered into the van.

The engine sputtered as the key turned. He stepped on the accelerator and we lurched forward.

"Luc and Peace got a Benz while we got this rust bucket?" I asked as he backed out and we bounced onto the unpaved driveway that curved toward the scrapyard's gate.

"Trust me, we don't want to be driving a fancy car in town," he replied, pushing a fob on his key chain to open the gates. "We want to blend in."

David swung onto the main road, maneuvering around cars, motorcycles, and the occasional pedestrian who didn't seem to have a sense of their own safety.

"How are we gonna find out where they're going?" I said, looking around me. "It's busier than when we drove in this morning."

"It's Friday," David said. "The market opens today."

We gave each other a look.

"The baskets!" I said.

David slapped his forehead.

He gunned the engine and overtook a taxi, the old van protesting loudly as he did. "There's only one way to the market from here," he said, his eyes on the road. "We should catch up soon."

I scanned the traffic, watching the minibuses, family sedans and flatbed trucks zipping around us, my eyes peeled for two shiny black SUVs.

"They've done this before," said David more to himself. "Should have guessed."

I turned to him. "Hey, you know a lot about these people. How long have you been watching them?"

"A while," he said, after a moment.

"Why?"

He sighed and looked away.

"If we're on the same team, which is what I'd like to think, why are you hiding stuff from us?"

"I'm not hiding anything," David said, giving me an angry look.

"Watch out!" I said, as a man jumped across the road in front of us.

David swerved around him and straightened the van.

"Jeepers. That was—"

"There!" I said, sitting up and peering through the windshield. "That's them. Look!"

We got ourselves exactly three cars behind the SUVs. The roads were busy, which meant we could follow discreetly. We kept our distance and drove silently, moving forward with the surge of traffic.

Fifteen minutes later we were pulling into the parking lot of Nairobi's city market.

The lot was really a huge dusty wasteland where everyone parked haphazardly as they wished. The two black vehicles took a prominent spot near the entrance, right next to a parked police vehicle.

"Wow," I said as we drove in, "that's pretty bold."

"The old man's got ties to everybody in town. Even the police," David said, shaking his head.

As we watched, the back door of the second SUV opened, and the drivers shooed out young girls like they were dogs being let out of their cages.

I craned to catch their faces but couldn't make anyone out. We were too far away.

We waited in the van until the wives had entered the market with the girls in tow. The women in the burqas walked abreast, swishing their robes as they wobbled forward. They were not small women by any means and took up the entire pathway. Anyone coming from the opposite direction had to scoot to the side to pass.

The two drivers followed the women in the back.

We got off the van and trailed them from afar.

I saw one of the drivers jab a girl with his hand. She stumbled forward, almost falling on her face. Even from where we were, we could hear the men laugh coarsely. I clenched my fists. *The bastards.* The girl regained her composure and hastened her steps, without even looking to see who'd harassed her.

"You'd better get a hijab," David said, pointing at my hair. "Best to look the part. Plus, you won't attract attention."

"What about you?"

"I look local."

"Yeah, right."

"People here know me. They think I'm the son of a Jewish immigrant. They think my father came to set up an export business here and I don't dispute that." He shrugged, like what others thought was inconsequential. "Anyway, I've just got to open my mouth and they know I'm native. Not like you."

I bought a headscarf and a pair of dark sunglasses from the first stall that sold them. David got himself a safari hat for good measure.

I wished I could just get a hat too. The scarf reminded me too much of when I'd pretended to be Bibi in London. It symbolized everything that girl went through—a life bound by thousand year-old traditions that treated women like pieces of furniture. Her worth came from the men to whom she belonged and when they were done with her, they discarded her like you'd dump a used sofa in a landfill.

Zero used to say the burqa kept his sister's "honor" intact but what he really meant was she was his property, his slave. It was an easy way to justify her subjugation.

I hated my new look, but David was right. Men stopped leering as soon as I put that thing on. I sighed. *Why must women cover up because these dimwits can't behave like mature adults? These are the kind of men who give all men a bad name.*

Grumbling to myself, I followed David through the stalls. The Saudi entourage was heading toward the meat and fish area now. David led the way, stopping now and then to browse or talk to a stall owner about something or the other.

But we didn't linger.

The women in the burqas stopped at the beef stall. The three girls stood respectfully a few feet back, heads bowed, awaiting instructions from their mistresses, their owners.

The women began haggling over flanks of beef shoulder, shouting even though they were within a few feet of each other. It took me a while to realize this was their normal way of speaking. The man behind the beef counter stood quietly, doubled over, his hands clasped in front, nodding his head every few seconds. He was eager to please these wives of one of the most powerful men in town.

David pretended to examine a wood carving of a lion at a nearby stall. It was a crowded booth with half a dozen tourists bargaining for the best price, so there was no one to question or even notice us. I stood a few feet behind David, keeping an eye on the beef stall.

As I watched, the largest woman in the group turned around and snapped at the girls. She didn't have to speak twice.

The girls scattered in all directions with their baskets. One girl turned around so quickly she bumped into one of the burqa-clad women by accident. The woman didn't miss a beat. She raised a hand and whacked the girl across the head with a resounding slap. The girl reeled back.

"Hey, did you see—?"

David jabbed me with his elbow. "Shh..."

The girl hadn't objected or even raised her arm to protect her face. She merely turned around and walked toward the fish stalls, head down. I followed her with my eyes, feeling a surge of fury bubble inside me.

How wicked can they get?

That was when I noticed the second girl had her back to us and was kneeling to adjust her shoe. Like the others, she had wrapped her cotton scarf over her head and partially across her face. When she stood up, something glinted around her ankle.

An anklet?

In a trance, I took a step toward her. Then another. And another. I heard David say something urgently behind me but I didn't stop. It was like a force was pulling me toward her now.

The girl was walking over to the fruit stall. An old man was sitting behind a mountain of pineapples, fanning himself. He glimpsed her but didn't speak.

I pulled my own scarf across my face and stepped closer to the stall.

The girl's hand reached out to pick a fruit.

I knew that hand.

I stepped up to her, my heart in my mouth.

"Preeti?" I said.

Chapter Forty-four

Her hand stopped momentarily, hovering over the pineapples. I tried again.

"Preeti, is it you?"

The girl pulled her hand back as if she'd been bitten and turned around to leave.

"Hey, it's me, Asha," I said, stepping up behind her. "Please don't go. It's *me*."

She started walking away briskly.

"Preeti," I called louder, touching the girl's shoulder. She jumped like I'd prodded her with an electric rod. She swiveled around and gave me a stare.

My jaw dropped.

"Oh, my god!"

She gave me a glazed look.

I pulled the scarf off my head and tore off my glasses.

"It's me! Do you remember me? I came for you. I came all the way to find you—"

With a fearful look, she took a step back. And, another. And, another.

"Where are you going?" I looked at her, confused. "I'm here to rescue you. I've been waiting years to see you again. Come with—"

One of the robed women let out a stinging yell from the beef stall.

In a flash, Preeti turned back around, ran to the fruit stall and wordlessly held out her basket.

The man who'd been sitting casually snapped to attention, threw his fan on the ground, and picked three of the largest pineapples on top of the pile. He plopped them into Preeti's basket and grabbed the money she held out in one hand.

I heard a rustle near me. Someone was trying to grab me by the elbow. I pulled away.

"Hey, get out of here."

It was David, but I didn't have time for him.

"Preeti!" I called out.

One of the robed women gesticulated to Preeti under her robe. She looked like an angry black crow gone insane.

These women are demented. They're all raving mad.

David pulled on my elbow again. "Let's get out of here."

I turned around, furious. "That's my cousin! It's her! We have to *do* something—"

"Shh..." he said, putting a finger to his lips. "Keep it down, for god's sake. You have no idea—"

I didn't wait to hear what he had to say. I turned around to run after Preeti when David grabbed me, this time with force. I squirmed but his grip was too strong.

"Let go!" I said, punching his chest.

He caught my fists and pulled me in. "Are you trying to get yourself killed?"

"That's my cousin, you numbskull!" I said, struggling.

"I'm trying to save you here."

I pushed him away. "I don't need saving!"

"Keep your voice down, for heaven's sake."

"Git your hands off me!" I glared at him.

"Are you trying to get *her* killed?"

I stopped.

"What do you mean?"

He slanted his head slightly in the direction of the two drivers. I looked over. They were standing in a corner smoking, waiting for their mistresses. They laughed while we watched, like they were sharing a joke.

I turned away quickly and looked back at David.

"Do they..."

"They won't hesitate to kill a slave girl trying to escape," he said, his steely eyes boring into mine. "Or for trying to talk to outsiders."

"They'd do that out here in the market?"

"Oh, the police will come when they hear the gunshots," David said, gritting his teeth. "Someone will say it was an accident. Or she was trying to steal, so they had to stop her. This is a powerful man. They'll happily execute us and blame it on someone else."

I stared at him in dismay. I wanted to look back at the drivers to see if they noticed us, but I knew I shouldn't. I wondered how much they'd seen already.

Oh, my god, what have I done? Again?

"Is she..." I swallowed. "Is she in trouble? Is she going to be okay? Are they going to..."

David shook his head. "She's docile and obedient. That means she's useful to them. If they wanted to hurt her, they'd have done it in front of you."

I drew my breath in.

"They'll do that to punish you and make you regret your actions. Plus, it will be a lesson to the others."

"How do you know all this?"

"You think I haven't seen this before?" I noticed his lips were quivering like he was trying to control himself.

A yell made me turn around.

The Saudi women were calling all their slave girls. They were heading back toward the parking lot slowly, calm now they'd got all their provisions.

I watched as Preeti trailed behind them, in between the other girls, their baskets weighing them down. The men marched in front, leading the pack back to their cars, their compound, back to Preeti's prison.

My brain screamed silently, *Run, Preeti, run!*

But she didn't look back.

Chapter Forty-five

"Hey, where's the second SUV?"

I could see one in front of us, weaving in and out of traffic. The roads were light so we should have been able to spot the second car.

I swiveled my head. *Where did it go?*

We'd given adequate time for the Saudi group to leave the market and get back in their cars before we ventured out to the parking lot.

The few minutes we waited had also given me time to calm down and take stock of the situation.

My mind whirled at first. *Oh, my god, was that really Preeti? After all these years?*

Then, doubt crept in. *Did I dream that up? Maybe it wasn't her.* I shook my head. *Of course, it was her. She's alive!* My heart leaped. *I touched her. I touched Preeti!*

I took a deep breath to steel myself.

I've finally found her. Now to get her out.

I touched the revolver cloistered in my Kevlar vest, under my jacket. In my sheer panic and relief at seeing my cousin, I'd forgotten I had it on me. *Next time, I'm gonna use it.*

David had warned us not to get into rash gunfights, as that would be a surefire way for no one to survive. But I didn't care if I died trying. I was going to shoot the men who held Preeti captive. I needed all my strength now. My battle was just beginning.

Next to me, David was quiet, thoughtful, speaking in quiet tones and only to suggest our next steps.

The parking lot was full when we returned to our van. In place of the black SUVs in front were two more police cars. We jumped into our vehicle and got back on the road going toward the Saudi compound until we caught sight of the black SUV.

"Check behind," David said, keeping his eyes on the SUV up front.

I undid my seat belt and scrambled over the seats to the back of the van to get a better look. I scanned all four sides.

"Nothing," I called out. "They must have taken another route."

Without a warning, David swerved the van.

"Hey!" I called out, clutching on to the nearest door handle. "What're you doing?"

The U-turn made me swing from one side of the van to the other. David pushed on the accelerator and the van screeched like a hundred dying cats.

"What's going on?"

We were heading in the opposite direction from where we came, away from the Saudi compound. The engine stopped squealing as David slowed down to the speed of traffic. I scrambled over the seats and got to the front. I plopped on my seat, my heart pounding.

"What the heck, David?"

"Something isn't right," he said, his eyes scanning the road ahead. "We gotta find another way home."

Why? Did those men see me? Is Preeti going to be okay?

David threw me a flinty look. "You've no idea what a dangerous clan they are. They have so little value for human life." He paused to change gears and overtake a car. "We can't go in with guns blazing with these people. That's a surefire way to get killed and get everyone else killed, including your cousin."

"What do you suggest, then?"

"Outsmart them."

"How?"

"I don't know." He shook his head. "I just don't know." He hit the steering wheel in frustration.

He looked pale. There was a hint of pain in his eyes, one I didn't understand.

"I've been trying to get at them for years. Trust me, I know how you feel. I want to go in and blow those bastards to smithereens just like you do. But I know that will only hurt the innocents."

"What did…" I stopped and tried to find the right words. "What did that Saudi do to you?"

He was quiet for a minute.

"It was my sister," he said in a whisper.

I stared at him.

"You see," David said, not taking his eyes off the road, "my parents were stoned to death."

"*What?*"

"Killed for their religion." He took one hand off the steering wheel and touched the cross on his neck.

I looked at him, shocked. "The Saudi did that?"

He shook his head. "Not him. Yemen. They didn't tolerate us. They wanted our kind gone."

"Oh, my god."

"But my sis and I escaped. Our neighbor helped us get to a refugee camp. He put us in the trunk of his car and got us across the border. He risked his life for us."

I listened, frozen.

"The camp was taking in the Sudanese fleeing their famine, but they let us in because we were just two little kids. We were alone."

A frisson of fear went through me.

"One day…" He paused, turning the van onto a quieter road. "A group of men who said they were from the Islam brotherhood came and took me and my sister. They said they found families for us. That's what they told the refugee camp organizers, anyway. These Westerners…" He turned to give me an accusing look. "They believe anything anyone tells them, so they let us go with them."

"What happened?" I whispered, feeling my heart sink, not really sure I wanted to hear this story, but knowing I had to.

"They raped my sister the first night. All of them. She was only nine. I was seven. They tied me up and made me watch."

I closed my eyes. *No.*

"I stopped eating after that. They said I was not good enough to sell if I didn't eat, so they threw me out of the car, while it was rolling just outside Nairobi."

David's voice was calm but low, like he was simply telling a sad tale. But this was his own gut-wrenching, agonizing life story.

I shook my head, feeling numb.

"They took my sister to the Saudi man's compound here in Nairobi. It took me months to find her. I stole inside through the back gate. The one we're watching now."

"Oh, god."

"You know what they did when I tried to run away with her?"

I shook my head, unable to speak. It was like someone had reached in to my heart and was squeezing it, wringing every drop of blood out.

"They shot her."

My eyes welled up.

"In the head."

He banged his hand on the steering wheel.

Even after all I'd seen and heard about Bibi, about Win, about Tetyana, about Katy, it was so hard to hear these stories. *How can such things happen? How can humans be so cruel?*

My throat was too dry to speak, my heart too wrung out to think of the right words to say to this man who was pouring his own heart out to me.

"They laughed as they kicked me. Then, they threw me out to the street to die."

David was silent for a long time after that.

I wiped away the tears rolling down my cheek. How many more like him, like me, like us were out there? The tortured, the wounded, the exiled.

David cleared his throat. "At least I ended up in a good place. When I woke up, I was at the Jewish hospital in town. A good Samaritan had found me and taken me there."

He gave me a quick side glance. "I stopped you at the market because I didn't want you to see what I saw."

I gave a barely perceptible nod.

"I didn't want you to experience what it's like to watch the one you love die like an animal in front of you."

Chapter Forty-six

We took the long way back. We were driving along a quiet road in an industrial part of the town now.

Lined up along the road were skyscrapers grazing the sky. The roads were better paved and the streetlights looked more modern and slick than elsewhere. Everything was new here. Things were quieter too, it being almost the weekend.

"Business district?"

David nodded.

I wondered how Katy and Win were faring alone in the bus.

Luc and Peace couldn't return in case they were followed. The plan was for them to keep up with their pretense and drive to the ritziest hotel in downtown Nairobi and sleep over that night. Then, they were supposed to rent a car and drive back to the dojo the next day, leaving the yellow Mercedes to be picked up later.

I tapped my earpiece. Nothing. We were too far away to connect with my friends.

I gave a side glance at David. His eyes were fixed on the road.

He no longer looked like the intimidating, tattooed man I'd not want to meet in a dark alleyway.

"Hey," I whispered. "I'm sorry about what happened."

Silence.

"And I'm sorry I mistrusted you."

He gave a shrug, as if to say it was okay.

"It's just that I've learned not to trust anyone."

"Me too," he said, rubbing his eyes. "All I knew when I was a kid was I wanted to get bigger and stronger so no one could hurt me again."

"Is that why you took up Krav Maga?"

He nodded. "I wanted to learn to fight. It's how I got through college. I won enough championships they couldn't ignore me, but I'm not a naive little boy anymore."

I looked at him. There was no anger on his face, just grim determination.

But something steel-like was growing through my spine. I sat up straight. I felt my heart harden.

"David?"

"Yeah?"

"I want to get rid of the Saudi and his cronies. I want them to pay. For what they did to your sister. And what they're doing to Preeti."

He was silent for a while.

"Nothing will redeem what they did to my sister. Nothing." He shook his head. "But if I can help you save Preeti, I'll feel like I've done something."

"But I want them to suffer," I said, gritting my teeth. Kali flashed into my mind, the image of her holding the severed man's head burning brightly in my brain. "I want them to hurt so badly that when I'm done, they'll beg for mercy. They'll wish they'd never lived."

"Asha—"

"And I want to get back at the men from Boko Mines who killed my parents." My eyes flared with fury. "None of these thugs deserve to live."

"Did you say Boko?" he asked, squinting his eyes.

I nodded.

"We'll be passing their headquarters soon."

I peered out the windshield.

"Are you telling me Boko Mines is right here?"

"They're everywhere. They own most of the industrial complexes in Nairobi. They probably own the Saudi man's compound too. Plus the mines out in the desert. But their headquarters is here."

I stared out the window, scanning each passing building.

After a few minutes of silence, David cleared his throat. "Look, it's not my place to give you advice..."

I frowned. That was never a good way to start a sentence, but I didn't want to cut him off. Not after what he'd shared with me.

"It's just that you don't want to stoop down to their levels. If there's one thing I've learned from martial arts—"

"That's not the point." My mouth opened before my brain kicked in. "I want them all to stop hurting others. Don't you see?"

"Then, we have to be patient."

"For what?"

"For the right time."

"You're beginning to sound like Peace's father," I said, exasperated.

"We have world-class equipment. We have a good group now to put our heads together and work as a team. We'll figure things out so there's no collateral damage."

If David hadn't been there, I'd have driven right into the compound and confronted the Saudi. I'd have beaten him to a pulp for everything he'd done, even if that would have meant I'd get shot to death.

Kali lived inside me now. I had brought her across the ocean from India. All I knew was I no longer cared for my safety. I wanted to make them all pay. Badly.

"There it is," David said, looking out the window.

We were passing by an impressive building set in even more impressive grounds. With its swanky facade and tall tower, it outshone everything around it. In front of the building was the shiny five-foot-tall steel logo of the Boko Mines.

"Stop!" I yelled, pulling hard on the steering wheel.

"Hey!" David cried, screeching to a stop, wrestling my hand away.

I banged my door open and jumped out.

Chapter Forty-seven

"Oi! Come back!"

I didn't look back.

I put my shades on and kept walking toward the tower.

Behind me, I heard the van door slam.

I pulled on the main doors and was hit by the air-conditioned coolness. I shivered. I was in the middle of East Africa but it was like the Arctic in here.

The inside of the Boko Mines headquarters could have been the inside of any swanky firm in Toronto's financial district. The walls were made of white marble slabs and the floor gleamed like it had been polished by hand.

In the back of the lobby was the front desk, manned by three smartly dressed security guards. From the corner of my eye, I saw two more guards standing next to the bank of elevators. I guessed with their kind of operations, they had to be careful.

I marched confidently through the lobby toward the front desk, keeping my eyes straight ahead, not smiling, like I owned the place.

The men watched me nervously but didn't make any moves. There were advantages to being a five-foot Asian female. I was not a threat. Or so they thought.

I stepped up to the man in the middle.

"Good afternoon," I said, in my most crisp North American accent. "I'm here to see Sophie Dubois, please."

The guard's eyebrows shot up. The other men craned their necks to get a better look at me.

The guard cleared his throat and spoke almost deferentially, "Does she know you're coming today, miss?"

"I don't like to announce my visits."

"You...you are, I presume, a friend of Ms. Dubois?"

"A longtime friend."

They stared at me like I was an alien. Thank god I had my glasses on.

"We went to the International School of Dar Es Salaam together."

The men stood straighter at the mention of my school.

It was an elite place for children of foreign diplomats, politicians, and the wealthiest families in the region. The school also offered scholarships to a dozen kids whose parents worked at local not-for-profit organizations, but I didn't tell them that.

"I'm visiting from New York. I'm here with National Geographic."

They stared at me wide-eyed.

"I fly out tonight. It would be good to say hello while I'm still in Nairobi. Sophie would get mad if I didn't."

The guards looked at each other in alarm.

One of them picked up a phone and talked quietly into the receiver, while the others pretended to look at a file folder on the desk, but I could see they were discreetly checking me out, eyes traveling to my cargo pants and jacket. That should only build my credibility and American-ness, I was sure. If I'd come all dressed up, I'd have to had to put on a European or Asian accent or they wouldn't have believed me.

The elevator door opened.

I looked up expecting to see my old classmate, the daughter of the mining magnate. Instead, three businessmen in pinstriped suits, carrying leather briefcases, stepped out. With quick nods to the guards, they walked briskly across the lobby and out the door.

"Hullo, sir! Can we help you?"

I spun around.

David was standing at the doorway with a confused look on his face. I guessed those tattoos and muscled arms were enough to spook the guards.

"He's with me," I called out.

The guards turned and gave me a surprised look.

David walked up to me, glaring.

I'd be pissed off too if someone had jumped out of my car while it was still rolling. The screeching of the van's tires was still ringing in my ear.

We waited silently, David with his arms crossed, frowning. I was sure there would be words later, but I had a job to do now. I waited, my nose in the air, tapping my feet to show my New-York-style impatience.

The elevator doors opened again three minutes later and this time, it was a haughty woman who stepped out.

She wore a hot pink miniskirt and glittery heels that must have been five inches high. Her hair was died peroxide blonde. Even from where I stood, I could see those shoes cost more than twelve months the salary of the security guards. As she walked across the room catwalk style, an expensive perfume pervaded the entire lobby, suffocating the air right out of it.

As I watched her approach me, a flood of memories rushed to my mind. Sophie. This girl who bullied me in class, who laughed at my parents for their work, calling them hobos, who said I belonged with the "dirty, smelly locals."

"My secretary told me someone was here to see me from New York," she said, walking toward me. Like everyone who'd gone to international schools, her accent had become a mix of everything with a slight hint of British.

"Asha," I said, not taking off my glasses. *I see your snootiness and raise you.* "From ISL in Dar Es Salaam."

Her eyes looked me over.

"I heard you work here," I said, trying to sound as disdainful as she would. "Still in Nairobi, I see."

She looked me up and down again. "American fashion is so understated."

"You can't beat New York."

Her eyes blazed.

Got her.

She pouted.

"I've always wanted to visit America, but Daddy won't let me."

"Ma'am, do you know these, er, miss and sir?" one of the guards asked.

"Of course, I know them," she snapped, not even looking at him.

"Tanya's in New York too," I said. "But you knew that, didn't you?"

"Tanya?" She frowned. "Really?"

Tanya was the daughter of the former American ambassador to Tanzania. They were all part of an elite clique, but Sophie was Tanya's best frenemy.

On the surface, they hung out and got along, but everyone knew Sophie resented Tanya for being the most popular girl in school. For a moment, I glimpsed the old Sophie in this older version of her. Her face was a picture of malice now.

"I came by to say hello," I said, "thought we could catch up and share some gossip."

"Gossip?"

She hesitated only for a moment.

"Come," she said, looping her arm around mine. "Let's go outside and you can tell me all about New York. I needed a cigarette break, anyway."

Chapter Forty-eight

S ophie walked me over to the side of the tower and across a small pathway. I heard David following us at a distance.

We were going toward an outdoor patio set under a pristine white tent. It was an upscale smoking area, one built just for her, I was sure.

She pushed me into a luxurious sofa and plopped down across from me, and crossed her long legs.

"I know you," she said, taking a gold cigarette case out of her purse. "I remember you."

She watched inquiringly as David came over and sat next to me. He still looked upset but he was more curious than angry now.

"Lighter?" she asked him.

He shook his head. "Sorry."

With a dismissive sniff, she rooted in her purse until she found one and lit her cigarette herself. I watched her sit cockily in that extravagant getup, taking a nonchalant puff. *Even Tetyana looked classier in her red heels and leather skirt,* I thought.

"Don't believe Americans smoke any more. Or do you?" she said, holding her carton toward us. David and I held our hands up to say no.

"So you own Boko Mines now?" I asked as she blew rings of smoke.

"Huh!" she said, looking away. "Daddy does."

"It's a family business, isn't it?"

"I wish," she said with a shrug. She gave me an inquisitive look. "I thought you were dead."

The hair on my neck rose. Not with fear. With rage.

"One day you were sitting in the corner of class looking like a loser..." She stopped.

I watched her, my muscles tensing. At least she had the decency to check herself. I struggled to keep Kali from rising inside of me.

"One day you were in school and the next, you disappeared." She looked at me curiously. "No one would tell us why. It was like a big, fat secret."

You have no idea.

"What happened?"

I leaned in. "You wanna know what happened?" I felt my eyes glowing. If I could have spit fire, I would have. "Are you telling me you don't know?"

She drew back and stared. "Jeez. Relax. What's the deal with you?"

"The deal? You wanna know what the deal is?" I spat out. "The deal is your daddy killed my parents."

I didn't realize my right hand had balled into a fist. I half stood up when David pulled me back.

"Hey," he said. "Take it easy."

I let him push me gently back down.

Sophie stared at me with huge eyes, her lit cigarette now all but forgotten.

"Your father sent goons to kill my parents," I said, between clenched teeth. "We were on our way to a safari when they rammed us off the road. My parents died in a ball of fire. They were murdered in cold blood."

She was silent for almost a minute.

"Yeah, I can imagine Daddy doing that," she said finally, and casually took another puff. "Frigging bastard."

It was my turn to sit back in surprise.

"He's a vicious son of a bitch, that's for sure." She let out a hollow laugh. "What does that make me then? The daughter of a son of a bitch. Ha ha!"

David and I glanced at each other.

"You know," Sophie said, turning to me with a serious look on her face now. "I actually thought you'd run away to the market to live with Chanda. I truly did. I even asked her about you."

"You...you...Chanda?" I looked at her with my mouth open. "You *talked* to her?"

She scowled in disgust and took another puff. I noticed her hand was trembling. "What a question," she said with a sniff. "Have I talked to Chanda?"

I moved to the edge of my seat. "Do you know where she is?"

Sophie gave me a look of irritation. "Of course, I know where that whore is."

I stared at her.

She waved her arm grandly at the tower behind us. "She runs the whole gong show now."

Chapter Forty-nine

Within seconds we were whisked up in the elevator to the twenty-first floor.

A team of receptionists snapped to attention as we walked in. "Good afternoon, Mademoiselle Sophie," they chorused.

Without even the slightest acknowledgment of them, Sophie sailed by, marching toward the offices.

David and I followed her, stumbling on the lush carpet.

She'd been suspicious at first. "Did Chanda bring you here?" she'd asked.

"No," I said, shaking my head, "she doesn't know I'm here. I've been looking all over for her."

Her eyes narrowed. "Why did you come here?"

"I..." I stopped. *I came to find the people who'd killed my parents. But now, now Chanda is here.*

"What exactly does Chanda do here?"

Sophie gave an unhappy shrug. "Everything." She sat back and took a puff of her cigarette. "Every goddamned thing."

"Maybe it's a different Chanda?" David said, speaking for the first time.

"Oh, it's her all right. That ratty little chick who lived in the market. The daughter of a no-name market hairdresser," spat Sophie.

"Mrs. Ngozi," I said between clenched teeth.

"Whatever," she said, taking another puff. "That runt is my father's right-hand woman now."

"How?" I asked. "How did that happen?"

"By being a whore, that's how." Sophie's voice dripped with so much venom it made me shiver.

"When they brought her in, she was a scared little girl. But then she convinced Daddy to send her to school. That little bitch did so well, he made her his secretary. Can you believe that?" Sophie glared at me, her eyes flashing.

I didn't say a word.

"Thought he'd get rid of her like all the other little prostitutes he bought from that fat-bellied Saudi. But this one, *this one*, he kept. She wormed herself into his heart and his money. That's what that little tramp did. He didn't just keep her, he hired her. He told me she was so smart she'd become a manager one day. And then, she did. That conniving little harlot."

She's unhinged, I thought. I wondered how old Chanda had been when she was "bought" from the Saudi.

Sophie lit a second cigarette and smoked silently for half a minute. "She's Chief of Everything and even has an office on the top floor." She gave me a pointed look. "Daddy gave me a tiny office on the ninth floor and calls me his 'Brand Ambassador.' It stung when he did that. It really stung."

She blinked away tears.

"Do you think I give a shit about the brand? I just wanna run this show." She pointed her cigarette at me, her hand shaking. "Your little friend's gonna inherit all this while I get leftovers. She's pushed me out of what's due to me!"

There was nothing for me to say. I was struggling to digest everything Sophie was telling me, trying to separate reality from her paranoia.

"Hey," I said, sitting up. "Can you get me to her?"

She glared. "Why? So you can join her plot against me too?"

"Of course not." I leaned toward her and lowered my voice. "Her mother's not well. I'm afraid she won't live very long. I came here to give her a message to return home."

Sophie looked at me like she didn't believe me.

I tried again. "I came to take her back home with me."

"Back to Dar Es Salaam?" she asked in a high-pitched voice.

I nodded.

That was all she needed to hear. She threw her unfinished cigarette to the ground, scrunched it with her shoe and picked up her handbag.

"This way," she said, stepping onto the pathway and sashaying back to the building.

And that was where we found ourselves. On the top floor of the Boko Mines headquarters, marching toward the Chief Executive Office.

After sailing through reception, we stepped inside an imposing office, the size of an apartment really, overlooking the city of Nairobi. Halfway across the mahogany-lined room, set on a luxurious Persian rug, was a presidential desk and an executive leather chair. The desk was flanked by two flagpoles, one carrying the Tanzanian flag and the second, the insignia of Boko Mines. But the big chair was empty.

"Monsieur Charles Dubois, Chief Executive Officer." I read the lettering on the gold nameplate on the desk.

"Yeah," Sophie said, scrunching her nose. "That's what he calls himself, but she's the one who does everything. Now where's that little bitch?" She looked around impatiently. "Maybe in the bathroom?"

"Wait here," she barked, before stomping out of the office.

I hovered near the desk, wondering what to do next. I was glad to have David with me. He'd been quiet and unassuming during this whole charade, even though he was probably mad as hell. I sensed his warmth, a comforting, powerful presence that made me feel safe.

"Thanks for being such a sport," I said with a sheepish smile.

"I still can't believe you jumped out like that," he said, shaking his head. "Could have got yourself killed."

"I'm sorry. I just had to come here and see this place for myself. I didn't think you'd agree to stop. I'm sorry for dragging you here."

"I'm glad I came because if I hadn't been here, you'd have socked that woman and got arrested by now," he said with a small smile.

I smiled back, embarrassed. "I owe you one."

His face turned somber again. "Listen, we need to—"

A side door to the office banged open.

We stepped back, startled.

Set among the rich mahogany wall panels, I hadn't even noticed that door. A youngish man in a gray suit stepped out with a phone stuck to his ear. He looked like an intern or a junior employee of some kind. He didn't even notice us, his face staring at the carpet, his attention on the phone conversation.

He listened intently for a few seconds. Then, he shook his head. *"Pas maintenant,"* he said in a low voice. *"Je suis dans un reunions tres important." Not now. I'm in an important meeting.*

He twiddled with the phone to turn it off and pulled the side door open to walk back in. Just as the door shut behind him, I walked up and silently pried it open an inch. I held my breath, hoping no one would notice.

Male voices, speaking in English but in different accents, came through the opening.

I opened the door a few inches more.

Whoever was in there was deep in a heated discussion. It was probably why they hadn't realized the door was slightly ajar.

I leaned in to listen, making sure to hide behind the door.

"...continual supply from war camps..."

"... Any issues with foreign...?"

"...don't suspect a thing..."

"... I told you. Very healthy, young and dependable..."

"... both genders..."

"... are you sure they're in good condition...?"

"... Transportation is available..."

"Ah! She in there?"

I looked up, startled.

Sophie had come marching back in. "Should have checked the boardroom first."

Pushing me brusquely aside, she pulled the door fully open and stomped in. I stood by the door, stunned.

Everyone turned to look.

"Sophie, *ma cherie!*" cried an old man. "What are you doing here? We're having an important meeting."

Sitting at the head of the table was a European man, his hair white and his face wrinkled and spotted with old age. To his left sat two middle-aged African businessmen, impeccably dressed like they'd just stepped out of a men's fashion magazine.

At the end of the table, opposite the old man, was the young French man we saw earlier, taking notes. But it was the woman next to him who made my jaw drop.

She was a beautiful, ebony-skinned woman about twenty years old, dressed in a smart white Chanel suit. She looked like a younger, healthier and much wealthier Mrs. Ngozi.

Gone was the giggly young girl with braided plaits who'd played with me at the Saturday market. Chanda had changed, but her features were unmistakable. She still had her large almond-shaped eyes, full lips, and high cheekbones I remembered from a long time ago.

She was now sitting with such poise and confidence it shocked me. *How can she work with these villains? How can she support a company that uses stolen children? How can she work for the very people who killed my parents?*

I felt blood rush to my head, making me dizzy.

Sophie leaned across the expansive desk. "Daddy, I have something important to discuss."

"But *ma cherie*, you can't come barging into meetings like this," the old man replied. "How am I ever going to get any work done, my dear?"

"This is important, Daddy. Super important."

"I thought we discussed this before," said the old man, his bushy eyebrows all scrunched up. "Unless the building is burning—"

"Chanda's mother's dying. And she needs to go home."

Chanda sat up with a loud gasp.

A wicked smile spread on Sophie's lips. She pointed at me standing by the doorway. "They're here to take you home."

Chanda turned to look at me.

She stared.

I glowered back.

Chapter Fifty

Sophie didn't leave anything to chance.

She marched around the boardroom table and pulled Chanda up by the elbow. With her other hand, she grabbed Chanda's handbag.

David and I stepped back into the room quickly as Sophie strutted toward us, dragging a confused Chanda behind her. Sophie kicked the door shut and positioned herself in front of it with a fierce look on her face.

Chanda stood in the middle of the room, uncertain of what was going on.

"What are you doing here?" I asked her, my tone harsher than I expected.

She took a small step toward me, a worried expression on her face.

"Tell me about my mother." Her voice was soft, scared even—not what I'd expected from a smart Chanel-wearing businesswoman.

"She's not well," I said. "I found her dying. Alone. At your home. A few days ago."

Chanda's face scrunched up like she was being pulled apart.

"I'm sorry," I said, suddenly feeling pity for her. "We took her to the Dar Es Salaam hospital."

"How is she?" she whispered.

"Recovering. They're taking care of her. But she misses you."

Chanda looked away. Her eyes had a faraway, sorrowful look.

"It broke my heart to see her like that," I said, still angry at her for abandoning her mother for a lavish life here at Boko Mines, of all places. "She was ready to die alone and would have, if we hadn't found her." What I also wanted to ask was, *What the hell are you doing here?*

Chanda swallowed a few times like she was trying to compose herself.

I looked her in the eye. "I've been through hell and back to find you and Preeti."

At the mention of Preeti's name, Chanda's eyes grew wide.

"Do you know where she is now?" I asked, giving her an accusing look. "And what she's going through?"

I felt David's hand on my shoulder. He gave me a light squeeze.

Sophie was still standing at the door, arms crossed, with a smirk on her face. It was like she was enjoying the scene.

I ignored her.

"Why the hell didn't you go back home?" I cried out to Chanda.

Chanda shook her head and gave me a strange look. "You don't understand."

"I know how you got here. I also know I played a part in it. Just do the right thing and come home to see your mother. It may be your last time."

She stared at me for a moment, her eyes blinking, as if she was considering something.

Then, she stepped around the desk and pulled out a fancy scarf and a pair of shades from a drawer. She stepped up close to me and said in a low voice, "Let's go."

Before I could answer, she turned around and walked out into the plush corridor.

From behind me, I heard Sophie snicker.

Without giving Sophie another glance, I followed Chanda out, trying to keep up with her fast steps. David came after me, close by my heels.

Chanda marched toward the elevators, slipping the scarf on her head as she walked. She waited for us to enter the lift and without a word, took us down to an underground parkade.

Executive and VIP Guest Parking Only said the sign when the doors opened up.

She walked briskly out the sliding doors and into the car park, heading toward a gleaming white BMW. *Does everyone with luxury cars tint their windows here?*

She pulled the driver's door open, took off her beautiful Chanel jacket and threw it in the backseat carelessly with her handbag.

I took a step back in shock.

Strapped around her upper waist was a silver handgun. *What's she doing with that?*

"Jump in," she said to me.

I stared at her. *That gun.*

I felt David's hand lightly on my shoulder—a warning.

"We're just parked outside," he said. "We'd be happy to follow you, but we'll come in our vehicle."

She glared at him.

"I didn't mean *you*. Just her."

I took another look at her weapon.

"Er," I said. "I think I'll come with him."

"Who's he?" she asked, giving David a skeptical look.

"A friend," said David.

She cocked an eyebrow.

"I'm here to make sure Asha doesn't do anything ill-advised," he said.

A cold silence followed his statement, like we were all waiting to see who'd give in first.

"Do you trust him?" Chanda finally asked, looking at me.

I didn't know what to say. *Do I trust an old friend I'd lost touch with and who's now working for an evil organization? Or do I trust the man I'd just met who also carries a weapon, but seems to be on my side?*

I took a deep breath. "Yes," I said, "he comes with me."

She turned to David, her eyes traveling slowly down his chest and settling where he kept his holster.

"I want you to know," she said, her voice low and dangerous. "I can draw faster than you can even imagine."

David didn't move for a minute. Then, to my surprise, he started rolling up the shirt sleeve on his left arm.

"What are you doing?" *Is he planning a fist fight?* "David, what in god's name—"

He thrust his tattooed forearm toward Chanda. "Do you recognize any of this?" he asked.

Whatever it was, it had an astonishing effect on her. She took a step back and looked at him in shock.

I peered at his arm, wondering what they were seeing. His tattoo was a tribal design that looked more like a piece of intricate native art than anything else.

"What?" I said, scrutinizing David's arm. "What are you guys looking at?"

Chanda pointed a fob on her key ring at the garage door. The long door rolled up effortlessly, letting daylight stream in.

"I'll see you both outside," she said in a brisk voice, got in her car and slammed the door shut.

David took my hand and gently pulled me outside.

From behind us, I heard Chanda starting her car.

"What was all that about?" I asked, trying to keep up with David's long strides. "What's going on?"

His face had taken on a dark expression. "Do you know who we just saw right now?"

"Something on your—"

"No, I mean in the boardroom upstairs."

"That business meeting?"

"The most powerful men in this country."

"Sophie's dad, you mean."

"I meant those two lawyer-looking crooks at the table. They're the sons of the most influential and corrupt politicians in Kenya."

We were just about to get into our van when Chanda screeched to a stop next to us. She leaned out her window, holding a piece of paper.

I reached over and took it.

"I'll be waiting for you. Don't even *think* of following me."

With that, she rolled up her windows and took off like a rocket. We could hear the roar of her engine long after she'd disappeared around the corner.

I looked at the paper. The address meant nothing to me.

"Let's see it," said David, taking it. His eyes narrowed. "That's a bit of a drive."

"How far?"

"A bit out of town."

I looked down the road where Chanda had disappeared.

"We have to go," I said. "I can't lose her now." Not again.

We got in and David started the van.

"Hope Katy and Win are doing okay," I said, feeling slightly guilty for leaving them by themselves. Our earpieces were out of range and we were getting further every minute. "Do you have a phone on you?"

"I do, but *they* don't. Couldn't find encrypted mobiles in time. Sorry."

"Let's check what Chanda has to show us first. We'll head back right after."

"They have food, water, and a working toilet, good for a week if needed. There's even a change of clothing in the cockpit if they don't mind wearing my old T-shirts and a few uniforms."

"Uniforms?"

"Police, army, medical personal stuff." Seeing my expression, he added, "Disguises, costumes I picked up in case of an emergency."

Once again, I wondered where David found the bus and the equipment. He still hadn't opened up about it yet.

"Is the scrapyard safe?"

"As long as they don't walk out of the bus and start rooting near the compound, they'll be fine."

We drove out of the business district, through Nairobi's main streets and onto a ramp that led to the freeway.

"Where's she taking us?" I asked.

"To a small town nearby."

"Hey," I said, giving David a steely look, "what do you have on your arm?"

"What do you know about Chanda?"

A question for a question. I sighed. "She was my best friend when I lived in Tanzania."

"How old was she when you last saw her?"

"Twelve. We were both twelve."

He gave me a quick side glance. "Have you spoken to her after that?"

I shook my head.

"Didn't you notice?" he answered. "When she took off her jacket?"

"That gun? Why the heck would she carry that? I can't believe it."

"I'd have one too if I was working for those men."

"What do you mean?"

David kept his eyes on the road. "You didn't notice that little star on the crook of her elbow?"

I tried to think, but all I remembered was that shiny silver gun nestled against her tailored white suit. It had been so shocking, I hadn't registered anything else.

"She had this too," David said, pointing to the crook of his left elbow.

I squinted to see what he was showing me.

There, in the middle of the tribal motifs that swirled around his arm, was a tiny star. I'd never have noticed it if he hadn't pointed it out.

"I didn't know Chanda was Jewish," I said, sitting back perplexed.

"This is not David's star, Asha," he said with a sigh. "This means she was brought into this country the same way I was."

"What do you mean?"

"What do they do when they sell cattle to a new farm?"

I took a sharp breath in. "They *branded* you?"

Another tattoo flashed across my mind. The one I'd seen on Win when I first met her. She covered it up with jeans now, but I remembered seeing it in London. That angry dragon on her thigh, visible just below her miniskirt, tattooed by the Chinese gang that had brought her to Europe. Marked like an animal, I thought.

But what does it mean? I already knew the Saudi man had kidnapped Chanda and brought her to Nairobi. That didn't exonerate her from what she was doing now.

David was silent, his focus on the road.

Very soon, we'd left the bustle of the city behind us and were passing small villages clustered along the highway. Outside, it was open savannah land with lone acacia trees in the distance. A flood of memories came, memories of long drives with my parents on sunny weekend afternoons.

"There's the exit," David said as he took a ramp off the highway.

We were entering a small town. It was quieter here, less cars on the road and fewer people on the streets.

We drove past rows of single-story houses with old cars parked outside. There were no fancy BMWs or glass towers here. It seemed like a quiet farming community. Behind the houses were fields of corn, going for miles on end. Occasionally, we'd meet a small truck rumbling through, piled high with corncobs in the back.

David swung onto an unpaved road.

We drove through miles of cornfields on either side until we came to the end and stopped in front of a solid iron gate. A tall brick wall surrounded the place. Tamarind trees lined the wall on the outside.

"A rich person's estate," I said.

That was when I spotted the barbed-wire fencing on top of the wall and two small cameras perched on either side of the gate.

"Or a government facility."

"Or part of the mining company," David said.

There was a small brass plaque on the gate. I leaned out of the window to inspect it.

"Service - Love - Salvation," I read out loud. I looked around but saw no button or bell or intercom.

"Think it's a church or a hospital," I said finally.

"But how do we get in?" David asked, peering through the windshield.

I looked at the piece of paper Chanda handed to us, but there was no phone number to call.

Then, without warning, the gates were rolled open by unseen hands.

We looked at each other nervously. This was creepy.

"Do we go in?" he said, more to himself.

"Yes," I said. "I want to know what Chanda has to show us."

The gates closed behind us as soon as we rolled onto the grounds.

We drove silently through a paved path lined with trees. Modern light posts stood every few feet. The driveway was unusually long and eerily quiet. When we finally came to the main grounds, a large post-colonial mansion stood in front of us and next to it was a long, flat structure.

A warehouse?

As we got closer, I realized the long building was a schoolhouse. The walls were painted a sunny yellow with pictures of planets, animals, and flowers. Next to it was a children's playground complete with swings, slides, a jungle gym, and even a tree house. But it was empty.

The front door of the mansion opened and a tall, dark figure appeared on the threshold. Someone was waiting for us.

David pulled up carefully, his eyes flitting back and forth, watching for problems. He parked next to Chanda's BMW, his worry lines deepening. Then, keeping his head down, he pulled out his gun and racked the slide before tucking it back in the holster.

"Stay close," he said in a low voice before opening the door.

From somewhere in the back, I heard a child's playful shrieks.

"What *is* this place?"

Chapter Fifty-one

A giant of a man was waiting at the front door.

Looks like a bouncer from hell, I thought.

Somewhere in the back, a kid yelled. A holler and then, an excited whoop.

The man gave me a brief nod. "She is waiting for you," he said in a sonorous voice. He turned to David. "You can stay in the car, sir."

"No," I said, "I'm not—"

Chanda's face peeked from underneath the man's elbow.

"Let him in," she said. "He'll want to see this too."

The bouncer stepped aside and watched us as we walked inside.

We followed Chanda through a long corridor to the back. David and I walked silently, looking at the finger paintings and amateur sketches adorning the wall. We walked by a dorm room filled with rows of pint-sized bunk beds. Then we passed a noisy kitchen where three young women in chef uniforms were cooking something up, the warm smells making me realize I hadn't eaten for hours. They called out and waved at Chanda but gave David and me cautious glances.

At the end of the corridor, a large woman wearing a long traditional dress and a bright yellow head wrap stepped out of an office. It was like she had known we were coming.

"This is Asha," Chanda said, pointing at me, "an old, good friend of mine."

An old, good friend?

"Mama Abudu," Chanda said.

I gave the woman my hand. She grasped it tightly.

She squinted at David.

"David," he said in a friendly voice.

She nodded and shook his hand. I noticed she blinked rapidly when she spotted the tattoo on his arm.

That was when we got ambushed.

A dozen kids ran up, hollering Chanda's name, and surrounded her. She stooped to hug the children, laughing as she did. A few of them peeped at us, smiling shyly, but I noticed they gave us a wide berth. Chanda's face no longer looked like the cold, calculating businesswoman who carried a gun. She almost looked like the girl I knew from long ago.

"This is Asha and David from Nairobi," Chanda told them. A little girl gave us a wave. We waved back. That made everyone giggle.

"Go now and play outside," said Mama Abudu. "And remember we're having ginger cake for tea today."

The children ran outside, whooping.

I turned to Mama Abudu and Chanda.

"Who are these children?"

They looked at each other.

"Let's find a place to sit," Chanda said in a quiet voice, picking up her handbag and glasses that had fallen during the melee.

"It's too hot in my office," said Mama Abudu, as she ushered us into a classroom.

The walls were lined with bookcases filled with children's books. Chanda pulled out a kid's chair and took a seat at a tiny table. The woman joined her, making the chair creak as she sat down.

"Take a seat," she said amiably.

David and I glanced at each other and joined them. We sat surrounded by the miniature furniture, staring at each other for a minute. No one spoke.

"Nobody knows this place exists," Chanda said finally. "Nobody except for the cooks and the security team. The people in town think this is a government-run orphanage."

"Are they really orphans?" I asked.

Chanda's face took on a pained expression. "This is where I bring the youngest ones."

"Where are they from?" David asked.

"The trucks come every month," said Mama Abudu. "They bring children from desperate places. Sometimes from the south, but mostly from the north, Congo, Sudan, Somalia refugee camps, war zones. Sometimes the big international aid organizations hand the kids directly to them. The gullible ones think they're helping. The corrupt ones do it for money."

I didn't look at David, but I wondered what was going through his head right now.

"They bring them to a big warehouse in Nairobi," continued Mama Abudu.

"The same warehouse I was brought into," said Chanda, not looking up.

"They like the small ones because it's easy for them to slip down the mine shafts," Mama Abudu said. "They spend all day in dark tunnels. They work till they suffocate in the mines or are beaten to death by their supervisors."

Her eyes flashed angrily. She wiped her face as if that would stop what she was feeling. "When you buy a diamond from Africa, you buy the life of an African child."

No one said anything for a moment.

"This is a halfway house," said Chanda.

"What does that mean?" I asked.

"I bring the children here. At least the ones I can save."

I stared at her.

"From here, we send them to shelters across the region," Mama Abudu said. "Chanda has been very generous. We have private estates like this in every country nearby. That way, the kids get to go back to the culture and language they are familiar with."

"What about their families?" I asked.

"Their families don't want them back, especially the girls," said Chanda. "They consider them soiled. They are, in essence, exiled." She looked away.

Just like you, I thought, feeling my heart constrict to see her like this.

"And the company doesn't suspect anything?" asked David quietly.

"I pay the drivers hush money," Chanda said. "I always worry, but I give them enough to buy cars and send their kids to school. So far, they've been loyal."

"It's a risk," said Mama Abudu. "But then, everything in life's a risk. I should know. That was my career at Boko."

I looked at her in surprise. "You worked at Boko too?"

"I was head of risk management. I reported directly to the executive committee."

I couldn't help myself. "Why would you work there?"

There. I asked the question I was dying to ask Chanda.

Mama Abudu let out a sigh and looked down.

"I was a single mother from Lunga Lunga who was lucky to get a break. I got a university scholarship in accounting, graduated at the top of my class so they offered me a job. I really thought I hit the jackpot then. Until the day I learned how they operated. A few years later, I resigned, telling them I was immigrating to Canada."

"So they think you've left the country?" asked David.

She nodded. "This means I can never leave the house. I can never show my face outside."

"You sacrificed everything," I whispered.

She shrugged. "Everyone thinks this is an orphanage for kids with AIDS. That keeps most people away. But I worry someone's going to start asking questions about all the security we have." She paused and looked out the window. "Still, I'd rather do this than anything else. It's all about risk management." She gave us half a smile. "In a very different context this time."

"Won't someone in the company realize the kids go missing every month?" I asked.

"I pick the youngest ones and only a handful at a time," replied Chanda. "That way, they don't notice. It's worked so far, anyway. When I can get away with it, I pick the girls who fight back because I know what happens to them. They're used to teach others a lesson."

Next to me, I saw David give a shiver.

I felt sick, remembering his sister's terrifying demise at the hands of the same people.

"I hate choosing," said Chanda, looking down at her hands, her voice getting softer. "That's the hardest part."

She gave me a sad look. "I'm fighting from the inside."

I didn't know what to say anymore.

"It's risky but effective," said Mama Abudu. "All those non-profits clamoring to get funds get hampered by either bureaucracy or corruption or both."

"Plus, I get to use Boko profits against them and they don't even know it," said Chanda.

"You're siphoning their money too?" David asked.

"In small amounts at different times, so they don't notice."

"We have access through their Social Responsibility department," said Mama Abudu. "All public companies were legally required to set one up five years ago. Everyone knows it's just a scam. Well, I thought to make ours the most useful scam in town. I set it all up before leaving and as the head of Risk Management, I had a lot of leeway. But yes, it's a dangerous game we're playing."

"They'll kill me if they ever find out," said Chanda. "No question about that."

I swallowed. "I didn't even know—"

Chanda reached out and touched me on the arm. "I brought you here because I want you to pass a message to my mother."

I looked at her in surprise. "But aren't you—"

"I want you to tell her what I have done, what I'm doing here."

"But, but...you can come with us. We can leave right now and we can take you to her."

She shook her head gravely. "I can't drop everything and leave. They depend on me to keep up this shelter and rescue these kids every month. How can I go now?"

Chanda looked down at her star tattoo and rubbed it as if wishing it would disappear. "My village knows what happens to girls who are taken away. If I return, it will only bring shame on my mother."

"But your mother's not—"

"This is not my decision." She blinked as if trying to hold back tears. "This decision was made the day they took me. I can never go back."

Chapter Fifty-two

"We have got a problem, Ma!"

We all turned around. The bouncer was standing in the doorway, his face creased with worry.

"Are the children okay?" Chanda asked nervously, rising.

"They're okay. It's..." He gave a suspicious glance at David and me. "Something else."

"You may speak freely, Geoffrey," said Mama Abudu. "What's the issue?"

The man gave David and me a pointed look. "We think someone followed you here."

"Us?" I said.

"We are the only building in this cul-de-sac. Only the garbage truck and the postal van come this way. Unless these companies upgraded their vehicles, something's definitely not right."

"What do you mean?" asked David.

"My men noticed a luxury SUV with tinted windows come up the street ten minutes after you arrived," said Geoffrey. "A black Porsche. Does that sound familiar to you?"

My heart sank.

David swore, deepening the frown on Geoffrey's face.

"They're gone now," said Geoffrey. "They headed back, but I sent one of my boys to check them out."

"Are they still in town?" I asked.

He shook his head. "They got back on the highway to Nairobi about five minutes ago."

Mama Abudu's face had gone pale. "Now they know of this place."

"The risk of that is high, Ma," said Geoffrey. "After they left here, they drove around town, pulling up to every building, stopping here and there. They were looking for information. We got the license plate and my boys are checking it against our databases as we speak."

"I don't feel good about this," said Mama Abudu. "I don't feel good about this at all."

"It's the old Saudi man's goons," I said, a sinking feeling in my stomach.

David stood up, shaking his head. "This is my fault. I wasn't paying attention. I should have detected them. What can I do to help?"

"You can leave," Geoffrey replied, his face stoic.

Chanda let out a sigh. "I don't think this is solely your doing." She looked at us, her face crestfallen. "I've been getting this feeling for the past two months that I'm being followed."

"Followed?" Mama Abudu asked. "Why didn't you tell me?"

"It was just a feeling. I had nothing to pinpoint it on, so I didn't want to worry you."

"But you should have, my girl. You're always trying to carry the world on your shoulders."

Chanda shook her head and looked down at her hands. "If they followed you here, it's because they suspect me."

Mama Abudu sat up. "It's time for us to move."

"Move?" I asked.

"The children have gone through so much. Moving to another safe house is nothing compared to what would happen if we got found out."

"I'm sorry," Chanda said, still not looking up.

"It's not you!" I cried. "It's us. They followed us here."

"It doesn't matter who they followed, what's done is done," said Mama Abudu, her voice taking on a sharp tone. "We can move fast if we need to." She turned to Geoffrey. "Let's expedite our process this week. Get ready to send these kids tonight."

"Where to, Ma?"

She thought for a moment. "Take them to Dar Es Salaam. It's the fastest route," she said. "I'm coming too," she added as an afterthought.

Geoffrey nodded. Shooting us an accusatory glance, he turned to leave.

"At least we have backup plans. As I said, this is all about risk management," said Mama Abudu as she pushed her chair back to get up. She didn't seem angry as much as nervous.

As I got up to follow her, I felt a cold shiver run through me. "Hey, David. If they found us here, do you think they'll find Katy and Win near the Saudi compound too?"

"The Saudi compound?" asked Mama Abudu, her eyes widening. "What are you doing in that godforsaken place?"

"We've, er, got a surveillance setup," said David. "Our friends are in a shelter nearby. Bulletproofed and out of sight."

Chanda shook her head. "I'm not even going to ask how you arranged that. But you're really brave. Even I don't dare go near the compound as a Boko employee."

I looked at David in alarm.

He was already at the door. "I think we've done enough damage here."

"Take my car," Chanda said, pushing her keys toward me on the table. "It'll be faster."

My eyebrows shot up.

"What about you? Where are you going?"

"I'll figure something," she said. "Geoffrey will get a car for me. Go check up on your friends."

She paused, as if she was fighting to control her emotions. Years of living a double life probably taught her to conceal her feelings, but this was hard for her.

Her eyes met mine.

"Will you tell my mother I think of her every day?"

I stared at her for a moment. "I will," I mumbled.

"Tell her I've dedicated my life to doing something she'll be proud of. It may not look like it from the outside, but tell her I'm doing my best."

Mama Abudu put an arm around her shoulder. "Your mother would be proud of you."

"I have no more tears left," said Chanda. "I cried for years and then I learned I had to let go."

I struggled to find the right words. "Will I see you again?"

I wanted to run up to her and hug her, but something told me she wouldn't want that. Not because she didn't want to, but because keeping things at arm's length made her job easier, her life safer. She had exiled herself and there was no going back.

Chanda shook her head, averting her eyes.

"This is goodbye, Asha."

Part SIX

Don't let the bastards grind you down.
Margaret Atwood

I swung Chanda's car onto the highway, cutting off a corn truck that was lumbering up the ramp.

From the corner of my eye, I saw David grab on to the dashboard.

"Where did you learn to drive like that?"

"Just want to get back to Katy and Win," I said, moving my foot to the clutch and changing gears, my full focus on the road. It was nice to be behind the wheel of a machine like this.

The last time I'd driven a powerful car was when I took out Mrs. Rao's underutilized Land Rover, the car she'd made me clean every week. I still remembered the day I took it on a crazy dash across Toronto with Katy as we fled Dick and Jose.

"Slow down," I heard David say.

"I will, when we get within hearing range," I said, tapping my earpiece.

We drove in silence for ten minutes. I was going as fast as the law would allow, overtaking as many vehicles as I could.

"Hey!" David suddenly yelled.

"Don't distract me when I'm driving."

"Behind you!"

I checked the rearview mirror and my stomach sank. There was a shiny black SUV right behind me, looking as big as a tank, revving down on my bumper.

"How did they find us?" I yelled.

"Go!" cried David. "Faster!"

I thrust my foot down and revved the car to its maximum RPM. The engine growled happily and we shot ahead of the Porsche in a flash.

Thank goodness the highway's clear.

But the respite was short-lived. Within seconds, the SUV had caught up to us.

From the corner of my eyes, I saw David pull his sidearm out.

My heart beat wildly.

What do I do? What do I do?

"Take that exit!" David shouted, pointing to a faraway sign.

I pushed the car, praying for it to go faster. There were a few vehicles in front of us now. I passed them quickly on the right lane with the SUV on my tail.

The exit sign was getting closer. I moved over to the left lane.

The Porsche was taunting me, speeding ahead and slowing down like this was a game. I kept my foot down and my eyes on the road, praying for the highway to remain clear until we got off it.

"Watch that car!"

"Oh, my god!" I pulled off the accelerator. I hadn't realized how fast I'd been driving. I'd caught up to a sedan in the slow lane within seconds. Two little heads turned around and looked at me through the rear window, their eyes as round as saucers. *Kids!* It was too late to brake.

I pulled a hard right, swerved onto the highway shoulder, accelerated and got back to the road again.

Behind me, the car honked madly.

"Sorry, sorry, sorry," I whispered.

I was playing with the lives of innocent families. I had to find a safe zone. Maybe a police station. Anything to keep us away from these men. I sped up to the exit ramp and rocketed off of the highway.

David had turned around and was watching the back window, the gun in his right hand.

"They're coming after us!"

In front of us was a line of cars waiting at a stop sign.

"Oh no!"

I slammed on the brakes and screeched to a stop. I braked within milliseconds of hitting the car in front of us. Suddenly our car lurched just as the vehicle in front of us moved ahead. My head snapped forward.

"What the heck was that?"

"Those thugs bumped us."

My heart was beating like a jackhammer inside my chest. I looked at my side mirror and saw the SUV looming behind me like an ugly black monster. I prayed they wouldn't get out and try to grab us here. A panicked glance around confirmed all doors were locked and all windows were up.

How did they know we're in here? The windows are tinted. Or are these people after Chanda and not us?

"I'll keep an eye on them," said David. "Let's hope they won't do anything stupid with people around. Keep with the traffic."

"Are they after Chanda? They don't know we're in here, do they?"

But David was too occupied to answer.

"Come on, hurry, hurry!" I said, willing the vehicles in front of me to get out of the way. They were taking their sweet time, stopping to check both ways before moving along. Like they were supposed to. But they didn't have Saudi goons on their tails.

David had the gun in one hand and was watching the mirror like a hawk, his face taut. His other hand hovered over the window button, ready to open it and fire at a moment's notice.

I turned my eyes back on the road. There was only one car in front of us now. The sign in the front showed two arrows. To my left was the entrance to the highway again. To my right was a single-lane country road with fields on either side. It looked desolate.

I put my turning signal to the right. We needed every spare second we could get.

As soon as I got to the intersection, I turned a hard left and went roaring toward the highway ramp. I think I jumped over a barrier because the car went airborne and fell back with a thud on the pavement.

"Jesus Christ!" I heard David exclaim.

This car had amazing suspension. I gave a quick thank-you prayer to Chanda. We'd have been killed by now if we'd taken the rickety van.

But the SUV was not far behind.

"Faster!" I shouted at the car, pushing the accelerator all the way down. "Come on! You can do it!"

A glance at my rearview mirror told me the SUV was catching up. Soon, it was on my left, traveling at the same speed as I was.

"Keep driving!" David shouted. "I'll take care of 'em!"

That was when I noticed a second SUV on my right.

"What the hell?"

The second car was driving alongside us on the shoulder. I was flanked by both vehicles, all of us zooming at two hundred on a highway built to do a hundred kilometers an hour at best. I didn't see anyone on the road ahead, but this traffic-free zone wasn't going to last. We were coming up to another exit, another town, which meant cars, families, children.

The SUV to my right veered toward me. I tacked to the left but the SUV on the left didn't budge. They had us pinned.

The window of the Porsche to the right rolled down. A face poked out. It was one of the Saudi guards who'd driven the women to the market. He grinned lecherously. That was when I saw the barrel of a gun pointing at us.

"Hey!" I cried as the SUV to my left banged violently against us. I took my foot off the pedal and swerved, but it was too late. I'd been going too fast.

The car spun around like a top and I found myself moving the wrong way on the highway. I slammed on the brakes and swung left to avoid a car coming toward me. It passed, honking crazily as it did.

The two SUVs turned around in record time and were gunning toward us now.

I pushed on the accelerator to the floor.

We were all speeding the wrong way on the highway.

I heard the whoosh of the wind rushing in as David brought his window down.

"What the hell are you doing?" I asked.

"Keep moving!" he yelled. A loud bang made me jump. Then another. And another as David pumped bullets into the SUVs behind us.

That was when I felt our car get hit. Once. Twice.

"Get back in!" I cried.

"Don't stop!" David shouted.

I revved the car. I heard a loud crash from behind me but I didn't dare look.

"Got him!" David pulled back and brought his window up. He reached into his vest and pulled out a new magazine.

How are we still moving? Did Chanda bulletproof the heck out of her car?

'Watch out!" I screamed as a motorcycle came whizzing by. It veered at the last minute.

I scanned the road in front for cars and looked for an exit. I kept to the shoulder which slowed me down, but I didn't want to risk hitting anyone. This meant the remaining SUV could catch up soon, but I had little choice.

Next to me, David inserted the new magazine in his gun and scrambled over to the backseat.

"Keep your speed!" he yelled. "Keep driving!"

I heard the back window go down. More gunshots in rapid succession.

And that was when I saw it.

"Noo!" I screamed.

Hurtling toward us was a massive monstrosity, an eighteen-wheeler truck in the fast lane. It blasted its horn. The SUV swerved toward us. I pushed down on the accelerator and shot out of the way just as I heard a burst of gunfire.

The SUV skidded across the road. The truck blasted the horn again. I heard the screech of heavy brakes and a horrifying crash from behind me.

I couldn't look. I had to keep my eyes in front.

David pulled back in.

"Go! Go!" he yelled from the back seat. "Let's get outta here!"

I raced on the shoulder till the next exit. Then, as soon as the road was clear, I turned the wheels around and jumped through four lanes toward it.

Finally, we were off of the highway.

I brought the car to a stop on the side of the road, my heart pumping like mad, my body trembling, and my hands shaking so much, I couldn't hold on to the steering wheel any more.

I glanced quickly over at David, who was scrambling back to the front.

He plopped into his seat, panting. He wiped the sweat off his face and stared back at me, his gun still in his hands.

"We got them," he whispered. "We got the bastards."

Chapter Fifty-four

It took us half an hour to get back to Nairobi.

We drove silently, shell-shocked. I tried not to think too much about the consequences. The past hour had felt surreal, like a nightmare come to life in broad daylight.

A few people stopped to stare as we drove through the busy Nairobi streets. It took me a while to realize they were gawking at the car's bullet-ridden body. The front and back windshields were cracked, and I was sure there were golf ball-sized dents on the panels.

Whatever Chanda had done to upgrade this car, it had been spectacularly well managed. It was a miracle we survived.

Using David's directions, I followed the quieter back roads toward the scrapyard, praying we'd not bump into an inquisitive cop who'd wonder about the car. Or worse, any of the Saudi goons.

David tried to contact Luc and Peace through his earpiece as we crossed the upper end of the city where their hotel was located. But all we got was dead silence. There wasn't even a whir or a click to tell us the system was on air.

"Peace? Luc?" David called. "Where are you guys? Give us a signal, man."

He tried the girls next.

"Katy? Win? Are you there? Can anyone hear me?"

Nothing. It was like everyone had stopped talking.

"Maybe the system's down?" I said.

He leaned over and plucked the earpiece from my ear and scrutinized it, together with his.

"Jeepers, she's turned them off," he said. "Or someone's made them shut it down."

I felt that sinking in my stomach again.

"Something's very wrong," said David.

We drove in glum silence toward the scrapyard, unsure of what to expect.

David jumped out of the car before I could park. I got out, slammed the door and ran after him.

We burst through the bus doors.

"Asha!"

"Katy! Win!" I said in relief.

"Are you both okay?" asked David.

"Where were you?" Katy's voice sounded strained.

"Why did you disappear like that?" Win looked like she'd been crying.

"Why didn't you guys answer us?" asked David. "We've been trying to reach you from halfway across town."

"Luc and Peace never got out," said Katy.

"*What*?" said David.

I grabbed on to the steel bench, my legs feeling like jelly. "What do you mean they never got out?" My voice had gone hoarse all of a sudden.

"The guards pulled them out of the car just as they were going through the gate. And they took them back inside," Katy said, her voice shaking. "Happened two minutes after you left."

"They found their earpieces," Win said, "so I shut everything down."

"Where are the boys now?" asked David.

Win pointed at the largest screen. A grainy picture was showing the inside of the Saudi man's house.

I leaned in to see better. It was the same room they'd been in before, the living room with the tusks in the corners, the murals on the walls and the luxury carpeting on the floor. The entire room was visible to us now. With a shudder, I realized why. Luc and Peace were at the very back of the room looking toward the old man.

Are they tied up? Are they alive?

I could make out the Saudi sitting on his cushions. He was entertaining visitors now, three men. They were sitting with their backs to us, smoking hookah pipes and drinking coffee. Behind the old man stood the two guards carrying their scimitar swords. As I leaned in to squint at the screen, a guard looked directly at the camera and scowled. I drew back in shock.

"Can they see us?" I asked, as a cold tremor passed through me.

"Impossible," said David, shaking his head. "Those are cameras. They feed only one way. He was looking at Luc or Peace, not us."

"We can see, but we can't hear anything," said Katy.

"They've been there all the time," said Win, her voice high-pitched. Overflowing with stress.

"Both cameras stayed alive the whole time?" asked David.

"They roughed them up at the beginning," replied Katy, "but after that, they've been sitting in that room opposite the old man. For hours now."

"We don't know if the cameras are still on the boys though, do we?" I said.

Everyone looked at me.

"They could have found the cameras and placed them across the room so we'd see whatever it is they want us to see. We don't know for sure if Luc and Peace are even in the room."

Win's face went paler.

David started pacing, his arms crossed and an angry frown on his face.

"We gotta get them out," Katy said.

"And Preeti too," I said.

David stopped pacing and gave me a thoughtful look. "You know what?"

We waited.

"I got you into this mess. I'm gonna get you out."

"How are you going to do that?" I asked, narrowing my eyes.

He stretched his palm toward me.

"Car keys, please?"

I handed them over.

"Where are you going?"

"I never thought this would get this serious. We need backup now. Serious backup. At least I'm gonna try to get them to help us."

"Who?" Katy asked. "The police?"

"Better than the police."

"Can you tell us?" I said, feeling exasperated and not for the first time. "Are we on the same side or not?"

"I've risked my life for this campaign," he said. "I'm so on your side, you can't even imagine."

Katy and I exchanged glances.

He opened the door. "Don't do *anything* until I come back."

He stepped down, closing the door behind him with a click.

Chapter Fifty-five

"**S**he's coming."

Katy and I whipped our heads around.

Win was hunkered over a keyboard, typing furiously.

"What're you doing, Win?" I asked.

"Chatting."

I raised my eyebrows.

"With Tetyana."

Katy and I scrambled toward her and leaned over her shoulder.

"Where is she?" I asked.

"Dar Es Salaam," Win replied, not looking up. "She just landed."

"How'd you know?" asked Katy.

"She emailed me."

"That's an empty inbox," I said, pointing at the side window which showed zero messages.

"That's 'cuz we delete messages after reading. That way, no one can find out what we said to each other."

"Does she know where we are?" Katy asked.

"I gave her our coordinates in the last email. I know David doesn't want us to tell anyone anything, but I told her everything." Win gave us a stubborn look. "We need her."

I nodded. *That much is true.* I squeezed her shoulder.

"Atta girl. You did the right thing. We couldn't have come this far without you."

"But that doesn't get Luc out," she said, her voice cracking. "And Peace."

"We'll find a way, honey," I said, my brain whirling, trying to think of rescue ideas. I had no idea what David was up to. I trusted him more than before now, but I didn't like how cagey he was. I also didn't know how long it would take for Tetyana to get here, or if she could at all.

"You said we need to rescue Preeti," Katy said. "Is she inside?"

I nodded. "I saw her at the market. She saw me too but ran back to the Saudi women. Maybe she was drugged or something. I couldn't do anything."

"Stockholm syndrome?"

"Don't know. Maybe she was scared they'd shoot her."

"We saw them come back," said Win.

"You saw Preeti?"

"The women and the three girls," said Win. "We don't know what Preeti looks like."

"Did they...did they do anything to the girls?" I asked haltingly, unsure if I wanted to hear the answer.

"Like what?" asked Win.

Like shoot them in the head. But I couldn't get those words out.

"They just walked back into the small house, carrying their baskets," said Katy, pointing to the screen that showed the women's quarters.

It was quiet inside the compound. I turned to the first screen, which showed the old man's living room.

"Who are these men?"

"They never looked this way and they're sitting far away, so it's hard to say," said Katy. "But you know what? I can't help feeling..."

She stopped and stared at the screen, chewing her lower lip.

"What?"

She shook her head. "Maybe it's my imagination, but that guy," she said, pointing to the man in the middle, "he looks familiar."

"Can we get a better view?" I asked Win.

"When I try to zoom, everything gets totally fuzzy. Those pen cameras are super tiny. I'm surprised we can see them at all."

I squinted at the blurry image.

"It's the way he moves," said Katy. "It's a funny feeling."

"I don't think I've seen him before." I got closer to the screen. "No, wait. You're right, Katy. The other two look vaguely familiar to me too. Or is it my imagination?"

We watched them for a while. They were in deep conversation, nodding, gesturing, drinking coffee. It could have been a bunch of regular middle-aged men having a meeting, if we'd not known what the old Saudi was up to.

"Hey!" Win said, pointing at the screen that was showing the women's quarters.

Katy and I gathered around her.

"That just came in."

A black SUV drove in and parked next to the women's house.

Didn't we just ruin two of them? How many of these SUVs do they have?

We watched as two men got out of the vehicle. One of them opened the back hatch and pulled something heavy out.

Oh no!

It was a girl, no, a woman, with her hands tied behind her back. She stumbled out.

"Chanda!" I screamed.

I turned around and ran to the door, before Katy caught me and pulled me back.

"What the heck are you doing?"

"They're gonna kill her! You think I'm going to sit here and watch while they assassinate her?"

"We don't know that—"

"Yes, I do! These goons followed us. We took Chanda's car back to town and they shot at it, so I'm sure they don't want her to live!"

Katy let go of me, her face pale. "They shot at you?"

Win was staring at me from her perch at the bench.

"Chanda's saving some of the kidnapped kids and she takes them to a secret orphanage," I spluttered, trying to explain. "She's being doing this for years. I think the company figured it out. They followed us to the orphanage."

Katy and Win listened with shocked expressions on their faces.

I looked at the screen desperately. "Where's she now?"

"They took her to the back," Win said, pointing at the women's quarters. "Maybe they put her with Luc and Peace."

Katy's eyes flared at the mention of Peace.

"I'm going in," I said.

"It's a suicide mission," Win whispered to herself, but I heard her.

"A rescue mission," I said, correcting her.

"Whatever," Katy replied, her eyes flashing. "But you're nuts if you think I'm letting you go by yourself."

Chapter Fifty-six

Katy pushed the intercom button.

We waited.

We were standing in front of the white cement wall that wrapped around the Saudi compound. It had looked much smaller on screen. Right now, as I stood in front of it, my heart beating like mad, I felt like I was trying to penetrate Fort Knox.

I glanced nervously at Katy. *Thank goodness, Win's not here with us.* She was watching from the safety of the bus.

I wondered where Luc and Peace were being held now. I prayed they were alive here, somewhere together with Chanda.

A small door next to the gate creaked open and an Arab man poked his head out, startling us.

It was the same man who'd pulled Chanda out of the SUV. Like the other guards, he carried his curved sword dangling from his belt.

He frowned when he saw us.

"What you want?" he snarled in Swahili.

I gave him my most professional smile. "Good afternoon, we're here to cater for your festival celebrations," I replied in English.

He took a startled step back.

We had cleaned up in the washroom at the back of the bus. We didn't have many options and even less time. All I knew was I had to do something drastic when the men pulled Chanda behind the women's quarters, leading her like an animal to slaughter.

Katy, Win and I all had skin in the game now. We worked quickly, trying to figure out the best way to penetrate the compound and get to our friends.

I remembered David telling me he had a hamper of clothes in the back somewhere, and that was what Katy and I rooted through. Using the medical personnel uniforms, police shirts and matching caps that vaguely reminded me of those worn by the Indian airport agents, we'd concocted something that looked like semi-professional catering cum delivery people. It wasn't perfect, but it was better than our dusty cargo pants and T-shirts.

While Katy and I had been making ourselves more presentable, Win had prepared a new tablet with a fake website full of mouthwatering images of sumptuous desserts of all kinds. The camera and mic on the tablet had been turned on and were now sending audio and video footage back to the Mother Ship, as Win had dubbed the bus.

The man looked us over with squinted eyes, lingering over Katy's red curls strategically placed in front so they cascaded down toward her waist. There weren't too many redheads in this region. She was a rarity. There were, however, many families who'd relocated from India to East Africa, so my looks weren't a major distraction. Between Katy's hair, my American accent and our new uniforms, we'd find a way in. Or so I hoped.

I crossed my fingers.

"Your madame invited us to deliver French cakes next week," Katy said, with her bright smile that could charm anyone. "We'd love to speak with the ladies to find out exactly what they're looking for."

His eyes traveled down our clothes. He looked confused, clearly unsure where to place us.

We weren't covered up the way women in his tribe were supposed to be. We spoke English. And we were talking to him directly, making eye contact—something the women here would not dare do. Coming from a place where women walked seven steps behind men and knew their place, we were probably as outlandish as aliens from another planet.

"Haven't you seen us? We were on TV," said Katy sweetly. "We're known for our European pastries." She pointed at our red shoes. "We're the famous Red-Heeled Rebels."

"Rebels?" He raised his eyebrows.

"No, no," I shook my head, "not rebels from the desert. We're from New York."

He looked at us with renewed interest. "New York?"

"Absolutely," I said with a fake smile.

His eyes wavered behind us. "Your car?"

"Oh, our chauffeur dropped us," said Katy, waving her arm grandiosely. "He'll be coming to pick us up in half an hour."

"Who told you to come?"

"We were invited by the wife," I said.

"Which wife?"

"The youngest one. She wanted to surprise their husband with some delicious foreign sweets this year."

"They won't be disappointed," Katy said, flipping her hair back and jutting her chest out. She gave him a sexy pout. "And I believe you won't be disappointed either."

The man gawked at her.

Katy and I had gained several inches around our busts. It served two purposes. One to distract these men if the need arose, and second, to hide our guns. The Kevlar vests we had on underneath had pockets in exactly the right places, so they did double-duty.

The man's eyes traveled over Katy's bosom. I could tell she was struggling to keep from looking repulsed, but he wasn't paying any attention to her face. He licked his lips. I tried not to cringe.

"And if you want," Katy said in a husky voice as she stepped closer to him, "you might get some extra sweets from me."

The man visibly quivered in pleasure. "Very nice," he said, nodding lewdly. "Very nice."

I felt like throwing up.

"Shall we?" said Katy, boldly taking another step toward him, toward the door.

Careful, Katy.

With a creepy grin, the man pulled the door open, his eyes firmly on her chest.

She flicked her hair and walked in with an extra swing to her hips, brushing past him. I squeezed in behind her, trying to not touch the man who'd positioned himself so we had no choice but to do so.

When we were both in, he slammed the door behind us and locked it.

"There is wifes," he said, pointing at the smallest house in the compound.

I nodded. "Thank you."

"I'll see you soon," said Katy with a smile that could have melted steel.

I glanced around me, feeling a strange sense of déjà vu. I'd seen the layout of this compound so often it was like stepping into a place I'd been to before.

We walked up to the house he'd pointed to. There were no gardens or flowers here, just a dusty yard with bland concrete buildings.

We could hear women's voices coming from somewhere inside the small house.

"Hey, be careful with that Neanderthal," I whispered to Katy as we stepped up to the door.

"Don't worry. If he tries anything, I'm shooting him right between the eyes."

The door opened before we could knock. Two young boys, ten years old or so, ran out pushing us out of their way, hooting and hollering as they did so. One rudely stuck his tongue out at me before racing out to the yard. They didn't seem fazed to see two strange-looking women standing at the threshold of their home.

We peeked inside.

We were looking into an open kitchen and living area of sorts. The place was in chaos, smelly, messy. A half a dozen children ranging from two to nine in various stages of undress were whining, yelling and running around.

Two heavily made-up women, dressed in gaudy Western dresses and heels, were in the kitchen screaming at a servant girl. An obese middle-aged woman sat sunk in a large armchair, glued to a television screen. Her robe lay carelessly at her feet, looking like an ugly black puddle.

My eyes scanned the room. *Where's Preeti?*

At the stove was a young girl. She didn't look our way, too busy trying to reach an empty iron skillet on the far end of the stove. She was on her tiptoes. *How old is she? Twelve?*

In the other corner, where the sinks were, stood another girl. I'd seen her before in the old man's living room. She gave me a scared look before bowing her head to continue cleaning a pot that was almost as big as her.

Servants, I thought. *No, slaves.* What difference did it make anyway? They were trapped in a lifetime of bondage, kept down by tradition, greed or both, doing menial work that others didn't want to do or were too lazy to.

One of the kids raced by the servant girl screaming at the top of his lungs. He reached out to her as he ran by, pulling on her hair. The girl doubled over and dropped her soap on the floor. And that cost her.

With a banshee-like wail, one of the women marched over to her, her hand raised. The girl cowered. Before we knew it, the woman gave an ear-splitting whack across the girl's face.

I recoiled in horror. Katy drew her breath in sharply.

Sobbing, the girl bent to pick up the soap with trembling hands.

Still shouting, the woman pulled the hot skillet from the stove and held it up to slam it on the girl.

No!

"Oi!" I yelled without thinking.

Everyone stopped where they were and turned around.

"Hi there!" Katy said with a wide, fake smile. "How are y'all doing?"

They stared at us openmouthed.

"Who you?"

It was the youngest of the wives. She could have been seventeen at the most.

"We're here to bring you French cakes and sweets and desserts of all kinds," Katy said in her happy voice. "For your festival celebrations!"

The younger wife called out something in Arabic to the other women.

"Would you like to see our menu?" Katy asked. She turned on the tablet and stepped toward the youngest wife.

The woman's eyes grew wide as photos of mouthwatering desserts dazzled their way across the screen.

"Look at all these beautiful, delicious treats," Katy said, scrolling through cakes, flans, pies, pastries and sweets of all kinds, decorated to the hilt. "They don't have too many calories either. You can eat these and still look skinny like all the beautiful French girls. It's magical!"

"Hai!" the youngest wife exclaimed excitedly. "I want!"

The two other women walked over to see what they were missing. The older woman turned to glance at us, and with a warthog-like grunt turned back to her television.

"So many cakes. You just have to pick what you love," Katy said, in a singsong voice. "All for you."

"For me?" squealed the youngest wife, snatching the tablet from Katy's hands.

"No, for me!" cried another wife, grabbing the tablet and walking with it to the kitchen island. The younger woman cried out in protest, but the other woman ignored her.

At least they've forgotten all about the girl, I thought in relief.

The two slave girls kept working, bent over their duties, not daring to look up.

The three wives were crowded around our tablet on the kitchen counter, jostling each other, exclaiming loudly as they scrolled through the photos, while their children pulled at their skirts, trying to see what the fuss was about.

While they abhorred Western culture, we knew they loved Western goods, especially luxury items. It was all the rave in the Middle East.

While Katy and I had been busy putting our disguise together, Win had made the site as enticing as possible, gratuitously adding blonde women swathed in extravagant gowns in between the pastries to give that exotic flavor. One thing was for sure. When it came to technology and design, Win was a miracle maker.

"We can bring each of you a cake." Katy's voice was dripping in syrup. "Which ones do you like the best?"

They ignored her.

Katy and I glanced at each other.

We hadn't had much time to plan our foray. The hardest part, we'd thought, was to get inside the compound. Now we were inside, we had to figure out what do next.

I looked around the house. A passageway led out of the kitchen to what looked like bedrooms. I tried to think. If Katy could keep the attention of these women, I could slip out and look for Preeti, Chanda and the boys.

My eyes fell on the black robe lying at the feet of the older woman. The television was still on but the woman was dozing now, eyes half-closed, spittle forming on one side of her mouth.

I took a quiet step toward the old woman, my eyes moving between her and the robe.

Someone thundered on the door.

I jumped.

I whirled around to see Katy reaching into her top toward her weapon. I did the same.

The door burst open and the guard who'd let us in now stood at the doorway, his sword drawn. In his other hand, he held a pistol, pointed directly at Katy and me.

The house erupted. The women shrieked and screeched.

"You!" the man shouted. "Out!"

The older woman sat up, suddenly awake. With a few sharp words she shut the other wives up, and made them run and put their robes on. She turned to the man at the door and said something.

Katy and I stood side by side, hands ready to draw.

I had to think fast. There was no way we were going to get to our weapons before he jumped on us, slashing us or worse, shooting us point-blank. Plus, if we were going to have a bloody battle, we needed to get away from the kids.

"Out!" he growled at us. "Get out!"

Chapter Fifty-seven

The man kicked me in the calf as I stepped out of the house.

Katy and I walked in front of him, our hands in the air.

He pushed us along the pathway that led to the main house at the other end of the compound. I was glad we'd thought of placing mini backup cameras on our shirts. If we hadn't, with the tablet now in the women's quarters, we'd have lost all contact with Win.

"That way!" he shouted as we came across a fork in the path.

I felt the end of the scimitar on my back. I stumbled but straightened up quickly.

I turned to the right as instructed, holding my head up and keeping my back straight. My breath was coming fast and shallow, but one thing kept rolling in my mind. *If I'm gonna die today, I'm going to die standing up.*

We followed the path around the women's quarters and toward the man's larger house.

We'd just turned around the corner when I heard a gasp from Katy.

I stopped.

The man swore.

Blood drained from my face.

"Chanda?" I barely whispered.

"Go!" A knife prodded my back.

But I didn't move. I couldn't.

In front of the old man's house was an open patch of bare ground. In the middle of that was a stake about six foot tall. Tied to the stake with her hands behind her back was my childhood best friend. Chanda was still wearing her white suit, but it was torn and soiled, stained with dust and mud, like she'd been dragged along the ground. She looked pale, exhausted.

She turned and looked my way, her eyes watery with pain.

"Chanda!" I cried out.

"Go!" The knife jabbed me. A searing pain went through my back. I careened forward, almost falling on my face. I pulled myself upright just in time.

"Master waiting!"

Katy and I lurched toward the main door. I gave Chanda one last desperate glance before stepping inside the house.

The man pushed us through a metal barrier. I was sure Katy and I were going to set off all the alarms with our guns, but nothing happened.

I gave a silent prayer to David. I still didn't know who he really was, who he worked for or where he got this equipment from, but for the moment I was glad we had access to his stuff.

We walked through the same long corridor Peace and Luc had walked through earlier.

This was a palace compared to the women's dingy quarters. Fancy light fixtures and oriental paintings lined the walls. The floor was covered in a beautiful patterned rug.

The role of women in this compound was clear. They were nothing more than baby-making machines who managed the slaves. And it was the slaves who did the heavy work from cooking, to cleaning to probably even pleasuring the men. This compound revolved around the men. Women were insignificant chattel. For a moment, I wondered which century I'd time traveled to.

The closer we got to the end of the corridor, the faster my heart beat.

Are Luc and Peace in here? Are they okay? Oh, god, please let them be alive.

I gave Katy a side glance.

Her face was flushed but stony. If there was one thing I knew about Katy, it was you never push her into a corner. That was when she turned into a roaring lioness. *Good,* I thought summoning my own Kali from within me. *We need all the ferocity we can muster.*

When we got to the end of the corridor, the guard pushed us into the old man's chambers. It looked even more luxurious in real life. And sitting comfortably in the middle of all his opulence was the Saudi.

He looked bigger and fatter than I remembered. A hookah pipe and a tray of small coffee cups were next to him. The three men we'd seen on camera were seated in front of him. Their heads were bowed down, intently watching or reading something on the rug.

I peeked behind me quickly.

Peace! Luc!

At the other end of the room were the boys. They were kneeling on the ground, backs against the wall, their hands tied behind them and their mouths gagged. But they were very much alive.

It wasn't by accident the pen cameras weren't removed from their pockets. They'd been strategically placed so we'd see what was going on, so we'd come to rescue them, so they could capture us too.

"Peace!" Katy called out. "Oh, my god!"

The boys looked at us in shock.

A hyena-like laugh made me swivel around.

To my horror, seated among the piles of cushions were three men I never thought I'd see again.

First was Franky with his sickly smile. Next to him was Jose. His gentlemanly façade pulled away to reveal his predator mask, his face set in a sneer as he regarded us. But he was wounded now, his arms and face covered in bruises. I wondered who did that to him. Too bad they hadn't finished him.

In the far end sat Charles Dubois himself, Sophie's father, the head of Boko Mines, hunched over. With trembling hands, he adjusted his glasses and squinted at us through his bushy white eyebrows.

How did they all get here? How do they all know each other?

"Ah, Mohamed, you brought in new guests, I see," said the Saudi, his bulgy head making him look even more like an ugly toad. The man who'd pushed us in here, bowed to his master and moved to the side, sword still in hand.

Behind the old Saudi stood two more guards with savage expressions on their faces, their brutal scimitars dangling from their belts. *I'd rather be shot than be chopped by those knives.* I shuddered.

"You thought you could get away with your silly little girls' game, didn't you?" the Saudi asked, his eyes boring into mine.

I glared back.

"You look familiar," said Sophie's father, searching my face. "I never forget a face. We've met before, somewhere. I am sure."

"Daddy, who are you all talking to?"

Katy and I gave a start.

Sophie?

"Seems like we have guests, *ma cherie.*"

Where is she?

"Can you turn me around so I can see?" said Sophie's voice, slightly electronic.

"*Quoi? Ma cherie?*" Charles asked, looking down at the laptop.

"Lift me up!"

With trembling hands, her father picked up the laptop and put it on his lap.

"Daddy, you need to turn me around!"

The old man looked confused.

"And higher!"

Jose leaned over and took the laptop from the man. He settled it on a pile of cushions and turned it around with a pompous expression on his face.

I looked at the laptop, flabbergasted. Sophie's pink-lipsticked face filled the screen.

What's she doing here?

She let out a loud cackle when she saw Katy and me. "So you found them, then? I'll need to give the boys a raise."

So, she was the one who sent those goons to follow us to Chanda's orphanage. *Well, they're dead,* I thought with a smidgen of satisfaction. Crushed under a truck, on the highway.

Another cackle. "Too bad I can't be there. I'd have loved to see your face close up when you saw everyone here."

I glared at the screen.

Sophie beamed back.

So you thought Chanda was the head of the company?"

"What have you done to her?" I spat out.

"Only what's due to her. I've been suspecting her but I could never track her. But today, you helped us. Thank you, you guys were really great."

The image of the children running to hug Chanda at the orphanage burst into mind. *Oh, my god. Did they get away in time? What have I done?*

Sophie's smile widened at my reaction.

"Chanda's a secretary Daddy uses on and off. A glorified prostitute, really. The company belongs to me and Daddy. Well, his team does all the work, but I own everything. I loved that you believed my little story. I'm such a good actress, I'm thinking Hollywood is next." She giggled.

Someone called her off screen. She nodded to them and turned back.

"I'd totally love to join you all, but I gotta go. There's a big celebrity party in Jo'burg and I don't wanna be late. Daddy, I'm taking the Beech jet this weekend. Tell me all about it all on Monday."

"Ca va, ma cherie," nodded her father, who'd been listening to the conversation doubled up, his ear almost touching the laptop.

Sophie's smile vanished and her face turned hard.

"Asha," she said, her eyes piercing through the screen, "I always thought you were a loser. Daddy did the right thing to get rid of your parents. They never deserved to live and you don't either."

With that, the screen went blank.

Chapter Fifty-eight

The Saudi man picked up his cup and settled back with a sordid smile.

"So you are the ringleader of this little boys and girls club then?" he said with a sneer.

We were in his territory now. He had the men, the weapons and my friends hostage. We were outgunned in every way, but I wasn't going to make this easy for him.

"I'm not here to play games," I said, glaring at him. "I'm here to take my friends home."

The men laughed.

"How naive," said the Saudi.

A quick movement in the back of the room caught my eye. A slave girl was walking in with a fresh pot of coffee or tea in her hands. It was the girl from the kitchen, the one who almost got hit with a hot iron skillet. She kept her eyes down.

"You thought you could get away from us that easily, haa?" I heard Franky say with a snort.

Jose laughed out loud.

I turned back to the men.

The Saudi was shaking his head. "Don't think we can't track anyone down."

"Ah yes, that much is true," said Charles, who had one hand cupped to an ear now. He gave me a grandfatherly smile. I felt sick to my stomach just to be in the same room as this man who'd given the order to kill my parents.

"We may disagree in some aspects and we may compete with each other, but we're connected across the world, more than the United Nations," he said.

"Better than even INTERPOL and the FBI," Franky said with a sly smile, his head nodding sideways, Indian style.

"Do you think we're stupid?" asked the Saudi, his eyes flashing in anger. "A quick call to Fred was all I needed."

I felt a chill go down my back.

"He told me some very interesting stories," said the Saudi, glancing behind us at Luc and Peace. "About all of you."

While we were talking, the slave girl had quietly filled everyone's cups and was now leaving the room. Just before she disappeared through the heavy curtains in the back, she gave me a quick glance and an odd gesture from her hand before leaving. *Was that a wave? Or some sort of signal?*

I turned my attention back to the men.

"I've heard some interesting things about you too," I replied, straightening my back and crossing my arms.

"Oh, is that so?" The Saudi raised his eyebrows and glowered.

I stared back, thinking only of what I'd like to do to him for what he'd done to Chanda and Preeti.

"Tell me," he said, leaning forward, "who do you work for?"

I didn't reply.

"You can't lie to us," said Jose, with an amused look on his face. "We'll get to the truth one way or the other."

"You're nothing but scum," I heard Katy say next to me, her voice low but furious. "Sick, pond scum."

Good for you, girl.

I kept my gaze steady.

Jose stared at Katy.

I could feel the fury emanating from her as she glared right back—back at the man she'd thought she loved, but who had betrayed her in the most unspeakable way.

"We were told large sums of money are being depleted from Zero and Vlad's accounts," the Saudi said, watching me carefully.

My heart jumped but I kept my face straight.

"The money was tracked to places that correspond to where you were. Now, was that a coincidence?"

I gave him a blank look. I was thankful Win was out of harm's way, still in the bus, safe and sound.

"Answer me, woman!" he roared, making everyone in the room jump. "I'm more powerful than you foreign rats can even imagine."

"I'm sure you are," Katy said.

"Shut up, you vulgar woman, or I'll thrash you to death!" The Saudi hurled his cup across the room. "I said, who do you work for?"

"No one," I replied, trying to look as calm as I could, though it felt like a tornado was whirling inside of me.

He spat on the ground. Jose had stopped leering at Katy and was giving me a nasty look now.

Behind them, I caught sight of two dark eyes peeking from behind the curtains. *Is that the slave girl again?*

"You say you work for FBI," said Franky, giving me an accusing look.

I remained silent. I never said such a thing. It was his imagination that gave him that impression, and I was not about to clarify anything for him.

The Saudi man's face flushed red, his lips contorting into a snarl. "You're not getting out of here alive," he growled.

"I'm not afraid of you," I said, keeping my face straight. "Or of dying."

I knew they were not above torture. The image of Chanda tied in the yard haunted me, but I wasn't going out like a coward.

"Stupid women," said Franky, "think they're men. Women must shut up and stay in the kitchen. That is what I say."

The Saudi sighed. "This is what happens when you give women a Western education," he said with a sniff. "That's why I keep mine locked up in the back and beat them when they don't behave."

"Well," said Charles, clearing his throat. "I think women can be just as good if not better at some things. Look at my dear Sophie now. She's the most intelligent woman I know. Even smarter than all of you, I would say."

The Saudi and Franky shot him annoyed looks.

Charles sat up. "Look, messieurs, I'm afraid I don't have time to sit and talk about these interesting cultural insights with you. I am too old for these lengthy meetings. Can we finish with this business so I can get back home?"

"Yes, let's finish this business right now."

When I turned back to the Saudi, I found myself staring down the barrel of a gold-plated revolver.

"I can shoot you in your head." He laughed crudely, brandishing his fancy gun my way. "Or right in your heart."

I stared at the weapon. I had my own tucked under my shirt, but by the time I could get to it, I'd be dead. It was a miracle the guards hadn't physically searched Katy and I and found what we were carrying concealed, but they probably didn't expect girls to carry firearms.

I kept my eyes on the Saudi, steady and firm. Something about this place and that gun didn't make me feel as frightened as I should have been.

If someone had pulled a gun on me two years ago, I'd have caved right in. But now, after fighting for my life more than once, and getting so close to reclaiming the two people I'd been desperate to find most of my adult life, that weapon pointing at me only made me feel stronger.

It was peculiar, but I felt at peace. I'd made mistakes, yet I'd done everything in my power to right my wrongs and help those who needed me. Though I hadn't been successful, I'd done my best.

I quickly scanned the room. Charles was peering at me through his bushy eyebrows, trying to follow along, but it was Franky and

Jose who caught my attention. I could see through their smirks. They were worried. No, anxious.

That was when I realized. They could have easily finished Katy and me the moment we'd entered the compound. We didn't need to have this nonsensical, elaborate discussion. The Saudi man's finger wasn't even on the trigger.

There's a reason Peace and Luc are still alive. They think we work for someone powerful, a rival gang who's stealing their money. That's the only reason we're having this conversation.

I felt a steel thread work its way up my spine, strengthening me. Kali was still inside of me, alive and kicking, stronger than ever. As much as I hated her frightening and violent side, she gave me so much strength. I took a deep breath and called on her.

I uncrossed my arms and took a step toward the Saudi, looking him in the eyes. He flinched as I came close. I took another.

"If you let my friends go and promise to never follow or contact them again, I will stay and give you all the information you need."

I heard Katy give a small gasp from behind me.

I didn't take my eyes off the man. "That includes Chanda, who's tied outside. And all the slaves in this compound."

He stared.

"They get out safely and I'll talk."

No one said anything for a while.

It was Franky who broke the spell. He laughed out loud, a hollow laugh. Jose grinned but I could see the glint of worry in his eyes. He knew what we were capable of. In another life, in another place, we'd outsmarted him. I was sure he remembered.

"My goodness gracious. You bargain hard," said Charles, who'd scooted closer to me so he could hear.

The Saudi man's eyes flared. It was a brief reaction but I didn't miss it.

"Go ahead," I said. "Take me down and you won't learn a thing. Not about the money. Not about our connections."

I waved my hand toward Katy and the boys in the back. "They can't tell you anything because they don't know. They're helping *me*."

The Saudi glared at me for a full minute, his expression a mixture of hatred, curiosity, outrage. He looked like he was about to explode.

"Throw them in the well!" he yelled.

Chapter Fifty-nine

I was plunged into pitch darkness.

At the Saudi man's command, the guards had whipped out their swords and descended on us like a pack of wolves.

They'd pulled us out of the room, pushing Peace and Luc behind us. I'd expected them to take us outside to the grounds where Chanda was tied up. But instead, they'd forced us through a door, halfway along the corridor.

They kicked me inside first, followed by the others.

I stood petrified, my heart hammering, trying hard to breathe.

"What in god's name—?" I heard Katy exclaim as the steel doors slammed behind us.

"Mmmm..."

"Luc?"

"Mmmm..." Luc replied, in a high-pitched tone now.

They're tied up!

"Let's free the boys," I said.

I groped through the dark.

"Where are you guys?"

I touched someone.

"Is that you, Luc?"

"Mmmm...."

I pulled him over and felt for his hands. It took several tries to untie them in the dark. My own hands were shaking. Whoever had bound him had done a good job, plus they had had light to see. I didn't.

"Merci," Luc said breathlessly after I tore the gag off his mouth.

"Thanks, Katy," I heard Peace say from somewhere in the back.

"You guys okay?" I asked.

"I was sure he was going to *shoot* you." Peace's voice came through the darkness.

"I thought he was gonna cut your head off," said Luc.

"Did they lock us in?" Katy asked.

Someone rattled the door.

"Let me try," I heard Peace say.

More rattling.

"Pressure tight," said Peace.

"What *is* this place?" Katy asked.

"He said a *well*, but this is a corridor," said Luc. I heard his hands sliding across the wall. "Small enough for only two of us to stand side by side."

I reached over and touched the wall next to me. It was made of stainless steel, or so it seemed, smooth and cold, like the doors of a refrigerator.

"What do we do?" Katy asked.

Suddenly, I felt a wisp of fresh air from somewhere in front of me. No, from below.

"I think it opens this way," I said, taking a step forward, holding my hands out in front of me.

"Didn't that dude say a *well*?" Luc asked. "Better be care—"

I stumbled. "Oh!"

Someone grabbed my shirt.

"Watch it!" I heard Katy call out from behind me.

"Steps," I said. "Steps going down."

I cautiously reached out with the tip of my toes.

"Could be a trap," Luc said. "Or a hole."

I stepped down.

"What are you doing, Asha?" I heard Peace from the back.

"There's a staircase here," I called out. "Trying to see where it goes."

"Wait!" I heard Peace say, then the rustle of feet and shuffling behind me. Someone pulled on my shirt.

"Hey!" I said, startled.

"It's me," said Peace. "I've got you."

"And I got you, man," I heard Luc say.

"And I'm holding on to you, Luc," Katy said.

Great. Now if I go down, they'll all come tumbling with me.

I stepped down once, twice, and three times, feeling every inch of the way, keeping all my senses alert to anything that would indicate an abyss below.

The stairway spiraled down. The walls grew narrower and narrower until only one of us could walk through. The darkness and the tight space made me dizzy and claustrophobic.

After a minute, my eyes slowly adjusted to the darkness. I could see the silhouettes of my friends if I looked behind, but I couldn't see much else.

Step by step, we made our way down, with me counting each step out loud.

I got to the thirtieth step and felt around with my foot. The floor was flat.

"Guys, I think we're at the bottom," I called out.

"Careful," Peace said. "Could be a hole or trap anywhere here. Walk slowly."

We were three stories below ground. *What would they have here?*

I felt my way around the darkness, hearing the rustle of the others moving as well.

"It's a small room," said Luc.

"An entranceway," said Katy.

"To what?" I asked.

"Hey," called out Peace, "found something."

I stepped up to his voice.

"Here," he said, feeling for my hand and sliding it along the wall.

I felt a small, smooth, round object. It was cold to the touch.

"A door!"

I turned the doorknob slowly.

"Stop!" whispered Katy.

I froze.

"There's something in there," she said. "Or someone."

We stood silently next to the door, leaning in, not daring to breathe.

"I don't hear—" whispered Luc.

"Shh…" said Peace.

"Someone's crying," I said.

"An animal?" Katy whispered.

We waited for a few minutes, our ears pressed against the cold steel door.

"Footsteps," I whispered. "It's a person."

"I'm going in," I said.

"What?" Katy said.

"Unless you want to stay stuck in this place forever?"

No one replied.

I took that as a no.

"Asha," I heard Katy whisper urgently. "Your gun!"

I reached under my shirt and felt for my pistol and pulled it out.

"Stay back," I whispered before turning the knob.

I opened the door gingerly, pointing my weapon forward.

A single beam of light slipped through the crack. I tried another inch. More light streamed out. The sounds from the other side had stopped. I opened the door a few more inches and peeked in.

"Oh!" I said in shock and yanked open the door.

"Oh, my god!" Katy cried out.

Chapter Sixty

F ive girls huddled in a corner, on a bed of straw and dirty blankets. They must have been barely twelve or thirteen years old.

"What the hell?" said Luc.

I lowered my gun.

They withdrew into their corner, looking terrified. They were wearing torn shorts and T-shirts. They had bruises on their faces and their hair was matted like they hadn't had a wash in days, if not weeks. Next to their bed of straw was a bucket from which a foul stench was coming. I tried not to gag.

A single naked light bulb hung from the middle of the ceiling, the only light in the vicinity. The room was not more than twenty feet by twenty feet. The walls were built with stainless steel. It was like we were inside an oversized freezer compartment. A draft of cool air was coming from somewhere nearby, making it just bearable.

"So, this is the well," said Luc, staring at the girls.

I put my gun back in my holster and crouched down, hoping I didn't look intimidating. For a split-second, I got a flashback from India, when I'd tried to reassure the little girl in Kristadasa's room.

"Hey," I whispered at the girls. With a fearful glance at me, one girl pulled a blanket over herself.

Katy and Peace came over and knelt next to me.

I glanced behind to see Luc still standing at the threshold. He had placed himself against the doorframe and was watching the stairway. He saw me look.

"I'm staying right here," he said. "In case anyone decides to come down."

I turned back to the children. They looked like animals in a zoo. I wondered how long they'd been here.

They were staring back at us now, with more curiosity than fear. One of them leaned forward to get a better look at us. *We don't look like the men who ordinarily come down here*, I thought with a cold shiver.

"Hey guys," Luc called out in a low voice.

I whipped around.

"Do you hear that?" he whispered.

We listened.

"Up there," he said, pointing.

Katy, Peace and I got up and tiptoed toward the door and strained to listen.

A faint rustle from the stairway.

There," said Luc in a whisper.

I pulled my gun out. Katy already had hers in her hands.

Peace and Luc had lost their knives during the initial search, but I wondered what use knives would be anyway against those murderous scimitars and who-knew-what-else those men kept under their robes.

We turned to watch the stairs. There was someone up there fiddling with something. Whoever it was seemed to be trying to keep quiet, but not successfully.

I tiptoed out of the room and positioned myself in front of Luc. Katy followed me. We knelt down and trained our guns at the dark stairwell.

Is it a guard with his curved sword? Is it Franky, Jose or one of the other men?

Suddenly, two small sandal-clad feet appeared on the highest step visible to us. They stopped moving as if feeling our presence. The feet were brown, scarred and dirty. On one ankle was a silver bracelet—

"Preeti?"

The feet took one step down and stopped. Then another. And another. Then, a small, brown face dipped down to look at us.

I dropped my weapon with a clatter.

"Oh my god, Preeti!" I jumped up toward her.

She stepped back in alarm at my sudden move.

I stopped. "It's okay." I backed away slowly. "It's okay. It's me. Asha."

Preeti climbed down, one step at a time, her eyes flitting from one person to the other. She'd never met Peace or Luc or Katy.

I stopped breathing and waited patiently, not daring to make a move in case she ran away again.

She got to the last step, stopped and stared at me with those big dark eyes. She looked so emaciated. A pang of sadness mixed with joy burst inside me. This was my cousin who'd patiently taught me my father's language. We'd walked to school together, played together, laughed together. She was the only family I had left on this earth. Tears streamed down my cheeks.

"I've been waiting so long to see you again," I said in a trembling voice. Suddenly, I felt like the world collapsed around me. I fell to the ground sobbing. "I'm so sorry, Preeti. I'm so sorry for everything."

I felt my cousin's thin arms around me. I pulled her in and hugged her close, crying into her shoulder, not wanting to let go of her.

I don't know how long we sat on the floor like that. Preeti hadn't said a word, but her closeness meant everything. *She recognizes me. She knows I came for her.* That was all that mattered.

"Guys!"

"Asha!"

I looked up.

"Someone's opened the door," said Peace.

He was right. This time, there was no stumbling.

People were yelling in Arabic, shouting.

Preeti shot me a frightened look. I stood up, picked up my sidearm from the floor and took position in front of her.

"Stay inside," I said to her, pointing at the room. "It's safer."

Katy and I trained our guns on the stairs once again. The boys flanked us. I was glad Peace was with us. His decades of Krav Maga training might come in use, after all. We stood close together, blocking the entrance to the room where the children and Preeti were.

More yelling upstairs.

Then, it sounded like a troop of soldiers were stomping down the stairs.

I kept my gun steady, pointing up, ready for whatever was coming down.

Chapter Sixty-one

A powerful strobe light panned the stairwell.

I blinked. I wanted to shoot, but I couldn't see to aim.

"Ah! So nice to see you again."

It was Franky's voice. He slanted the torch downward so we could see him.

Franky and Jose were standing in front of us with nasty grins on their faces. This time, they meant business. Jose was pointing an AK-47 machine gun right at us.

"We have some catchup to do now, don't we?" said Jose, leering at Katy.

"Our good Saudi friend said to come down and persuade you," Franky said, baring his yellow hyena teeth.

I watched him warily.

"You can first please put your playthings away," he said, giving my handgun a contemptuous look.

I didn't move.

Franky flashed a grin at me. "When did you learn to play with those anyway, haa? I thought you were just a little baker."

I knew all Jose had to do was pull the trigger and he'd mow us all down within seconds.

"The last time you came to my office in Goa, didn't you say you bake cakes to pay for your air tickets? Ha ha!"

We held our stance.

"Put your guns down, you stupid girls," Jose said, his face turning hard.

"Do as he say and nobody get hurt," Franky said, nodding amiably.

"What do you want?" I snapped, keeping my position.

Franky's eyes widened. "You're such a street mutt, you think you're not scared of anything, ha?"

I glowered back.

"Okay now, this is the question. Tell us how you found the money and how you got it all out. Tell Uncle Franky everything. Be a smart girl."

Good, I thought. *This means Win's still safe.*

"If I do, what do we get in exchange?"

He gave me a surprised look. He turned to Jose and shook his head. "We're here with much bigger gun. Six guards waiting upstairs, and she want to negotiate?"

"Let me get rid of the little bitch," said Jose, turning his weapon on me. "I told you from the beginning she's too much trouble."

Franky put a hand on Jose's arm and turned to me.

"So, you want to bargain, ha? Like a vegetable seller in the market? You have some Indian blood in you, that's for sure." He laughed at his own joke.

I glared.

"Okay, I'm listening. Tell Uncle Franky everything, please."

"My position hasn't changed," I replied. "You let everyone go, including Chanda outside and the slave girls in the kitchen, and...," I swallowed in distaste, "the little girls in here."

"How we know you tell us whole truth if we let everyone go, ha?"

"I have nothing to lose by telling you what I know. In fact, it might be a good thing for everyone."

He narrowed his eyes. *That confused him.*

The thing about Franky and his ilk was they were too proud to admit when they didn't understand something, especially when they were confronted by a woman.

He flashed his hyena smile. "You were such naive little girl. Look at you now, looking like a Miss Rambo."

He's diverting the conversation.

"I like her like this, you know."

We all turned to look at Jose. He was ogling Katy.

"A sexy, female Rambo." He turned to Franky. "Hey man, give me a few minutes with her, will you? You can go about this interrogation business after."

Franky frowned at his colleague. "Information is the most priority right now."

"Why can't I have some fun first?"

"My god, man, you sound like Zero. We are here to do business."

"How do you know Zero?" I snapped. My curiosity had got the better of me.

"Aah," said Franky, "you not know as much as you think you know. Zero is special friend. I hired him to find you in London." He flashed his sick smile. "And he found you, no?"

"Franky," Jose said, "for god's sake, can we finish this quickly? I just want a woman. That little girl last night wasn't enough. Screaming like a cat—"

A dull thud spooked all of us, making us jump.

Jose crumpled to the ground, clutching his chest. His rifle flew to the side of the room with a clatter on the steel floor.

Luc leaped across the room and scooped the weapon up.

Franky stared at me in shock.

It wasn't me who shot Jose.

"That was me," said Katy.

Without a warning, she shot Jose a second time, point-blank, in the heart.

I looked at her stunned.

The gunshot didn't echo against the steel walls.

The silencer!

Thank you, David, I prayed quietly.

"Oyo!" wailed Franky, suddenly realizing what was happening.

In a second, Peace jumped on him and pinned him against the wall, his hand clamping down on his mouth.

On the floor, Jose's eyes bulged and his body writhed. Then, his head fell to the side and blood trickled out of his mouth. He didn't even have time to realize who shot him.

We stood staring at his body, dumbfounded, breathing hard, listening carefully, in case the guards came trooping down.

But nothing.

"Aiyo!" Franky mumbled from underneath Peace's hand, struggling to get out.

Peace slammed him against the wall, making his head give a sickening crunch.

"Shut up!" Peace said in a low voice.

Then, he pulled Franky into the little room.

I didn't have time to fully register what Katy had done. Katy hadn't either. She retook her position next to Luc, her gun forward, trained at the stairwell in case anyone else came down.

I could see her chest heaving. She had done the unimaginable—the unimaginable, but fully justified in my eyes.

Luc was holding the AK-47 now. I noticed his hands were slightly shaking. I was glad David had trained us, though we'd never thought in a million years we'd have to handle this weapon in a hurry.

I picked up the torchlight from the floor and followed Peace inside, thinking of how to restrain Franky so he wouldn't call any more attention to us.

Inside, Preeti was pressed against the far wall, her arms wrapped around the terrified girls, their faces buried against each other's shoulders.

I hoped to god they hadn't seen Jose get shot. They'd probably witnessed enough for a lifetime of nightmares. They didn't need any more.

Peace dragged Franky against the wall furthest away from the girls. I walked over and shone the torchlight in Franky's eyes.

He blinked, giving me a desperate look.

"Let him talk," I said.

Peace removed his hand slowly from his mouth but kept the man immobilized against the wall.

"Please don't kill me," Franky sniveled.

I stepped up to within five inches of his face and pushed the barrel of my gun against his chest.

"You bring any attention to the men upstairs and I'll happily send all these bullets inside you," I said in a low growl. "Understood?"

He withered under my glare.

"Now, I believe it's you who owes me information. Tell me, who is the mastermind behind all this?"

He whimpered. "I am just middleman. I was only doing what he told us."

"Who?"

"The Saudis."

"What about Fred?"

"Never seen him. No idea who."

"How did you know where we were?"

"They told me. They were following you."

He tried to wiggle out, but Peace pushed him back. Franky groaned.

"Who's they?"

"I don't know."

I glared at him. I wondered how many little girls and boys he'd sold over the past few years. I thought of their tears, their anguish, their stolen childhoods.

Franky whined. "Let me go. I don't know anything. I was only trying my best to help your family."

My family?

Something in me snapped. I nodded to Peace to let him go. As soon as he moved aside, I stepped forward, raised my arm high and whacked Franky's face with the gun.

He doubled over, clutching his head, moaning in pain.

"One more lie from you and you're a dead man." My voice was so guttural even I didn't recognize it. It felt like something stronger was coming out from within me. Kali was awakening.

"Please, I'm a god-fearin—"

I kicked the side of Franky's stomach with such force he doubled over. I kicked again. And again. And again. I couldn't stop myself. I could no longer hear or see anything other than the depraved man in front of me. My blood boiled so much at the mention of my family that I forgot the girls at the other end of the room.

Franky fell to his knees, crying.

I gave him one last whack on the head with all my might.

He slithered to the ground, whimpering, blood streaming down his face.

Suddenly a volley of gunfire broke out from upstairs.

Peace and I whirled around.

Through the open door I could see Luc kneeling, the AK-47 in hand, watching the stairwell.

"What's going on?" Peace called out.

"Coming from upstairs, inside the house," Luc replied.

More gunfire. We looked at each other. *Who's shooting at who?*

"We gotta be prepared if they come down," said Katy.

As if on cue, the upstairs door banged open.

"Get ready!" Luc shouted. We ran toward him and lined up, shoulder to shoulder.

From behind us, I heard Franky yell. "You good-for-nothing daughter of a bitch." I knew he was talking to me. "I will make you pay one day so all your family and generations will feel my wrath."

I kept my eyes on the stairs. Franky was not worth the trouble right now.

That was when I heard Preeti scream.

I whirled around and ran back inside the room.

Franky had grabbed one of the girls and was holding her by the throat like a puppet.

"Aii!" Preeti shouted, grabbing the girl, struggling to loosen his grip. For a heart-stopping second, I thought the little girl would get ripped apart.

Then, as if realizing he had more important prey nearby, Franky dropped the girl and hooked his elbow around Preeti's neck, choking her.

"Drop her!" I yelled.

Preeti kicked and punched him furiously.

"Why?" Franky snarled, tightening his grip on her neck. She pulled on his hands, struggling to breathe. "She tricked me. Just like you."

"Preeti!" I yelled and cocked my gun. "Duck!"

I took aim and shot Franky right in between his eyes.

The gunshot echoed around the steel room, deafening me.

The girls screamed.

Chapter Sixty-two

"**S**top!" shouted Peace from outside the room. "I said, stop right there!"

My heart was beating a million miles a minute and my vision was blurred. The weapon in my hand throbbed, like it was alive. I wanted to feel shaken, but instead I'd gone numb. I just killed a man. I killed Franky.

His body lay lifeless at my feet with his blood splattered all over the floor. If I'd looked long enough, I'd have thrown up.

The girls had taken refuge at the other end of the room and were staring at me terrified.

A volley of gunfire came from somewhere up above us. Someone screamed in Arabic. It sounded like chaos upstairs.

"One more move and I shoot!" Luc shouted, panic in his voice.

I didn't have time to reassure the girls or Preeti. With a quick glance at my cousin who was pulling the girls toward her, I ran out of the room.

Luc and Katy were aiming their guns at the staircase. Peace was standing in his prepared-to-fight position, fists clenched in front, feet apart, ready to kick whoever was coming down.

Where I'd seen Preeti's sandals a few moments ago were two red leather boots.

"Wait!" called a voice from the staircase.

Katy and I looked at each other. She raised an eyebrow.

More screaming and yelling came from upstairs. *What's going on up there?*

The boots took a few cautious steps down.

"I'm here to help."

I vaguely recognized that Eastern European accent. Something about it made me stand back. It was a muffled voice, but clearly a female one.

My mind whirled. *It can't be her. She can't have gotten here that soon.* Then, a dreaded thought came to mind. *What if someone's pretending to be her?*

Luc shot me an uncertain look but didn't move. I guessed he was thinking the same as me.

The red boots took another step down.

"Who are you?" Katy asked.

"I'm with the Red-Heeled Rebels," said the voice. "You lost me in Marseilles."

I lowered my gun, relief washing over me.

"Are you all insane?" asked Peace, looking confused. He reached across to pry the gun from my hands. I jerked back. Just then, the boots jumped down and an extraordinary apparition stood in front of us at the bottom of the stairwell.

We stared.

It was a tall woman carrying a semi-automatic rifle. She was wearing army fatigues and a heavy-duty Kevlar vest. Slung across her chest was a second long-barreled firearm. An ammunition belt around her waist held magazines and hand grenades. Tied around her right thigh was a pistol holster, and around her left a knife holder.

Tetyana looked like she was prepared to fight World War Three all by herself.

Her head was wrapped in a black balaclava, the sort of thing you'd see on a bank robber, with only her green eyes visible through the slits. That's why her voice had been unrecognizable.

"Oh, my god," Katy said, lowering her gun.

"I don't believe this," said Luc.

Is it really her?

She stepped casually over Jose's body and pulled her mask off to show the face we'd all been hoping to see.

"You're alive!" cried Luc.

Tetyana looked at Peace, who was gaping at her.

"This is Peace," I said. "from Dar Es Salaam. I knew him as a kid."

"*Peace?*" She raised an eyebrow.

"This is Tetyana," I said to him. "Ukrainian special soldier."

They gave curt nods to each other.

More gunfire came from above us. More shouting. It was like a madhouse upstairs.

"What's going on up there?" I asked.

"Don't have much time," said Tetyana. "Good thing you had cameras on. Win told me where to find you."

"Is she okay?" Luc asked.

"She sent this." Tetyana pulled something from a pocket in her vest. "Got four of 'em," she said, holding her palm out.

"Earpieces!" I grabbed one and plugged it in right away.

"Oh, my god!" Win's squeals came into my ear, almost deafening me.

"Win!" Luc cried out.

"Luc!"

"Are you okay?"

"Don't worry about me. Get out and come back to the Mother Ship, okay?"

More bursts of gunfire from above.

"We need to move now," Tetyana said.

I pointed at the room. "You need to see this."

"Good frigging lord," she whispered, seeing the girls and Preeti huddled in a corner.

She gave a cursory glance at the body on the floor.

"Who did that?" she asked, turning to me.

I looked at Franky, not feeling anything. No sense of satisfaction, no triumph, not even distaste at my deed.

"Me."

Tetyana clapped me on the back. "Good job. Clean shot. I'm impressed."

She turned to the girls and waved. "Come on out. We're getting out of here."

I didn't know if they understood her, but they followed Preeti's lead out of the room.

It was getting crowded in the small stairwell now.

"We need to get Chanda too," I said to Tetyana. "She's in bad shape outside."

She nodded. "We'll get there soon. David's keeping things at bay for now."

"David's here?" I said, surprised.

"Not really, but you'll see."

She reached over her shoulders and pulled the rifle off her back. "Hand your weapon to Peace. You'll need this. It's locked and loaded. You got thirty rounds."

I passed my pistol and the torchlight to Peace and took the heavy-duty weapon with both hands, almost dropping it as I did.

"Sling it," she said. "Won't feel too heavy then. It's got a hell of a recoil, but David said you guys got training."

She bent down, pulled a knife from her boots and handed it to me. "You'll need this too." I took it and tucked it in my belt.

My eyes flickered to the girls and Preeti, who were staring at us, trying to follow the conversation.

Katy and I locked eyes for a second. None of us knew what we were getting into. I could feel the tension rise in the room. I was scared and nervous too, but I couldn't show it. I gripped my rifle tighter.

Tetyana turned to Luc. "You got a good piece there. You'll need to back up me and Asha, got it?"

"Sure thing," Luc said.

She addressed Katy and Peace next. "You two shepherd these kids safely out through the back gate and into the bus."

"With these?" asked Peace, looking in dismay at the small revolver in his hands. It appeared insignificant compared to what Luc and I were carrying.

"That's risk mitigation. Luc, Asha and I will cover you all the way. We're your front line. Understood?"

Peace looked unsure.

"And don't ever stop even if any of us get hit."

Peace and Katy stared at her.

"Your priority is the safety of the girls. Clear?"

This time, they nodded.

"Good," she said, "just get everyone safely in the bus and we'll join you when we're done here."

"Wait," I said. "What about the girls from the kitchen? We can't just leave them."

She nodded. "We'll get to them. Just follow my instructions, okay?"

I looked at her curiously. Tetyana seemed to know a lot for the little time she'd been here.

"David?" Tetyana said, tapping her earpiece. "All good?"

"In position." David's voice came clear over the airwaves.

Chapter Sixty-three

"What's the status?" Tetyana asked.

"They're regrouping," said David. "Women and children leaving in SUVs out the front gate now. Six men in a huddle, all have handguns. You got two minutes."

"We're coming out."

"I've got your back."

"Ready?" Tetyana said, looking at us.

"Ready," Katy and I said at the same time.

"Let's do this!" Luc said, looking more confident than he felt, I was sure.

The group started to move.

Tetyana climbed up first. Luc followed, his weapon at the ready.

Peace and Katy walked in the middle, Peace holding the torchlight with him so the girls could see in the dark. Preeti followed gripping the hands of the two youngest ones. They were eerily silent.

I took the back.

When we'd all got to the top door, Tetyana opened it gently, while Luc gave her cover.

One shot at us and you shoot back, were her instructions. But there was no one outside. It was deadly silent. I wondered about the guards and their swords. *Where are they?*

We trooped out of the darkness and into the well-lit plush hallway of the Saudi man's home. To our right was the main door that led to the yard and the small back gate. To our left, the corridor to the living room. But there was no sign of anyone.

"They're in the master bedroom," Win's voice came through the earpiece.

Who?

Tetyana tapped me on my shoulder. "Go bring the girls. Join us when you're done."

"The servant girls?" I asked.

But she was already walking stealthily over to the front door, waving for the others to follow her.

Preeti pulled on my arm urgently.

"This way," she said. "I know where it is."

I walked in front of her, stepping softly, keeping my rifle aimed forward, swiveling it at each open doorway, just like I'd seen soldiers do in the movies.

Why are we going back here? Shouldn't we be getting out of here? I tapped my earpiece. David and Win were silent. *What's their plan?*

"Master bedroom," whispered Preeti, pointing at a massive wooden door just outside the living room's entrance.

A dark shadow lay on the ground at the threshold of the living room. It was one of the Saudi guards. His sword was next to him, useless now. *Who did that? Tetyana? Are those men still in there?*

Training my gun on the bedroom door, I turned the knob slowly. Not a sound.

I opened the door wider, my finger on the trigger, ready to shoot the place down if I saw any movement.

It was a chamber fit for the king of the desert. An oversized bed sat in the middle of the room piled with luxury cushions and blankets.

"Stay back," I said to Preeti as I scoped the place, looking for any nook or cranny that could hide a Saudi guard with a curved sword.

Something rustled.

"In there," Preeti whispered.

I followed her finger to the ornamental wardrobe next to the bed. I stepped up to it and opened it cautiously, weapon trained forward.

My jaw dropped.

Crouching inside were the two servant girls from the kitchen. They each had backpacks on like they were ready to go on a trip. They clutched at each other at the sight of my firearm, but their faces relaxed when they saw Preeti.

"Come," she called to them, motioning urgently with her hands. "Come!" They clambered out to join her, giving me wide berth.

"It's okay," I said. "I'm here to help you."

They gave me frightened looks.

"Let's go," I said, turning around and walking toward the door.

I looked out. At the other end of the corridor, Tetyana was talking to Katy and Peace. It looked like she was giving them instructions.

Luc spotted us and waved. "Come on!"

I stepped out, followed by the girls.

That was when I heard the cry.

"Aidez moi." Help me.

It was a man's voice, a trembling man's voice. I stopped in my tracks. Something stirred in my gut. I knew that voice.

Tetyana and the group were walking out the door now.

"Go!" I said to Preeti and the girls. "Run!"

They didn't hesitate. They bolted toward the front door, after Tetyana and the group.

I turned right and stepped inside the living room. And gawked.

A tornado had ripped through the room, tossing furniture and overturning coffee tables. All the windows had been shattered like someone had shot through them.

The bodies of three guards lay facedown on the floor. They'd all been shot on the forehead. Dead center. Tetyana's words came back to me. "Good job. Clean shot. I'm impressed."

The old Saudi had been shot twice, once through the head and another through the back. His monstrous body now lay lifeless, unable to do any more harm.

"Ici!" Here!

I saw movement from under a pile of cushions.

I walked up and tossed them away with the butt of my gun, to discover Charles Dubois's frightened face. He was struggling to sit up. There were no signs of wounds on him. He'd escaped death by getting buried in here just in time. Or Tetyana didn't see the need to waste her bullets on him.

"What are you waiting for?" the old man snapped. "Help me up, girl."

I stared at him, my throat dry.

"Get me out of here!"

"You..." I watched him struggle among the cushions. "You *killed* my parents."

He looked up at me, startled.

"Asha?" Tetyana's voice came in my ear, irritated. "What are you doing? Get out of there now!"

I ignored her. I couldn't take my eyes off this man who was responsible for everything that had happened to me.

"You destroyed them," I snarled. "You ruined my entire family."

"What are you babbling on about, stupid girl? I said, help me out of here now!"

A fire was raging inside me—one that had been ignited the day my parents burned to cinders in that car crash.

I gritted my teeth. "My parents worked for Environ Africa," I said, looking Dubois right in the eyes.

He stared back at me with a callous and cruel glare.

"You didn't like what they did, did you? You didn't like them finding out about your child labor camps, so you *killed* them in cold blood."

"Asha," David's voice came through the earpiece. "You must leave now."

I didn't budge.

"It was you. It was *you* who ordered their assassination."

His eyes cleared. "Look, business is business—"

"How dare you?" I screamed. "How *dare* you?" My fury was an inferno now, spreading through my belly, my heart, my arms.

I lifted my rifle and aimed at his head.

"No!" he cried, holding his hands up. "No! Please, for the love of—"

I pulled the trigger.

Chapter Sixty-four

"What the hell are you doing?" Tetyana's angry voice grated in my ears.

"Get out, Asha." David's voice was calmer.

I turned and ran back through the corridor, the gun weighing more heavily on my back now.

Everyone was huddled outside the front doorway. Tetyana and Luc had their guns trained outward. Peace and Katy were shielding the girls and looked ready to dash out. Katy turned as I ran toward them and motioned me to hurry.

I didn't have time to think or regroup.

"Okay, boys and girls," Tetyana cried as soon as I caught up. "Cover me!"

She stepped out firing like mad. Single shots fired back from somewhere in the back of the compound.

Luc and I sprang after Tetyana, firing in their direction.

"Katy! Peace! Now!" Tetyana screamed.

From the corner of my eye, I saw them scramble out with Preeti and the girls. They ran toward the back gate, doubled over, darting from building to building, following a path I was sure Tetyana had given them. Tetyana, Luc and I moved with them, covering them, jumping backward, shooting forward.

"Keep going!" Win said. "You're getting close."

The Saudi guards were hidden behind the houses in the back and were shooting all over the place. Their talents lay in swords, not guns, I hoped. But it was hard to pinpoint them and I was sure we'd get hit any moment.

"Katy, Peace, you're good now," I heard Win say in my ear. "It's clear outside the gate."

"Got it," said Katy's voice. "Almost there."

"Sending the girls out first," said Peace.

"Make it quick, you people!" Tetyana called out. "For Christ's sake, get out now!"

"Down," I heard David's steady voice in my ear.

What?

"Everyone down!" screamed Tetyana.

I threw myself on the ground just in time to hear the whistle of a bullet go by.

A man let out a yell from behind one of the houses.

We shot in his direction. More yelling and screaming. *Good. I hope we got them.*

"Peace!" I heard Katy scream from behind me, her voice filled with terror.

I glanced back. The last of the girls were slipping through the gate. But Peace had fallen to the ground.

"Get back, everyone!" yelled Tetyana. "They're shooting from the left!"

I fell to my tummy and crawled over to Peace. A red stain was forming on his shirt. I put my hand to his chest. He pushed me away. "I'm fine," he said.

Katy came dashing toward us from the gate, a look of horror on her face. "Peace! Oh, my god, oh, my god, what happened?"

"Get down, Katy!" Tetyana yelled angrily from somewhere.

Katy flung herself on the ground

"Take him," I said to her. "I'll cover you."

I turned around and sent a volley of shots in the other direction as Katy and Peace crawled on their stomachs to the gate.

"Everyone's out," said Win. "Tetyana, Asha, Luc! You're the only ones inside."

"And Chanda!" I cried out.

"Down," David said in his calm voice.

This time, I knew what to do. I slammed to the ground as the bullet whipped by.

Another surprised yell from behind the women's quarters.

"Keep down," he said.

Another shout came from behind the second building.

"Good job," said Tetyana before jumping back up.

"Forward!" she yelled. Luc and I jumped up and followed her.

A bullet kicked the dust near my feet.

"Second building to the right," Win's voice crackled through the earpiece.

"Down," said David.

We slammed down.

A whistle. A yell. Then quiet.

"Got him," said David.

Where is he?

"They're regrouping in the back," said Win.

The shooting stopped as suddenly as it had started.

Tetyana, Luc and I watched carefully, training our guns forward, ready for anything.

"Moving to new vantage point," said David in my earpiece.

We headed forward slowly, shoulder to shoulder, hardly breathing, our guns trained in front, moving from side to side. My eyes flitted from one building to the next, expecting a crazed Saudi to jump out and shoot us dead.

"To your left," said Win in my ear. Her voice sounded strained. "She's right there."

"Chanda!" I cried, as she came into view.

"Go!" Tetyana shouted. "We'll cover!"

I broke off from them and ran to her.

Chanda opened her eyes and gave me a lifeless look. Her body looked slack, her limbs drooping. She wasn't going to last very long.

I pulled the knife out of my belt.

"I'm gonna get you out of here," I said, as I put the knife on the rope. "It's okay, Chanda. You're gonna be just fine."

Gunshots. I whipped around.

Tetyana and Luc were hunched against a nearby wall, shooting. Someone was shooting at us from inside one of the buildings. They were dangerously close. I turned back to focus on Chanda's knots.

"Just a few more, a little bit more," I said more to myself than her, as I desperately sliced through the rope.

"Ow!" I said, as I cut myself. Ignoring the blood trickling from my palm, I cut faster, harder, using all my strength. Suddenly Chanda seemed to wake up. She yanked on the cable.

"Yes! Keep pulling. That's good," I said urgently. "You're doing great. Keep pulling!"

"Almost out of ammo!" someone yelled in my ear.

That was Luc. And that was not good.

"Done!" I said, as I tore the rope away from Chanda. She leaned against me like she didn't have any energy left.

"Down," said David.

I pulled my friend to the ground just as the bullet whistled past us.

"Chanda's free," I heard Win's voice vaguely in my ear.

"Go!" It was Tetyana. "Get out now!"

I pulled Chanda up and threw my arm around her shoulder. "We've got to run now. Do you understand?" She gave a slight nod. I thought she was going to faint on me. *Dear god.*

Then, propelled by some unseen force, she grabbed my hand. I grabbed it back.

"Run!" I yelled.

We started running toward the gate, holding hands. I felt like we were moving through mud, Chanda weighed down by her wounds and me by my weapon.

"Almost there!" I heard Win say in my ear, "You're almost out!"

"I got you covered!" yelled Tetyana from behind me.

"Keep going!" shouted Luc.

I dropped my gun. I needed to focus on getting Chanda out. With renewed energy, I ran faster, pulling her along with me.

We reached the gate and scrambled out.

Chanda and I stumbled over a dead body and fell to the ground.

It was the guard who'd been standing outside these gates looking bored. He had a bullet wound neatly in the middle of his forehead. *David's work.*

I got up, pulled Chanda to her feet and pushed her against the wall. It was safer here, the concrete acting as a barrier from the bullets.

"Tetyana?" I cried in my earpiece. "Luc?"

"Coming!"

Suddenly, they came dashing out of the compound.

"Jeepers!" I heard David say in my ear.

We looked at each other in alarm.

"What?" Tetyana snapped.

The faint sound of a siren came from somewhere.

"Someone's called the cops."

"We still have to get to the bus," I said, looking at Chanda, who was leaning against the wall, her eyes closed.

"We have to distract them," said David.

The sirens were getting closer.

"Cars are at the front gate now," said Win.

Tetyana pulled two grenades from her waist belt and stood up with a look of determination on her face.

"You guys start walking. Don't look back."

Luc took one of Chanda's arms and slung it around his shoulder while I grabbed the other. We crossed the road toward the scrapyard, half carrying, half dragging her, walking as fast as we could.

"Cops are at the front gate," I heard Win say. "They look confused but they've got guns."

"Tetyana, get out," David said. "I can't shoot the police."

I glanced back just once to see Tetyana's arm swing like she was throwing a baseball.

Then the whole compound blew up.

We flew across the road, dust swirling around us like a mini hurricane.

Chapter Sixty-five

It took us ten minutes to get into the scrapyard.

Following directions sent by David into our earpieces, we crawled behind vine bushes and trees, moving away from the Saudi compound. Luc and I held on to Chanda while Tetyana took the rear, alert to anything or anyone coming our way.

The back lane was deserted and it was getting dark, so things were in our favor. For now.

"Everyone's here," Win's encouraging voice came over the airwaves. "We're waiting for you. You guys are doing great. Almost there."

But the wailing of the police cars didn't stop. Behind us, a fire was raging inside the compound.

Suddenly, a new and louder siren screeched through the air.

"What's that?" I asked.

"Fire trucks," David said. "Three of them. A few streets away. Coming toward the front gate."

I prayed they wouldn't send helicopters.

The fire engine sirens seemed to give Chanda a burst of energy. Even in her weakened state, she hastened her steps, holding on to Luc and me.

We could hear the fire roaring behind us. Thank goodness the women and kids got out earlier. Anyone left behind deserved to get burned to shards. Kali's fierce blue image sprang to my mind. This time, she had a wicked smile on her face.

"Hurry!" David voice came through my earpiece.

He guided us through a narrow opening in the wall. We had to get on our hands and knees to crawl in, but it was our passageway to safety. We got Chanda to go in first. Luc went next and then me, Tetyana insisting on being the last one in.

I breathed a sigh of relief once we all were inside.

A hundred feet in front of us was the dark shadow of the bus, its tinted windows not giving away the people or equipment inside. Behind the bus lay the crumbling house, looking more menacing than ever. A rustle of leaves from a nearby tree made me look up.

David was clambering down the tree with a long-barreled weapon slung across his back.

A sniper gun!

One by one, we got into the bus without speaking.

Preeti and the girls were already inside, seated at the back, leaning against each other, clutching the water bottles Win had handed to them as they'd come on board.

Preeti opened her eyes when I walked over. She gave me a relieved look. I settled Chanda next to her and bent down to give her a long hug, one I'd been wanting to offer for years.

"We're safe now," I said to her. "No one's going to hurt you anymore."

She nodded, giving me a tired look.

Chanda had her eyes closed, too exhausted to speak. She opened them briefly to look at me.

I leaned in and squeezed her shoulder. "It's over now," I said. "We're going to take you home. You'll get to see your mom soon."

Without a word, she lay back on her seat and closed her eyes as if all this was too much to take.

I checked up on the other girls. They were sitting quietly in their seats, looking like deer in headlights. I realized then, they needed far more help than we could give them. But first, we had to get them to safety.

I walked to the front row of the seats where Katy was bandaging Peace, ignoring his protests.

"I'm fine. No need to make so much fuss."

"It only grazed him," Katy said, when I leaned over to look. "Still, would be good to find a doctor."

I nodded.

We need to get out soon.

Up front, near the cockpit, Tetyana and David were conferring about something serious.

I stopped by Win, who hadn't budged from her station in front of the computers. She hardly noticed Luc take the seat next to her. He put his arm around her waist and kissed her on the cheek. She gave him a peck on his lips before turning back to the screens.

I took the empty seat on the other side of her and peered at the screens. *Did two hand grenades do all that?* It looked like a bomb had hit the compound.

"No one saw you guys," Win said. "They're all busy now trying to put the fire out."

"But they'll start searching the area soon," I said, frowning.

I noticed two familiar backpacks on the bench next to her.

"What's that?"

"David's idea," Win replied.

I remembered seeing the servant girls with these bags when I discovered them inside the Saudi man's bedroom. I flipped one open and peeked in. Inside were tablets, phones and a handful of flash drives. I pulled one out. The label was in Arabic.

I looked at Win. "What's all this about?"

"Tetyana told them to pick up all the Saudi man's electronic stuff and wait for you in the bedroom closet. The girls were hiding at the back of the living room when she shot the men. They thought she was going to shoot them too."

I remembered how scared they looked when I found them.

I studied the flash drive in my hand. "Are these any good?"

Win shrugged. "Don't read Arabic, but I think I can decrypt them for David to read."

I squeezed her shoulder. "What would we do without you, Win?"

She smiled shyly.

"Thank you for everything," I said.

"I'm just happy you guys got out okay," she replied.

"Buckle up, everyone," David called out from the front. "That goes for you too, Win and Luc," he said, glancing at them.

Luc reached over and slipped a seat belt across Win, who had turned back to the screen with her usual monomaniacal focus.

Tetyana was standing behind the driver's seat, her rifle leaning against the window, frowning at her phone. I slipped into the passenger seat in front just as David started the bus with a push of a button. The cockpit lit up but the engine didn't roar like I'd expected it to. It didn't even purr.

"Electric?" I asked.

David nodded, switching on more buttons. "Been charging it all day."

"Good thing it's quiet," said Tetyana from behind us.

"Take a seat, Ms. Superwoman," he said. "I'm not responsible if you get hurt."

Tetyana grabbed the seat behind me.

Without another word, David maneuvered the bus out of the scrapyard.

Chapter Sixty-six

"**W**hatever happened to the backup you promised?"

David didn't reply, his eyes on the road.

Behind us, Tetyana was still absorbed in her phone.

I was too nervous to close my eyes because I kept expecting a horde of police cars to come screeching by and cart us off to jail.

We'd been driving in silence for a while, navigating through back roads. We were now in the outskirts of Nairobi, heading toward the Tanzanian border.

All of us, except for Preeti and the girls we'd rescued, had passports on us. We had no idea how to get everyone across, but Tetyana suggested we tackle that when we got to the border.

Right now, our priority was to get as far away from the Saudi compound as possible without attracting any attention.

In the back, everybody was asleep. The lights were dimmed down in the bus, but I could see everyone curled up in their seats, dead to the world. Even Win had shut down her bank of computers and was sleeping, nestled against Luc.

I tried again. "Did you and Tetyana know each other before?"

"Nope. Never met her until today," said David.

At least he's talking, I thought. "So if it wasn't Tetyana, who were you going to ask for help?"

"We did fine without outside help, didn't we?"

"Your sniping was pretty amazing. Where'd you learn that?"

"Been training with the Mossad since fourteen."

"The *Mossad*?"

"The Israeli intelligence agency?" Tetyana asked, leaning in between the seats, suddenly interested in the conversation. "You know." She paused. "I kinda guessed something like that."

David gave a nonchalant shrug.

"So that's who you're working for," I said to myself, seeing more pieces of the puzzle now. I remembered the beefy men sparring at the dojo the first evening we arrived.

"The dojo is their training gym, isn't it? And that's why you have a firing range in your backyard."

"It's one of them," said David. "They train in a few places."

"Probably like to switch it up," said Tetyana. "For security."

"What happened to them?" I said. "Why didn't they help us?"

He sighed. "Because I realized at the last minute that asking for their help was a bad idea."

"Why?"

"'Cuz they'd throw me in jail for life."

"For what?" Tetyana and I asked at the same time.

"To start, for not telling my superiors what I'd been up to."

I was scared to ask, but I had to now. "Like what?"

"Running a sting operation without their consent. And..." His voice trailed off. "Stealing equipment."

"Like this bus?" Tetyana asked.

He didn't reply.

"And the guns? The knives? The computers? The cameras?" I asked.

Behind us, Tetyana chuckled. "Some nerve you have. I'm impressed."

"I'm a reserve member," David replied in a quiet voice. "They'll put me away for life for this."

I took a deep breath in. "So they don't know any of this?"

"Not really." He paused. "Not yet."

"And we're running away in a *bus*," I said. "We're not going to get that far."

"I removed the tracking device," he said. He pushed his foot on the accelerator, lurching us forward. "Plus, this thing has more power than that BMW you trashed."

"Won't they miss it?" asked Tetyana. "I'm sure the Mossad keeps excellent books. Not to speak of noticing this gone from their warehouse or parking lot."

"Well, technically..." David paused, as if unsure if he should continue. "The bus belongs to the CIA African branch. I, er, kind of borrowed it."

Tetyana let out a low whistle.

"The CIA?" I said stunned.

"I told them a Mossad special forces team needed it for training, so they let me sign it out. I sent a requisition from my boss's computer. The two departments have an agreement to share equipment so I just, er, helped myself."

Tetyana leaned over and slapped him on the back. "Atta boy! This is frigging fantastic."

I couldn't keep a smile from crossing my face. "So, Monday morning, they're all going to be asking questions of each other and find out no one has the bus?"

"We'll be in Tanzania by then," said David. "I'll ditch this thing somewhere."

"Well, you just gave up a perfectly pensionable job, my man," said Tetyana.

"I was trying to help," said David. "Plus, I've been waiting all my life to get back at these men."

Tetyana's face turned serious. "Tell me. What exactly are the CIA and Mossad doing out here in East Africa?"

"Joint ops. Operation Black Dawn. They've been here for years trying to shake down the Saudi man and the Boko Mines."

"Why didn't they get the job done?" I said. "They're much bigger than us."

"Politics," quipped Tetyana from the back. "Am I right?"

He nodded. "You remember those two lawyer-like guys we saw at the Boko HQ?"

"Yeah," I said.

"They've been stonewalling the entire operation. They and their powerful politico families. On the surface, everyone's working hard to stop trafficking and child labor. They even get millions of dollars in international aid for it. But under the table, the politicians are getting paid by Boko Mines. So the Saudi man got away with murder."

"And kidnapping," I added. "And torture and rape and..."

"Corruption at its finest," said Tetyana dryly.

"I've been waiting for years to finish them off," said David, a grim look on his face. "And we took them all down in one day."

"There's still Sophie," I said, worried. "She runs the show now."

"She's crippled though," said Tetyana. "Their human resources channel has just been cut short. But you're right, they'll find a way to rebuild."

"What about Fred?" I asked.

"He's going to be lying low for a while too," said Tetyana.

"That leaves the CIA and Mossad," I said, shaking my head. "Maybe we can outsmart people like Fred and the Saudi. But how are we going to outrun the two most powerful agencies in the world?"

"We'll figure it out," Tetyana said. "I fought the Russian army, didn't I? At least part of it. They're gonna think twice before they come after me now." She pointed her chin to the back of the bus. "Besides, this has all been for a good cause."

I looked over at Preeti sleeping with her legs curled under her. Yes, the risks were well worth it.

"We got them all out alive," said Tetyana, a catch in her voice. "And that's all that matters."

"Hey." I turned back to look at her. "I'm sorry."

She stared at me uncomprehendingly.

"I'm sorry about your brother."

She looked down and was silent for a while.

"I'll never forget his face, the way he looked when he saw me. He knew I'd come back to find him and take him away. But they shot him before I could."

David and I listened silently.

"What helps me sleep at night is that I told him I loved him before he left us." Her voice cracked. "I'll be forever grateful for that moment."

• • • •

I EVENTUALLY DRIFTED off to sleep.

The past few weeks had caught up to me, and I slept so soundly I didn't even hear Tetyana and David stop the bus along the highway to exchange the driver's job.

We reached the Tanzanian border at one in the morning and stopped at a small motel on the Kenyan side to catch up on sleep, take showers, get food and recharge the bus. Katy and Peace went to the front desk, pretending to be overnight tour guides, and booked a block of rooms for all of us in one wing.

When dawn broke, Peace, Katy and I took a taxi to the nearest store to buy a change in clothes for everyone. We found a shop selling second-hand clothes, throwaways from a disaster recovery program from a few years back. There was a good choice of jeans, shirts, and T-shirts of all sizes for cheap. Anything was better than the blood-stained, dust-covered clothes we had on, especially if border guards decided to inspect the passengers.

On our way back to the motel, Peace made a stop at the local liquor store to get the most expensive whiskey in town—"gifts" for border patrol officers who might want to ask too many questions. It works every time, he said, and he was right.

When we were ready to cross the border, Peace took over the driver's seat.

He pulled in slowly through the main barriers and stopped at the Customs gate. On his lap were our passports, each with a wad of cash stuck in between the pages.

The rest of us sat in our seats, not making a sound. The girls were all hiding under blankets right at the back of the bus. We'd already packed the computer gear in boxes, tucked them under the bench and covered them with blankets.

We caught the word "tourists" as Peace spoke rapidly to the guards in Swahili. He offered two duty-free bottles of whiskey as a "gift." Then, I saw our stack of passports being handed out the window and returned.

There was a lot of smiling, laughing and handshaking. Despite his wound and the fact that he had to leave his treasured Jeep back in Nairobi, Peace was happy to be of use. He charmed his way through and no one even bothered to come inside.

We all breathed a sigh of relief when the gates opened and the guards waved us into Tanzania.

It was a few minutes before anyone said anything.

"We just smuggled people over an international border," Katy said. "How many years do you get for that?"

Tetyana gave her a grim look. "Best to not think about it."

"Technically," pointed out Luc, "We un-smuggled them. We should get a medal."

"Just don't say anything to Father," Peace said from up front.

Part SEVEN

Everything you've ever wanted is on the other side of fear.
George Addair

Half an hour after we crossed the border to Tanzania, I shook Chanda awake to tell her the idea that had been swirling around my brain for hours now.

We were driving through a long stretch of desert, yellow dust whirling around us. There was not much to see outside. Everyone except for David, Tetyana and me were asleep at the back.

Chanda had taken a strong painkiller, wrapped herself with a blanket and gone to sleep in her seat. She needed the rest badly so I didn't want to bother her. Until now.

We had to find proper care for the seven girls we'd rescued from the Saudi compound. Tetyana and David had no idea what to do with them. But I knew one person who could help, if only she'd agree to it.

Chanda didn't even wait till I finished.

She asked for Tetyana's phone to call the orphanage in Dar Es Salaam. To my relief and surprise, Mama Abudu said yes to the extra girls without hesitation.

With Geoffrey's help, Mama Abudu had taken the children and fled to their satellite shelter in Tanzania, as soon as David and I had left their orphanage the day before. They were in a small town near the capital city now, a half an hour's drive from Dar Es Salaam.

Chanda's funds had allowed for several smaller buildings in the region, but none as secure or established as the one they had in the outskirts of Nairobi. The important thing was the kids and Mama Abudu were safe now.

David parked the bus outside the shelter and waited in the driver's seat while everyone got off.

"Hey Win," he called out, almost casually as we were getting ready to disembark. "Say goodbye to the Mother Ship."

"Oh no!" she cried. "Can't we keep it? Please?"

"Sorry, not a good idea."

"Too bad," I said, unsure I was ready to lose the comfy and secure bus so soon either.

"Where are you going to ditch it?" Katy asked.

"Return it," he corrected her. "The Mossad has a warehouse in town. Least I can do."

"Won't they catch you?" I asked.

"Don't plan on it. Will park it a kilometer away. They'll find it soon enough."

"Want me to come with you?" asked Luc.

David shook his head. "Best I do this alone."

The girls had followed Preeti out of the bus and were now saying hello to Mama Abudu. She was embracing each one of them like they were her own lost daughters. Tetyana, Luc, Katy, Peace and Win had left the bus.

"Hey," said David, turning to me and lowering his voice, "this should take me three hours tops but don't wait up for me, okay?"

I looked at him, startled.

"And if I disappear, don't go looking for me."

A pang crossed my heart, but words eluded me.

He reached out with his hand. I took it in my limp one.

"Stay safe," I whispered.

With a quick nod, he turned around and started the engine.

There was nothing to do but let him take care of his job. I descended, feeling heavy with melancholy. I'd grown fond of David, maybe even liked him a bit. Okay, more than a bit.

I had the same feelings in the pit of my stomach as when we were all leaving Luxembourg only a few weeks ago. It was that dreaded sensation this would be the last time we'd see each other.

* * * * *

THE REST OF US WALKED into the shelter to help Mama Abudu orient the girls to their new home.

Geoffrey, his security team, the young chefs and all the kids had arrived safely with her, and she welcomed the extra help we offered. Geoffrey merely gave me a curt nod to acknowledge my presence. He still seemed angry at the chaos we'd thrown his life into.

I tried to forget my feelings about David and help Mama Abudu and her team. I joined in with the rest of the crew, making beds, sorting old clothes piles, cleaning the backyard, and playing sous-chefs in the kitchen.

Win sat on the floor of the orphanage playroom absorbed in the screen in front of her. Before David had driven off, she'd snuck out a laptop without him even knowing. I hoped the Mossad would so be happy to get their bus back they wouldn't mind one minor missing device.

She worked on it, surrounded by the phones, tablets and flash drives we'd taken from the Saudi compound.

"How's it going?" I asked, coming to check in on her after a while.

She gave me a self-satisfied smile. "I cracked it."

"You got into his phone?"

"All of them," she replied. "He used the same password for everything."

I narrowed my eyes. "What did you find?"

"Most of the stuff is in Arabic, but I found one in English. Contact names and routes and distribution centers all over the place. I'm uploading them and tagging them to INTERPOL right now. They've got translators, right?"

I nodded, frowning. "Hey, they won't be able to trace all this back to us, right?"

"Nope." Win shook her head. "Same thing when I uploaded the stuff from Zero's computer in Brussels. They'll get the info but they'll never know who shared it. How cool is that?" She grinned.

I took a deep breath in. Sometimes I wondered if she thought of this as a real-life video game.

"You're a genius, you know that?"

She flashed another cheeky grin.

David returned forty minutes after the promised three hours, unscathed but unnerved, just as I was about to give up on him.

My heart did a jump at the sight of him walking into Mama Abudu's kitchen. He came over to give me a hug.

"I left an apology note inside," he said, sheepishly.

Will that be enough to keep him out of jail? I wondered.

After saying goodbye to Mama Abudu and the girls and promising them we'd return soon, we bundled into two taxis and headed to Peace's home. Mr. Mudenda was beginning to ask too many questions, and we could only hold out for so much longer.

Peace had dutifully called his father every night, even phoning him from the bus while stuffed with Tylenol on our way to the Tanzanian border.

But Mr. Mudenda was a smart man, and Peace had been too cryptic for his liking. We'd been gone for ten days now and he smelled something fishy. It took another call from me to beg him not to send a search party or call the police.

Our return trip to Mr. Mudenda's home was a somber affair. There was no joy or celebration in our hearts. The past few weeks had changed each of us immeasurably.

I was not the Asha who'd left Tanzania a long time ago. I was also not the Asha who ran away from India or from Toronto. The images of the frightened girls in their cramped underground prison, and the slave girls in the kitchen cowering under their owners' blows, would keep me awake for the rest of my life.

I still didn't know Preeti's and Chanda's full stories and was aware that hearing them talk about their pasts, if they ever opened up, would be gut-wrenching.

Taking Franky's and Dubois's lives, however evil they'd been, was not helping me feel any better. My instinctual actions and their violent deaths weighed heavily on my mind. I was a murderer now.

I tried to bury these memories somewhere deep inside so I didn't have to face them every day. But one thing was sure. I had changed. Irrevocably.

Chapter Sixty-eight

"You all have some serious eating to do. Eat up!"

Mama Gladness plunked a huge casserole dish right in front of Preeti's nose. She was paying special attention to Preeti, who looked like a skeleton of her former happy schoolgirl self.

We were all seated around Mr. Mudenda's massive dining table. Finally together. A remarkable homecoming. All twelve seats were occupied except for one, which was waiting for Mama Gladness to stop fussing about and join us.

Mr. Mudenda was sitting at the head of the table. Mrs. Ngozi sat across from him at the other end. She looked pale but had a soft smile on her face and was holding tightly to Chanda's hand, like she'd never let her go. Chanda, a younger version of her mother, was now wearing a pair of jeans and T-shirt and looked so much prettier without the Chanel dress and all that makeup.

Peace and Katy sat together to Mr. Mudenda's right. I wondered if Peace's father knew they had something special going on. Luc and Win were sitting together too. They had been inseparable since our bus ride.

Mr. Mudenda had welcomed us back cautiously, even David and Tetyana, who were strangers to him.

And we stuck to our story.

We had found Preeti and Chanda working as maids on the outskirts of Nairobi during our investigative work. We'd managed to get them out quickly with the help of David and Tetyana, who worked nearby. The only casualty of the venture had been Peace's Jeep, which had been left behind in our hasty departure. Tetyana promised him she'd find a way to get it back.

We didn't lie. We just didn't tell the whole truth.

Mr. Mudenda blinked a few times as we told our tale in earnest, his eyes flitting to each of us to see if he could detect a fault line.

I worried about Preeti, but she managed to keep a straight face throughout.

When he asked why we hadn't called the police right away, Peace explained that we simply hadn't had the time. Besides, Peace said, they could have kept Chanda and Preeti in the country as witnesses, and they were safer here than in a foreign police shelter or worse, a jail cell.

I knew his father didn't fully believe us, but for now, he seemed relieved we'd all returned in one piece with the two people we'd been searching for.

But that didn't stop the uneasy feeling gnawing at my stomach. The others felt it too. One unanswered question hung in the air like a dark, thunderous dark cloud.

Why hadn't the Mossad, the CIA, or the police tracked us down yet? Why hadn't Fred or Sophie's men come crashing through the door to get us back for destroying their businesses? Maybe we were no longer a threat. Maybe they had other priorities. Maybe we'd never find out. Then again, maybe these events were just being postponed for another day, yet to come. We simply didn't know.

"The good news is," Mrs. Ngozi said, picking up her glass. "The good news is everyone is here safe and sound." She turned to Chanda with a smile. "I don't want to ever lose you again." Chanda leaned in and touched her mother's forehead with hers. "Me, neither."

"And the even better news is," said Mama Gladness, adding a spoonful of mashed potatoes on Preeti's plate despite her protests, "no one is leaving this home until you get more fat on your bones. I don't know what shenanigans you kids got up to, but right now, you must get healthy."

We dug in quietly, passing the dishes around. Next to me, Preeti ate shyly. I squeezed her hand. She squeezed mine back. I'd found the only family I had left in the world, and I wasn't about to lose her again.

Preeti was keeping to herself, still struggling to come to terms with the sudden shift in her life. I remembered how Win used to stare into space for hours after we'd taken her out of the brothel. It took a while for her to shed that look of an animal under attack. But all the racing around, and the opportunity to use her talents with us cheering her on, helped her overcome those demons and approach some normalcy in life.

Preeti had been forced to marry that vile Kristadasa at a much older age than when Win was abducted from her village. I was sure Preeti would recover. I didn't tell her about my encounter with that man yet, how I left him bleeding between his legs, howling. The time for that story would come.

For now, I ate my supper sitting next to her, feeling whole again after a very long time.

For a moment, I thought the most pleasant sound in the world was the clinking of forks on plates and the murmurs of satisfaction from my closest friends and family around the dinner table. *I've finally found a home,* I thought. I wanted every day to be like this. Warm. Safe. Loving.

"Hey," Win said suddenly, looking at me. "Don't forget Chef Pierre's still waiting for you to call him back."

"I didn't think he'd have anything to do with you anymore," said Tetyana, giving me a curious look.

"He's been trying to get ahold of Asha for weeks now," said Katy. "Tweeting it out to the world."

"Who is this Chef Pierre?" Mama Gladness asked, narrowing her eyes.

"Apparently," Luc said, "Asha's cakes impressed him so much he wants her to join him and open a café in New York."

"In America?" Mr. Mudenda's eyebrows rose.

"A café?" asked Mama Gladness.

"So what do I tell him?" Win asked.

Everyone stopped eating and looked in my direction.

I needed time to think.

This had been my dream ever since I used to bake cakes with my mother on those happy Sunday mornings long ago. This was the dream I'd hung on to, to survive those dark days in Goa and in Toronto. It was what linked me to my mother.

I badly wanted to keep my mother's legacy alive, but I wondered if I was capable of it anymore. *You can't handle a semi-automatic, rescue a few slave girls, knife a pedophile, kill a couple of evil men, and still hold on to the same dreams of your childhood. Or can you?*

"Do you know Chef Pierre's super famous in Europe?" Win was saying. "He even catered to the queen's party in London last year."

Mr. Mudenda gave me an approving look. "This is very impressive. I'm proud of you." He frowned slightly. "But does this mean you will be traveling again?"

I looked down at my plate. An idea had been growing in the back of my mind. I wanted to help Mama Abudu take care of the children, especially since she'd lost her only sponsor. Chanda was no longer in a position to fund her work.

How's she going to feed all those kids? How's she going to help out others who may still need to be rescued?

I looked over at Win. "Tell him we'll need to negotiate a price first."

She gave me a thumbs up and went back to her food.

"Who is this man who thinks he's so famous?" Mama Gladness asked the table in a stern voice. "Does he cook better than me?"

"Of course, not," Katy said quickly.

"He only knows how to bake sweets," Luc said. "You make real warm, hearty, amazing food."

A chorus of murmurs went around the table, agreeing, even from those who'd never heard of Chef Pierre until now.

"You're the best, Mama Gladness," chipped in Win. "This is yum."

"That's true," said Chanda, helping herself to more, "I could stay here and eat your food forever."

"Me too," nodded David. "And I've eaten all kinds of food, all across Africa."

"Best home-cooked meal I've ever had," said Tetyana. "And I've been all over Europe."

"You're such good girls and boys," Mama Gladness said, beaming at us.

I looked around the happy table, thankful for the presence of everyone here. I only wished my parents and Aunty Shilpa could join us. *What would I give to have them with me, right here, right now?*

A slight breeze suddenly ruffled the dining room curtains, lifting the sheer inset. It fluttered like a bird ready to take flight.

I looked out the bay windows toward the quiet, sunny garden. My parents and Aunty Shilpa were gone from this world. But something told me they would always be close, watching over me, showing me the way.

• • • •

—THE END –

• • • •

Read the First Chapter of the Next Red Heeled Rebels Book Here.

Chapter One

The shrill scream of a terrified woman reverberated through the house.

I whipped around.

Katy had been strolling around the hall, admiring the murals on the walls—the ones with austere men in robes riding black Arabian horses across golden dunes. She was now standing next to a display of scimitars, those ancient curved weapons of the desert.

She stared at me with a horrified expression on her face.

"Did you hear that?" she asked, almost in a whisper.

"I think so," I said, unsure myself.

We remained motionless, heads tilted, waiting to see if we'd hear the cry again, wondering if we'd imagined it.

We were alone in the dining hall that morning.

This room was unlike any dining room I'd been in. Though that was what the ambassador's head of staff had called it when she'd ushered us in here an hour ago. I thought it was more like a mini-museum dedicated to the Orient, not a room for eating in a luxury suite in downtown New York.

Until that strange cry, I'd been sitting deep in thought, reviewing the official papers the head of staff had left on the antique dining table.

I still couldn't believe I was holding this contract in my hands.

I'd been waiting for this moment my whole life. A jolt of pride went through me when I saw the logo on top of the document. I'd pointed it out to Katy.

"Check this baby out," I'd said.

"We've made it!" she said, giving me a high five.

It was our brand new Red Heeled Rebels logo. It had been Katy's idea. To make us official, she'd said. And now, next to the Saudi Arabian Embassy's formal insignia, it made us look distinctly professional.

Katy was right. We'd made it. Finally.

This was my foot in the door to my dream career and good money. Respectable money. Made legally, for a change.

But I couldn't ignore the eerie feeling I got every time I stepped into the ambassador's sprawling residence in the sky. Even Katy said this place gave her the heebie-jeebies.

Something didn't feel right.

Neither of us could pinpoint what it was, but I felt a warning tingle on my back whenever I walked out of those fancy elevators and the security personnel escorted us through the front doors. Every time, it felt like I was entering a time machine and taken back to a medieval world where I'd get trapped. Never to escape.

But that was ridiculous. We were in a modern apartment, in a modern city.

The luxury penthouse was eighty-five floors high in an exclusive residential skyscraper in midtown Manhattan.

In this house, multi-million-dollar sculptures that looked like they'd been loaned from MoMA sat awkwardly next to antiquated Bedouin furniture right out of *Lawrence of Arabia*. Everything was bunched together wherever they found space. Whoever decorated this place had been more concerned with showing off their possessions than creating a pleasant interior.

Then, there was the sickly smell of expensive men's cologne that pervaded every inch of this home. Maybe that was what made the house claustrophobic. All this opulence sucked the oxygen right out.

I looked at the contract in front of me again. The offer on the table was good. It was so good I was forcing myself to ignore my instincts.

"Lemme go!"

I jumped.

This time, I didn't imagine it.

It was a girl's voice. With a distinct Arabic accent.

"I heard that!" Katy said. "That was real."

I swiveled around to check the door.

It was still closed. The head of staff had shut it behind her. I'd thought it was to give us privacy while we looked over the contract, but now, I wasn't so sure.

Katy and I stared at each other, wondering what we'd got into this time.

I pushed my chair back and stood up. Reading my mind, Katy followed me to the door. I was halfway there when the door banged open.

We jumped back in alarm.

"Bibi!" Katy and I cried out at the same time.

Without acknowledging us, Bibi whirled around, closed the door firmly behind her and turned the bolt, locking us in.

"What's going on?" I asked.

She looked like she'd seen a ghost.

"You okay?" asked Katy, concern on her face.

"They're coming," Bibi hissed.

"Who?" I asked.

"Those bad men," she replied, wiping her nose with her sleeve.

"Which men?"

"When they come, act normal."

"Normal?" I asked. "But you just locked us in here."

She averted her eyes. I noticed the sweat running down her face, ruining the dark goth makeup she insisted on wearing. Yes, even to our diplomatic client visits.

"Bibi," I said. "It wasn't you that screamed just now, was it?"

"No," she said and gave a furtive glance behind her. "But we need to get out of here."

"Why?" Katy asked. "And who are these men?"

Bibi's face was scrunched like she was about to cry. "Bad people. Can we go now?"

Bibi was multilingual, English being her fourth language, which she'd only learned recently. But right now, something besides language had her tongue-tied.

Her past gave her ample reasons to not trust anyone. Even us. She'd gone through more in her seventeen years than most adults did in a lifetime. Even now, I'd forget she was just a teen, unpredictable at times, struggling to adjust to a normal life.

"Hey, you can tell us what happened," I said, reaching over to touch her arm. "Do you know who screamed? Is someone in trouble?"

Bibi's eyes darted from side to side.

"It's like I'm back home. This is a bad place." She sniffed and looked away. "Can we go now?"

Katy and I glanced at each other.

I was supposed to get back to the head of staff with a signed contract in half an hour. We were invited guests at the Saudi Arabian ambassador's house. We couldn't just walk away. Or lock ourselves in our hosts' dining room. That just wasn't done.

"Why don't you two stay here," I said. "I'll go talk to the head of staff and ask her what's going on, okay?"

"No!" Bibi said, clutching at my arm. "Don't do that. They'll come and get us too."

"Sweetie," said Katy, "we're in New York. No one can hurt you here anymore."

A scraping sound on the door made us turn around. Someone was trying to open it.

Bibi slipped behind Katy and hunkered down. "It's them!" she whispered.

I felt the hair on the back of my neck stand up.

The door handle depressed slowly. It didn't sound like a bunch of scary men trying to swarm in. It was more like someone was trying to slip in quietly. Stealthily.

My mind raced. It was my turn to overreact.

Katy and I had stopped carrying our weapons to business meetings after we moved to New York. Not because it was illegal, but because we never had a reason to. But Bibi's reactions had unnerved me.

David kept a serrated Japanese knife in our vehicle's glove compartment and a handgun in the overhead bin. "Just in case," he'd said when he'd tucked them there months ago. But our car was now eighty-six floors down in the underground parking garage.

I crossed the room and pulled a small dagger from the open scimitar display. I touched the blade with my finger and pulled away quickly. The knife was ancient, but it had been sharpened recently.

"Better than nothing," I whispered to Katy. "Just in case."

I stepped up to the door.

• • • •

CONTINUE THE ADVENTURE...

Do you want to know what Asha, Katy and the Red Heeled Rebels get entangled in next?

You'll find out in the fourth book of the series.

Asha is sure she's finally made it when she gets a catering order for the swankiest party in Manhattan. But she doesn't realize the lavish banquet is a ruse for something far more perilous than she can imagine...

The Girl Who Broke Free is a gritty tale of crime and deception that will take you on a mad scramble under the bright lit night skies of New York, to the seedy underground world hidden beneath all that plush, opulent veneer, where you'll discover the worst of humanity.

Yes, The Red Heeled Rebels are coming to New York City!

Click link below to get the next book, **The Girl Who Broke Free: www.books2read.com/TheGirlWhoBrokeFree**[1]

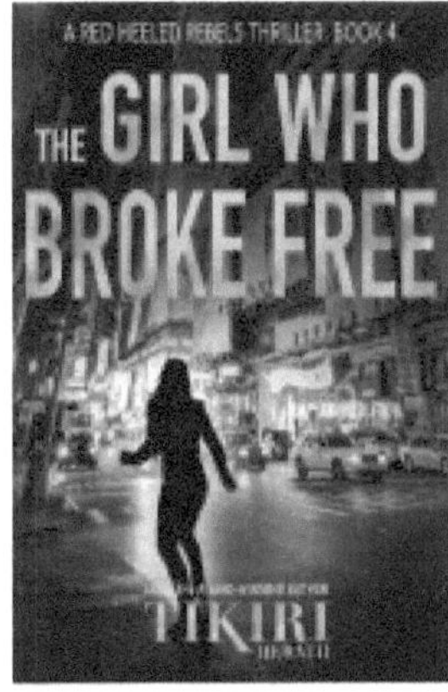

---

1. http://www.books2read.com/TheGirlWhoBrokeFree

Your Gift

· · · ·

Did you get your copy of the TOP SECRET CIA dossier on the Red-Heeled Rebels yet?

Get the backgrounds of each Red-Heeled Rebels member and learn why the biggest intelligence agencies in the world have them on their radar.

Download the Top Secret CIA dossier to the Red Heeled Rebels here.[2]

www.BookHip.com/WSWTCV[3]

---

2. http://dl.bookfunnel.com/k8jx8jp7u2

3. http://www.BookHip.com/WSWTCV

THE RED HEELED REBELS Series

• • • •

IN A WORLD WHERE JUSTICE no longer prevails, six iron-willed women rally together to seek vengeance on those who stole their humanity.

This is a story where the thrill of *Kill Bill* meets the wrath of *The Girl with the Dragon Tattoo.*

If you like gripping thrillers with flawed but gutsy heroines, vigilante action in exotic locales and twists that leave you at the edge of your seat, you'll love these books by multiple award-winning Canadian novelist, Tikiri Herath.

Pick up the Red Heeled Rebels books for a heart-pounding international adventure without having to get a passport or even buy an airline ticket!

• • • •

WHAT READERS ARE SAYING on Amazon and Goodreads:

- "Fast-paced and exciting!"

- "An exciting and thought-provoking book."

- "A wonderful story! I didn't want to leave the characters."

- "I couldn't put down this exciting road trip adventure with a powerful message."

- "Another award-worthy adventure novel that keeps you on the edge of your seat."

- "A heart-stopping adventure. I just couldn't put the book down till I finished reading it."

- "Kept me mesmerized and captivated with the rich descriptions which made me feel like I was actually inside the story."

- "This is a fantastic read that will have you traveling the globe. I absolutely loved this book. You won't be able to put it down!"

- "A real page turner and international thriller. Reminds me of why I've always loved to read. Because I can visit worlds and places I wouldn't ordinarily get to see."

To learn more about this addictive series, go to www.RedHeeledRebels.com[4]

• • • •

PREQUEL: THE GIRL WHO Crossed the Line

A reckless girl. A grave mistake. A fateful destiny.

All she wanted was to belong. Then, she committed an unforgivable crime...

• • • •

BOOK ONE: THE GIRL Who Ran Away

An estranged orphan. A treacherous plot. A perilous journey that could kill her.

She'd just survived a fiery car crash in the middle of nowhere. Both her parents are dead, but that's nothing compared to what she would face next...

---

4.   http://www.RedHeeledRebels.com

• • • •

BOOK TWO: THE GIRL Who Made Them Pay

A kidnapped friend. A forbidden house. A precarious journey to escape their captors.

They are fleeing a fate worse than death. They think they're finally safe in London, when one of them is snatched into a waiting black cab. And now, she will do anything to find her friend...

• • • •

BOOK THREE: THE GIRL Who Fought to Kill

A lost cousin. A heinous crime. An impossible rescue that risks it all.

She was ready to cross oceans to hunt down her stolen cousin. But she didn't know the terrifying stakes waiting for her on the other side that will test her resolve and courage...

• • • •

BOOK FOUR: THE GIRL Who Broke Free

A sweet sixteenth birthday banquet. A missing diplomat's daughter. A menacing family secret.

She thought she'd finally made it when she was invited to cater for the swankiest party in upscale Manhattan. But she didn't realize the birthday girl's family has other plans and the banquet is a ruse for something more perilous than she could ever imagine...

• • • •

BOOK FIVE: THE GIRL Who Knew Their Names

A glittering Hollywood gala. An actress with a dark vendetta. A cold-blooded murder among the stars.

She thought she'd snagged the most coveted catering job in Los Angeles, and a chance to meet A-list celebrities. But she didn't realize she was about to confront the most powerful predator in town on her first day...

• • • •

BOOK SIX: THE GIRL Who Never Forgot

A girl from the swamps. A family gripped by darkness. A killer on the loose at the Mardi gras.

She was invited to cater a lavish ball where New Orleans' blue-blooded families celebrated Mardi gras in style, away from the cacophony of common street parades. But she didn't realize a murderer was lurking in the shadows, waiting to frame her for their deed...

• • • •

AWARDS & PRAISE FOR The Red Heeled Rebels books:
- Grand Prize Award Finalist - 2019 Eric Hoffer Award, USA
- First Horizon Award Finalist - 2019 Eric Hoffer Award, USA
- Honorable Mention General Fiction - 2019 Eric Hoffer Award, USA
- Winner First-In-Category - 2019 Chanticleer Somerset Award, USA
- Semi-Finalist - 2020 Chanticleer Somerset Award, USA
- Winner in 2019 Readers' Favorite Book Awards, USA
- Winner of 2019 Silver Medal - Excellence E-Lit Award, USA
- Winner in Suspense Category - 2018 New York Big Book Award, USA
- Finalist in Suspense Category - 2018 & 2019 Silver Falchion Awards, USA
- Honorable Mention - 2018-19 Reader Views Literary Classics Award, USA
- Publisher's Weekly Booklife Prize – 2018, USA

Truth Is Harsher Than Fiction

The state of women around the world:

- 33,000 girls become child brides every day.

- Women in rural parts of Africa spend 40 billion hours a year collecting water.

- Most of the 3.9 billion people not connected to the internet are poor, less educated rural women and girls.

- Globally, women are just 13 per cent of agricultural land holders.

- Only 6 countries give women equal *legal* work rights as men.

- Women are 47% more likely to suffer severe injuries in car crashes because safety features are designed for men.

- It will take 108 years to close the gender gap.

2019 Sources:
World Economic Forum
United Nations

. . . .

"THE WORLD WILL NOT be destroyed by those who do evil, but by those who watch them without doing anything." - Albert Einstein.

. . . .

AS I RESEARCHED, PLANNED, and wrote these novels, I spoke with women and men from around the world, some of whom I'd never met before. They included women who are tirelessly fighting for equality and dignity in South Asia despite the push back and hostility from their own families and communities.

They included former military officers and peacekeepers who had been deployed to conflict zones and saw the heart-wrenching plight of children, but had neither the resources nor the permission to assist them.

Regardless of where they came from, they all shared with me their stories. They read mine. Most importantly, we discussed the difficult topics in these books frankly and without prejudice. I gained many insights through these chats, but one lesson I took away was there are good people everywhere.

These are the good people who do not apologize for harmful traditions nor tolerate cultural dogma. These are the good people who yearn to change age-old customs that subjugate our daughters and alienate our sons. These are the good people who desire to create a better world for all humanity, for now and for the future.

I was surprised to see how much of our world views we share, regardless of differences in gender, vocation, political views, sexual orientation, or nationality.

We all have more in common than not. And this gives me hope, hope for a wiser, kinder, open, and more connected global community that uplifts us all.

How would you like to write your own life story?

The Rebel Diva Self-Empowerment Series
www.RebelDivas.com[1]

The Rebel Diva books are life-changing practical guides that take you on an adventure of a lifetime. Uncover your purpose, your passions, and your talents to create a step-by-step masterplan to achieve your life goals.

You'll create a story in these Rebel Diva books and that story will be yours.

· · · ·

WHAT READERS ARE SAYING:

- *"One of the most motivational and thought-provoking books I have ever read."*

- *"This book is phenomenal! This book is written for real people; no platitudes or empty promises."*

- *"A very inspirational read. This is highly recommended, especially if you're seeking to do and make a difference."*

- *"The author is teacher and cheerleader. She gives solid guidelines to help you figure out your goals and action plans, and she truly comes across as someone who cares."*

- *"This isn't just another self-help book—instead, this incredibly useful book includes a clear method and helpful ex-*

---

1.   http://www.rebeldivas.com/

*ercises to help you uncover your dreams, passions and pur-
pose."*

● *"Very inspiring. Even though I am older, this book made
me want to go after some of my dreams that I thought I was
too old for. The book comes with a link that you can download a 100-page workbook. I plan on giving my daughter a
copy too."*

● *"Proudly considering myself a Rebel Diva after taking this
journey to self-discovery!"*

● ● ● ●

SIGN UP TO GET YOUR exclusive Rebel Diva gift!

The Fear Buster is a short Rebel Diva workbook that shares
three essential tools to help you overcome any fears or doubt and
make both small and big decisions quickly. Go to the Rebel Diva site
to get your personal copy as a gift.

www.RebelDivas.com/FearBuster[2]

---

2. http://www.RebelDivas.com/FearBuster

Dedication

This book is dedicated to Stéphane. Thank you for twelve wonderful years and thank you for teaching me about the beauty of life.

Acknowledgments

To my fantastic international team of beta readers who helped me through this adventure, who cheered me on as I toiled, and who gave me their frank feedback, thank you.

(In alphabetical order)

- Carolyn Pennett-Staresinic, Canada
- Cyndi Wannamaker, Canada
- Otivbo Akhigbe, Nigeria
- Paula Mathews, USA
- Five anonymous beta readers, Hidden Gems, USA

· · · ·

TO MY AMAZING, TALENTED, superstar editor, Stephanie, thank you for coming on this literary journey with me and for helping make these books the best they can be.

· · · ·

TO ALL THE GENEROUS readers who take the time to review my novels and give their frank feedback, thank you. I owe you all a debt of gratitude and a glass of wine (or several) when you come to Vancouver next!

About the Author

Tikiri Herath is a multiple-award-winning Canadian author.
Born in Sri Lanka, a tropical island in the Indian Ocean, she spent her childhood in South East Africa, and has lived and worked in Southeast Asia, Continental Europe, and North America.
She started her adult life as a lone immigrant girl, but went on to receive a bachelor's degree from the University of Victoria, British Columbia and a master's degree from the Solvay Business School in Brussels.
For fifteen years, she worked in risk management in the intelligence and defense sectors, including in the Canadian Federal Government and at NATO.
Tikiri's an adrenaline junkie who has rock climbed, bungee jumped, rode on the back of a motorcycle across Quebec, flown in an acrobatic airplane upside down, and parachuted solo.
When she's not writing or plotting another thriller scene, you'll most probably find her baking in her kitchen with a glass of red wine in hand and jazz playing in the background.
To say hello and get free travel stories from around the world, go to www.TikiriHerath.com.[1]

---

1. http://www.TikiriHerath.com

www.ingramcontent.com/pod-product-compliance
Lightning Source LLC
Chambersburg PA
CBHW021548110726

47902CB00004B/1076